HOLLY TAYLOR

Night Birds' Reign

Silver Imprint
Medallion Press, Inc.
Florida, USA

Dedication:

To my mother, Patricia Ann Flowers Taylor, who always believed in me.
I miss you, Mom.

Published 2005 by Medallion Press, Inc.
225 Seabreeze Ave.
Palm Beach, FL 33480

The MEDALLION PRESS LOGO
is a registered tradmark of Medallion Press, Inc.

Printed in the United States of America

Library of Congress Cataloging-in-Publication Data

Taylor, Holly, 1965-
  Night birds' reign / Holly Taylor.
      p. cm.
  ISBN 1-932815-53-8
  1. Arthurian romances--Adaptations. I. Title.
  PS3620.A945N54 2005
  813'.6--dc22
                              2005019794

The court of Lleu Lawrient lies
Stricken and silent beneath the sky.
The thorns and blighted thistles over
It all, and brambles now,
Where once was magnificence.

Harps and lordly feast, all have passed away.
And the night birds now reign.

Taliesin
Fifth Master Bard
Circa 270

CHARACTERS
Y Dawnus (The Gifted)

The Dreamers
Gwydion ap Awst var Celemon: Dreamer of Kymru, brother of Amatheon, half brother of King Uthyr

Dinaswyn ur Morvryn var Gwenllian: former Dreamer, aunt to Amatheon and Gwydion, Myrrdin's sister

Cariadas ur Gwydion var Isalyn: Gwydion's daughter and heir

The Dewin
Myrrdin ap Morvryn var Gwenllian: Ardewin, uncle to Gwydion and Amatheon, brother to Dinaswyn

Rhiannon ur Hefeydd var Indeg: former heir to the Ardewin, mother of Gwenhwyfar

Amatheon ap Awst var Celemon: Gwydion's brother, Dewin to Hetwin Silver-Brow

Elstar ur Anieron var Ethyllt: Myrrdin's heir, daughter of Anieron, wife to Elidyr

Llywelyn ap Elidyr var Elstar: Elstar's oldest son and heir

Arianrod ur Brychan var Arianllyn: cousin to Gwydion and Rhiannon

Cynan ap Einon var Darun: Dewin to King Uthyr, later Ardewin, uncle to Gwydion, Amatheon, Rhiannon, and Arianrod

The Druids
Cathbad ap Goreu var Efa: Archdruid, Myrrdin's cousin

Aergol ap Custennin var Dinaswyn: Cathbad's heir, Dinaswyn's son

Sinend ur Aergol var Eurgain: Aergol's daughter and heir

Menw ap Aergol var Ceindrech: Aergol's son

The Bards

Anieron ap Cyvarnion var Hunydd: Master Bard, Rhiannon's uncle

Elidyr ap Dudod var Llawen: Anieron's nephew and heir, husband to Elstar

Dudod ap Cyvarnion var Hunydd: Anieron's brother, Elidyr's father, Rhiannon's uncle

Cynfar ap Elidyr var Elstar: Elidyr's youngest son and heir

In Gwytheryn

Rhufon ap Casnar: a descendant of the last steward of Cadair Idris

Tybion ap Rhufon: Rhufon's son

Lucan ap Tybion: Rhufon's grandson

In Gwynedd

Uthyr ap Rathtyen var Awst: King of Gwynedd (House of PenHebog), Lord of Rhos, half brother to Gwydion, Amatheon, and Madoc

Ygraine ur Custennin var Elwen: Uthyr's Queen, sister to Queen Olwen of Ederynion

Arthur ap Uthyr var Ygraine: Uthyr's son

Morrigan ur Uthyr var Ygraine: Uthyr's daughter

Madoc ap Rhodri var Rathtyen: Lord of Rhufonoig, half brother to Uthyr

Cai ap Cynyr: Uthyr's Captain, the PenGwernan; his wife Nest and his son Garanwyn

Susanna ur Erim: Uthyr's Bard, Griffi's lover

Griffi ap Iaen: Uthyr's Druid, Susanna's lover

Neuad ur Hetwin: Uthyr's Dewin

Arday ur Medyr: Uthyr's steward

Duach ap Seithfed: Uthyr's doorkeeper

Greid ap Gorwys: Master Smith of Gwynedd

Donal: gatekeeper of Tegeingl

Trachymer: Uthyr's chief huntsman

Jonas: Bard to Diadwa of Creuddyn; his wife Canna

Diadwa ur Trephin: Gwarda of Creuddyn

Berwyn ap Cyrenyr: Diadwa's Captain

Glwys ap Uchdryd: Diadwa's Druid

In Prydyn

Rhoram ap Rhydderch var Eurneid: King of Prydyn (House of PenBlaid), Lord of Dyfed

Geriant ap Rhoram var Christina: Rhoram's son and heir by his first wife

Sanon ur Rhoram var Christina: Rhoram's daughter by his first wife

Gwenhwyfar ur Rhoram var Rhiannon: Rhoram's daughter by Rhiannon

Efa ur Nudd: Rhoram's second wife, sister to Erfin, Lord of Ceredigion

Achren ur Canhustyr: Rhoram's Captain, the PenCollen

Aidan ap Camber: Achren's lieutenant

Ellywen ur Saidi: Rhoram's Druid

Erfin ap Nudd: Lord of Ceredigion, Efa's brother

Dafydd Penfro: Rhoram's counselor

Tallwch ap Nwyfre: Rhoram's doorkeeper

In Rheged

Urien ap Ethyllt var Gwaeddan: King of Rheged (House of PenMarch), Lord of Amgoed

Ellirri ur Rhodri var Rathtyen: Urien's Queen, sister to Madoc, half sister to Uthyr

Elphin ap Urien var Ellirri: Urien's oldest son and heir

Owein ap Urien var Ellirri: Urien's second son

Rhiwallon ap Urien var Ellirri: Urien's youngest son

Enid ur Urien var Ellirri: Urien's daughter

Trystan ap Naf: Urien's Captain, the PenDraenenwen

Teleri ur Brysethach: Trystan's lieutenant

Esyllt ur Maelwys: Urien's Bard, March's wife

Sabrina ur Dadweir: Urien's Druid

Bledri ap Gwyn: Urien's Dewin

March Y Meirchion: Urien's huntsman, Esyllt's husband

Hetwin Silver-Brow: Lord of Gwinionydd

Cynedyr the Wild: son of Hetwin Silver-Brow

In Ederynion

Olwen ur Custennin var Elwen: Queen of Ederynion (House of PenAlarch), Lady of Ial, sister to Queen Ygraine

Elen ur Olwen var Kilwch: Olwen's daughter and heir

Lludd ap Olwen var Kilwch: Olwen's son

Angharad ur Ednyved: Olwen's Captain, the PenAethnen

Emrys ap Naw: Angharad's lieutenant

Talhearn ap Coleas: Olwen's Bard

Iago ap Cof: Olwen's Druid

Regan ur Corfil: Olwen's Dewin

Llwyd Cilcoed: Dewin of Caerinion, Olwen's lover

Alun Cilcoed: Lord of Arystli, Llwyd's older brother

HISTORICAL FIGURES

Arywen ur Cadwy: the Fifth Archdruid, one of the Great Ones of Lleu Silver-Hand

Bloudewedd ur Sawyl var Eurolwyn: wife of Lleu Lawrient the last High King, lover to King Gorwys

Bran ap Iweridd: the Fifth Dreamer, one of the Great Ones of Lleu Silver-Hand

Lleu Lawrient (Silver-Hand): last High King of Kymru, murdered by Bloudewedd and Gorwys

Gorwys of Penllyn: consort of Queen Siwan of Prydyn, lover of Bloudewedd, murderer of High King Lleu

Idris ap Coachar: the First High King of Kymru

Macsen ap Edern: the Second High King of Kymru

Mannawyddan ap Iweridd: the Fifth Ardewin, brother of Bran, one of the Great Ones of Lleu Silver-Hand

Taliesin ap Arthen: the Fifth Master Bard, one of the Great Ones of Lleu Silver-Hand

The Shining Ones

Cerridwen: Protectress of Kymru, Mistress of the Wild Hunt, Queen of the Wood, wife of Cerrunnos

Cerrunnos: Protector of Kymru, Master of the Wild Hunt, Lord of the Animals, husband of Cerridwen

Annwyn: god of death, Lord of Chaos and the Otherworld, husband of Aertan

Aertan: goddess of fate, the Weaver, wife of Annwyn

Taran: father god, King of the Winds, god of the Bards, husband of Modron

Modron: mother goddess, the Great Mother, goddess of the Druids, wife of Taran

Mabon: King of the Sun, Lord of Fire, god of the Dreamers, husband of Nantsovelta

Nantsovelta: Queen of the Moon, Lady of the Waters, goddess of the Dewin, wife of Mabon

Camulos: god of war, twin to Agrona, Y Rhyfelwr—the warrior twin

Agrona: goddess of war, twin to Camulos, Y Rhyfelwr—the warrior twin

Sirona of the Stars: goddess of stars, wife to Grannos

Grannos the Header: god of healing, Star of the North

Part 1
The Dream

The dim night is silent,
And its darkness
Covers all of Kymru.
The sun in the bed of the sea,
And the moon silvering the flood.

Math of Falias
First Master Bard
Circa 148

Prologue

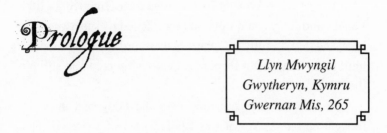

Calan Llachar Eve

The Dreamer dismounted from his tired horse. Bran's long, sweat-soaked, auburn hair hung lankly around his drawn face, strands of it tangling in his close-cropped beard. His silvery eyes glittered as he surveyed the now still battlefield.

Too late, he thought. He had come too late, and there was nothing to be done now but to search for the body of the friend he had loved. As a drowning man clings to a scrap of floating wreckage, he clung to a ragged hope that he would find his friend still alive. But although he resolutely refused to acknowledge it, his heart already knew the truth.

He held out his hand and called Druid's Fire, for night had long since fallen, and it was Calan Llachar Eve, so there was no moon to illuminate the bloody scene.

The fire flickered orange and blue as it danced in the palm of his hand as he began to search the still faces of the dead on the shores of Llyn Mwyngil.

1

He had not thought there would be so many bodies. But Lleu's warriors had fought hard to save their High King's life. Fought until they could fight no more; felled by superior numbers, and the carefully laid plans of their lord's betrayer; fought until every last one of them was dead, lying cold and still on the breast of Kymru.

He stooped down, turning over the body of a man he thought he knew. Yes, it was Rhufar, Lleu's huntsman. The dead man's tanned, leathery face was peaceful now, but his cold hand was still clutching his spear as though he had not yet given up, as though he still had hopes of fighting on. And there was Clydno, Lleu's doorkeeper, his face upturned to the sky. There were so many wounds on his body that it was not easy to tell which one might have killed him.

Bran went forward over the blood-soaked ground, knowing that Lleu was here somewhere; knowing Lleu had not escaped; knowing Lleu was dead; knowing he had come far, far too late.

Oh, he had come as soon as he had known. But the Shining Ones had not seen fit to send him a dream, so he had not known in time. He had only known a few hours ago when a dread had settled on his heart as he journeyed to Cadair Idris, thinking to spend Calan Llachar with Lleu and his Great Ones. He had tried to Mind-Speak to his friend, to apprise the High King that he was coming and had met only blank silence.

He had cried out and urged his horse to a dead run. He had Wind-Ridden, casting his spirit ahead for a glimpse of Cadair Idris, trying to see what had happened. And he had seen Bloudewedd, Lleu's wife, waiting at the top of the steps of what was a strangely emptied hall. Then he had seen King Gorwys of Prydyn, consort of Bloudewedd's sister, ride up in the company of his warriors. Their clothes were stained and torn, but they were laughing and shouting in victory. Gorwys had thrown the reins of his horse to his Captain and mounted the white, shining steps of the High King's mountain hall. He had taken Bloudewedd in his arms and bent his head to kiss her savagely. He had torn the sleeve of her gown and bent to kiss her white shoulder. He had picked her up and she had smiled up at him, locking her slender, white arms around his neck. They had entered the hall and the Doors had closed behind them.

Bran had cried out again when he saw this on the Wind-Ride, knowing now what they had done and why they had done it. He searched the rest of Cadair Idris, seeking his fellow Great Ones, knowing that they must be in prison or dead, or else they would have found a way to tell him what had happened.

He found them in a dark cell in the bowels of the mountain. Dull lead collars, the dreaded *enaid-dals*, hung around their necks. Arywen's dark hair was tangled and dirty; Taliesin's face was pale and bloodied; Mannawyddan's arm hung at an odd angle. He wanted to Wind-Speak to them, to tell them that he was coming, but they would not have been able to hear him, not with the cursed soul-catchers around their throats.

Then he had cast his awareness to the sky once more, seeking to find Lleu. Instead he had found the aftermath of a battle on the shores of Llyn Mwyngil, just a few leagues west of Cadair Idris. So he had made for that spot as quickly as he could.

The glint of golden hair in the light of the fire that danced in his palm stopped him in his tracks. He stood stock-still, looking at the form that lay at his feet. The man was lying on his side, facing away from Bran, cradling something beneath him.

Bran knelt beside the body. He reached out a trembling hand to turn the corpse so he could see its face. But he knew. Oh, yes, he knew who it was. His heart had already told him. He turned the body over.

Bran's breath rattled in his throat as the fire illuminated Lleu's upturned face. Lleu's tunic was slashed and stained with blood, so much blood that Bran could scarce believe a man could bleed so much. Lleu's hands—both his normal hand and the hand of silver—were still wrapped around the hilt of Caladfwlch, the object Lleu had been cradling. The golden, eagle-shaped hilt glittered coldly in the light of Druid's Fire. The eagle's bloodstone eyes shifted in the flickering light as though unwilling to look upon what had happened here, to acknowledge the truth about its master.

Tears streaming down his checks, he reached out to take Lleu in his arms.

And then Lleu opened his sapphire blue eyes.

Bran's heart stopped, then consented to beat on. "Lleu," he whispered. "You're alive."

"Waited for you," Lleu breathed.

"I—I am sorry I am late."

"Aren't late," Lleu whispered. "In time." Feebly he tried to raise his sword, to hand it to Bran. But Lleu was far too weak. He succeeded only in pushing it toward his friend.

"Take it," the High King whispered.

"Lleu—"

"Take it, Dreamer."

Bran took the sword, holding it with one hand while he cradled Lleu's dying body in the other. "I have it," he rasped.

"You know where."

4

"Yes, I know where to take it."

"Came from the water," Lleu said laboriously. "Must go back."

"Yes, I know. I was there when you first found it."

Lleu smiled the warm smile that had first won Bran over so long ago. "Knew you'd come."

Bran could not answer through his tears so he held his dying friend tighter.

"Bloudewedd—"

"I saw," Bran said shortly. "Bloudewedd and Gorwys. Her own sister's husband."

"Don't kill her," Lleu insisted weakly.

"I won't let her get away with—"

"I know. But don't kill her."

Knowing now what Lleu meant, Bran merely nodded.

"And Gorwys." Lleu hesitated, searching for the strength to talk. "You know what to do."

"Yes," Bran said. "I know."

"The others?"

"Are alive," Bran said steadily. "And in the dungeon of Cadair Idris."

"Get them out."

"I will."

"And tell them—"

"Tell them what, Lleu?" Bran prompted quietly when Lleu fell silent, searching for the strength to continue.

With a great effort, Lleu whispered. "Tell them I wait for them in the Land of Summer. That never had a High King such faithful Great Ones as they."

"I will tell them. Be at peace, my friend. And wait for us. We will join you in Gwlad Yr Haf when our lives are done.

And there we will sit with you. We will sing the songs of Taliesin together. You know how much he likes that."

Lleu smiled weakly, and nodded.

"And Arywen will teach us how to dance, as she always threatened to do. And Mannawyddan will make us laugh, for he always knew how."

Lleu's smile began to fade as the light in his blue eyes started to dim.

"And one day the Wheel will turn, and you will be returned to Kymru in her hour of need, as you always have been," Bran promised, his voice soothing.

Lleu gave a single sigh, then his chest hitched once, and his breath stopped.

Bran stayed by Lleu's dead body for some time, cradling Caladfwlch in one arm and Lleu's steadily cooling corpse in the other.

The sword must be returned to the Lady of the Waters. He must ensure that it would be found again, when the time was ripe. He had a feeling that many years would pass before Caladfwlch was returned to the light of day.

Bloudewedd and Gorwys must be dealt with. They would pay for today's work, but not with their deaths. That would be too easy.

Cadair Idris must be closed to begin its long wait for the next High King. The Four Treasures, those implements needed to make a High King, must be hidden away for now, to be found when they were again required.

Yes, he had much to do. He had promises to keep, and a future to safeguard.

He rose, holding Caladfwlch in his hands. He looked down at Lleu's body. Overhead the stars were beginning to dim as the sky began to lighten. It seemed to him that the sound of a hunting horn was borne to him on the wings of the wind. The Wild Hunt, perhaps, saying farewell to the High King of Kymru.

Preparing, already, for the day when he would return.

Chapter One

Suldydd, Lleihau Wythnos—night

Gwydion slept on the Dreamer's pallet in Caer Dathyl, twisting restlessly under the light of the waning moon that streamed through the glass ceiling. His dark brows were drawn together in concentration, and the lids of his closed eyes twitched rapidly.

For the Dreamer's heir was dreaming.

And the Shining Ones smiled, satisfied.

HE WAS STARING at Cadair Idris, the deserted hall of the High Kings of Kymru. The mountain stood tall and silent, closed and dark, as it had been since the murder of Lleu Silver-Hand, over two hundred years before.

The waning moon was rising over the mountain, bathing the still plain in faded, silvery beams. In Calan Llachar, the forest west of Cadair Idris, even the leaves on the trees did not move. But from Galor Carreg, the standing stones that guarded the burial mounds of the High Kings, he saw movement.

8

Three figures made their way from the shadowy stones to stand at the base of the dark mountain. Silently they mounted the broken and time-stained steps that led to Drwys Idris, the bejeweled Doors that guarded the entrance to the hollow mountain.

The golden Doors glittered palely at first, then began to glow as the ghosts of the High Kings approached. Verdant emeralds and azure sapphires vied with milky pearls and fiery opals. Rubies shone like drops of fresh blood while clear diamonds, orange topaz, and purple amethyst glowed warmly as though in sweet welcome.

When the three ghostly figures reached the top of the stairs they turned their backs to the Doors, facing outward toward the plain, toward Gwydion who now faced them from the bottom of the steps.

He knew them, for he had seen them before in his dreams, the dead High Kings of Kymru.

Idris, the first High King, had silvery eyes in a face lined with years of bright laughter and unspeakable sorrow. Macsen, Kymru's second High King, was tall and broad-shouldered, his honey-blond hair held back from his good-natured face by a band of gold. Lleu Lawrient, the last High King of Kymru, stood in the center. Moonlight spilled across his silver hand and his golden hair.

Each of them wore an identical, massive torque formed of twisted strands of silver and gold. At the center of each necklace was a figure eight studded with onyx, the sign of Annwyn, Lord of Chaos. A luminous pearl and a sparkling emerald hung to the left of the onyx, while a glittering sapphire and a fiery opal flashed from the right.

As one the High Kings pulled the ghost of a sword from

the scabbards hung around their waists. Each shining sword was a duplicate of the other two, for all three of them had once carried Caladfwlch, although where the real sword was now, no one knew.

The gold and silver sword flashed in the moonlight. The hilt was fashioned like an eagle with outspread wings. The eagle had eyes of bloodstone and wings of onyx, and the remainder of the hilt was scattered with emeralds and pearls, sapphires and opals.

The three High Kings stood silently, ghostly swords raised, scanning the sky above the shadowy plain.

At last Gwydion found his voice, sure that the question in his dreaming mind was the right one. "What do you here, High Kings of Kymru?"

Idris answered his voice like the rushing of a storm through the trees, "We are waiting."

"What do you wait for?"

"For the next High King," Macsen replied, his voice hollow, echoing with dead power.

"It is time?" Gwydion asked, his heart beating faster. For Kymru only had need of a High King when the land was in danger.

"The time is coming," Lleu answered, his voice resonating across the moonlit plain.

"Betrayal endangers the life of the one we wait for," Idris said.

"Betrayal, Dreamer," Lleu said, "is what killed us all."

Before Gwydion could reply he heard the faint strains of a hunting horn, borne on a suddenly quickening breeze. The moon seemed to shine even brighter and the stars glittered sharply. A fierce cry sounded out over the plain. Gwydion could hear the beat of wings overhead and turned sharply to see.

The largest eagle Gwydion had ever seen soared effortlessly over the dark mountain. Silhouetted against the bright moon, its wings outstretched, the eagle cried out again as it folded its wings and dropped down, coming to rest before the three kings at the top of the stairs.

The eagle was brown, with tail feathers of shimmering blue. Around its breast it wore a massive torque of gold exactly like the torque's that glittered from the necks of the High Kings. The eagle cried out again, its call fierce and commanding.

As one the High Kings laid their ghost-swords on the stones before the eagle's talons. But as the eagle stooped to take the swords in its beak, the weapons shimmered and disappeared.

At that moment the shadows on the plain began to twist and moan, melting together, forming a pool of darkness that coalesced at the bottom of the steps. Gwydion retreated, stepping backward up the stairs, his heart caught in his throat.

The shadowy darkness reared up, looming formless and menacing over Gwydion and the eagle, crying in a voice like the rushing of the wind across a dark sky, calling for the eagle's blood.

The High Kings vanished, blown away on the winds that had risen. The shadow stretched out dark arms, reaching for the eagle, death in its cry.

"No!" Gwydion cried, as he sprang in front of the eagle.

The things dark arms plunged through Gwydion's chest, parting his flesh like water. Icy cold terror gripped his heart and his back arched in pain.

"No!" he cried again as he fell to his knees, all strength drained from him. "No!"

11

"No!"

The echoes of his scream still ringing hideously in his ears, Gwydion sat up, his heart pounding, his lean body bathed in sweat although he felt cold inside. His dark, sweat-stained hair hung lank around his face, tangling in his short beard. His gray eyes, dilated with horror, were almost black. His chest heaving as though he had run many leagues, he did not hear the footsteps of the others as they pounded up the stairs and burst into the Dreamer's chamber.

They rushed to his pallet, Aunt Dinaswyn reaching him first. Her long black and silver hair in disarray, she grabbed his face between her cool hands, steadying him. "Look at me," she commanded, her voice level. "Look at me, Gwydion. Tell me."

When he did not answer immediately, she turned her head slightly to the young man behind her. "Amatheon, bring wine," she snapped. Without a word, her youngest nephew turned to the small table by the door, grabbed up a goblet and pitcher, and poured. He brought the cup to Gwydion and placed it in his brother's shaking hands.

As Gwydion drank, still trembling from the terror of his dream, Dinaswyn sat back on her heels next to his pallet. "Arianrod," she said to the young woman who had halted by the door, "bring the Book of Dreams."

Arianrod hesitated, her face pale and washed out by the moonlight. "Will he be all right?"

"Of course he'll be all right," Dinaswyn said, impatiently. "Go." Without answering, Arianrod left the room.

Amatheon crouched down next to Dinaswyn as Gwydion remained on the pallet, trying to force his shaking body into some semblance of calm. They glanced at each other over

Gwydion's bowed head.

"You ever have a dream as bad as this?" Amatheon asked quietly.

Dinaswyn shook her head.

Arianrod returned clutching a leather book with an ink-well and quill balanced on top. She set them on the low table, picked up a taper and, touching it to the glowing brazier, lit the candles. Amatheon went to the table, opened the book and dipped the quill in the ink, sitting cross-legged on the bare floor. "Ready," he said, his voice steady.

Dinaswyn stirred up the fire in the brazier, then turned to Gwydion. "All right. Tell us."

Gwydion looked up from the depths of his goblet. In the fitful light from the burning brazier Ystafell Yr Arymes, the Chamber of Prophecy, seemed to have more shadows than could be accounted for. The clear light of the waning moon streamed through the glass dome overhead. The jewels, which studded the four round windows of clear glass set around the circular chamber, gleamed in the vagrant lights of moon and fire. There were sapphires for Taran of the Winds around the north window; and pearls for Nantsovelta, Lady of the Waters to the east. Opals for Mabon, King of Fire framed the south window; while emeralds for Modron, the Great Mother surrounded the west. The jewels winked and glimmered slyly, as though holding a secret. The floor shimmered and shifted as light played over the onyx of Annwyn, Lord of Chaos and the bloodstone of his mate, Aertan, Weaver of Fate.

As he gathered his thoughts, he looked up at the three people who waited to hear the dream.

Dinaswyn's face was impassive. Around her slim, proud neck the Dreamer's Torque glittered. Thick strands of gold intertwined to form a massive collar. The center clasp was formed of two circles, one inside the other; both studded with fiery opals. Firelight and moonlight turned her high cheekbones into sharp, hard angles. Her gray eyes, so like Gwydion's, were cool and watchful. Yet in them he saw that she understood the power of the precognitive dreams that reached through time and space into the mind of the Dreamer. She understood, for as the Dreamer of Kymru she had guided her country for many years. Distantly, he wondered that he, the student, should have this dream, while she, the teacher, had not.

Amatheon, Gwydion's younger brother, looked at him calmly, with an encouraging smile on his fresh, young face. Amatheon wore the Dewin's torque, strands of silver clasped with the shape of a pentagon from which a single pearl dangled. As he always did, Gwydion saw echoes of his beloved father in his brother's face, in his clear, blue eyes. But he would not think of that now. His father's death was still too raw, too painful to dwell on for long.

Lastly, Gwydion looked at Arianrod, his beautiful cousin. She was vain, selfish, and powerfully sensual. As he well knew, her long, thick, honey-blond hair was silken to the touch, and her almond-shaped amber eyes promised many things, all of which she could and would deliver—if she chose. He had shared her bed now for a few years, and he knew that he wasn't the only one—which had never bothered him, for she had touched his body, but not his heart. Never, never would he allow any woman to have that kind of power over him, not after . . .

He shied away from that thought, as he always did. Now was not the time to think of his festering wounds that would never heal. Now was the time to tell of the dream. Gwydion sank back on his pallet and began to speak.

GWYDION FELL SILENT, staring into the brazier. The only sound was of the quill racing across the Book of Dreams, as Amatheon recorded the threat to the unknown High King.

"Interpretation?" Amatheon asked crisply, his pen poised.

Gwydion looked up quickly. "Guess," he said bitterly.

"Interpret the dream," Dinaswyn said, her tone clipped

Gwydion took a deep breath and let it out slowly. He raised his head and looked up at the night sky, past the uncaring stars that glittered through the clear ceiling of the shadowy chamber.

"The eagle. It was Arderydd. The symbol of the High King." Gwydion shifted restlessly on his pallet and got to his feet. He began to pace the room. "Which means a new High King. They said it was time."

"Which means war," Arianrod said in a hollow voice. "High Kings are only born for warfare."

"And born to be betrayed," Gwydion said, his throat tight. "All three of the High Kings were betrayed to their deaths."

He fell silent for a moment, thinking of those betrayals. Idris had died from wounds received in battle against his own son. Macsen had died in Corania where he had gone to fetch his bride, killed by Coranian oath-breakers. Lleu Silver-Hand had been murdered by his wife and her lover.

He closed his eyes briefly; his throat tight, for he still suffered from the raw wounds of betrayal himself.

"But who is the betrayer that endangers this High King to be?" Amatheon asked. "Who would wish him ill?"

"Who can tell?" Gwydion asked wildly. "Any one of Dinaswyn's fellow Great Ones might perceive a High King to be a threat to their way of life, for now they are answerable to no one. Or, if it comes to that, any one of the Rulers of the four kingdoms might have cause. They, too, are used to doing things their own way. Perhaps they would wish ill to one who would rule them."

"Was there nothing in the shadow that you could identify?" Dinaswyn pressed.

Gwydion shook his head. "Nothing. It was a figure made of darkness and it threatened the eagle. But who—or what—the figure stands for, I cannot tell."

"Do you think it one person, or many?"

"I think . . . I think that it is one person. But I cannot be sure."

"Than we leave it for now. If the Shining Ones had meant for us to understand who the shadow is, they would have sent some detail to help you. Perhaps they still will. We move on, then, to the identity of the High King."

"Yes, who?" asked Amatheon curiously.

Gwydion continued to pace. "I don't know."

"For something that important, there must be a clue. There must be something," Dinaswyn insisted.

"I tell you, there was nothing," Gwydion said impatiently, still pacing.

"Color?" Dinaswyn asked.

"Color." Gwydion paused, frowning, trying to remember. And he did. And as he did, he hesitated. Two out of the three people in the room he would trust with his life. But the third . . .

"Arianrod," Gwydion said sharply, "go to bed."

Arianrod bristled. "Why?"

"Because you aren't doing any good here," Gwydion said

pointedly.

"I see," Arianrod said, her voice beginning to rise. "You are getting almost as good as Aunt Dinaswyn in sending people away."

"Arianrod," Dinaswyn began. Her face was impassive but her voice strained, for the bone of contention between them was old and much gnawed over.

"Wait and see, Gwydion, what your welcome is the next time you are begging for a place in my bed," Arianrod went on, as though Dinaswyn had not even spoken. "If you are expecting . . ."

"As always I expect nothing from you," Gwydion said swiftly. "Not even the common courtesy to do as I ask."

Fuming, Arianrod left the chamber, slamming the door behind her.

Amatheon whistled and shook his head. "You are a brave man, Gwydion. There aren't many who would give up the chance to spend their nights with Arianrod."

"I didn't give up the chance," Gwydion said absently. "She'll take me back."

"Because it's not really you she's angry with," Dinaswyn said quietly. "It's me."

"And that will never change," Gwydion said.

"Unless you somehow produce her parents for her, safe and sound after all these years," Amatheon said. "And I don't believe you can do that."

"I sent them away," Dinaswyn said, "to Corania, as my dream demanded that I do. I cannot help it if they didn't come back."

"True, Aunt," Amatheon said. "So when will you stop trying to make it up to Arianrod?"

"We have wandered far from our task here," Dinaswyn said sharply. "The question was, who is to be the next High King of Kymru?"

"I know who," Gwydion said quietly. "The eagle was brown. And his tail feathers were blue. Bright, sapphire blue."

"Blue and brown. The colors of Gwynedd," Amatheon said slowly.

"Uthyr of Gwynedd's son?" Dinaswyn inquired.

"Uthyr doesn't have a son!" said Amatheon.

"Not yet. But Ygraine's time will be soon. Their first child is due within the week," Dinaswyn replied.

Gwydion stopped pacing. "My brother's son," he whispered. "The High King."

"Maybe," Dinaswyn said cautiously.

"Maybe? You just said . . ."

"You have to be careful with these things," she said mendaciously. "Dreams are rarely so straight-forward. You should know that by now."

"Dinaswyn," Amatheon said abruptly. "Did you dream at all tonight?"

She stiffened as she turned to face her youngest nephew, rage in every line of her body. She stared at him, but she did not speak.

"Did you?" he asked urgently.

"Amatheon . . ." Gwydion began.

"Did you?" Amatheon pressed.

Slowly the fury drained from her as she looked into Amatheon's blue eyes. "No," she said finally. "I did not dream. The dreams have passed on tonight, in Gwydion's first night alone in the Chamber of Prophecy. Gwydion is the new Dreamer of Kymru. My work is done."

"Done?" Gwydion was stunned. "But I have another year of training yet!"

"No," she said. "You don't. The dream was yours. And so is the burden that goes with it. You are the Dreamer now." She fumbled at her neck, releasing the catch on the torque. The necklace came off and she clutched it tightly for a moment. Firelight washed across the golden surface and glittered on the double circle of blazing opals. She thrust the necklace into Gwydion's unwilling hands. "It's yours, now. Take it. Take it all." Her head held high and her face a frozen mask, she left the chamber.

"It's too soon," Gwydion whispered, staring after Dinaswyn as she made her way down the stairs. "I'm not ready."

"Be ready," Amatheon said.

Addiendydd, Lleihau Wythnos—dusk
THE LAST RAYS of the setting sun filtered through the trees surrounding the clearing and the songs of the birds began to quiet for the night when Gwydion reined in his horse and dismounted. Behind him Amatheon did the same.

"I take it we are stopping here," said Amatheon.

Gwydion said nothing. Amatheon sighed. For four days now they had been on the road to Tegeingl. In all that time his brother had barely spoken.

Amatheon had been patient, for that was his nature. But there was also a time for action. He was done waiting. To-night he would get Gwydion to talk to him. He would not learn anything he didn't already know, for he knew his brother very well. But maybe Gwydion, hearing his fears spoken aloud, would find some peace in that. Amatheon had a feeling that peace would always elude his older brother, and his heart ached with that knowledge.

Silently they set about making camp, their movements economical and smooth. The day had been warm and both men wore tunics laced up the front with no shirt beneath. Gwydion's tunic of black with red lacing, the colors of the Dreamer, reached just below his upper thighs. His breeches were black and tucked in to black leather calf-length boots. His shoulder-length dark hair was tied back at the nape of his neck with a strip of leather. His cheekbones stood out stark and hard, and the shadows under his silvery eyes showed that true, restful sleep continued to elude him.

Amatheon was dressed similarly, but where Gwydion wore black and red, he wore sea green and silver, the colors of the clairvoyant Dewin.

"You realize, of course, that we don't have to do this. Camp out, I mean," Amatheon said somewhat irritably. By the Law of Hospitality any farm hold, any village, any manor would take them in, feed them, treat them as honored guests, shelter them for the night, and send them on their way with full saddlebags—and no questions asked. Of course, they would no doubt be recognized, but their hosts would preserve the laws with the polite fiction that they did not know who their guests were. But every night they had slept under the stars at Gwydion's insistence.

"What's the matter, brother? Your bones getting old and brittle? Need a soft bed?"

"You're just jealous," Amatheon said smugly. "Because you're older. And always will be."

Gwydion did not answer, but set about scraping a pit for the fire. The clearing was small, surrounded by birch, rowan, and ash trees. Amatheon spread a cloth over a small, flat rock, and began cutting bread and cheese.

"Don't really understand why you build a fire," Amatheon said, "when you won't even cook anything over it."

"I told you," Gwydion said absently, "that I hate to cook."

"What you mean is that you don't know how. I, on the other hand, am an excellent cook, and if you had brought anything else except dried meat, I'd show you." The conversation had the comfortable ring of familiarity. They had said the same thing every night since leaving Caer Dathyl.

Gwydion gathered small branches and heaped them into the hollow. Holding his hands over the pit, he briefly closed his eyes, his breathing deep and slow. Then a small, flower-like flame appeared in the middle of the branches. Shaped like a rosebud, it grew larger until the petals of fire burst from the glowing rose as the flame blossomed and the fire took hold.

"I do love watching you do that," Amatheon said casually.

"Druids Fire-Weave all the time," Gwydion pointed out. "It's hardly new for you to see that."

"Oh, yes," said Amatheon. "But they don't have your sense of style. You get that from Da, I see."

Gwydion did not answer. Amatheon had not thought he would.

Twilight descended as Gwydion tended the fire, feeding small branches into the crackling flames. As he leaned forward to feed more branches, the firelight crawled hungrily over the double circle of opals hanging from the Dreamer's Torque, symbol of Mabon, Lord of the Sun.

Amatheon's torque of silver with its pendant of pearl glowed in the dusky twilight, the symbol of Nantsovelta, Lady of the Moon.

Slight rustles in the forest spoke of small animals making

their ways back to their homes, or beginning their nightly hunt for food. Far off, a wolf howled at the ebon glory of the night sky. Gwydion continued to stare into the fire as if it held all the answers to his questions. He scratched his short beard absently.

"You always scratch that thing," said Amatheon.

"It itches."

At least it was an answer. "Why grow it then, if it itches?"

Gwydion shot a look to his brother, his gray eyes gleaming. "It does what it's supposed to do."

"Hide you, you mean?" Gwydion made no answer so Amatheon continued. "There are many ways to hide, brother mine, and you know them all. Tell me what's wrong. What's bothering you so? Maybe I can help."

Gwydion was silent for a long time. Just when Amatheon was sure that his brother would not answer, Gwydion drew in a deep breath, then let it out with a sigh. He looked over at his brother, a hint of desperation in his gray eyes. "I'm the Dreamer now. And it's . . . it's too soon. I thought it would be years yet before this happened."

"And?" Amatheon prompted.

"And I barely know what I'm doing. It's too soon."

"Come now, Gwydion. The Dreamer interprets the dreams that the Shining Ones send and acts—or doesn't act—accordingly. What's so hard about that?"

"You're over simplifying," Gwydion accused. "It's a lot more complicated than that. Suppose I interpret something wrong? Then what happens? Look, here's an example. Twenty years ago Dinaswyn has a dream. And she interprets that dream as telling her that Arianrod's parents must go to Corania to spy on the enemy for a time. And they never come back. Now you tell me, did they never come back because Dinaswyn misinterpreted the dream? Or, were they supposed to go and never come back? And, if so, why?"

Amatheon shook his head. "You're too impatient Gwydion. It's too soon to know the answer to that."

"Too soon? Twenty years?"

"A blink of the eye for the Shining Ones. You know that."

"Amatheon, that's not the point," Gwydion said impatiently, waving away his brother's comment. "The point is that the dreams are my responsibility now. Mine to interpret."

"And?" Amatheon pressed.

"And nothing," Gwydion muttered.

"And you might get them wrong, is that it? You might make a mistake. And if you do, what happens?"

Gwydion hesitated, then said in a rush, "Then I fail. And I can't. I can't do that."

"Why?"

"Why?" Gwydion repeated, shocked.

"Yes. What's so terrible about failing? People do it all the time and the world goes on turning. They pick themselves up and try again. Why should you be different?"

"Because I'm the Dreamer, Amatheon," Gwydion said quietly. "The Shining Ones have sent me a dream. I have tasks to perform . . . things I must do, and do right."

"Ah. So, lesser mortals can make mistakes?" Amatheon asked lightly. "But not you—you aren't allowed."

"I am one of the Great Ones now," Gwydion said, staring into the fire. "I take my place with the Master Bard, with the Ardewin, with the Archdruid. Soon a High King will come and I will do all I can to protect him from whatever threatens him. In that—and in any other tasks the Shining Ones give

23

me—I cannot fail."

"What else is wrong?" Amatheon asked quietly. "That's not all of it."

Again the silence descended over them both as Gwydion left his brother's question unanswered. "The torque becomes you," Amatheon said at last.

"She didn't want to give it up," Gwydion replied. After a pause he went on, "They never do want to do the things they should."

"They?"

"Women." Silence again.

"It was a difficult thing for Aunt Dinaswyn to do. You know that. She had been Dreamer for many years. She never had anything else. Or anyone."

More silence. Amatheon sighed and began again. "Arianrod was angry with you. But, as you say, she'll take you back to her bed."

Gwydion's eyes brightened with amusement. "Did you think that was bothering me?"

"No," Amatheon said quietly. "I don't think anything Arianrod does would bother you. You would have to care about her first."

Gwydion sighed. "I give her what I can."

"No. You give her what you want to. Nothing more."

"And you think it should be more?" Gwydion asked.

"No." Amatheon said promptly, "I don't. Not with her. She will only take and take, and then take some more."

"You don't make sense. First you seem to tell me that I should love her, and then you say that I shouldn't. Is there a purpose to this, or are you just bored?"

"I only want to point out that it's your habit. You judge all women by just a few. Arianrod is selfish and demanding. But all women are not like that. And Mam—"

"No." Gwydion cut him off, eyes blazing. "I will not discuss Mam with you."

"If you can't talk about her with me, then with who?"

"Not with anyone."

"Gwydion . . ."

"I said no. You weren't there. You didn't see. I . . . I can't." Again the silence, the wall, back higher and stronger than ever. Gwydion went back to staring at the fire.

Amatheon looked up at the stars, silently asking for patience. A few could be seen, but the trees around the clearing obscured most of them. Amatheon took a deep breath and held out his hand. "Come. Let's Wind-Ride."

After a momentary hesitation, Gwydion grasped his brother's hand. "Where do you want to go?"

"I just want to get a good look at the sky. Follow me. With that, both men closed their eyes. Their breathing slowed until their chests barely moved. And when they were ready, a portion of their awareness leapt from their bodies, and soared up into the night sky.

As they flew upward, leaving their bodies sitting by the fire, Amatheon Wind-Spoke to Gwydion, his words echoing in his brother's mind, "*You see that? It is the constellation of Llyr the Great who first brought us into this land. And there, not far off, the constellation of Penduran reaching her arms out to Llyr. It was these two who saved a remnant of the Kymri when Lyonesse sank beneath the sea. These two, in partnership, taught their children well. And these children became the leaders of the next generation—the Dreamer who guides Kymru, the Ardewin who leads our clairvoyants,*" *the Master Bard who heads our telepaths, the Archdruid who rules our psychokinetics. Without Llyr and Penduran, the Kymri would have perished."*

Gwydion replied, his mind-voice bitter, *"Yes, I see those constellations. And there, do you see the constellation of Dahut, the woman whose evil caused Lyonesse to sink? Do you see her, too? Or only what you want to see?"*

Abruptly, Amatheon returned them both to their bodies. As both men opened their eyes Gwydion rubbed his head gingerly. "You didn't have to be so rough."

"Maybe I did," Amatheon said shortly. "Look, you can live your life any way you choose. I only want to point out that when you distrust half the human race, you lack balance. And without balance you can make mistakes. And mistakes, as you so recently pointed out, are not things you can tolerate."

"Women do not deserve to be trusted," Gwydion said shortly. "I shouldn't have to tell you that, of all people."

"All women are not like Mam," Amatheon said. "They don't all do what she did."

"Well, I can assure you that no woman will ever have the chance to do to me what she did to Da," Gwydion said coldly. "Ever."

"Because you will never let one get close enough to touch your heart."

"All I want is to be free, not to be entangled with a woman's faithless heart. What's wrong with that?"

Amatheon sat quietly, looking out into the night. At last he said, "Loneliness can be the price of freedom, brother."

"A price I am willing to pay," Gwydion said firmly.

"Then so be it," Amatheon replied sadly.

Chapter Two

> Tegeingl
> Kingdom of
> Gwynedd, Kymru
> Gwernan Mis, 482

Meirgdydd, Lleihau Wythnos—dusk

Gwydion and Amatheon arrived at Tegeingl at dusk the following day. The strong, high stone walls loomed out of the gathering gloom, towering over the two men as they rode out of the forest and up the slight incline to the west gate. Tegeingl's walls formed a huge triangle with three towers, one at each joining of the walls. The torches in these towers were just being lit and the city gates were closing for the night. One massive, iron door was already shut, and the other was halfway closed.

"Whoa," Amatheon called out to the gatekeeper. "Not yet, man."

The gatekeeper, a slender man with a long, mournful face peered distrustfully into the gloom. "Who goes there?"

"The sons of Awst," answered Gwydion.

The man gave an exaggerated sigh and shook his head. "Almost shut the gate on you two." He paused, eyeing them. "Might not have been a bad idea at that."

"You're hilarious, Donal," Amatheon said dryly. "Don't tell me that you didn't see us coming."

"Oh, I did. That's why I almost shut the gate."

Amatheon eyed Donal and casually blew on his nails and buffed them against his tunic. "May I remind you," he said airily, "that you are addressing two of the Y Dawnus of Kymru?"

"Wonderful," returned Donal, in a bored tone. "Can't wait to tell everyone that I was lucky enough to speak to those with the gifts. That will make me the envy of all."

"Smart mouth," Amatheon returned, without rancor.

Donal pulled back on the door, widening it just enough to allow their horses to get through. Amatheon gave him a jaunty wave, which the gatekeeper ostentatiously ignored.

They rode east, down the main street of the city. Torches burned in brackets set at intervals on the outside of the stone buildings that housed the brewery, the smithy, and the public baths.

"Deserted," Gwydion remarked, as they came to the empty marketplace. The wooden stalls were locked up for the night. From down one of the side streets, lined with wooden houses, a dog barked. Smoke filtered through the chimneys of the cheerfully lit houses.

"Of course it's deserted. Everyone's having his or her dinner. Everyone except us, of course."

Gwydion eyed his brother's lean frame. "Hungry?"

"Always."

They passed Nemed Gwernan, the grove of alder trees where the eight festivals of the year were celebrated, and where the Queens of Gwynedd bore their children. A slight breeze rustled the leaves of the darkening wood as they rode by.

"No one is there. Ygraine must not be in labor," Amatheon said.

"A few more days yet, I think. I wouldn't be surprised if she has the child at the Calan Llachar festival."

"What makes you think that? Did you dream it?"

"No, but this year there will be an eclipse on Calan Llachar, as there is every eighteen years. It seems momentous, fated, because Idris, Macsen, and Lleu were all born on Calan Llachar, all born on the day of the eclipse. If Uthyr's son is truly the one he will be born then, too."

They lapsed into silence as they passed Bryn Celli Ddu, the burial place of the Rulers of Gwynedd. The standing stones that marked the entrance to the barrows stood gray and silent, sentinels to another world. The only sound was of the horses' hooves striking the cobblestones as they rode by.

And then they were at the walls of Caer Gwynt, the House of Winds, the fortress of the Rulers of Gwynedd. Torches burned on either side of the gate. The proud Hawk of Gwynedd, outlined in sapphires on the silver-plated doors, stretched his wings into the night.

"Ho, there," Amatheon called. The gate slowly opened, and a young man with golden hair and a sharp, intelligent face stepped out.

"Welcome, travelers," the young man said, bowing. "King Uthyr ap Rathtyen var Awst welcomes the Dreamer of Kymru, Gwydion ap Awst var Celemon, the great Dreamer of Mabon the Bright."

"How did you know I was the Dreamer now?" Gwydion asked curiously.

"Oh, Dinaswyn Wind-Spoke to Susanna a few days ago— she's our new Bard here, by the way," the young man said casually. "But you're interrupting my speech," Duach went on in a reproving tone.

"Oh. Sorry."

With a flourish, Duach continued, "And welcome also to Amatheon ap Awst, one of the Dewin of the House of Llyr, beloved of Nantsovelta, White Lady of the Moon."

"Nice, Duach," Amatheon said admiringly. "Very nice."

The young man grinned. "You like it?"

"Very much. You the doorkeeper now?"

"Just appointed last month," he said proudly. "Come in."

The two men dismounted as grooms came out to lead their horses to the stables that rested just inside the gate. Dogs from the kennel on their right began to bark as Gwydion and Amatheon followed Duach across the well-lit courtyard.

They passed a long, low, wooden building that housed the King's warriors. No lights shone now in the windows, for they were all at dinner in the hall. As they passed the King and Queen's ystafell they noticed that a light was glowing from a window in the second story of the polished wooden walls. "The Queen?" Gwydion asked.

"She's not feeling well enough to leave her chambers."

"I imagine not," Gwydion said dryly. "It should be within the next few days."

"That's what Cynan says," Duach replied. "But Griffi's holding out for the end of the week. They've got a bet."

"Who's Griffi?"

"New Druid. Just came about two months ago to replace Cathbad, now that he's the Archdruid's heir."

"I hear the Archdruid is very ill," Gwydion said, "and not expected to last much longer."

"No doubt," Duach said. "I think he's only holding on

long enough to train Cathbad. After all, no one expected the tragedy and Cathbad doesn't have the training an heir would normally have."

"What do you think of Griffi?" Amatheon asked.

"Good man," Duach replied. "Of course we'll miss Cathbad."

"We'll all miss Cathbad," Gwydion said, for the Druid was a good friend. "I am glad that he will be Archdruid, but sorry for his brother's sudden death. Dorath was a good man, and would have made a good Archdruid."

"Cathbad was very broken up about it," Duach said. "He said that a man never had a better brother than Dorath."

"Well, I don't know about that," Amatheon said, with an air of exaggerated innocence. "I think Gwydion has just about the best brother anyone could ever wish for in the whole wide world."

"Yes," Gwydion said blandly. "There's no better brother than Uthyr."

"Ha, ha," Amatheon said flatly.

"Oh, do you two want a bath first or do you want to go to the hall?" Duach asked.

"You saying I need a bath?" growled Amatheon.

"Well, it wouldn't hurt," Duach grinned.

"We'll go to the hall first," Gwydion replied, for he was eager to see Uthyr.

As Duach opened the doors to the Great Hall, bright lights and cheerful noise spilled out. The hall was filled with people, some sitting at the long tables, some standing in front of the roaring hearth fire, some dicing in the far corners. Most of the people were the men and women of the King's *teulu*, dressed in the brown breeches and blue tunics of Gwynedd's warriors.

They had bright daggers at their belts and brown leather boots to the knee laced with strips of blue cloth.

Bright banners of silk hung on the walls. The banner over the east wall showed the Battle of Naid Ronwen, when Queen Gwynledyr put to death the treacherous Coranian husband who had tried to steal her throne.

The banner of the Hawk of Gwynedd, shimmering brown on blue silk and worked with sapphires and silver thread, hung on the west wall. Under the banner the dark, polished wood of the King's table shone in the firelight.

Surrounded by people, King Uthyr sat at the table, his massive oak chair tilted back precariously, his legs stretched out and crossed negligently at the ankles, resting on the table's surface. He was paring his nails with a knife and laughing at something, his even, white teeth gleaming in his tanned face. His brown hair with just a touch of red was tied back with a thin silver chain, and his auburn beard was closely cut. Around his neck he wore the silver Torque of Gwynedd, studded with sapphires. He wore a huge, sapphire ring on his right hand. His blue tunic was embroidered with silver and worked with sapphires, and his breeches were brown. His leather boots were turned down at the top to reveal a lining of blue cloth. Uthyr's deep set, dark eyes under heavy brows glanced toward the door and widened at the sight of Gwydion and Amatheon.

"Brothers," he roared as he leapt from his chair and over the table. His long strides ate up the distance between them and, as he reached them he enveloped each brother in a fierce bear hug, actually lifting them off their feet and swinging them around.

"Little brothers!" he said, setting them back on their feet with a thump. "The Shining Ones bless you both for coming."

"Uthyr, you've got to get over this shyness of yours," Amatheon said, grinning, while Gwydion tried to set his rumpled tunic to rights. "And your tendency to treat important men like the Dreamer with overwhelming respect. It gives the wrong impression."

Uthyr grinned back and flung his arms around their shoulders. "We're just about to eat. Come, you two sit with me."

As they made their way through the press, the warriors of Uthyr's *teulu* shouted greetings and a few good-natured, rude remarks. "Hey, Gwydion," someone shouted from the back of the crowd. "Learned to use a sword yet?"

"No," Gwydion shot back. "Have you?"

"Amatheon," a warrior called, "ready to lose at dice?"

"Ready to take your money," Amatheon retorted with a grin.

Amid the laughter and jokes, they slowly made their way down the length of the hall. As they neared the King's table, a young man with curly red hair and an engaging grin in a freckled face rose from the table and bowed. His brown, hooded robe, embroidered in green around the hem and sleeves, proclaimed the man to be a Druid. The pendant on his slender golden torque was a circle inside a square, with an emerald glittering in the center. "Griffi ap Iaen," the Druid said, offering a slightly exaggerated bow, along with an impish grin.

A young woman in a sleeveless gown of blue over a snowy white smock rose from a graceful curtsy. Her girdle was a fine silver chain, wrapped once at the upper waist and doubling back over her hips. The front of her bodice was laced with white silk ties, and her torque had a triangular pendant from which a sapphire dangled. Her long, red-gold hair was loosely wrapped with a blue ribbon. She had a generous mouth and bright, blue eyes under slender red-gold brows. She held out her hand to Gwydion. "Susanna ur Erim, Uthyr's Bard."

"Been here long?"

"No, I just arrived last month." Her eyes cut to Griffi. "I haven't been here much longer than he has." As she looked at the young Druid, her eyes glowed, finding an answering glow in Griffi's fresh face. She bowed to Amatheon. "You are both most welcome here."

A tall, older man with dark hair lightly silvered and mild gray eyes stood by diffidently, patiently waiting to be noticed. He wore a sea green tunic and his torque was silver with a pentagon-shaped pendant, a single pearl dangling from it. Amatheon caught the man's eye and grinned. "Uncle Cynan! You look well," he said, slapping the man's back. "Being Dewin here must agree with you."

"It does, Amatheon, it does." He smiled, and made a slight bow to Gwydion. "Greetings to you, Dreamer," he said.

"So formal, Uncle Cynan? I remember when you dawdled me on your knee and fed me sweets."

"Oh, yes. That always made Celemon angry." At the mention of his mother, Gwydion froze. Amatheon's eyes cut sharply to Gwydion, but he did not speak. Cynan colored slightly and looked to Uthyr. Absorbing Amatheon's more relaxed stance, Uthyr laid a light hand on Gwydion's arm. "Come, I have somebody else for you to greet."

Uthyr led Gwydion to a man waiting at the other end of the table. The man stood stiffly, a fixed smile on his face. His reddish gold hair hung in curls to his shoulders. His red tunic and leggings were embroidered with silver-threaded hawks. His boots were red, dyed to match the tunic and the tops were turned down, showing flashing rubies. His blue eyes were cold.

"Madoc," Gwydion murmured. "That popinjay! What's he doing here?"

"Why he's here for the birth."

"He hoping for a still born?" Gwydion asked, bitterly.

Uthyr froze and turned slowly toward his brother, his eyes wide with shock. "Is that what you have dreamed? Is there something wrong with the child?"

"Oh, Uthyr, no. No." Gwydion put his hand on his brother's arm, gripping it hard. "It's just, it's only . . ."

"It's only that you hate Madoc? He's my half brother, Gwydion. The same as you and Amatheon are. He is Lord in Rhufonoig and serves me faithfully. You will treat him politely. Come, do as I bid you."

Gwydion raised one eyebrow, his mouth tightening.

"All right, Gwydion," said Uthyr in an exasperated tone. "Do as I beg you, then. Greet him and try to be polite. His wife just gave birth to a daughter, and died doing so."

"I'm sorry for that," Gwydion said quietly. "Bri was a lovely woman. And she deserved better than the husband she got."

"Most of them do," Uthyr said dryly. Together, Uthyr and Gwydion approached Madoc, who had been watching them narrowly.

"Madoc," said Gwydion, as he briefly inclined his head.

Madoc smiled even more widely, but his blue eyes were cold. "Gwydion. How very, very good to see you!" He nodded toward Uthyr. "Perhaps, Gwydion, you can calm him down. He's as nervous as a cat about Ygraine. I keep telling him that nothing will go wrong. Women have babies every day."

"I was sorry to hear about Bri," Gwydion said quietly, his eyes never leaving Madoc's face.

Madoc's smile faded slightly. "Yes, poor Bri. I miss her sorely. But the child does well, so we must be thankful for that."

"Hear anything from your father?" Gwydion asked casually.

Madoc's eyes narrowed. "Not a thing. Just after the Queen died he went to Prydyn and stayed there for a little while with his nephew, King Rhoram. And then he was off. Wouldn't say where he was going, just that he wanted to be left alone. Of course, my father's bitterness isn't really surprising. After all, he had just had final proof that his wife did not love him. A pity that she died of grief over the murder of your father. And such a murder! Dead at the hands of his own—"

"Madoc," Uthyr cut in with a tone of steel. With one look at Gwydion's white, set face, Uthyr took Gwydion's arm and led him away from Madoc, who was smiling again, this time with a hint of satisfaction.

"Sit down," said Uthyr, steering Gwydion to the chair next to his at the King's table. Uthyr nodded to Griffi who raised up both hands and said, in a carrying tone, "Be seated, all." The crowd took their places and the room began to quiet down. Griffi lifted his hands again and intoned.

The peace of lights,
The peace of joys,
The peace of souls,
Be with you.

"Awen. So let it be," the crowd replied in unison.

"Just a few announcements," Griffi began. "For those of you who have been inside a wine jug for the last week or so and don't know what day it is—"

"He means you, Cai," someone yelled. Amid the catcalls and laughter, Griffi grinned, and again raised his hands for (relative) silence.

"Tomorrow is Calan Llachar Eve. The hunt for the stag begins at noon. Since Ygraine's not feeling up to leading it this year—"

"Can't blame her for that," a warrior called out.

Griffi continued, "She has appointed the Bard, Susanna ur Erim, to lead this year."

"Go get him, Susanna!" someone called as she rose and bowed slightly to the crowd. "How about we call the stag 'Griffi'? Then she'll be sure to lead us to it." Susanna, blushing bright red, abruptly sat down.

Griffi, his face an interesting shade of mauve, cleared his throat and valiantly continued. "On Calan Llachar itself, there will be a full eclipse of the sun beginning at midday. We'll be running the race to choose the King of the Wood in the morning, so it shouldn't interfere with that. We should be dancing around the tree by the time the sky begins to darken."

As he sat down, the servers began to bring in heavy platters to each table. Gwydion speared a few slices of venison with his belt knife and laid them on his plate, passing the platter to Uthyr on his left. Preoccupied with his thoughts, he did not notice his other companions, but ate in silence.

Finally satiated, he took a deep breath and glanced up. Susanna was leaning forward slightly to talk to Griffi who sat opposite her. Uthyr had turned to say something to Madoc. He glanced across the table. Arday ur Medyr, Uthyr's steward, sat directly across from him. At his glance, she smiled slowly. Her black hair had a blue sheen in the firelight. A green ribbon held her hair back from her face. Her arched black brows cut startlingly into her milky white skin. Her lips were full and her pointed chin emphasized the heart-like shape of her face. She was dressed in a forest green gown, the

37

bodice tightly laced, clearly outlining her firm breasts.

"Arday," said Gwydion. "I'm sorry, I didn't see you before."

She laughed lightly. "That was obvious! I was making sure that this magnificent feast got to the tables. How goes it, Gwydion?" Her dark eyes, full of promise, held his.

Gwydion smiled quite ready to take the lady up on the offer in her eyes.

Amatheon, who was sitting on Arday's right, chose that moment to speak. He gestured to the lean, brown-haired man sitting next to him. "Gwydion, you remember Cai, don't you?"

"Of course," Gwydion said pleasantly, hiding his annoyance at being interrupted. "How goes it, Cai?"

Cai's dark brown eyes brightened. "It goes well, Gwydion. And you? Any good dreams lately?"

Gwydion's smile froze. "No," he said harshly.

Taken aback, Cai glanced quickly at Amatheon. Stepping into the sudden silence, Amatheon said, "Cai's hoping the Shining Ones sent you a dream about him! He's just been named Captain of Uthyr's *teulu*."

"Congratulations, then, to the PenGwernan," Gwydion said, recovering swiftly from his blunder. "Here's to the Head of the Alder!" Gwydion lifted his cup and drank, while Amatheon and Arday did the same.

Cai grinned somewhat uncertainly at Gwydion, his face flushed.

"Ah," Gwydion went on. "I remember the dream now. You see, a weasel was leading Uthyr's *teulu* and they got lost in the forest—"

Uthyr's laughter soared above the rest. "He's got you on that one, Cai. You do look like a weasel. Lean, brown, shifty-eyed."

38

"Shifty-eyed!" Cai retorted. "I'll have you know that my wife says my eyes are my best feature." He batted his eyes rapidly at Uthyr.

"And you're sitting on your second best—your brains," retorted Uthyr.

"That's not fair. Everyone's against me." Cai leaned forward to call to the end of the table, "Trachymer! Help me out here."

Trachymer, Uthyr's chief huntsman, a taciturn man with a leathery face, didn't even glance up from his meal. "Whatever it is, you deserve it, Cai."

"What's he mad at you for?" asked Amatheon curiously.

Cai looked at Amatheon in surprise. "Oh, he's not mad. If he was mad, he'd be smiling." Trachymer merely grunted, and kept on with his meal.

Susanna abruptly turned to Gwydion. "Tell me, what do you hear about Rhiannon ur Hefeydd?"

"Rhiannon?" he said in surprise. Rhiannon was a woman of the House of Llyr, and a cousin of his. She was the Ardewin's heir, and would replace his uncle, Myrrdin, when the time came. But Gwydion barely knew her, for they had been at different colleges throughout their training. "What do you want to know about her?"

"Surely you knew that just a few months ago Dinaswyn sent Rhiannon to Prydyn to have a child by King Rhoram. I just wondered if you knew how she was, that's all."

"Dinaswyn didn't mention it. The bloodlines of Llyr were still her responsibility at that point. Has Rhiannon conceived yet?"

"Not yet, I don't think. But I heard Rhoram was quite taken with her. Things have been pretty rough with him since his wife died last year."

"Then all appears to be as well as can be expected," he said coolly. "Why are you concerned?"

"It's just—well she's a good person. A little quiet and shy. She went to Y Ty Dewin, of course, but I got to know her since she was always coming around Neuadd Gorsedd to look for her father. He was a Bard."

"Why did she have to look for him at the Bardic college? He could have gone to Y Ty Dewin to see her anytime. It's a school, not a prison."

Susanna frowned. "Oh, he would never do that. He avoided her on purpose."

"Why?"

"Oh, I never really knew for sure. Her mother died giving birth to her, and he always blamed Rhiannon for that, I think. And for something else, too, but I never knew what. Look, it's just that . . . well . . ."

Bards were facile with words and the fact that Susanna was having trouble alerted Gwydion that she had something to say that he probably didn't want to hear. "It's just that what?" Gwydion asked impatiently.

Susanna took a deep breath. "People like you, and like Dinaswyn, you have your dreams. And you have your Book of the Blood to tell you who should mate with who, and when. You command men and women of the House of Llyr to mate with kings and queens. And, sometimes, like with your father and Queen Rathtyen, they find love. And sometimes they don't, they just grit their teeth and do what needs to be done so that they can carry on the bloodlines. And the Dreamers never seem to care about the people that they order around. I was just hoping that Rhiannon would be happy living with

Rhoram and bearing his child. And I was hoping that when the time came for her to leave Rhoram and return to Y Ty Dewin she would be able to bear it. I want her to be happy, because she always seemed so sad."

Was Susanna really telling him that he should care about people's love lives? He was supposed to be concerned about this along with all the other duties of the Dreamer? Susanna wanted him to care if some woman was happy? "She is doing her duty. Most of us can never ask for, or have, anything else," he said shortly.

"You know, Gwydion, you are one cold bastard." Susanna stood, looking down at him. "Even if you are the Dreamer of Kymru. Or maybe because of it."

As she swept away from the table, somebody called out, "A song, Susanna. A song!" The shout went up around the hall. Susanna smiled tightly, as someone brought her harp.

"Chose a song, Gwydion," she called her smile mocking. "What song shall I sing for the mighty Dreamer? Do we not all live to serve you?"

But he would not be mocked—not by Susanna, not by anyone. "I call for Bran's Song," he said.

Susanna's smile faded away. The hall grew hushed as people wondered why the Dreamer should ask for that song. Into the sudden stillness, Susanna sang.

Saplings of the green-topped birch,
Which will draw me from the fetters,
Repeat not thy secret to a youth.

Saplings of the oak in the grove,
Which will draw me from my chains,
Repeat not thy secret to a maiden.

41

Saplings of the leafy elm,
Which will draw me from my prison,
Repeat not thy secret to a babbler.

The Wild Hunt with their horns are heard.
Full of lightning, the air,
Briefly it is said; true are the trees, false is man.

False is man, Gwydion thought to himself. Very false indeed.

BY THE EARLY morning hours, the gutted candles were flickering feebly in Uthyr's chambers. A huge bed with an oak frame and a thick mattress stood against the wall, covered with a blue silken bedspread with the Hawk of Gwynedd embroidered on it in silver thread and brown silk. Bearskin rugs were scattered on the polished floor. The fire in the large fireplace had burned down to glowing embers, casting its light fitfully over the three men gathered there.

Gwydion sat cross-legged on the stone hearth, cradling a gold cup of barely touched wine in his hands. Amatheon reposed on Uthyr's most comfortable chair, for he had declared that the youngest never got anything good and dared his brothers to prove him wrong. Uthyr himself sat on a low stool, drawn up close to the hearth. The three brothers had talked far into the night, and dawn was now not far away.

Uthyr stirred slightly. "And so, soon after I received the Ruler's Torque, King Rhodri just left. Didn't say good-bye to anyone. Just left."

"I'm sorry for that. Deep down he is a good man, I think," replied Amatheon.

"He was jealous of my mother and your father. You can't blame him, really. I think he truly loved her," replied Uthyr.

"Rathtyen did love Rhodri, I think. As much as she could," said Amatheon.

"Not enough for him." Uthyr sighed, and glanced at Gwydion, who was sitting quietly, half turned on the hearth to gaze into the fire.

Gwydion's hands were clasped tightly around the cup that he held. They are getting close, he thought. Too close. Any minute now they will start talking about how Rathtyen died of grief. Start talking about how Da died. About how—not even to himself would Gwydion finish that thought. He swallowed hard and turned to Uthyr, desperate to change the subject.

"And Ygraine?" he asked. "How is she?"

Uthyr chuckled. "Oh, fine, fine. She threw her brush at me this morning."

"Ah," Amatheon smiled. "The same as ever."

"Yes, well," Uthyr shifted on the stool and touched his ear thoughtfully. "Of course, she's a little slower, what with the birth being only a day or two away. The brush barely nicked my ear."

"That must have truly made her mad," Gwydion smiled, scratching his beard.

"Why do you grow that thing if it itches?" Uthyr asked curiously. Amatheon's eyes gleamed.

"I like it," Gwydion replied defensively.

"The birth," Uthyr said, after a pause. "Have you seen nothing?"

Gwydion hesitated. Was Uthyr's child truly the one? He could not be sure. He trusted Uthyr completely, but there was nothing to be gained by speaking out of turn. "Were you expecting something?" he hedged.

"Sometimes," Uthyr said hesitantly, "I put my hand on Ygraine's belly and touch the baby growing there. And sometimes, I think I feel something very . . ."

"Something? What?" Amatheon asked, leaning forward to stare intently at Uthyr.

Uthyr closed his eyes and was silent. Then he spoke in a hollow tone. "I see a throne in the shape of an eagle. It is all of gold. And there are eight steps leading up to it. Each is inlaid with precious stones—one is of topaz, one of amethyst. One of emerald, and one of pearl. One of ruby, one of onyx, one of opal, and one of sapphire. They glitter in the golden light that floods the room. But the room is empty."

Amatheon said nothing, his face carefully still. Gwydion was also silent, looking at his half brother without expression.

"You know something," Uthyr said flatly. "You both do. I just described the throne room of the High King's at Cadair Idris that has been shut up now for over two hundred years. And you both just sit there and look at me as though you cannot imagine what I am talking about."

Gwydion sighed and placed his hand on his brother's arm. "Uthyr, if I truly knew, if I had truly seen, if there was anything I could tell you, I would. But there is not. The child isn't even born." Gwydion paused. "But brother, I tell you this. Trust no one. Tell no one what you have told us. It could be dangerous—for all of us."

"I have told no one," Uthyr answered. "Not even Ygraine. I thought that perhaps it was nothing. Only fancies." He looked Gwydion square in the face. "If you tell me it is dangerous, then it is. I will say nothing."

"It's late," Amatheon said, rising. "We should all get

some sleep."

"Yes," said Uthyr, "And the Calan Llachar hunt will begin soon. Why don't you both sleep here? You can bed down in front of the fire. To tell you the truth, I don't really want to be alone tonight."

"I think we'll just stay here, then," said Gwydion, as he rose from the hearth.

"Arday will be disappointed," Amatheon said, his eyes glinting in amusement.

Uthyr and Amatheon laughed, and even Gwydion smiled sourly. Gwydion stretched and laid down on the rug as Uthyr threw another bearskin over him. Silently, Gwydion began murmuring the Dreamer's Prayer, calling on the Shining Ones to protect him and enable him to dream true.

Annwyn with me lying down, Aertan with me sleeping.
The white light of Nantsovelta be in my soul,
The mantle of Modron about my shoulders,
The protection of Taran over me,
And in my heart, the fire of Mabon.
If malice should threaten my life,
Then the Shining Ones between me and evil.
From tonight till a year from tonight,
And this very night,
And forever.
Awen.

With that, Gwydion fell asleep. And dreamed.

HE WAS STANDING in a forest clearing. The trees were fresh and green. Even the bark seemed to glisten in the light of the sun that streamed through the trees, bathing the forest in a golden glow. The ground beneath his feet was covered with marigolds and the delicate white flowers of the rowan tree. They made a carpet of silver and gold on the forest floor.

In the distance, he heard the sound of a hunting horn. It echoed, again and again, shattering the still air. He heard the baying of hounds, coming closer. He heard a rustle in the leaves overhead. Looking up, he saw a young eagle, terror in its eyes.

"Are they hunting you, little one?" Gwydion asked, lifting his arm out to the young bird. "I will not harm you. I will save you from them."

To his surprise, the eagle flew to him and perched on his shoulder, its talons digging into his flesh. He could feel the bird trembling as it pressed itself against his neck.

"Do they hunt you? Hush, I am here." He gently lifted the bird from his shoulder and cradled it in his hands, stroking its blue and brown feathers. "I will not let them hurt you."

The horns, the baying, came closer. The eagle shifted restlessly, but Gwydion held the bird firmly. "No, no, young one. You are safe with me. They will bypass us."

He sent a thought to the baying hounds, telling them to pass by, that there was no one there. But instead, the baying became even more insistent. He could hear horses now, crashing through the trees.

Suddenly the hounds leapt into the clearing. Gwydion gasped in surprise, for all the hounds were white, with red ears. They seemed to grin at him, surrounding Gwydion and the young bird that he held in his hands.

"This eagle is under my protection," Gwydion said sternly. "You may not touch him." The hounds backed away a little then continued to circle, panting and baying for their master.

And then their master was there, his white horse stepping

delicately into the clearing. The horse wore no saddle or bridle. The rider's chest was bare, and his breeches were made of deerskin. His leather boots were studded with topaz gemstones. He had the face of a man but his eyes were the topaz eyes of an owl, staring at Gwydion, unblinking. Most alarming of all, he had antlers growing from his forehead, like a stag. The rider seemed to glow in the light of the sun.

Oh gods, thought Gwydion. Oh gods.

"Yes, gods are here," uttered the rider. "I am Cerrunnos. I know you, Dreamer."

Gwydion swallowed hard. "I know you, Cerrunnos. Lord of the Wild Hunt, Protector of Kymru." Gwydion managed a bow, of a sort, careful to keep the eagle out of reach.

Another horse, black as midnight, stepped into the clearing, and Gwydion gaped at the woman on the mare's back. Slender and lithe, her skin was tanned and smooth. Her midnight hair cascaded down her back. Her shift was a glowing white, the length of the skirt barely reaching her calves. A silver belt sparkling with amethysts circled her slim waist. Her boots were leather, studded with amethysts, and her amethyst eyes studied Gwydion, cool and serene.

"Goddesses greet you too, Dreamer. I am Cerridwen."

Again, Gwydion bowed. "Mighty Cerridwen. Queen of the Wood. Protectress of Kymru. Your beauty stops my heart and stills my tongue."

Cerridwen laughed. "Strong words from a man who has vowed never to care for a woman!" She shrugged, as Gwydion looked up quickly, stricken. "It matters not to me, Dreamer. But we will trouble you for that eagle. He is ours."

Gwydion took a deep breath. "I cannot oblige you, Lady. I have sworn to protect him from the Hunt."

"No one can be protected from the Hunt," Cerrunnos said bluntly, his owl eyes as bright as topaz. "The Hunt comes for all."

Gwydion took another deep breath. "He trusted me, you see. And so I cannot give him to you."

"If you do not, Dreamer, do you know what happens to your world? Without a High King you are all doomed."

Gwydion glanced down at the eagle he still cradled in his arms. Lightly he stroked the bird. And then he raised his head, looking at the god and goddess squarely. "He does not want to be High King. He wishes to be free."

"All men wish to be free. But in this world, it cannot be. The High King has his duty. It is not for you to help him to shirk it," Cerrunnos replied.

"If he is High King, will he be happy?"

"It is not for him to be happy, Dreamer," said Cerrunnos. "And neither is it for you. He must be who he was born to be."

"Listen, Dreamer, and listen well," Cerridwen said. "For this is the first of your tasks. You must protect him, hide him, see to it that he suffers no harm."

"There are traitors among the Kymru," Cerrunnos said. "Understand this. Hide him well. And remember that those you can trust are few."

"Who? Who can I trust?" Gwydion asked.

"That is for you to discover," Cerrunnos said sternly.

"Can't you—"

"Next," Cerridwen interrupted, "your task will be to find Caladfwlch, the sword of the High Kings, hidden by Bran long ago. But you may not begin this task without the aid of those who will be revealed to you."

"When?" Gwydion asked.

"In good time," Cerrunnos said. "Now, give the eagle to us. He is ours. It is not for him to be free. It is for him to be what he was born to be, until his turn on the Wheel is done."

Cerridwen's voice rang like silver bells through the clearing. "Men do not ask for pain, for grief, for sorrow. But it is their lot to bear it. Men ask for happiness and perhaps it comes to them, in some measure. This young eagle that tries to escape us runs only from himself. We are the Wild Hunt. We are the Protectors of Kymru. And we will see to it that this eagle does his duty. It is for this that he is born."

Her voice lowered, and it seemed to Gwydion that there was some pity in it. "And for you, Dreamer, a different lesson. You know only duty. You depend on no one, and in this way you protect yourself. I tell you that someone will come to whom you will open your heart. You will fight it, but in the end, you will win by losing the battle. It will happen after many years of pain, and toil, and hardship. They will be long years. There will ultimately be a measure of happiness, however, even for you, who seems to care so little for it. But who longs for it deep within."

The glade was silent. "Now," said Cerridwen, "give him to us. The Hunt will train him, and protect him through you, our tool in the waking world. We will see to it that, when the time comes, he will lead Kymru in her time of need, as he must."

Gwydion slowly raised the bird and placed him in Cerridwen's outstretched hands. She snapped gold and silver jesses to the eagle's talons. The bird shivered, then was still. Cerridwen gazed deeply into the eagle's eyes. "You belong to Kymru, to the Hunt. Remember."

"Farewell, Dreamer," said Cerrunnos. "You have done

what you must do. No man can keep another from the pain of his destiny. Dream well and true, for the storm is coming." And with that, they were gone.

Chapter Three

Calan Llachar Eve

Gwydion stood in Nemed Gwernan as night began to fall. The huge grove of alder trees was filled with the exultant, expectant people of Tegeingl—over a thousand men, women, and children waiting for the Calan Llachar Eve ceremony to begin. Warriors lined the perimeter, each one holding a torch, bathing the clearing in fire. The light flickered off the smooth bark of the trees, and the shining dark green leaves turned black as night deepened its grip.

To Gwydion it seemed as if the trees themselves were huddled around the people of Tegeingl, as though the people needed their protection tonight. And perhaps they did. Never had a festival made him uneasy before. He tried to dismiss these thoughts, but he was tense and wary. He knew his uneasiness was, in part, due to his dream the night before. The rest of his uneasiness could probably be attributed to the fact that he was well on his way to being very drunk indeed.

He had refused to join the hunt for the stag earlier that day.

After his dream the thought of hunting anything at all fairly turned his stomach. Instead, he had remained in Caer Gwynt, sitting by the hearth in the Great Hall, slowly drinking goblet after goblet of rich, blood-red wine, wondering dully why he couldn't seem to get drunk enough to pass out. Whenever he closed his eyes he saw the eagle in Cerridwen's hands, with chains on its talons and hopelessness in its eyes.

And an accusation. An accusation he deserved. For he had promised the eagle to protect it from those that hunted it. But he had not. He had surrendered the eagle to the Wild Hunt. In doing so, had himself betrayed the animal.

He knew what it was to be betrayed. He knew what it was to trust in someone and to have that trust destroyed by a faithless heart. He knew the bitter taste of treachery, and yet he had meted it out himself in his dream.

And so he drank.

How was it, he thought, as he had sipped his wine, that Amatheon could seem to live with what had happened to Da so much better than Gwydion himself could? How could Amatheon rise above it all, retaining his calm, his good nature, and his warm heart? Gwydion did not know how this could be, except that it had always been that way, even from the time they were children. Gwydion supposed that perhaps, when he was very young, his heart had been warm and merry. Perhaps. If so, he did not remember. But it might have been so—before the damage had been done.

He remembered the icy pain in his heart that the shadow had dealt him in his first dream, and wondered, yet again, what thing the darkness would do that could cause his heart to be any colder than it already was.

He had not really thought it possible.

Later, when the hunt had returned, he had refused to go with the men to cut down the tree for the festival. Amatheon had given him a keen glance but Uthyr had only shrugged and led thirty men to the forest outside the town walls to cut down the tree.

When the men had returned, carrying the seventy-foot alder tree across their shoulders, they set it up in the market-place. At last giving in to Amatheon's urging Gwydion had gone to see them set up the tree. With much straining and swearing, they had maneuvered it into position and dropped the trunk into the hole that had been dug for it. The women of the city had moved in to decorate the tree, hanging long ribbons of orange and purple—the colors of Cerrunnos and Cerridwen. Then Uthyr himself had climbed up and set the crown of orange marigold and white rowan flowers at the top-most branch.

Amid the laughter, the teasing, the bright noise, Gwydion had stood silent and withdrawn. The rumor that the Dreamer had been having dreams that were not to his liking traveled swiftly through the town. People were uneasy, and gave swift glances to Gwydion that he did not see. But no one had the nerve to brave his forbidding aspect and they left him alone, asking no questions.

Now the lights of hundreds of torches flickered over the faces of the people in the grove. The feast was over, the stag had been eaten, jokes had been told and songs had been sung. The crowd waited patiently for Griffi to begin the ceremony of Calan Llachar Eve, celebrated at the time of the new moon in the month of Gwernan when winter was truly gone and spring had begun.

Four fires made up of different woods had been laid out

in the four quarters of the huge clearing. Gwydion stood now, along with about two hundred other people, at the unlit fire made of rowan wood on the south side of the grove. Later, when bidden by Griffi, he would light the fire as part of the ceremony.

The unlit fire on the north side of the clearing consisted of birch wood. The Bard, Susanna, would light that fire, which symbolized the element of air. She stood there now, talking quietly to Cynan. She had not spoken one word to Gwydion since the night before, but her eyes had followed him, questioning his preoccupied silence.

At the east of the grove another unlit fire was laid, this one made of the wood of the ash tree, the symbol of water. Amatheon stood there, waiting to light this fire. Surrounded by people, Amatheon joked and laughed with Duach, Uthyr's doorkeeper, but his eyes were wary. Gwydion wondered if he, too, felt the undercurrent in the air and thought he probably did for Amatheon was very good at that.

Finally, to the west, Uthyr stood next to the pile of oak wood, the symbol of earth, that he would light. A glint of golden hair, ruddy in the torchlight, alerted Gwydion that Madoc had chosen to stand at Uthyr's fire. Gwydion noticed that his old friend, Greid, the Master Smith of Gwynedd, was also at Uthyr's fire. Greid's powerful shoulders strained against his tunic. His short, gray hair bristled and his dark eyes flickered in the firelight. Uthyr was talking to Greid, but for a moment he looked Gwydion's way, catching his eye. A small smile flashed across Uthyr's face then was gone.

In the center of the massive grove a large, flat stone had been set. On it now stood four tall vessels, flickering gold in the torchlight. Small, delicate rowan flowers and orange-yellow marigolds were strewn across and around the base of the standing stone.

Gwydion shifted slightly, unintentionally jostling the people packed around him. Arday was one of these. Obviously undeterred by her lack of success in cornering Gwydion the night before, she stood quite close to him, glancing at him often. She had tried, at first, to engage him in conversation, but his clipped replies had finally had an effect and she had at last begun to talk to Nest, Cai's wife, who stood on Gwydion's other side. Cai joined his wife, kissing her in greeting and nodding pleasantly to Gwydion and Arday.

At last, Griffi made his way through the crowd and up to the stone altar. Eight unlit torches were stacked next to the stone. One by one, Griffi picked up a torch, closed his eyes briefly, and the torch burst into flame. Each time he did this, small children oohed and aahed. As each torch was lit, Griffi set them in brackets around the stone until it seemed surrounded by a wheel of fire.

"This is the Wheel of the Year before us," Griffi intoned as he gestured to the burning torches. "One torch for each of the eight festivals when we honor the Shining Ones." He pointed at each torch, traveling clockwise around the circle. "Alban Haf, Calan Olau, Alban Nerth, Calan Gaef, Alban Nos, Calan Morynion, Alban Awyr, and Calan Llachar, which we celebrate now."

Griffi lifted his hands, his voice loud in the hush. "We gather here tonight to honor Cerridwen, Queen of the Wood and Cerrunnos, Leader of the Wild Hunt. We honor these two Shining Ones, the Protectors of Kymru."

"We honor them," the crowd responded as one.

Griffi went on. "Let the rest of the Shining Ones be

honored as they gather to witness the Hunt. Taran, King of the Winds. Modron, Great Mother of All. Mabon, King of Fire. Nantsovelta, Lady of the Waters. Annwyn, Lord of Chaos. Aertan, Weaver of Fate. Y Rhyfelwr, Agrona and Camulos, the Warrior Twins. Sirona, Lady of the Stars. Grannos, Star of the North and Healer."

"We honor the Shining Ones," the crowd responded.

Then Uthyr spoke the first of the ritual questions, his voice deep and assured, carrying effortlessly across the wide grove. "Why do we weep tonight?" he asked.

Griffi responded, "We weep for Cerrunnos who is dead. For Cerridwen killed a mighty stag as she hunted in the forest. And as the noble beast fell with her arrow through its dying heart, the enchantment lifted and she saw that she had killed Cerrunnos, Master of the Hunt. And Cerridwen wept for what she had done. We sorrow also."

"The Master is dead, and we weep in sorrow and anguish. Shall we weep forever?" Uthyr called out.

"Behold," Griffi replied. "Cerridwen called upon the four greatest of the Shining Ones to watch over the body. First she called on Mabon the Bright, the King of Fire, and he came." Griffi gestured to Gwydion and the unlit pile of rowan wood. Gwydion stared at the pile of branches, and a sunburst of flames hovered in mid-air. Some people gasped at the sight, as the blue and orange flames lowered onto the pile of wood. As the fire took hold and roared hungrily, Gwydion heard voices in his mind. "*Show-off*," Susanna and Amatheon Wind-Spoke in chorus.

"Taran, King of the Winds, came at her call," Griffi went on, gesturing at Susanna and the fire of birch wood. She lit the fire with her torch and it blazed up instantly.

"Nantsovelta, Lady of the Waters, came at her call." Griffi gestured to Amatheon who touched his torch to the ash wood, the flames crackling loudly in the stillness.

"And she called on Modron, Great Mother of All," continued Griffi, gesturing to Uthyr to light the oak fire.

As the fires burned and crackled, Griffi continued. "And so these Shining Ones guarded the dead Lord of the Hunt as Cerridwen left the forest and traveled through sky, and stars, and deepest night to Gwlad Yr Haf, the Land of Summer, where the dead await rebirth. And there she spoke with Aertan, Weaver of Fate, mother of Cerrunnos. And Cerridwen begged the Shining One for a way to return Cerrunnos to life. And Aertan answered Cerridwen's plea.

"Then did Cerridwen return to the forest, to carry out the commands of Aertan. She laid the body of Cerrunnos beneath the alder tree. And she hung the tree with marigold and the flowers of the rowan. And she played her harp and her song of sorrow caused ivy to twine and grow about the body. And behold, Cerrunnos returned to life and seeing Cerridwen, he loved her, and claimed her for his own. The two became one. And now they ride the land of Kymru, and lead the Wild Hunt together."

"Blessed be to Cerridwen and Cerrunnos," the people responded.

Four of Uthyr's warrior stepped forward. Each picked up a golden vessel from the altar as Griffi joined Amatheon at the fire of ash. One warrior went to each fire, passing the vessel to each person gathered there. Each man or women reached into the container and pulled out a piece of bread. Some looked at the bread eagerly, some with trepidation. The ones who chose the burned pieces would have to jump through the flames.

Gwydion heard a shout and looked over to see that Greid had chosen the burned piece from the vessel that was passed around the Uthyr's fire. He held the burned piece aloft, waving his hand and laughing.

Another shout and Gwydion saw that Susanna herself at her own fire had chosen the burned piece from their vessel. She gave a graceful bow to the crowd.

As the bowl came to Arday on Gwydion's left, he heard more commotion—Duach had picked the burned piece at Amatheon's fire. The golden-haired doorkeeper held the burned piece aloft, a grin on his cheerful face.

Arday reached into the golden bowl and pulled out a piece of bread, holding it up for all to see that it was unburned, and passing the bowl to Gwydion with a sigh of relief. He reached in and pulled out a piece that he did not need look at to know it was unburned.

He passed the golden bowl to Cai, who reached in and pulled out the burned piece. Laughing, he held it up for all to see.

A hush spread over the crowd. He looked over to Uthyr's fire and saw Greid take his leap through the flames.

And then it was Susanna's turn. It was silent in the grove as she leapt through the fire. Everyone cheered and she waved briefly at the crowd.

At Amatheon's fire Duach lightly jumped through the fire.

Then it was Cai's turn. Uthyr's Captain leaped, landing safely on the other side of the flames.

It was in that moment that Gwydion saw figures flicker into being beside each fire. He recognized them, instantly, although he did not understand how he knew them. But the knowledge was there, already in his soul.

The figure by Uthyr's fire was a woman, her long, black hair held back from her face by a golden tiara sparkling with emeralds. She wore a robe of forest green, trimmed with bands of brown, the color of fresh-turned earth. A cloak of bull hide was fastened to her slim shoulders with golden clasps. He knew it was Arywen, Archdruid to the murdered High King Lleu.

The glowing figure by Susanna's fire was clothed in a robe of silver trimmed with bands of sea green. He held a golden staff in his hands, and a cloak of white swan feather cascaded down his back, fastened at his broad shoulders with pearl clasps. Patience and wisdom were carved into his calm face. Gwydion knew it was Mannawyddan, Lleu's Ardewin.

The figure that materialized by Amatheon's fire had alabaster blond hair and wise eyes of light green. He wore a robe of deep blue, trimmed with bands of white. In his hand he held a golden branch hung with tiny bells, and his cloak was made of the feathers of songbirds—thrushes, sparrows, robins, and bluebirds. He was Taliesin, the Master Bard of Lleu.

The man who flickered into sight by Gwydion's fire wore a robe of black, trimmed with bands of red. Fiery opals fastened his cloak of raven feather to his shoulders. He had dark hair and eyes of piercing gray—almost silver in the glowing light. And Gwydion knew him. It was Bran, Lleu's Dreamer; the man who had found Lleu's body on the shores of Llyn Mwyngil; the man who had engineered the downfall of Lleu's faithless wife and her lover, sentencing them to a kind of half-death that still had the power to make Gwydion shiver. This was the man who had hidden away Caladfwlch, the High King's sword, who had closed the High King's mountain hall so that none could enter there.

Gwydion could tell from the lack of reaction that the people around him did not see the glowing figures. Until his eyes cut to Amatheon and he saw his brother blink in astonishment. He saw, too, that his Uncle Cynan, also Dewin, was staring at these figures with wide eyes.

"*Remember.*" Bran's Mind-Speech hammered into Gwydion's brain. "*Remember those who jumped the fires this night.*"

"*Why are you here?*" Gwydion silently asked.

But Bran did not answer him. Or, perhaps, he did give an answer, after a fashion. "*Remember the four who leapt the flames. They shall do their part, when the time comes, to ensure the High King's safety.*"

With that the four figures around the fires of earth, water, air, and fire flickered and disappeared. Gwydion's eyes traveled to Greid, to Susanna, to Duach and to Cai, for these were the four who had jumped the fires.

He would remember.

Calan Llachar—dawn

GWYDION FELT A cool breeze on his face and wondered where he was. He slowly realized that his arms were stretched across the shoulders of two men, one on either side of him. Both men carried torches and the flickering light hurt Gwydion's eyes. Looking down, he focused on the road beneath his feet, noting with surprise that he appeared to be walking. This didn't strike him as a good idea, and he came to a sudden stop.

"Keep going, brother. Not too far now," Uthyr's voice said.

"We'll never get him back without having him throw up in the middle of the road. I just know it," Amatheon said. They tugged at him and he continued walking.

Gwydion was surprised to discover that he was talking rapidly. He couldn't seem to stop himself. "And then I saw Cerridwen and Cerrunnos. I gave them the eagle. But that was wrong because the eagle trusted me. But it was wrong not to give him up. So what do you do? What do you do when all the choices are wrong?"

When they made him no answer, he stopped again, digging in his heels. He grabbed Uthyr's tunic by the shoulders and drew his brother to him until their faces were inches apart. "What do you do?" Gwydion shouted into Uthyr's face. "What do you do when there is no right thing to do?"

A pained expression crossed Uthyr's face as Gwydion's breath hit him full force. "Take it easy, Gwydion. You're drunk. Just come with us, all right?"

"Drunk?" Gwydion replied in astonishment. "I'm drunk? Impossible. I never get drunk. You know," he continued in a confidential manner, "I tried to get drunk all afternoon, but it never happened. Did you know that?"

"I heard," Uthyr said shortly. "Come along, little brother."

"Where are you taking me? And what do I do when I get there? I've got to know the right thing to do. Then I've got to do it. Got to do the right thing. If you do that, then everything will be all right. But you always have to do the right thing. Can't let anything stop you from that, you know."

"Yes, Gwydion, I know, I know," Amatheon said soothingly. "Everything will be all right. Just come with us."

"Someone's coming," Uthyr said, "from Caer Gwynt." They heard the sound of running feet rushing down the road toward them. Duach burst into the torchlight. As he saw Uthyr, he grinned. "The Queen," he panted. "The Queen's in labor. She's on her way now to the grove. She's right behind me."

Uthyr stood stock-still, staring at Duach, a panicked look on his face. "In labor. The baby? Now?"

"Ygraine is right behind me. She's asking for you. And for Amatheon and Cynan, too. She needs the Dewin, she said."

Uthyr dropped Gwydion's arm and took off up the road at a dead run. And stopped almost immediately to avoid running into his wife.

"I told you she was right behind me," Duach said plaintively.

Uthyr slowly reached out to his wife. Ygraine stood still, Uthyr's tense expression at odds with the calm, detached look on her face. Even though her body was swollen and misshapen, she was still beautiful. She was fair-skinned, with rich auburn tresses that cascaded down her back, woven lightly now with a red ribbon. She wore a loose, white robe, fastened in the front with pearls. Her look was haughty, as always. Her eyes were dark, glittering coolly in the torchlight. Midnight eyes, Gwydion had always thought. She seemed to feel no pain at the moment. She probably doesn't allow pain, thought Gwydion. It would be undignified, almost human.

Her dark eyes rested on Uthyr for a moment as he took her hand. She smiled at him—the only time she ever smiled was when she looked upon her husband. He touched her smooth face with a gentle hand. "All is well with you, *cariad*?" he asked.

"It is well with me," she answered, her voice cool. She glanced at Gwydion, supported now by Amatheon and Duach. "How interesting to see you, Gwydion. Perhaps you would care to go back to Caer Gwynt and sleep it off." It was not a question.

Suddenly, shockingly, Gwydion was stone cold sober, as if a pail of freezing water had been dashed in his face. Ygraine always seemed to have that effect on him. Slowly he drew himself up, standing unaided. "Thank you, Ygraine. But I think I'll stay awake for this."

"As you wish," she said, indifferently. She turned to Amatheon. "Brother of my husband," she said formally. "You will attend?"

"Of course. I would be honored." He left Gwydion's side and moved toward Ygraine, making her a deep bow as he took her arm.

She nodded toward Gwydion. "Much as I would love to stay and chat with you, Dreamer, I must go to the grove. I hope you can make it back to the fortress unaided."

Gwydion was not deceived. She hoped that he would break his neck, that's what she hoped. She calmly moved on down the road, supported on one side by Uthyr and on the other by Amatheon. Gwydion waited until she was out of earshot. "That woman hates me," Gwydion said absently. "They both do."

"Both?" Duach asked.

"Ygraine and her sister, Queen Olwen of Ederynion."

"But why?"

"Oh, just a little misunderstanding I had with Olwen, once. A long time ago."

"A little misunderstanding?" Duach asked curiously. "About what?"

"Um, it was regarding a personal matter."

Duach's jaw dropped. "You didn't! With Queen Olwen?"

"She wasn't Queen, then."

"And you didn't freeze your—"

"Never mind," Gwydion said hastily.

Duach grinned. "My lips are sealed. But you are a brave

man, Gwydion ap Awst. I'll say that for you. I would not have thought anyone to ever trifle with Queen Olwen."

"I didn't trifle with her," Gwydion said irritably. "How was I to know that she would expect more than I had to give?"

"Ah, Gwydion, they all do. Didn't you know that? Now, let's go back to Caer Gwynt and put you to bed."

"No, I must go to the grove. For the birth."

"Gwydion, you're drunk."

"Not any more," he said absently, looking down the road that headed back to the grove. As the two men started back down the road, Gwydion grabbed Duach's arm. "Do you hear that?"

Duach cocked his head, listening intently. "I don't hear anything. Just the wind."

Just the wind, Duach had said. But Gwydion had heard more than that. It seemed to him that far away, rushing on the wind, he heard the sound of horns—the horns of the Hunt, calling across the sky.

Calan Llachar—early afternoon

GWYDION STOOD BY the Calan Llachar tree waiting for the runners to come into sight. The marketplace was filled with people talking, eating, drinking, and singing. Occasionally some craned their necks to the west road, looking for signs of the men competing in the race to the tree. The bright colors of the fine, spring morning stung Gwydion's eyes, and it was hard to separate the pounding in his head from the noise of the crowd that surrounded him.

Several hours had passed since Ygraine's labor had begun. Gwydion had followed Uthyr and the rest to the grove, but Ygraine had sent everyone away except for Uthyr, Amatheon, and Cynan. Gwydion had tried to remind Ygraine that since he was the Dreamer, and as Dreamer's had all the gifts he was as fine a doctor as Cynan and Amatheon. But Ygraine was adamant that Gwydion not be present. Uthyr had quickly asked Gwydion to take his place and judge the race to the tree.

Uthyr had meant that as a kindness, but Gwydion could have strangled him. The day was far, far too bright. Gwydion gingerly turned his aching head to Susanna and Griffi, who were standing next to him.

"It's taking a ridiculously long time. Does it always take this long?"

"The runners have practically just left." Susanna answered, surprised.

"I don't mean that. I mean the birth."

"Oh. It's not taking long. First babies can take up to eighteen hours or more."

"I don't think I could stand waiting that long," muttered Gwydion.

"Just think how Ygraine feels," Griffi grinned.

Across the square a group of young men and women had started an impromptu dance. People were buying food and drink from the gaily colored booths that lined the square. Some booths sold drink such as ale and cider; others sold skewers of highly seasoned meats, along with cheeses and freshly baked bread. This time of year there was no fresh fruit to be had, but people polished off their meals with nuts and pastries.

Watching all those people eat made Gwydion feel a little queasy. Susanna noticed it, of course. "Not feeling too well are we?" she asked loudly.

Gwydion winced. "There's no need to shout."

Susanna grinned. "Perhaps I should fetch Arday. She

might want to do something about the hangover of yours."

"If you so much as think about it, Susanna, I swear I'll—"

"You'll what?" she challenged.

"Now, now, children. No fighting." Griffi said in a paternal tone. "I think I hear the runners now."

A shout went up from the crowd. People rushed to clear a space for the runners. Twelve men sprinted across the square, legs pumping, sweat pouring down their faces.

Griffi and Susanna took up their positions next to the tree, a purple ribbon stretched between them, held tightly in their hands. Gwydion saw that Cai and Madoc were in the lead. He wondered what had possessed Madoc to enter the race. He had always thought the man far too indolent to do such a thing.

Neck and neck the two men raced to the finish line. At the last moment, Cai, in what seemed to be a superhuman burst of speed, pulled ahead and broke through the purple ribbon a fraction of a second before Madoc did.

The crowd cheered wildly, for Cai was a favorite with the people of Tegeingl. Gwydion grabbed Cai's arm and raised it high in the air, shouting, "I declare Cai ap Cynyr, the PenGwernan of Gwynedd, winner and king of Calan Llachar!"

Chest heaving, his face wreathed in smiles, Cai staggered back as his wife burst through the crowd, throwing herself into his arms. He swung her around, laughing, and planted a quick, hearty kiss on her lips. Then somebody yelled, "You can do better than that, boyo." Cai grinned and gave Nest a long, leisurely kiss, which the crowd cheered even more wildly.

"Hmm, who do you think Cai will chose for his festival queen?" Griffi asked.

"Looks like Arday has been disappointed again," Susanna said, nodding to the sight of Arday wiping Madoc's perspiring face.

Gwydion's jaw dropped open. "Arday and Madoc?"

"You just weren't fast enough, Gwydion. With some women you've got to be pretty quick," Griffi replied.

"That woman's got no taste at all," Gwydion said sourly.

"Why do you think she went for you first?" Susanna asked. "Oh, look, Cai's starting his climb."

With a mighty leap, Cai grabbed hold of one of the lowest branches on the huge tree and began to climb amid catcalls from the exuberant crowd. As he neared the top, he reached for the crown woven of rowan flowers and marigold. The delicate white of the rowan and the hardy orange of the marigolds seemed to flash in the sun as he reached for them. Perhaps that was why he lost his balance and slipped from the branch he was standing on. The crowd gasped, but Cai caught himself just in time, grabbed the branch and hauled himself up again. He waved at the crowd and carefully picked up the crown.

Cai descended, the crown clutched tightly in one hand. Proudly he made his way up to Nest and, placing the crown on her shining brown hair, knelt at her feet.

Voice trembling with tenderness, Nest spoke the ritual words, "I call to the King of the Hunt, the Lord of the Wild. To the woman be man. To the Queen, be King."

"I seek no kingdom. But as Protector, I answer. Hunt with me and I will be man to your woman. And King to your Queen." Cai replied steadily. Nest held out her hand to her husband and Cai rose, the ritual complete.

"Great king of Calan Llachar, what are your orders?" Gwydion called out.

"To dance!" Cai shouted gleefully. At his signal, dozens of men and women formed two rings around the tree. Those in the inner ring, Cai and Nest among them, grasped the orange and purple ribbons hanging from the lower branches. The others placed themselves within the outer ring. As Susanna grabbed her harp and struck up a tune the dancers in the inner ring began to circle the tree, twining the ribbons around the trunk as they danced. The dancers in the outer ring circled in the opposite direction, while those not dancing began to clap their hands in time to the music.

After a moment Susanna began to sing and others picked up the chant.

Fair season, welcome noble Spring.
Flowers cover the world.
The harp of the wood plays melody,
Color has settled on every hill.
Tender fruits bud,
The speckled fish leaps on high.
The glory of great hills is unspoiled,
Every wood is fair.
A joyful peace is spring!

Everyone shouted the last words. At the shout the dancers changed direction, untwining the ribbons as they danced. The verse was sung again, and when the crowd shouted, "A joyful peace is spring!" the dancers again changed direction, once more twinning the ribbons around the trunk of the tree.

Gwydion glanced up at the sun. It looked like some unimaginable giant had taken a tiny bite from the edge of the great glowing disk. He glanced over at Griffi. "You called it. It begins right on time."

"Of course I called it. We Druids are astronomers, you know."

At that moment, Cai shouted to Gwydion. "Over here,

man! Dance with us."

The orders of the king of Calan Llachar could not be disregarded, but Gwydion tried anyway, shaking his head. He hated to dance.

"I command you, Dreamer of Kymru, to dance!" Cai shouted again. A few hardy souls grabbed Gwydion by the arms and hauled him up to a grinning Cai. Laughing, Nest and Cai each grabbed a hand.

"Now, Dreamer, dance with us!" Cai said. Gwydion did, executing the complex steps perfectly.

"Why, Gwydion, you're a wonderful dancer," Nest complimented him. "I never knew that!"

"That's because he never dances," her husband replied.

"Why not?" Nest asked curiously.

"I don't like it," Gwydion replied shortly.

"Dancing's too fun, right? Never met a man who hated to have fun as much as you do. Except for Madoc."

"There's no need to be insulting, Cai." Gwydion said stiffly.

"Come now," Nest laughed. "If Cai didn't insult you then you'd need to worry!"

When the dance was over Gwydion slipped away from the ring. The sky was darkening perceptibly.

"When's the next one?" Cai asked to Griffi, nodding up at the eclipsing sun.

"Exactly eighteen years from now," Griffi replied.

"I wonder where we'll all be then?" Cai mused.

"Oh, we'll all be old and fat, I'm sure. Isn't that right, Gwydion?" Griffi asked, grinning.

Gwydion hesitated. He cleared his throat, absently scratching at his short beard. "Of course. We'll all be old and fat. Particularly Cai, here."

"Why do you grow that beard if it itches?" Nest asked curiously.

"I like it," Gwydion replied shortly.

"Sky's getting darker," Susanna said.

"I'm going to the grove." Gwydion announced. "That is, if the king of Calan Llachar will allow me?" He gave Cai a mock bow.

"Indeed, you may go my good man." Cai replied haughtily. "You may give Ygraine my best regards."

"Oh, sure. That's one way to get beaten to a pulp," Gwydion said sourly as he began to make his way out of the square. As he walked through the crowd he was so intent on his own thoughts that he did not notice that people instantly give way before him, fairly melting out of his path.

As he neared the grove, the ring of alder trees shivered. The wind was coming up, as the sky grew dim. Making his way through the trees, Gwydion noticed that the birds had stopped singing. An unearthly silence was spreading over the grove, broken only by the occasional rustling of leaves stirred by the stiffening breeze.

Ygraine was walking the perimeter of the clearing, supported by Uthyr, who was speaking in low, encouraging tones. Her white over-robe discarded, she wore a short rose-colored linen shift, now drenched with sweat. Her hair was braided tightly to her scalp, and her still imperious back was to Gwydion.

Amatheon stood by the altar stone, arms folded, absently eyeing the darkening sky. On the grass next to the stone a wool blanket had been spread, a low backrest squatting on the blanket. The back was covered with a cushion, the Hawk of Gwynedd embroidered on it in silver thread. The wooden arms were polished to a smooth, satiny finish.

Cynan was standing on the other side of the stone, supervising a small fire, where a pot of water was boiling. Another pot of water sat on the ground close by. A tiny woolen blanket, a large golden bowl, and a jar of oil rested on top of the stone.

"How goes it?" Gwydion asked Cynan.

"Oh, hello, Gwydion. It won't be long now." Cynan's eyes darted nervously across the grove to Ygraine. "I don't think she wants you here."

Cynan looked decidedly uncomfortable. He, too, had seen the figures last night. Perhaps he also feels the tension in the air, Gwydion mused. Now that his hangover was beginning to subside, Gwydion was aware once again of the feeling that something—that someone—was coming.

A flicker of movement out of the corner of his eye caused him to turn quickly. He stared hard at the trees, but nothing looked out of place.

"Who won the race, Gwydion?" Amatheon asked, joining them.

"Cai did. Madoc came in second."

"Gwydion, I really don't think Ygraine—too late," Cynan sighed.

Slowly, with Uthyr's aid, Ygraine crossed the grove and stood before the three men. Uthyr looked anxious and weary, but he stood firmly by his wife's side.

"What are you doing here?" Ygraine asked. "I told Cynan to allow no one else." She stopped abruptly, a spasm of pain rippling across her face. Then she turned her cool, dark eyes on Gwydion.

"Let me guess," Gwydion said. "You want me to leave."

"Out."

Gwydion withdrew from the grove without argument. He wasn't going to tangle with her over such a minor issue. He could observe the birth from the shelter of the surrounding trees. Quietly he returned to the edge of the clearing, screening himself behind the trees. The sky drew darker by the minute. Soon they would have to light the torches. He squinted up at the sky. The sun was almost two-thirds covered now and the wind was picking up.

"Didn't go too far, did you?" Amatheon spoke in his mind.

"No one's going to keep me from this, brother. Or don't you recall who is being born today?" Gwydion replied.

"I know."

Uthyr continued to walk with Ygraine at a steady pace around and around the grove. Amatheon and Cynan lit torches as the sky continued to darken.

Flicker. Again that movement—just out of one's range of sight. Gwydion turned his head quickly, but could not see anything out of the ordinary. Yet there was something there. He knew it. Every muscle in his body was tense, and he shivered as the darkness continued to swallow the grove.

"Now, I think." Ygraine said to Uthyr. He guided her to the blanket and helped her down onto it. She lay propped up against the backrest, her hands gripping the wooden arms, her legs drawn up and apart, as Amatheon knelt in front of her. Cynan dipped a cloth into a bowl of cool water, and gently sponged her face.

"All right, Ygraine," Amatheon said quietly. "Push."

Ygraine took a deep breath and bore down.

"Again," Amatheon said.

The wind moaned through the trees. To Gwydion it

sounded like a howling beast. Or horns, he thought suddenly, the horns of the Hunt.

Flicker. Again the brief movement at the edge of his vision. And again, nothing there. The darkness was almost complete. A thin, fiery ring was all that remained of the sun, the center filled with darkness.

Then the light was gone. The stars seemed to spring from the sky, shining coldly in the sudden night.

"Again," Amatheon ordered.

Ygraine took a deep breath and pushed. "Now. Oh, Shining Ones," she gasped.

Suddenly, in the very center of the grove, two figures appeared. To Gwydion's eyes, they seemed to glow in the darkness. One figure had antlers springing from his forehead, untamed topaz eyes glimmering. The other was a woman with long, black hair and a pitiless, amethyst gaze. His dream had come to the grove as Cerrunnos and Cerridwen, standing motionless, stared down at the woman on the blanket.

Neither Uthyr nor Ygraine gave any sign that they saw the two glowing figures. But Gwydion saw Amatheon's and Cynan's eyes widen, and heard them draw in a quick breath. But at Uthyr's anxious, questioning gaze they shook their heads, indicating that nothing was amiss.

Then Cerrunnos raised a horn to his lips, and, as Ygraine's single, shocking scream tore through the air, he blew the horn. The two sounds mingled in a dreadful counterpoint, and then the grove was quiet. The figures were gone. A small, pitiful wail rose up into the dark sky.

"A boy," Amatheon called out in delight. "A beautiful, sturdy, healthy boy." Gently, he laid the squirming baby on Ygraine's belly. She reached out a trembling hand to the child.

"A son," she whispered. She turned her head slightly to look at Uthyr, crouched next to her. "My love, we have a son!"

Uthyr stared at the baby, then gently kissed Ygraine's forehead. "Yes, *cariad*. We have a son this day."

Amatheon reached for the child. With woolen thread he quickly tied off the birth cord, then severed it. Then he picked up the baby and handed him to Cynan. Cynan gently laid him in the golden bowl of lukewarm water, washing him carefully. Dipping his hands into the jar of oil he cleaned the baby's ears and nostrils with his little finger. Then he dried the tiny body and put the child into Uthyr's large, sword-callused hands.

Uthyr stood for a moment, looking down into the face of his tiny son. The child stopped crying, looking up at his father with wide eyes.

"His name?" Amatheon asked Ygraine, for the mother alone named her child.

"I name him Arthur. Arthur ap Uthyr var Ygraine."

Slowly, Uthyr raised his hands over his head, lifting the child to the sky, which had just begun to brighten again.

"I name him Prince of Gwynedd, son and heir to all that I have." Uthyr said in a tone of quiet wonder.

Gwydion, watching through the trees heard voices on the wind, the sound of silver bells, the sound of golden chains. "*We name him High King of Kymru; heir of Idris, heir of Macsen, heir of the mighty Lleu. We name him Arderydd, High Eagle, quarry of the Hunt. We name him ours.*"

Chapter Four

Tegeingl
Kingdom of
Gwynedd, Kymru
Gwernan Mis, 482

Lludydd, Cynyddu Wythnos—dusk

Gwydion's horse stumbled. Jolted out of his reverie, he noticed that dusk was beginning to settle over the quiet forest.

"Sorry, Elise," he said to his horse. "I didn't realize it was so late." He dismounted and, looking around spotted a clearing just a few yards to his right. Leading the way through the trees, his horse followed with exaggerated patience. When they reached the clearing and Gwydion took off the saddle to rub the horse down, he thought the animal was looking at him somewhat critically. "I said I was sorry," Gwydion said defensively. Elise did not deign to answer. Instead, the horse slipped away from under Gwydion's hands and, ambling over to a nearby bush, began to eat. Gwydion sighed. Elise was not the forgiving type.

Leaving Elise to his meal, Gwydion began to gather wood for the fire, digging a shallow pit with his small shovel and resuming his interrupted musing.

75

He did not want to go back to Tegeingl and do what he must do now. But there was no way to avoid it. He had not been to his brother's city for four years, since the year Arthurs was born. Over and over he had avoided Uthyr's invitations to return, citing excuse after excuse. It wasn't that he didn't want to see Uthyr. It was simply that he could not bear to look on Uthyr's beloved face, knowing what he knew about Uthyr's son, and not yet being prepared to speak of it.

He had even avoided returning to Tegeingl two years ago, when his niece had been born. He had been told that tiny Morrigan was a replica of her mother, but that she had her father's smile and easy charm.

Yet now he had to return whether he liked it or not. Because, in just four days time, young Arthur ap Uthyr would undergo the Plentyn Prawf, the test given to all children of Kymru to determine if they had the gifts. The test would be public, and, unless Gwydion's plan worked, all of Kymru would discover that Arthur was destined to be High King. And that was something that had to be avoided for now, no matter what the cost. The child's safety still lay in anonymity.

The words of Cerrunnos hammered in his brain as he continued to set up camp for the night. "There are traitors among the Kymri," the Lord of the Hunt had said. "Remember that those you can trust are few."

But that, of course, was something Gwydion had always known. There were very few people he trusted, in any case.

He knew it would have been better, safer if he had taken Arthur away the day of his birth. But he had found it impossible to do so. He could not have deprived his brother of his firstborn son—not then. The time would come, and it would be soon, when he would have to do just that. He could not wait much longer. He must hide Arthur away soon and do what he could to ensure that the trail grew cold as quickly as possible.

The wood laid, he stood back for a moment and passed his hand over the pit. The shape of a lion, glowing golden in the solitary clearing seemed to leap from the ground at Gwydion's feet and fall hungrily onto the wood, setting it aflame. Elise looked over curiously but did not stop nibbling at his dinner. The horse could not be startled with the shapes Gwydion chose to light the fire any more—he was far too used to it by now.

Gwydion smiled tightly. Once again he had proven to himself that the great Dreamer was not afraid of fire. Of course he was the only one to prove it to at the moment. But it was best to stay in practice. For it would be unthinkable for the Dreamer, whose element was fire, to be afraid of it. Unthinkable.

The reddish gold of the crackling fire reminded him of his own little daughter, Cariadas, for her hair was exactly that shade. He smiled again, a true smile this time, at the thought of his tiny, perfect little girl. Although he had suffered much to get her, he was glad now that he had paid the price. As he stared into the fire, he thought on how it had all begun.

He remembered well that day two years ago when Dinaswyn had come to the conclusion it was time for him to pass on his seed. She had consulted the Book of the Blood and given Gwydion a choice—go to Rheged to mate with Eurgain, the sister of King Urien or to Prydyn to mate with Isalyn, the sister of King Rhoram. Either one would do, she had said coolly.

He had not even mentioned to Dinaswyn that directing the mating of the Children of Llyr was his task now. It had been difficult for Dinaswyn to give up the position of Dreamer so soon—much sooner than either one of them had anticipated.

Although he was occasionally irritated by her refusal to surrender her authority, he did not demand that she do so. He wasn't cruel enough to humiliate her like that.

So he had let it go, and chosen to go to Isalyn in Prydyn, for no other reason than that he had business to take care of there. And the business was of an unsettling nature. His cousin, Rhiannon ur Hefeydd, had been sent to Prydyn by Dinaswyn two years before to bear the child of King Rhoram. After that task was completed, Rhiannon was to return to Y Ty Dewin to begin training with Myrrdin as the next Ardewin of Kymru.

Rhiannon had gone to Prydyn as ordered; had the child as expected; and then had simply broken all the rules by falling in love with Rhoram and refusing to leave him. And King Rhoram, equally besotted, had let her stay; treating her as if she was his Queen—who she most emphatically was not, and never could be. For Rhiannon was a woman of the House of Llyr and one of the Y Dawnus. Her refusal to return to Y Ty Dewin had constituted a major crisis.

And for this, for Rhiannon's refusal to do her duty to her House, Gwydion had determined to go to Prydyn and shake her until her teeth rattled. If necessary he would drag her back to Y Ty Dewin himself, in spite of Rhoram's warriors.

But when he had arrived in Arberth, Prydyn's capital, he found that she had disappeared three days before. Rhoram had fallen in love with another woman, and Rhiannon, in a jealous rage, had left Arberth in the dead of the night, taking her child with her.

At first everyone had assumed that she had finally given way to Dinaswyn's continued demands and left for Y Ty Dewin. But she and her baby girl never arrived there. The two had simply vanished. Even now, two years later, they still had not been found.

Just thinking about it could still enrage Gwydion. Rhiannon was irresponsible. Spoiled. She had refused to do her duty. Gwydion often wished that some day he would confront that stupid woman and tell her just what he thought of her.

He hadn't thought much of King Rhoram's behavior, either. The man had been frantic, tearing his kingdom apart to find Rhiannon, all after having fallen in love with another woman, which had driven Rhiannon off in the first place. Rhoram had published embarrassing, heartrending pleas for her return. Gwydion loathed a man who couldn't make up his own mind. Worse still, he loathed someone who let himself be ruled by a woman's whims. He already knew what that led to.

The King's behavior had also exasperated Efa ur Nudd—the woman Rhoram had thrown Rhiannon aside for. But Efa was clever. She had aided Rhoram in his search and comforted the King when he returned empty-handed, again and again. Isalyn, Rhoram's sister, had said that Efa wanted to be Queen and was just biding her time. For Isalyn had not liked Efa at all.

Isalyn. What a horrible time he had with her. At first he had been pleasantly surprised, for she had been beautiful and anxious to please. Then he had discovered that she had fallen in love with him. They had mated, as was his duty, and when she became pregnant Gwydion had prepared to depart, his task done. But, to his shock, Isalyn had gone into hysterics, begging him to stay with her—at least until the baby was born. Rhoram had added his pleas to hers and Gwydion had reluctantly consented to remain.

He had tried to stay with as much grace as possible but it had been one of the most trying times of his life. Her constant clinging, her anxious tears, her continuous need for reassurance had battered at Gwydion every day as he waited through the long months for his child to be born. He had chafed at his prison, eating his heart out in this enforced captivity and trying not to show it. But, in spite of his best efforts, Isalyn had known how he felt.

That last month before the birth she had finally stopped asking him what was wrong, merely looking at him with her sad, blue eyes. He had been there on the day of Cariadas's birth, as she had wished. Isalyn had only screamed once, at the very end, and although this had elevated her considerably in Gwydion's estimation, it was not enough to make him stay. He wondered sometimes if, at the last, she had been just as glad to see the last of him as he had been to go. Just a week after Cariadas had been born he was on his way home, vowing that Dinaswyn would never make him do this again. One child would have to be enough.

But soon after his return home, he received the news that Isalyn had died in a hunting accident, falling from her horse and breaking her neck, leaving his little daughter motherless. So he had returned to Prydyn for the funeral and taken Cariadas back home to Caer Dathyl.

Just one year old now, his daughter had captured his heart from the very beginning. She crowed with delight whenever she saw him, and he took her with him on his long, solitary walks through the mountains surrounding Caer Dathyl, carrying her in his strong arms, plucking wildflowers for her, making daisy chains for her to play with, marveling at her beauty. She had his gray eyes and Isalyn's red-gold hair. And a grin that always reminded him of Amatheon. He wished she was with him now, but she was far too young for the five-day journey to Tegeingl.

He winced inwardly, knowing full well, now that he had his own child, just how Uthyr must feel about his young son. But he didn't want to think of that now. He couldn't. Or he would lose his nerve.

He wished Amatheon was here but his younger brother was in Rheged, for he had been posted to the court of Lord of Gwinionydd, Hetwin Silver-Brow. Amatheon seemed to enjoy his time there, finding a friend in young Cynedyr the Wild, Hetwin's son. The two would often get into trouble, Gwydion had heard, but it was nothing they had not yet been able to talk themselves out of.

Absently, still staring into the flames, he fingered the opal and gold Dreamer's Torque that hung around his neck, glittering in the firelight. He thought that he would be willing to trade this torque and all he had (except for Cariadas, of course) just to get a good night's rest—one without dreams.

He knew that there were heavy circles under his eyes. He knew he was too thin, for he hardly ever had any appetite these days. The constant repetition, the strain of reliving his first Dream, was grating on him. He had learned by now to keep his agonized tears locked firmly away, deep inside. But he had not yet learned how to live with the pain that the shadow brought to his heart, the pain he always brought back with him into the waking world in those first few moments when he started awake.

He glanced up. The waxing moon was on the rise. The stars of the Brenin's Torque, grouped in a semicircle, hung in the sky like jewels strung on a necklace.

A new Brenin, a High King, for Kymru had been born at last. It had been a long time. The last High King, Lleu Silver-

Hand, had died over two hundred years before at the hands of his wife and her lover. That was when Gwydion's ancestor, Bran the Dreamer, had shut down Cadair Idris in a rage ensuring that none but a High King could ever open the Doors. He had set the soul of dead Lleu's wife within Drwys Idris— the massive Doors of the High King's mountain, giving her the task to guard the deserted hall until the High King came again. He had punished her lover, Gorwys, binding him to the land with the task to guard the shores of Kymru. He had hidden Caladfwlch, the High King's sword. This would be another of Gwydion's tasks—to find the sword.

If he could.

Gwyntdydd, Cynyddu Wythnos—late morning
THREE DAYS LATER Gwydion arrived at Tegeingl. He dismounted as he approached the west gate, for the road was crowded with families who had come to have their children tested in the sacred grove this afternoon.

As he led Elise through the gates he made directly for the town smithy. He saw quite a few men and women gathered in front of the massive stone shed, talking, laughing, and greeting each other. The whole town was crowded and Gwydion knew this would make things all the more difficult for him. For the item that he had commissioned from Greid, the Master Smith of Gwynedd, was not for public eyes.

As Gwydion neared the smithy he saw Greid himself standing by the great anvil, laughing and joking with the crowd. His huge shoulders were bared and his sleeveless tunic of stiff leather was charred here and there, as was natural in the course of his work. He had a cup of ale in his right hand and he gestured with it often, spilling the contents as he bantered with his friends. Casually, Gwydion caught Greid's eye. The smith nodded slightly and cut his eyes to the back of the shed, but did not stop his cheerful conversation.

"Stay here," Gwydion said to Elise. "I won't be a minute." Elise eyed him doubtfully. Gwydion sighed in exasperation. "Just because I once forgot you were waiting . . ." His horse snorted, tossing his head.

Gwydion shook his head and walked around to the back of the smithy. As he did so, the door opened and Greid came out carrying a bucket in his right hand. In his left hand was a small, nondescript leather pouch. Casually, Greid slipped the pouch to Gwydion while brushing by him and continued out the back to dip the bucket in the full water trough. Gwydion tucked the pouch into a fold of his cloak and continued on around the smithy without stopping. As he came around the front again he went straight to Elise, grabbed the reins, and walked off.

"I told you," he said smugly. Elise merely snorted. As he made his way through the marketplace he kept his head down as much as possible. The place was crowded with families in a holiday mood. Booths selling cheeses, breads, nuts, and ale had been erected and were doing brisk business.

As he left the center of town he remounted, for the crowd was thinning. When he passed Nemed Gwernan he noted that several families had already entered the grove and were waiting for Susanna, Uthyr's Bard, to begin the testing. It would be a few more hours yet. Just enough time, he hoped, for him to do what he had to.

"*Susanna,*" he called out in the general direction of Caer Gwynt, Uthyr's fortress.

"*Gwydion? Where are you?*" Susanna's mind-voice

sounded a little breathless.

"I'm just at the grove. Where is Uthyr?"

"He's hunting for dinner tonight. He should be back within the hour."

"And Ygraine?"

"In her chambers, with Arthur."

Gwydion sensed that Susanna was distracted. *"What's wrong?"*

"Nothing. Nothing's wrong. I'll talk to you later," she said hurriedly.

Gwydion smiled. Now he understood. *"Tell Griffi hello, would you? And tell him I'm sorry for disturbing him."*

A slight pause. *"He says that you didn't disturb him in the least."*

"I thought not."

The great gate of Caer Gwynt was open and dozens of people were streaming in and out. He rode into the courtyard and scanned the crowd. Seeing a familiar face, he dismounted and hailed the young man who was hurrying across the courtyard. "Duach," he called.

The man turned and halted in surprise. "Gwydion! I didn't know you were coming."

"Listen, do you think you could do me a favor?"

"Of course," Duach said with a bow. "As doorkeeper of Caer Gwynt, servant to Uthyr PenHebog, the wise and noble King of Gwynedd, I am always at the disposal of the great Dreamer of Kymru, the Walker-between-the-Worlds—"

"Will you stop that?"

Duach grinned. "So, what's the favor?"

"I think," Gwydion said dryly, "that I've changed my mind."

"I know. You want to be announced. That's my job.

What, are you afraid I'll overdo it? Me?"

"Possibly. And, yes, I do want you to announce me. I need to see Ygraine and if we make a little ceremony out of it she may not kick me down the stairs right away."

"Come with me," Duach said slyly. "I'll take care of everything."

Gwydion sighed. "That's what I'm afraid of."

"Spoilsport." Duach gestured and a stable boy came over to take Gwydion's horse. Elise left without any further derisive gestures. A first, thought Gwydion.

As the two men made their way across the courtyard to the ystafell, Duach said in a serious tone, "You know, Gwydion, you don't look too good. You're not sick or anything, are you?"

"No," he said grimly. And he wasn't. Not in the way that Duach meant, anyway. "Do you know where Susanna is?"

"Oh, in bed with Griffi still," Duach said airily. "She just got back to Tegeingl two days ago. She's been conducting tests all over Gwynedd for the last three months. I think she and Griffi are making up for lost time."

"Duach, I'm going to need another favor. When Uthyr returns will you bring him straight to the Queen's chambers? Later, when I ask, will you get Susanna and bring her there? And tell her to bring the testing device. I need to check it."

"You're up to something," Duach said, looking at Gwydion speculatively. "But then, you always are," he went on cheerfully. "Count on me."

"I am. I must be out of my mind."

Duach merely grinned at him as he knocked at the heavy wooden door of the ystafell and waited. After a moment a young woman opened the door. She was dressed in a plain, gray gown and her light brown hair was bound back with a dark blue ribbon. Her blue eyes widened at the sight of Gwydion.

"Ah, Siwan, my dear. The most beautiful girl in all of Tegeingl," Duach said with a bow. "Allow me to introduce my companion, Gwydion ap Awst, Dreamer of Kymru." At Duach's signal Gwydion sketched a quick bow to the startled girl. "Ygraine's expecting us, my dear," Duach went on smoothly. "I trust we may come in?"

Siwan glanced nervously over her shoulder. "I don't know, Duach. She . . . she never said anything about this."

"No doubt it slipped her mind, what with the excitement of the testing today. It's all right, Siwan. Let us in and I'll take full responsibility."

"Well," she said dubiously, opening the door wide. "If you say so."

The large room was luxurious. Thick carpets made by the best weavers in Gwynedd were strewn on the floor in colorful profusion. Heavy, carved chests and small tables of dark, satiny wood lined the walls at intervals. A large, throne-like chair with brightly embroidered cushions stood under a blue velvet canopy. Intricate tapestries lined the walls with bright, colorful bursts. Polished wooden stairs with a curved banister arose at the far end of the room.

"The Queen is upstairs. With Arthur," Siwan said nervously. "I don't think—"

"Just go back to what you were doing, Siwan." Without pausing, Duach climbed the stairs, with Gwydion right behind him.

The two men stopped in the open doorway to Ygraine's bedchamber and looked in. This room was even more luxurious than the first. A large mirror hung against the far wall.

The silver frame studded with pearls gleamed in the noonday sunlight streaming through the open windows. Summer flowers stood in graceful gold and silver vases strewn on tables throughout the room. The huge featherbed was spread with a wool coverlet of white worked with silver thread and pearls. A canopy of the same material stretched over the bed, the curtains a dazzling white. There was a dressing table covered with small pots and jars of cosmetics and perfumes. A large silver jewelry box spilled pearls and sapphires onto the table. Tall wardrobes, exquisitely carved, covered one entire wall. Elaborate tapestries covered the remaining spaces.

In the corner by the large window, in a pool of sunshine, sat a cradle lined in blue silk. A coo from the cradle told Gwydion that tiny Morrigan occupied it.

Ygraine herself sat in a chair of oak, resting her hands on the curved armrests. She was dressed in white and her shining auburn hair gleamed. She wore a circlet of pearls around her forehead and her hair was elaborately curled. Another string of pearls encircled her neck twice then spilled down the front of her dress. Ygraine had not noticed the two men, all her attention bent on the child that played at her feet.

Arthur was small for his four years. Slender and delicate-looking, his eyes seemed too big for his face. A shock of sandy blond hair hung over his forehead. The child had a serious expression as he stacked small blocks of brightly colored wood to form a tower.

Duach cleared his throat. Arthur jumped slightly and the tower he was building teetered and fell. Unlike many children, Arthur did not cry at the destruction. He gravely looked at the ruins of his tower then glanced up at the two men. Obviously a fair child, his eyes held no blame for the mishap.

"My Queen," Duach said bowing deeply. "May I present to you a noble visitor. Gwydion ap Awst, Dreamer of Kymru, Walker-between-the-Worlds—"

"Thank you, Duach," Ygraine said dryly. "I believe I am aware of the identity of this uninvited guest."

Duach bowed again. "Is there anything else you wish, my Queen?"

"Yes. I wish for you to go," she said, her voice like winter snow. Swallowing hard, Duach bowed himself out.

"You scared him," Gwydion said mildly, his eyes never leaving Arthur.

"No I didn't. He expects that from me. He'd be frightened if I was nice to him," replied Ygraine, just as mildly, her eyes also fixed on her young son.

To gain some time before he faced Arthur, Gwydion went to the cradle by the window. Two-year-old Morrigan slept with a contented smile on her exquisite face, her auburn hair illuminated by the sun. She did indeed have her mother's delicate features, but Gwydion could see Uthyr in the set of her smiling mouth.

"She's beautiful," Gwydion said softly, lightly brushing his forefinger against her smooth cheek.

"Yes, she is," Ygraine said softly, but Gwydion noticed she had not taken her eyes from Arthur.

Gwydion crossed the room and knelt down beside the boy, who gravely returned his gaze. "Hello, Arthur. I'm your Uncle Gwydion."

Arthur swiftly looked up at his mother for confirmation. She nodded and Arthur returned his gaze to Gwydion, filing away this new bit of information.

"I'm sorry about the tower, Arthur. We didn't mean to

scare you." Another long pause. "Can you say hello to me?"

"Hello," Arthur said briefly, then stared down at the floor.

"Arthur is shy," Ygraine said softly.

"I was, too." He handed a block to Arthur. "Shall we build again?"

Arthur said nothing, but he reached for the block and set it on the floor. Gwydion placed a second block on top of the first and the two rebuilt the tower in silence. Then they sat back to examine their handiwork.

"What do you think?" Gwydion asked.

"Good," Arthur replied.

"Yes, it is good. I agree." Gwydion looked over at Ygraine. "A man of few words, I see."

"Yes," she replied.

"I wonder where he gets it?"

Ygraine almost smiled, but caught herself in time. She studied Gwydion, then said, "Tell me, and try not to lie for once. My son is being tested today. What are you up to?"

"Ygraine, he's my nephew," he said, with exaggerated patience, playing for time. "I'm just showing some interest."

"No you're not. You never show interest in anyone— unless you want to use him or her for something. So, tell me this, Gwydion, how do you intend to use my son? And what makes you think I will let you do that?"

Gwydion opened his mouth to reply, but at that moment the sound of horses hooves clattering in the courtyard below reached them. A babble of voices floated up through the open windows.

"Uthyr has returned. I hope the hunt was good," Ygraine mused. "Don't you want to go down and see him?"

"You want me to leave?" Gwydion asked innocently.

"Yes."

"I think I'll just wait here for a while. He'll drop in, I'm sure." As the two sat in silence Gwydion fixed his gaze on Arthur who had been quietly playing with his wooden blocks. The child had built another tower beside the first and was attempting to construct a bridge. "Need any help?" Gwydion asked.

"No, thank you, Uncle Gwydion," Arthur replied politely, not lifting his eyes from the construction.

Within moments Duach and Uthyr were at the chamber door. "He's here," said Duach, gesturing to Uthyr. "Shall I fetch Susanna now?"

"Please," Gwydion said getting to his feet.

"Gwydion! Brother!" Uthyr exclaimed, as he swiftly crossed the room and enveloped Gwydion in a gargantuan bear hug. "I didn't know you were coming!" Uthyr turned to Ygraine and kissed her lightly.

He went to the cradle and gently touched sleeping Morrigan's fresh face. Then he picked up his young son and tossed him high into the air. Arthur giggled delightedly. Uthyr caught the boy and held him close. Seeing them face to face Gwydion noted that the resemblance was very strong. Arthur would have his mother's auburn hair and dark eyes, but his face was Uthyr's.

"Well, boyo, are you ready to take a trip soon?" Uthyr asked, and Arthur nodded his answer.

"Where is he going?" Gwydion said sharply.

"Why, he's going to the graduation ceremonies at the colleges in Gwytheryn. They start in a few weeks. He's the heir, so he has to deliver the gifts for the graduates from Gwynedd."

"Are you going with him?" Gwydion asked.

"No. Susanna and Cai will go with Arthur. Ygraine and I will stay here this year, with Morrigan."

Gwydion nodded absently, his mind racing. A trip to Gwytheryn opened possibilities that could give Gwydion the chance he needed to settle Arthur's future.

"Isn't Arthur a little young to be going?" he asked.

Uthyr shrugged. "No younger than I was the first time. Well, little brother, it's good to see you! Are you here for the Plentyn Prawf then?"

Gwydion swallowed. Now it begins, he thought. "Uthyr. Ygraine. I need to talk to you both."

Uthyr's smile faded as he took a good look at Gwydion's tense, tired face. Gently, he set Arthur down and straightened. "What is it?" he asked in a tight voice.

"The testing. Please, Uthyr, sit down."

Uthyr drew up a chair next to his wife. "All right. I'm sitting," Uthyr said firmly. "What is it?"

"I've sent for Susanna. Arthur must be tested privately. Here and now."

"Why?" Ygraine asked coldly. "Heirs are always tested in public, just like all the other children."

"Because I think I know what we will find; and because the results must not be known publicly. Not yet."

"And what do you expect to find?" Uthyr asked slowly.

"I think you know."

Uthyr did not reply. Ygraine turned to her husband, but before she could question him, Susanna was at the door with Duach right behind her.

"Thank you, Duach," Gwydion said as he went swiftly to the door and pulled Susanna into the room. "I'll send for you if we need anything." Gwydion quickly shut the door on

Duach's surprised and curious face.

"Did you bring the testing device?" Gwydion asked.

Susanna wore a simple gown of gray wool. Her hair was loose and disheveled, and she was barefoot. "Yes," she said acidly. "I brought it. I was also busy when Duach came and hauled me over here. Griffi may never forgive you for this. I know I won't."

Gwydion said simply, "It's important, Susanna."

The Bard was instantly serious. "All right," she said quietly. "What do you want me to do?"

"I want you to test Arthur. Now."

Susanna's eyes widened in surprise. "But—"

"Please. Just do it." Something in his tone immediately stopped all protest. Slowly, Susanna moved to where Arthur sat on the floor, once again playing with his blocks. She knelt down beside him, taking a small square object from the folds of her gown. "Hello, Arthur. Do you remember me? I've been gone a long time."

Arthur looked at her, gravely considering her question. "Yes. You are Susanna. You play music."

"Yes," Susanna smiled. "And I do other things too. I travel all over Gwynedd and I meet many children. And when I meet them I do a little test, called the Plentyn Prawf, which means Child Test. And the test tells us if a child has a special talent. Like if they can talk to animals or see things in their minds from far away. Or if they can make things move without touching them."

"I can't do those things," Arthur said in a matter-of-fact tone.

"Well, you never know. I have a test to find out. Do you want me to find out about you?"

"Will it hurt?" He didn't seem apprehensive, just curious.

"No. You'll just feel a little prick at the end of your finger."

Arthur considered her request for a moment, then nodded for her to go ahead.

Susanna held out the small square box. The opening at one end was just large enough to insert a finger. The box was made of some kind of silvery material that glistened in the sunlight. The top of the box was decorated with jewels. In the very center there was a group of onyx stones, arranged in a figure-eight pattern around a bloodstone. Grouped around these stones were a large pearl, a sapphire, an emerald, and an opal. At the far corners other jewels nested—amethyst, topaz, ruby, and a diamond beside a garnet.

"You put your finger in here," Susanna explained, "and if you have a special talent, if you are one of the Y Dawnus, one of these jewels will glow."

Arthur leaned forward and gazed solemnly at the jewels. "Which ones?"

"Well, if you have the talent to be a Druid the emerald will glow. The emerald is for Modron, the Great Mother, and Druids belong to her. Or, if you should be a Bard, the sapphire, which is for Taran of the Winds, will light up. The pearl is for the Dewin, who belong to Nantsovelta, the Lady of the Waters. And the opal is for the Dreamer, who belongs to Mabon of the Sun."

"Like Uncle Gwydion."

"Yes," Susanna smiled. "Like your Uncle Gwydion."

"What about the others?" Arthur asked.

"The diamond is for Sirona of the Stars and the garnet for Grannos the Healer. The ruby is for Y Rhyfelwr, the Warrior Twins, Camulos and Agrona. Those don't light up, but are there for us to remember whom they represent. The amethyst and the topaz are for Cerridwen and Cerrunnos, the Protectors of Kymru. The topaz and the amethyst will glow for anyone who is Kymri. In the middle is the onyx for Annwyn, the Lord of Chaos and the bloodstone is for his wife Aertan, the Weaver of Fate, the King and Queen of the Otherworld."

"Just a moment, Susanna." Gwydion went to the windows, and closed the shutters one by one.

"It's too dark now," Ygraine said acidly. "I can barely see."

With a gesture, all the candles in the room lit at once with Druid's Fire. "Is that better?" Gwydion asked. Without waiting for an answer he nodded at Susanna. "Go ahead."

"All right, Arthur, just put your finger in this opening here on the side of the box."

Arthur did so and for a moment nothing happened. The box made a slight clicking sound and then began to whir quietly.

Suddenly, shockingly, every jewel on the box began to glow. Bright columns of light shot up from each jewel, mingling together on the ceiling. Brighter and brighter the jewels glowed and the humming sound grew louder and louder. Gwydion jumped to Susanna's side and pulled the box away from her frozen hands, pulling Arthur's finger out at the same time. Instantly the lights and the noise cut off, as though a door to another world had been abruptly shut.

Little Morrigan began to cry and Ygraine went to the cradle and swiftly picked her up, hushing her. Arthur, startled, did not cry, but his lower lip trembled. Uthyr reached down and picked his son up, cuddling him in his lap. The comfort of his father's arms quieted the child, but his eyes were wide.

"It was too loud," Gwydion explained. "Another minute and everyone would have come to see what was happening."

"Gods, I've never seen that before! I've heard of it but never—" Susanna said.

"It hasn't happened for over two hundred years." Gwydion said tightly.

Susanna, still shocked, turned to Uthyr. "Did you know?"

"I guessed," Uthyr admitted, his voice shaking.

"You never said anything to me," Ygraine said, coldly eyeing her husband as she continued to hush Morrigan.

"I asked him not to," Gwydion broke in.

Ygraine turned her cold stare to Gwydion. "Why?"

Gwydion took a deep breath. "This must be a secret for now. No one else must know."

"What?" Ygraine's voice was shrill. "How dare you? My son, *my* son is to be the High King. And you want to stop it? You can't stand the idea of a High King in Kymru again? Someone that might prevent you from doing exactly as you please? You—"

Gwydion face was pale with anger. "Shut up," he hissed. "You stupid fool, I'm trying to keep your son alive."

"You lie," Ygraine snapped.

Uthyr raised his hand and silence abruptly descended. "Susanna," he said quietly, "please take Arthur to the kitchens and get him something to eat. And please take Morrigan to her nurse." Ygraine handed Morrigan to Susanna as Uthyr went on. "And, until I tell you otherwise, what happened here today did not happen." Susanna nodded. Uthyr looked down at his son. "Arthur, do you understand? Not a word to anyone."

"Yes Da."

"All right. Go with Susanna. And, Susanna, not a word—not even to Griffi." Susanna nodded again and held out her hand to Arthur. The three left the room quietly.

Stern, Uthyr turned to his wife. "You will not speak again, Ygraine, until Gwydion explains himself." Gwydion had never heard Uthyr speak in that tone to his wife before. Apparently, neither had Ygraine. Her hands tightened on the arms of her chair until her knuckles were white, but she did not speak.

"All right, Gwydion. Explain. And it had better be good," Uthyr said grimly.

Gwydion hesitated, and then chose his words very carefully. "You know that the special talent of a High King is that he acts as a focal point. For instance, telepathy is limited in distance. A telepathic Bard can comfortably talk to another Bard up to fifteen leagues away. Beyond that, the conversation becomes garbled. Clairvoyant Dewin can see events that are happening at that moment up to thirty leagues away. And psychokinetic Druids can move objects only in their immediate vicinity—they have to actually see what they are moving. And the largest limitation of all is that groups can't act together. A group of Dewin all trying to see one event can't reach out any farther than thirty leagues." Gwydion paused, then went on.

"But a High King makes all the difference. Alone, he has none of these powers. But his presence augments all of them. He can direct and amplify these powers through those that possess them. A High King could empower a group of Dewin to see events many hundreds of leagues away. Or allow Bards to communicate, in concert, all over the country. He can augment the powers of a group of Druids to move or to set fire to objects many leagues away that they can't even see. With his help, Druids can bring a storm or fog. That's why a High King acts as the warleader for Kymru. He can coordinate communication across the land, direct a battle taking place many leagues away, even start a fire in the enemy camp, without getting anywhere near the place."

Gwydion paused again, looking down at the floor. "This is why a High King has been born to us now. Because sometime soon, we will have need of one."

Ygraine, who had never taken her eyes off Gwydion, stirred slightly. "You have told us there will be a need for a High King. Why, then, must it be a secret?"

"The Protectors have come to me in my dreams. They tell me that there are traitors among us. If Arthur's true nature is known, he will be in great danger. He will die." Gwydion leaned forward in his chair, willing them to understand. "He must be protected. I beg you, let me hide him. Let me protect him." He paused again, searching their faces. "I beg you," he whispered.

"You think that Uthyr cannot protect his own child?" Ygraine asked coolly.

Gwydion's gaze fell under Uthyr's stare. "No," Gwydion said softly. "He cannot. I must do this. The Protectors have given me the task."

"You are telling me that I must send my son away? For you to bring up? You will teach and care for him? You?" Ygraine asked bitterly.

"No, not I. Myrrdin will."

"Myrrdin? How can that be? He is the Ardewin. You can't hide Arthur at Myrrdin's side!" Ygraine exclaimed.

"I will persuade Myrrdin to step down as Ardewin and take up this task."

"And where will Myrrdin take him should we agree to your plan?" Ygraine asked.

"There's a small village that I know of, in Eryi. Myrrdin will take him there."

"To do what?"

"To herd sheep," Gwydion said simply.

"You want to raise my son as a shepherd?" Ygraine asked in outraged tones.

"For a time, yes."

Uthyr, who had not spoken a word, suddenly stood. He strode to the window, opened the shutters and leaned out, his hands resting on the windowsill, his back to his wife and brother. The room was silent as Ygraine and Gwydion waited for Uthyr to speak.

"And will you tell him who he is?" Uthyr said quietly. "Will he forget us?"

"Myrrdin will be sure that Arthur doesn't forget you."

"And if we do not agree to let you do this, what then?" Uthyr asked.

"Then Arthur will die. The Protectors have told me so. In my dreams there is a figure of darkness that menaces Arderydd, the symbol of the High King. Only because I protect him is the eagle still alive," Gwydion said simply.

Ygraine and Uthyr looked at each other. "I say no," Ygraine said firmly. "Uthyr can protect his own son. We will see to it that Arthur will be safe."

"Ah, Ygraine, you always did have such faith in me," Uthyr said, a sad smile on his face. He turned to Gwydion, with anguish in his eyes. "Take him."

"What?" Ygraine cried, stunned. "How can you—"

"I say yes. Gwydion dreams true. You seem to forget that, Ygraine. Whatever else you think of him, he dreams true."

"Maybe," Ygraine spat out. "But he doesn't tell all he

knows. I don't trust him."

"But I do. And I trust Myrrdin, too, to bring up my beloved son." Uthyr's voice broke. Clearing his throat, he went on. "It shall be done as Gwydion wishes. And what happened here today will never be spoken of." Uthyr went to Ygraine and took her hand, kneeling down by her chair. "Ygraine, *cariad*, it breaks my heart, too, to send my son away. But if we don't he will die. I believe this."

Ygraine gazed at her husband, tears in her eyes. She swallowed hard, and placed her other hand on top of his. She nodded slightly, but did not speak. Uthyr lightly touched her face, then stood. "When?" he asked Gwydion.

"When Susanna and Arthur go to Gwytheryn for the graduation ceremonies I shall go with them, to talk to Myrrdin. Three months from now I will return here, and take Arthur with me to the village where Myrrdin will be waiting."

"Three months," Ygraine said in a toneless voice.

"I'm sorry, Ygraine. But the sooner the better."

"I just had a thought," Uthyr said. "What about the Plentyn Prawf? How can we excuse Arthur not being tested publicly?"

"Oh, he will be," Gwydion said easily.

"But you just said—"

"Leave that to Susanna and I. Arthur will be tested this afternoon like everyone else. And his test will show that he has no special talents."

"But how?" Ygraine asked.

"Don't worry about it. Let's just say that I will be assisting Susanna very closely this afternoon. And leave it at that."

LATER THAT AFTERNOON, the children of Tegeingl were tested by Susanna, assisted closely by Gwydion ap Awst. In an unusual move, Susanna handed the tool to Gwydion to hold after each test was completed as she spoke gently to each child. Two clairvoyants and one telepath were identified, but Prince Arthur proved to have no special talents.

Nobody noticed that Greid, the chief smith of Gwynedd, watched the Plentyn Prawf with a quizzical look on his face. But some people did comment that Gwydion ap Awst must have been mad to wear long sleeves in such hot weather.

No remarked, for no one there knew, that the Dreamer of Kymru had always been good at sleight of hand.

Chapter Five

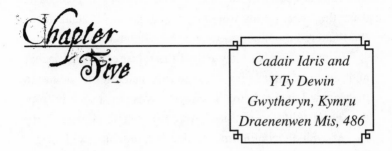

Gwyntdydd, Disglair Wythnos—mid-afternoon

It was a small party that left Tegeingl a few weeks later; just Gwydion, Arthur, Susanna and Cai. Susanna left her baby son behind with his father, Griffi, and, although Gwydion tried to ignore it, he was aware of Susanna's anguish. He had felt it himself when he left Cariadas behind at Caer Dathyl. He tried not to think too closely about how this would be nothing to what Uthyr and Ygraine would feel just a few months from now.

Arthur, young as he was, had proven himself to be his father's son. Every day he rode stoically on his small pony. Weary with travel, he fell asleep each night right after dinner, while Gwydion stared into the campfire each night, trying not to remember the look in his brother's eyes at the news that his son was to be taken from him.

Four days from Tegeingl they reached Gwytheryn, the High King's country located in the center of Kymru. When they came to the junction of Sarn Gwyddelin and Sarn Ermyn they turned eastward, making for Caer Duir, where the first of the three annual graduation ceremonies would be held. The route they were taking would lead them just past Cadair Idris, the shuttered mountain fortress of the High Kings of Kymru.

In mid-afternoon they exited the forest of Coed Llachar and reined in their horses to gaze in wonder at the mountain that loomed above them. The fortress rose majestically from the sea of wildflowers that covered the plain. Purple cornflowers, blue delphiniums, white snapdragons, and bright yellow tansy waved gently in the light breeze. Daisies and golden globeflowers bent and twisted under the hooves of their horses. The breeze sighed in remembrance of loss and sorrow, of loneliness and failure, of the death of dreams. But the mountain itself seemed to reach up and pierce the sky, as wild hope pierces the heart, and sets it to beating again.

To the east of the mountain the standing stones of Galor Carreg, the burial mounds of the High Kings, rose from the carpet of wildflowers, dark and silent. In their depths rested the bodies of Idris, the first High King and his High Queen, Elen of the Roads. Macsen, the second Brenin, also rested there, as well as Lleu Silver-Hand, the last High King of Kymru.

White alyssum and red rock rose twined over the once white stones of the eight steps leading up to Drwys Idris, the huge Doors that guarded the silent mountain, opening only at will of the Guardian. And the Guardian would open only to the one who brought her the lost Four Treasures of Kymru—the Cauldron, the Stone, the Spear, and the Sword. These Treasures would test a person who claimed kingship. And, if he survived the testing, he would be acknowledged as High King.

Gwydion glanced to his right, where Susanna and Cai had

reined in, Arthur between them. The boy seemed even smaller and frailer within the dark shadow of the mountain. "Do you know what this is?" Gwydion asked him.

Arthur nodded. "Cadair Idris."

"Yes, the fortress of the High King. Come, let's go talk to the Doors."

"Talk to the Doors?" Arthur looked carefully at Gwydion to see if he was being teased. "How?"

"You'll see." Gwydion dismounted and helped Arthur down from his pony. Taking the boy's hand, he curtly ordered Susanna and Cai to stay where they were. Susanna's lips tightened and Cai's face darkened, but they did not follow.

Gwydion helped Arthur mount the broken steps to the huge Doors, then pointed at the jeweled patterns that glittered and swirled. "Do you know what these mean?"

Arthur shook his head, never taking his eyes from the designs.

"These patterns represent the constellations named for The Shining Ones, and for the Four Treasures of Kymru. These are the Treasures," he went on as he pointed to each pattern. "Here is the Spear of Opals. And here is the Stone of Pearls. This is the Cauldron of Emeralds. And this is the Sword of Sapphires. The Treasures represent the four elements that come together to make all life: fire, water, earth, and air."

Arthur said nothing as he studied the designs. Gwydion continued to point out the constellations of the Shining Ones. Modron outlined in emeralds. Sapphires for Taran and pearls for Nantsovelta. Opals for Mabon. Rubies for Y Rhyfelwr, the Warrior Twins, Agrona and Camulos. Diamonds for Sirona of the Stars. Garnets for Grannos the Healer. Topaz for Cerrunnos and amethysts for Cerridwen, the Protectors of Kymru.

Black onyx for Annwyn, the Lord of Chaos and bloodstone for Aertan, Weaver of Fate. "And this last one, Arthur, is made of emeralds, pearls, sapphires, and opals. It is the constellation of Arderydd, the High Eagle. The sign of the High King."

As Arthur stared at the last pattern a humming sound came from the air around them, building in intensity, and the jewels began to glow.

Startled, Arthur stepped back quickly, but Gwydion held him still. "It's all right, Arthur. It's just the Guardian."

A voice, light and musical, coming from nowhere, from everywhere, began to chant softly.

Not of mother and father,
When I was made
Did my creator create me.
To guard Cadair Idris
For my shame.
A traitor to Kymru,
And to my Lord and King.
The primroses and blossoms of the hill,
The flowers of trees and shrubs,
The flowers of nettles,
All these I have forgotten.
Cursed forever,
I was enchanted by Bran
And became prisoner
Until the end of days.

An empty silence descended, broken only by the moaning of the wind. Then, the voice spoke again, "Who comes here to Drwys Idris? Who demands entry to Cadair Idris, the Hall of the High King?"

"It is I, Gwydion ap Awst var Celemon, Dreamer of

Kymru, who comes."

"The halls are silent. The throne is empty. We await the coming of the High King. He shall be proved by the signs he brings," the voice went on.

"We bring you no signs today. The Treasures remain hidden," Gwydion said.

"Then you may not enter here. I must still wait in silence and sorrow the coming of the King," the voice sighed, an echo of the mournful, empty wind that swept the plain. After a moment, the voice went on. "I know you, Gwydion ap Awst."

Gwydion bowed. "And I know you, Bloudewedd ur Sawyl."

"The name you give me is strange, Dreamer. It is long and long since I have heard it from the lips of the living."

"Yet it was once your name, High Queen."

"High Queen no more. The High King is dead and I wait in silence for the signs."

"I come here not to bring the signs but to show you hope."

"Hope grows old. Then it withers away. One silent day after another have I endured. The stars wheel overhead, ever changing and never changing. Season upon season and year upon year. In the beginning, with every rising of the sun I hoped. And with each setting of the sun hope died, until hope was no more. There was only silence."

"Yet there is hope, even for one such as you. For I bring with me one who will end your long wait."

The humming sound began again, building and building until the mountain seemed to ring with it. A bright, white light pierced Arthur as he stood within its startling glow. Then, just as suddenly, the light was gone.

"It is him," the voice whispered. "Oh, Shining Ones, it is him at last."

"It is," Gwydion said calmly. "But it is not time yet."

"But not long now," the voice breathed. "Not as I have learned to measure time."

"No, not long now." Gwydion laid a reassuring arm across the boy's thin shoulders. "But he's young yet."

Suddenly Arthur spoke. "Who are you?"

"I am the Guardian. I am Drwys Idris."

"I mean," Arthur explained, flushing in embarrassment, "who were you?"

"Ah," the Doors sighed. "I was Bloudewedd ur Sawyl var Eurolwyn, High Queen to Lleu Lawrient, many, many years ago." Bloudewedd's voice softened. "In this mountain we lived and ruled together." Her voice faltered. "A very long time ago."

"But—but you're still alive."

The voice laughed a wild sound that pierced like a knife through the soul. "I am neither alive nor dead. My spirit is bound to this mountain, cursed to guard the Doors until the High King returns. I cannot return to Gwlad Yr Haf to be reborn for another turn of the Wheel. This is what Bran did to me."

"But why?"

"For revenge. Because I plotted the death of Lleu Silver-Hand. And I succeeded."

"You killed him?" Arthur gasped.

"My lover and I did. And we were punished. My spirit was bound to the mountain. And Gorwys, my lover, was set to guard the shores. His task is to rise and warn the Kymri should invaders set foot on this land. And mine is to guard the Hall of the High King, until the next High King comes to claim the throne."

"And she cannot be released, Arthur, by any but the Dreamer, and then only at the High King's command. If released, another traitor must replace her. It is their punishment," Gwydion said solemnly. "Tell me, Bloudewedd, why did you do it? Why did you murder your own husband?"

"Lleu and I cared for each other. But Gorwys—" The sound of that dead name seemed to warm the cold voice, as embers are warmed by the memory of fire. "Ah, when I met him I forgot everything. Honor, duty, they were nothing to me. There was only desire. It meant nothing to me that he was my own sister's husband. Gorwys wanted me. I could deny him nothing, he held my heart in the palm of his hand."

"And now? Have you repented of your crime?" Gwydion demanded. "Or would you do the same again?"

The Doors were silent for some time. A mournful wind whipped across the plain, carving patterns in the wildflowers. A hawk, wheeling overhead, gave a lonely cry.

At last the Doors spoke. "I have no answer to that. Except to say that we are what we are. And that, Dreamer, is what the silence has taught me. We are what we are."

Meirgdydd, Tywyllu Wythnos—afternoon

TWO WEEKS LATER, having attended the graduation of the Druids at Caer Duir and the Bards at Neuadd Gorsedd, they arrived at Y Ty Dewin.

The huge, three-story, five-sided building of white stone glowed in the light of the afternoon sun. The banner of the Dewin, a silver dragon on a field of sea green, fluttered from the watchtower at the top of the keep.

As they neared the main entrance, young novices in silver-gray robes came up to take their horses. As they dismounted, a woman descended the front steps. She had long, light brown hair, tightly braided and wound around her head like a coronet. She wore a rich gown of sea green trimmed in silver. Around her neck was a silver torque with one large pearl. Her blue eyes held a smile as she greeted the party.

She bowed slightly to Arthur. "Greetings, son of Uthyr ap Rathtyen, King of Gwynedd. I am Elstar ur Anieron var Ethyllt, the Ardewin's heir. I welcome you to Y Ty Dewin in the name of Nantsovelta, Lady of the Waters."

Arthur, who had been well schooled in his reply by Susanna, bowed to the woman. "I greet the children of Nantsovelta, Lady of the Waters, Queen of the Moon, in the name of my father, Uthyr PenHebog, the King of Gwynedd. May we enter here?"

"Enter and be welcome to the house of Nantsovelta," Elstar replied formally. Then she smiled. "You did very well, Arthur ap Uthyr."

Slowly Arthur smiled back. "Thank you," he said simply. Fair as always, he went on, "Susanna taught me."

"And did an excellent job," she said, smiling at Susanna and giving her hand in greeting to Cai. She turned to Gwydion. "Your presence here lights my life and gives wings to my soul, oh great Dreamer. The fire of your eyes pierces my heart, and the power of your towering spirit warms my innermost being."

"Very nice, Elstar. You wouldn't be making fun of me would you?"

"I? Never. I adore you now and always," Elstar said, batting her lashes at him.

"Well, just don't tell Elidyr," Gwydion said, naming Elstar's husband. "He'd chop me in two."

"Nonsense. He'd have someone else do it for him. A Bard has to be careful of his hands. You must all be weary. Come, I'll show you to your rooms. By the way, Gwydion, Myrrdin wants to see you right away."

Gwydion nodded, as they were led through the huge doors of the college. The left door showed the sign for the ash tree, the tree sacred to Nantsovelta—one vertical line slashed with five horizontal lines of silver, all outlined in pearls. The right door displayed the constellation of Nantsovelta, also outlined in pearls.

Entering the cool building they took the stairs to the right of the entrance hall. "Yours is the first suite on the right here," Elstar explained, when they reached the second level. "The other heirs are housed in this corridor. Next to you is Geriant of Prydyn and his party. Then Elen of Ederynion. And then Elphin of Rheged."

She held her hand out to Arthur. "Come, let's go meet the Ardewin. You too, Gwydion."

Gwydion nodded for Susanna and Cai to settle in then followed Elstar and Arthur down the corridor to the open door of the Ardewin's chambers.

The room was bright, lit with the beeswax candles of Rheged, which augmented the light shining through the tiny glass windows. The walls were covered with tapestries made by the master-weavers of Gwynedd, bright colors woven to show scenes of forests, lakes, and mountains. The floors were covered with carpets in shades of green and silvery gray. A sideboard with glass decanters spun by the glassmakers of Ederynion stood to the right of the door, and the light played off the dark violet glow of the wines of Prydyn.

Myrrdin, the Ardewin of Kymru, splendid in a rich

robe of silver, sat at a small table before the hearth, frowning down in concentration at a playing board. His gray hair and short, gray beard glowed silver in the light. A younger man dressed in Bardic blue sat opposite, smiling slightly at Myrrdin's frown. An older man, tan and lean, reclined before the hearth, idly strumming on a harp, completely ignoring the two young boys who wrestled on the rugs.

"Llywelyn, Cynfar, stop that at once," Elstar commanded. The two boys sat up and hastily rearranged their clothing, trying without success to look innocent.

Myrrdin glanced over and, catching sight of Gwydion, leapt from the table with a smile on his face. "So, boyo, you've come to see your old uncle at last!" The two men hugged briefly, and then Myrrdin drew back to get a good look at Gwydion. The concern in his uncle's eyes told Gwydion clearly that the signs of strain and sleeplessness on his face had been noted. But Myrrdin forbear to comment and turned to Arthur, gazing down at the boy for a long moment. He stooped down and took the boy's hand. "Hello, Arthur. I'm Myrrdin ap Morvryn, your great-uncle."

"The Ardewin," Arthur said.

"Yes," Myrrdin smiled.

"My father says to tell you hello." Arthur paused. "Hello."

"So, you are a man of your word. I like that. Perhaps you would care to meet two young scamps that I know," he said, motioning for the two boys to come over. The elder boy looked to be about five years old, the younger one about three. "This is Llywelyn," Myrrdin said, touching the older boy's shoulder. "And this is Cynfar. Elstar is their mother. And Elidyr over there is their father. He is the heir of the Master Bard. I'm sure you saw him just a few days ago at Neuadd

Gorsedd, didn't you?"

Arthur nodded, as the younger man bowed briefly and smiled. Myrrdin motioned to the older man who was still strumming his harp. "And this is Dudod ap Cyvarnion. The Master Bard is his brother. He is Elidyr's father, and the Granda of these two imps." Dudod nodded and smiled, but did not cease playing.

Myrrdin turned to the children. "Now, you boys go outside. Why don't you show Arthur the gardens?"

As the children left Elstar called after them, "And don't get too muddy, and don't be late for dinner!"

"You're wasting your time, Elstar. They'll do both," Dudod said.

"Well, with you as an example, Uncle—" She shook her head.

"So, Gwydion, how was the testing at Tegeingl?" Myrrdin asked.

"Pretty good. Susanna found two Dewin and one Bard."

"Wasn't Arthur due to be tested this year?" Myrrdin asked.

"Yes indeed. No special talents," Gwydion lied smoothly. He turned to Dudod. The older man was lean and his face was tanned. Laugh lines bracketed his finely cut mouth. His fingers were long and supple, as they danced over the harp strings. His light brown, sun-streaked hair was caught at the back of his neck with a plain leather thong, and his light green eyes brimmed with life. He wore brown riding leathers and his soft leather boots were dyed Bardic blue. "What have you been up to, Dudod?"

"No good, as usual," his son, Elidyr, answered for him. "Flitting around Kymru from place to place. He'll never settle down."

"Tell me, Dudod," Gwydion said, "In all your travels, have you ever run across your missing niece?"

The harp strings jangled as Dudod struck a sour chord. "No, Dreamer," he said calmly, after a moment. "I didn't know you were still looking for Rhiannon." His light green eyes were bright with curiosity—and something else.

"Aren't we all? She's been missing now for over two years." Gwydion paused. "Do you think she's dead?"

"I do not," Dudod said shortly. He gave Gwydion a long, considering look. "What's your interest in this?"

"Only that she has managed to evade her duty. She was to be the next Ardewin."

"Elstar takes that place now, so you don't have to worry about it, do you?"

"Dudod," Gwydion said in exasperation, "people have obligations, particularly Y Dawnus of the House of Llyr. She is a powerful clairvoyant and telepath both. And Kymru needs her."

"Does it?" Dudod said shortly. "Or does it just offend you that she didn't do what she was told?"

"Both. Tell me the truth. Do you know where she is?"

Green eyes met steely gray, as Dudod returned Gwydion's stare. "I do not," Dudod replied, his gaze unwavering.

"And if you did, would you tell me?"

"I might. If you gave me better reasons than the ones I've just heard."

Before Gwydion could reply, a young woman entered carrying a tray piled high with bread and cheese. Her golden hair hung to her waist, shimmering against her journeyman's robe of sea green. Her smooth skin was flawless, and her blue eyes were the color of the summer sky.

"Neuad," Elstar exclaimed. "What are you doing? Journeymen aren't servants!"

Neuad set the tray down in front of Myrrdin with a dazzling smile. Although she answered Elstar, she never took her eyes off the Ardewin. "I was in the kitchens when the order came so I just thought I would bring it up myself."

As she continued to gaze worshipfully at the Ardewin, Myrrdin blushed. "Thank you, Neuad." He cleared his throat. "I'm sure you have many things to do, so we won't keep you."

"Yes, Ardewin." Her eyes never leaving him she backed out of the room.

Gwydion, his eyes wide, turned to his uncle. "I believe you have an admirer, oh great Ardewin."

Myrrdin moaned as Elstar, Elidyr, and Dudod began to laugh.

"Oh, Gwydion, it's so funny," Elstar said, giggling. "She follows him everywhere."

Myrrdin flushed. "I can't help that," he said testily.

"And the funniest part is how embarrassed he is about the whole thing," Elstar went on, still laughing.

Myrrdin scowled at his heir then turned to Gwydion in exasperation. "It really is awful. She never takes her eyes off me, and she's less than half my age. I'm old enough to be her father!"

"By the way, who is her father?" Gwydion asked.

"Hetwin Silver-Brow, Lord of Gwinionydd."

Gwydion raised his brows. "Amatheon is Hetwin's Bard. You'd better not let Hetwin's son get wind of this. They don't call him Cynedyr the Wild for nothing."

"Oh, Myrrdin could take Cynedyr any day of the week. And she is beautiful. I'm sure you'll both be very happy,"

Dudod said, with a grin.

"Stop that. It's not funny."

Dudod sobered instantly, showing an innocent face. "Of course not."

"And no more cracks either," Myrrdin warned.

"Now, now, Myrrdin. It's not your fault that you're irresistible," Dudod said in a soothing tone.

Myrrdin sighed. "Well, she graduates tomorrow, and I'm going to send her to the farthest reaches of Kymru."

"Oh, Myrrdin," Elstar said, "you can't do that. It will break her heart."

"She'll have to bear it," Myrrdin snarled.

"I think you should keep her here. Just getting to really know you would cure her," Gwydion contributed with a grin. "With a vengeance."

"Ha, ha," Myrrdin said flatly.

LATER THAT EVENING, Gwydion and his uncle walked in the gardens. The herb garden of Y Ty Dewin, where the physicians of Kymru learned to identify, harvest, distill, and preserve their herbal remedies, was legendary.

Trees of apple, willow, and hawthorn grew around the perimeter of the five-sided garden. Barberry and blackberry twined in glorious profusion over the low, stone walls. The shapely bell-like flowers of foxglove trembling slightly in the gentle night breeze. The heady aroma of various mints, of thyme, of rosemary, wafted in the night air. Five streams meandered throughout the garden, pouring into a deep, shining pond in the very center. The bright half-moon turned the streams into ribbons of silver.

Gwydion and his uncle had been wandering the garden for

some time now, walking the graveled paths, talking quietly of personal things. Of Gwydion's daughter and of Dinaswyn, Myrrdin's sister, back at Caer Dathyl. Of the latest group of apprentices, of the most promising journeymen.

Gwydion only fully trusted three people on this Earth; his brothers Uthyr and Amatheon, and his uncle, Myrrdin. Myrrdin had not only always been kind, he had also been wise, seeing early on the damage his sister, Celemon, was doing to Gwydion and Amatheon, and doing what he could to minimize it.

During the time he was Ardewin's heir, he frequently invited Gwydion and Amatheon to stay at Y Ty Dewin for as much of the holidays as his sister would agree to, sparing them lonely and tension-wracked days at Caer Dathyl.

All his life Gwydion had known that his uncle cared for him. But he also knew that his uncle cared greatly about his responsibilities as Ardewin of Kymru. And this was something he would find very hard to give up.

Their conversation grew more disjointed. Myrrdin was obviously waiting for Gwydion to unburden his heart. And Gwydion was waiting for the courage.

At last he swallowed hard and tried to begin. "Uncle . . ." He trailed off, not knowing how to say what he must.

"Ah, ready at last then? Here," Myrrdin said, gesturing to a stone bench. "Let me rest my old bones while you tell me whatever you are trying so hard to say."

"I tested Arthur privately. Just Susanna, Ygraine, and Uthyr were there."

"Why would you do that?" Myrrdin asked, perplexed.

"Because I knew what we would see. And we did. He has the makings of a High King."

Myrrdin blinked in surprise. "A High King? It is time again?"

"It is time," Gwydion agreed, grimly. "If I can keep him alive long enough," Gwydion rushed on. "I persuaded Uthyr and Ygraine to agree to have Arthur sent away and brought up in secret."

"How were you able to get them to agree to that?" Myrrdin asked in astonishment.

"By telling them the truth. That Cerrunnos and Cerridwen have come to me in my dreams and warned me that there were traitors among us. Ygraine said that Uthyr would be able to protect his own son. But I said that he could not."

"Traitors among us," Myrrdin said quietly, "who seek to harm the boy. Who seek to keep Kymru without a defender. And who are these traitors?"

"The Protectors would not say." He told his uncle of the recurring dream of the shadow that menaced the young eagle. "There was one other thing I told them that made them agree to it."

"And that was?" Myrrdin asked softly, his keen eyes searching his nephew's face.

Gwydion took a deep breath. "I told them that you would bring up Arthur."

"You told them what?" Myrrdin exclaimed, stunned. "But Arthur has to be brought up in secret! I can't do that as Ardewin!"

"That's right, you can't," Gwydion said steadily.

"Are you asking me to give that up? To step down as Ardewin and just disappear?" Myrrdin asked incredulously.

"Yes."

"Gwydion," Myrrdin said patiently, "I can't."

"Why?"

"For one thing, there's nobody to take my place here."

"There's Elstar. It's what you've been training her to do, after all."

"Elstar's too young," Myrrdin snapped.

"Myrrdin, she's my age."

"Oh, Gwydion," Myrrdin said impatiently, "you're too young. Didn't you know that?"

"What about Cynan at Tegeingl? He's of the House of Llyr."

"Cynan! Oh, he's a good man and a good Dewin, but he couldn't lead a horse out of a stable, much less the Dewin of Kymru." Myrrdin stood, looking down at his nephew. "I'm sorry. You ask the impossible. Don't you see that? Being Ardewin isn't about power, or prestige. It's about leadership and its burdens. It's about understanding the people who look to you. And, by understanding them, giving them the means within themselves to be the best that they can be. It's about guiding men and women to use their gifts, to explore within. I can't give that responsibility into uncaring or unskilled hands. And I won't."

"Uncle—" Gwydion pleaded.

"I tell you no. Get someone else to raise Arthur. I have a duty."

"Myrrdin, Arthur is your duty."

"You know nothing," Myrrdin said flatly. "Nothing."

Myrrdin turned to leave determined not to hear another word. Gwydion grasped his uncle's sleeve, refusing to let go. "Wait. He needs you. He's going to have power at his fingertips that you and I could never truly imagine," Gwydion went on, the words hastily tumbling out of his mouth. "And he's going to have to be taught how to use it. And how not to use it." Myrrdin stopped struggling to stare at his nephew as Gwydion went on, still clutching his uncle's sleeve. "He will have to be compassionate, hard, honest, cunning. He'll have to have a heart that can love but cannot be broken. Who else in all of Kymru could teach him these things? Who else but you?"

"No, lad," Myrrdin whispered. "Don't ask this of me, I beg you."

"I don't ask it of you, Uncle. Kymru itself beckons you." Unbidden, words came to him, as though from another place, at another's command. "The mountains of Gwynedd where the eagles nest in their aeries beg you to do this. The sands of Ederynion that ebb and flow with the ocean tides; the glens and forests of Prydyn where the wolves hunt; the wheat fields of Rheged, shining like fire in the noonday sun; all these beg you. Cadair Idris itself begs to hear more than the silent wind; it longs to listen to music and laughter again. Do this. Bring up the High King in secret. Your reward—"

"Do not speak to me of reward," Myrrdin flared. "Do not speak at all!"

"I understand—"

"You understand nothing, boy." Myrrdin gazed at the great keep of Y Ty Dewin as Gwydion's hand fell away from his arm. The white stones glowed silvery in the light of the moon. His gaze played over the garden, the stream, and, finally, to the moon herself. Myrrdin stood still as the moonlight washed over him and pooled at his feet.

Finally, he spoke, never taking his eyes from the glorious moon. His voice was quiet. "When I became Ardewin, I went to Nemed Onnen, Nantsovelta's sacred grove of ash trees here. I spent the night in the grove alone, listening to the beat of my heart, to the voice of the Queen of the Moon.

The moon was full, and she shone that night with a light that still breaks my heart to recall. She was so beautiful. I spoke to her in the silence. I vowed to lead the Dewin with all my heart, all my soul, all my mind, until the day I died. I made this vow to Nantsovelta, to Kymru itself. And now you tell me to break it."

The breeze chose that moment to send a gust through the garden with a gentle sigh. The stream laughed softly to itself. And the silver light of the moon shone, brave and quiet in the night sky.

Myrrdin turned to Gwydion, his eyes deep, dark pools, awash with agony. "I can't do it," Myrrdin said simply. "Good night."

GWYDION SAT MOTIONLESS, his uncle's departing footsteps echoing down the graveled path. He lifted his head and stared at the bright, shining moon. Suddenly, tears blinded him and the moon wavered, then spilled and ran down his face.

His uncle was right, he understood nothing. Nothing except that life could be so cruel.

She handed you a gift, then took away another. Or snatched it from you when you stretched out a hand to take it. She gave you pain to set you on your path then laughed when you fell on the way. And you fell and fell until your skin was scraped raw, until you were bruised and bloodied. And still she beckoned you on.

He thought of his own sorrows, his own festering wounds, how he had been unable to heal them and had now bled away too much of the man he might have been.

But he could not care about that. He could not care about Myrrdin's happiness; he could not care for his own. He would complete the tasks given him by the Shining Ones, using anyone and everyone to do it. Somehow he would make Myrrdin do this thing.

Only the task had meaning. It was the only thing that ever would.

Suldydd, Cynyddu Wythnos—afternoon
GWYDION STOOD BY himself at the back of the Great Hall, waiting for the ceremony to begin. A low buzz of conversation floated up to the high ceiling of the two-storied, five-sided chamber. The white stone gleamed in the light of hundreds and hundreds of candles.

Benches were lined up in the center of the hall. Dewin, journeymen, and apprentices occupied the first group of benches, while friends and family members of apprentices who were graduating to journeymen filled the next rows.

A huge banner of a silver dragon on a field of sea green hung on the wall behind the dais at the far end of the hall. Two more long benches had been set next to the dais. The bench to the right of the dais was empty, waiting for the graduates to enter. The long bench on the left was filled with the heirs of the four kingdoms and their escorts.

Arthur sat solemnly with Susanna next to him and Cai standing behind them. Next to Susanna sat the young heir of Prydyn. Nine-year-old Prince Geriant ap Rhoram's hair was golden like his father's, his face open and warm, and his blue eyes sparkled with excitement.

Achren, King Rhoram's Captain stood behind Geriant. Her black hair was braided tightly to her scalp, and her dark eyes were alert, constantly sweeping the hall for any sign of menace to her charge. Ellywen, Rhoram's Druid sat stiffly next to Geriant. Her dark brown hair was pulled tightly back from her face and confined with an emerald clasp. Her gray eyes made Gwydion think of thin ice, the kind that covered a very deep river. One misstep and a man might drown.

Princess Elen, the heir to Ederynion sat with all the dignity she had inherited from her mother, Queen Olwen. She was small for her eight years, delicate and slender, with rich auburn hair. The little girl would be a beauty like her mother one day. A slight smile crossed Gwydion's face, remembering his brief time with Olwen years ago.

Angharad, the Captain of Olwen's *teulu*, laughter in her light green eyes and her red hair braided and wound round her head, bent over to say something to Elen that made the little girl giggle. Young Iago, new to his post as Olwen's Druid, laughed with them, his dark eyes sparkling. It was obvious that he adored the child.

Prince Elphin, the eleven-year-old heir to Urien of Rheged, had brown eyes that brimmed with mischief as he chatted with Esyllt, King Urien's Bard. Esyllt had a sensuality that caught every man's eye. Her rich, light brown hair and sparkling blue eyes drew admiring glances. By the look in Trystan's green eyes, the Captain of Urien's *teulu* was interested in admiring even more of the lady. A good thing that March, the lady's husband, was not here to see it.

By rights Gwydion, as the Dreamer of Kymru, should have been sitting up front also. But for now, he preferred to lean against the stone wall next to the doors. He had not seen his uncle yet today, and he was far too tense to take a place where all eyes would be trained on him. As befitted the formality of the ceremony he wore the traditional Dreamer's robe of black, trimmed with red. Quite a few admiring glances from the ladies were sent his way. But he did not see them. All he saw was the memory of his uncle's eyes, dark with the pain that Gwydion's demand had given him.

The graduating apprentices and journeymen began to file in and onto the empty benches. The apprentices wore plain gray robes, while the robes of the journeymen were sea green. Elstar entered through a small door to the right of the dais, wearing a robe of sea green trimmed in silver. Around her brow she wore a silver circlet with a pearl in the center. She carried a silver staff and solemnly rapped the floor with it three times. As she did so the crowd fell silent. She lifted the staff and began the prayer to Nantsovelta.

O vessel bearing the light,
O great brightness
Outshining the sun,
Draw me ashore,
Under your protection,
From the short-lived ship of the world.

Then Myrrdin walked in slowly, mounting the steps to the dais and turning to the waiting crowd. His robe was silver, trimmed with green. Around his shoulders he wore the traditional Ardewin's cloak of white swan feather. He carried a staff of gold, and he looked haggard and haunted.

"Who comes here now before Nantsovelta, Lady of the Moon?" Myrrdin asked in a solemn voice.

Elstar answered her voice clear and light in the sudden hush, "Five apprentices who seek to become journeymen. May I present them to you?"

At Myrrdin's nod the five apprentices in gray robes came to stand before the dais. "I declare," Elstar went on, "that these are worthy. They have shown proficiency in herbal lore, in anatomy, and in surgery. They have mastered Anoeth, the secret language of the Dewin. They have learned the ways of clairvoyance and can Life-Read and Wind-Ride. I deem them worthy of becoming journeymen. Will you accept them?"

Myrrdin stepped forward and spoke to the first apprentice in line. "Are you, Llwyd Cilcoed, ready to dedicate yourself to Nantsovelta and the ways of the Dewin? Are you ready to accept the responsibilities of your gifts and to let truth guide your deeds?"

Llwyd Cilcoed spoke proudly in the silence. "As I walk in the ways of Nantsovelta may I show honor to the Lady of the Waters. May She continue to bless and guide me through this turn of the Wheel, and may I return to Gwlad Yr Haf when this life is done with wisdom and honor."

Myrrdin nodded and Elen of Ederynion stood, poised and dignified. "I declare that Llwyd Cilcoed is a true man of Ederynion," she said, in a high, clear voice. "For this, my mother, Queen Olwen, gives him a horse of his own, to aid him in his journeys."

Elstar then handed Myrrdin a round disk made of crystal that had been threaded with a long silver chain. The crystal was etched with three sinuous lines projecting outward, dividing the disk into three equal parts. "To you, Llwyd Cilcoed, I give the crystal triskale. Wear it with honor as a journeyman of Y Ty Dewin." Llwyd bent his head slightly as Myrrdin hung the crystal around his neck. "You are assigned to assist the Dewin at Neigwl in the cantref of Gwinionydd in Rheged. Serve with honor."

The next apprentice was a woman from Gwynedd, and Arthur stood to declare that Uthyr had given her a horse. His speech was letter-perfect, and, as the child spoke, Myrrdin watched him closely.

When the next three apprentices—two from Prydyn and one from Rheged—had received their horses and crystals and were assigned their posts, Elstar spoke, "I declare that these apprentices are now journeymen of Nantsovelta."

The new journeymen returned proudly to their seats as the crowd whistled and clapped their approval. A few raucous comments were shouted, then Elstar rapped again on the floor with her silver staff for silence. Again, she turned to Myrrdin. "Three journeymen there are who seek to become Dewin. May I present them to you?"

At Myrrdin's nod, the journeymen in robes of sea green stepped up before the dais. Gwydion knew the first two somewhat, for they were both from important families in Gwynedd. Regan ur Corfil was tall and slender, her wealth of dark brown hair spilling down her back. The other, Bledri ap Gwyn, had sandy brown hair caught up in a silver clasp at the nape of his neck, and his powerful shoulders strained against the cloth of his robe. The last journeyman was Neuad ur Hetwin, the woman who had been making sheep's eyes at Myrrdin last night. Today she stood silently before him, not even daring to lift her eyes, the candlelight turning her hair to molten gold.

The three stood still as statues while Elstar spoke, "I declare to this company that these journeymen have served in their posts with honor for five years. They are proficient healers. They are strong clairvoyants and use their gifts only to serve. I deem these worthy of becoming Dewin. Will you accept them?"

Myrrdin stepped forward then, framing Regan's face with gentle hands. "Regan ur Corfil, I deem you worthy of becoming Dewin, a true daughter of Nantsovelta." He nodded to

Arthur, who stood, clutching two rings in his tiny fist. The boy negotiated the steps to the dais laboriously then took his place beside Myrrdin. "My father, King Uthyr, declares that you are a true woman of Gwynedd and presents to you this ring of silver." Arthur handed the ring to Regan and she put it on the fourth finger of her left hand.

Then Myrrdin spoke, "Regan ur Corfil, I give you this torque of silver and pearl. Wear it with honor." So saying, he clasped the torque around her neck. "You will go to Ederynion, to the court of Queen Olwen in Dinmael, to serve her as Dewin. Serve with honor." She bowed to Myrrdin, and stepped back from the dais.

"Bledri ap Gwyn," Myrrdin said, his hands framing the young man's face, "I deem you worthy of becoming Dewin, a true son of Nantsovelta." Since Bledri was also from Gwynedd, Arthur again made his little speech and presented a silver ring. As Myrrdin clasped the torque around Bledri's neck he said, "You will go to Rheged, to the court of King Urien in Llwynarth, to serve as his Dewin. Serve with honor." As Bledri made his bow, Arthur returned to his seat, relieved that he had remembered his speech. Susanna smiled warmly at him, putting her arm around the boy's shoulders.

Then it was Neuad's turn. As Myrrdin framed her face with his hands the young woman blushed deeply. Elphin of Rheged rose and stood next to Myrrdin. "Neuad ur Hetwin," Myrrdin said gently, "I deem you worthy of becoming Dewin, a true daughter of Nantsovelta." Then young Elphin spoke, "My father, King Urien declares you a true woman of Rheged, and presents to you this ring of silver." After presenting Neuad with her torque, Myrrdin paused. His eyes searched the crowd, and when he saw Gwydion at the back of the hall their eyes met and locked.

Gwydion's eyes searched his uncle's. He saw sorrow and he saw pain. But at the last, he detected Myrrdin's faint, wry smile beneath his beard.

Myrrdin glanced down at Neuad's white, set face. "Neuad ur Hetwin," he said clearly, "You shall go to Gwynedd, to the court of King Uthyr at Tegeingl, to serve as his Dewin. Serve with honor."

At that moment, Gwydion understood what his uncle was saying, and he closed his eyes briefly with the knowledge. As the new Dewin sat down, Myrrdin turned to the hushed crowd. "I send Neuad ur Hetwin to King Uthyr's court, because Cynan ap Darun, the Dewin at Tegeingl, is being recalled to Y Ty Dewin. Cynan is a man of the House of Llyr, and he will take my place as Ardewin. I can no longer serve here."

Myrrdin continued to speak in the shocked silence. "I have suffered in secret for some time of an illness I will not detail. I can suffer in secret no longer, as my condition is becoming worse. I am no longer fit to lead the Dewin. If there is anyone in this hall who has ever cared for me, you will let me go in peace."

With that, Myrrdin started down the steps. Elstar, white faced, grasped his sleeve, but he shook her off. Pandemonium had broken out within the hall. Shocked faces started at Myrrdin as everyone spoke at once. But Myrrdin made his way down the hall, looking neither to the right or the left. Looking only at Gwydion. As he neared the huge doors, he stopped in front of his nephew.

Gwydion braced himself and looked into this uncle's eyes. They were undefeated and peaceful. The serenity in those dark eyes struck Gwydion like a blow. "Uncle, I—"

"*It shall be as you say, nephew,*" Myrrdin spoke within Gwydion's mind. "*May Nantsovelta forgive me my broken vow to her. And may Cadair Idris one day laugh again.*"

Chapter Six

Llundydd, Disglair Wythnos—midnight

Two months later, Gwydion rode slowly up to the closed west gate of Tegeingl. Torches set in brackets on either side of the closed doors burned fitfully in the hushed night. Overhead stars glittered coldly. The light of the full moon poured from above, turning the road into a path of silver.

Gwydion halted his horse, Elise, and waited. Within moments the gates of the city opened slowly, just wide enough for he and his mount to ride through.

"Any trouble?" Gwydion quietly asked the men who had opened the gate.

Cai, Uthyr's Captain, shook his head. The second man, Greid, the Master Smith, lifted Elise' legs, one by one, and tied sacks to the animal's hooves to muffle the sound. When this was done, Greid motioned Gwydion to proceed.

Gwydion passed through the silent streets of the sleeping city like a ghost. At last he reached the closed gates of Caer

Gwynt. He waited for a moment, staring at the hawk with out-spread wings incised on the gates of silver. A dark line parted the hawk in the center, as the gate silently opened.

Duach, Uthyr's doorkeeper, held a lantern in his hand that he handed to Gwydion. He silently motioned that he would hold Gwydion's horse and nodded toward the ystafell. Lights glowed at the windows of the two-story building that housed the King and Queen. Without a word Gwydion took the softly glowing lantern and made his way across the deserted courtyard.

As he approached the closed door of the ystafell, it opened, and Susanna, Uthyr's Bard, motioned him inside. Her eyes were red from weeping and her face was white and strained. "He's—he's almost ready," she said in a trembling voice.

"Has everything been done as planned?" Gwydion asked.

Susanna nodded. "Everyone believes that Arthur has been ill for the last three days. It helps that we have no Dewin here to examine him, since Cynan has left for Y Ty Dewin and Neuad has not yet arrived. We told everyone this morning that Arthur was worse, burning up with fever."

"And the burial?"

"We made up the shroud this morning and stuffed it with stones wrapped in rags until it was just the right weight. We will tell them that Arthur died tonight, and have the shroud ready in the morning for burial in Bryn Celli Ddu."

He didn't want to ask it, but he did. "And Ygraine and Uthyr? How are they taking this?"

"Sending Arthur away is breaking Ygraine's heart," Susanna said, her tone accusing.

Accusing him of—of what, exactly? Did she really think that it was a pleasure for him to deprive Uthyr and Ygraine of their only son? Did she think he was doing this for a whim? Did people think he knew nothing of pain, of bitterness, of despair simply because he had learned not to show it? Did they think he didn't live with agony each and every day, dream it each and every night? But he said none of those things, so bitter did he feel, so harsh was the flare of anger in his guts. To show this to Susanna—to show this to anyone, ever—would be showing too much.

"Children are sent away to be fostered all the time," he said shortly. "Even if the circumstances had been different she would have had to let him go soon anyway."

"It's not just that and you know it. She's afraid that she won't see him again. She doesn't trust you. And she loves her little boy more than she loves herself."

"If that's so," Gwydion replied, even more coldly than he meant to, "then she'll make this as easy as possible for everybody. I can't help it if she's wretched."

"No," Susanna said sharply. "But perhaps you could feel some pity for her."

"There's nothing I can do about Ygraine. And I can't tear myself up over it." Suddenly, his frustration, his anger boiled over. "I don't care what you think of me. I don't care if you hate me. I don't care if everyone hates me. I do what must be done."

"Would you care if Uthyr hated you?" Susanna asked quietly, her eyes malicious.

Gwydion clenched his fists. His face drained of all color. "Even that, Susanna," he said in a level tone. "Even that is a price I will pay. If I must."

Susanna said nothing for a moment, looking up into Gwydion's white, set face. "It's a price you won't have to pay.

You know Uthyr," she said gently.

"Don't pity me," he said, between clenched teeth. "I don't want it."

A sound at the top of the stairs made them turn. Uthyr, gently holding a sobbing Arthur, made his way down the stairs. He held the child carefully, as though he was holding his own heart between his hands. Uthyr tried to smile when he saw his brother; but the smile was stillborn on his white, strained face. His eyes were dry, but they had the look of a man dangling from a gallows tree waiting desperately for the moment when his body would cease struggling and hang lifeless, twisting in the wind, his agony over.

Gwydion knew that if he looked at his brother's eyes again, all his carefully won detachment, all his dedication to duty, all his walls would crumble into dust. And the future of Kymru would crumble with it. So he forced himself to look only at Arthur.

Uthyr gently deposited the sobbing child into Gwydion's arms. He brushed his son's hair lightly with the palm of his huge hand. "This is your Uncle Gwydion, Arthur. I know you remember him. Don't be afraid. He'll take good care of you. I'll—I'll come to see you as soon as I can. I promise." But the promise was empty, and Arthur knew it. Gwydion could feel the child's terror and pain as the boy shivered.

Gwydion looked down at Arthur, saying gently, "I will bring your father to visit, one day."

Arthur, who knew a true promise when he heard one, lifted his head, stopped sobbing, and stared solemnly up at his uncle. "I promise," Gwydion said again. Arthur twisted in Gwydion's arms, turning to look to his father. Uthyr was looking back at Arthur with a glint of hope in his face, hardly daring to believe Gwydion's words. "I'll see to it, Uthyr. I promise," Gwydion repeated.

Uthyr nodded, and reached out a trembling hand to cradle his son's wet cheek. "You be a good boy," he whispered unsteadily. Again, he tried to smile, but the smile never reached his tormented eyes.

Gwydion turned to go with the boy in his arms. As Susanna opened the door, he heard footsteps rushing down the stairs and then Ygraine was there, thrusting herself between Gwydion and the door. She wore a plain, shapeless gown of gray linen. Her hair was in disarray, and her feet were bare. Her movements were jerky and her eyes were bright, as though she burned with fever.

"Wait," she said hurriedly. "I just thought of something. Alban Nerth! The Alban Nerth celebration is in six days." She rushed onward, the words racing out of her mouth. "Why don't we wait until then? You could help us celebrate. Yes, that's what we shall do. You help us celebrate. And then— then you can take him."

Arthur began to cry again. He reached out his small arms to his mother. "Mam," he sobbed. "Mam."

With a moan like a dying woman, Ygraine tore Arthur from Gwydion's arms, holding on to the boy tightly. "No, no, I won't let you take him!" she screamed.

But Uthyr, his face white and desperate, leapt to hold Ygraine as Susanna tore Arthur from the Queen's arms. Ygraine screamed, twisting in Uthyr's grasp, raking his drawn face with her nails, sobbing for her son.

"Come on!" Susanna cried. She ran with Arthur in her arms into the courtyard and Gwydion was right behind her. Duach, seeing their haste, swiftly opened the gate of Uthyr's fortress.

As Gwydion mounted his horse, she tossed the boy up to him. Setting Arthur firmly in front on the horse's back, he Mind-Shouted at Elise to go. The horse took off from the courtyard at a dead run. The city streets streamed behind them as they made for the west gate. Cai and Greid, hearing Elise's muffled gallop leapt to open the gate and Elise shot through.

The horse did not stop running until they were far into the forest. As Elise slowed to a walk, Gwydion thought at first that Arthur was still weeping. But the harsh, dry, heartbroken sobs were not coming from his nephew's throat.

They were coming from his own.

Gwaithdydd, Disglair Wythnos—early evening
AT DUSK THE following day they came to a clearing in the forest, and Elise simply stopped walking. Gwydion blinked in surprise. Arthur, who had been sitting quietly on the saddle in front of Gwydion, craned his neck to look back at his uncle.

"Oh yes, so it is. Thank you," Gwydion said as he dismounted. He lifted Arthur from Elise's back and set the boy on his feet.

Arthur, who had not said a word since crying out for his mother the day before, finally spoke. "Who are you talking to?"

"Elise has reminded me that it's time to make camp. And he's right. It's late," Gwydion replied absently, as he grabbed the saddlebags.

"He talks to you?" Arthur asked in astonishment.

More than you do, Gwydion thought to himself. But he was relieved to hear Arthur speak at last. "In a way," Gwydion replied as he shuffled through the bags for something to eat—something that didn't require cooking. "It's something that telepaths can do with animals. You don't exactly talk with them—by which I mean that animals don't communicate with words. But you can sense what they are feeling, which is why they call it Far-Sensing. Telepaths talk to other people with their minds, too, which is called Wind-Speaking." He set out bread and cheese on the top of a flat rock, and gestured for Arthur to begin eating. Gwydion himself wasn't really hungry and he decided it would be a good idea to take a look around to be sure they were not being followed.

Without even thinking to tell Arthur what he was doing, Gwydion sat down on the ground, closed his eyes, and sent his awareness out of his body to hover over the clearing. He saw his own body sitting there, motionless and barely breathing, and Arthur's astonished expression. He scouted the land around them. Far to the north he saw lights, and, investigating closer, found a small farmstead. No problem there, the settlement was over five leagues away. As he scouted east he came close to Tegeingl, but shied away from investigating further. He scouted south and west, but saw nothing to alarm him.

Satisfied, he returned to his body. As he did so, he became aware the Arthur was frantically tugging at his sleeve, begging him to wake up. Gwydion was appalled at the fright on his nephew's face. The child must have been terrified, thinking that his uncle was deserting him, leaving him all alone in the great forest.

Hesitantly, Gwydion took the hysterical boy in his arms. "I'm sorry, Arthur. I should have explained. I was doing something we call Wind-Riding. It's a thing that clairvoyants can do. We leave our bodies for a short time, and we can see other places far away. I didn't mean to frighten you."

"I—I wasn't scared," Arthur lied.

"Oh, I know you weren't. Probably you were just a little startled, weren't you?"

Arthur nodded. "Could—could I do that?"

"Maybe someday. Clairvoyants can do another thing called Life-Reading. That's when they lay hands on someone and can 'see' what might be ailing them. That's why the Dewin are our doctors. Now, would you like to help me gather some wood for the fire?"

Arthur moved off, picking up branches from the forest floor and piling them in the center of the clearing, looking back often to be sure that Gwydion was still there. When enough wood had been gathered, Gwydion told Arthur to stand back. He stared at the pile of wood until it began to glow and then suddenly burst into flames.

"I've seen Griffi do that," Arthur said in a confidential tone.

"Yes. Griffi is a Druid."

"How do you do that?" Arthur asked, curiously.

"It's something all psychokinetics do. It's called Fire-Weaving. There are other things we can do, too, like moving objects with our minds. That's called Shape-Moving."

"You can do everything," Arthur said, in an admiring tone.

"Some people have a combination of two gifts. My father was both psychokinetic and clairvoyant. Your great-uncle Myrrdin is clairvoyant and telepathic. But most people who have the gift are only one thing. People who are telepaths become Bards. Those that are clairvoyants become Dewin. And psychokinetics become Druids. But only the Dreamer has all three gifts, plus others besides. The Dreamers practice something called precognition, which is being able to see the future. Sometimes, if it's very important, we can also do something called retrocognition, which is the ability to

135

see events from the past. There are many Bards and Dewin and Druids in Kymru. But in each generation there is only one Dreamer."

"And that's you."

"That's me."

"I can't do anything," Arthur said sadly.

"Oh, maybe you will, one day."

They settled down by the fire to eat and Gwydion absently scratched at his beard.

"Why do you do that?"

Gwydion stopped, and looked over at Arthur. "Because it itches," he said flatly.

"Oh," the boy said, understanding that further comments would be unwelcome.

After they finished their meal Gwydion rolled out a blanket for Arthur to sleep in. Arthur bundled himself up, and laid on the ground, watching the fire.

"Uncle Gwydion?"

"Hmm?"

"Where are we going?"

It was the first time that the boy had asked. "We're going to a little village called Dinas Emrys. The road we're on, Sarn Gwyddelin runs right through it. It's in the great mountain range of Eryi. We'll be there by tomorrow."

"What's it like?"

"Well, it's very small. Mostly the people who live there raise sheep."

"What will I do there?"

"You and your great-uncle Myrrdin will raise sheep, like everyone else. Now go to sleep, it's late."

"Uncle Gwydion?" Arthur asked, after a brief silence.

Gwydion began to look on Arthur's previous silence with nostalgia. "Yes?"

"When will I see Da again?"

Gwydion turned from the fire to look down at the small boy. Arthur's eyes were wide in an effort to keep the tears from falling. Gwydion reached over and picked Arthur up, settling him into his lap. "Your Da will come to see you as soon as I think it's safe, Arthur. It may be a while. But I will bring him. You remember that where you are is to be a secret, don't you?"

"Yes, Da told me. He said that I was a very important and special boy. He said I was so special that they had to send me to a place that would be very, very safe. He said Great-uncle Myrrdin would take good care of me. He said that he and Mam would miss me very much but that the most important thing in the world was that I be safe."

That was the longest speech Gwydion had ever heard Arthur make. The child was obviously too wound up to sleep. "Would you like to hear a story?" he asked.

"About what?"

"About Idris, the first High King of Kymru."

Arthur considered the question. "All right."

"Thank you," Gwydion said dryly. "The story begins four hundred years ago, when Lyonesse sank into the sea."

"Why?"

"That's another story for another time. May I go on?"

"Yes," Arthur said graciously.

"I appreciate that. As I was saying, Lyonesse sank into the sea. But some people escaped. About one thousand folk, all told, survived and landed on the shores of Kymru."

The moon was full, bathing the tiny clearing in a silvery

glow. Far off, a wolf howled. Elise shifted restlessly, then was still. The fire popped and crackled as Gwydion resumed reciting in a soft, singsong voice. "And these are the names of our greatest ancestors who survived the destruction. Llyr the Great, the first Dreamer. Penduran, the first Ardewin, the daughter of the Lady Don. Math, the brother of Don, the first Master Bard. Govannon the Smith, the son of Math, the first Archdruid. Elen of the Roads, the first High Queen. And, finally, Idris, the first High King.

"The people who survived the destruction banded together and began to build their lives again and survived that first, terrible winter. But their tiny settlement was attacked and destroyed in the spring. For the Coranians had come from across the sea and they wanted Kymru for their own. The Coranians plundered and burned and killed. And the survivors cried out for someone to lead them and save them from their enemies."

Gwydion glanced down at Arthur, but the boy was still wide awake. So he continued. "I have told you that one of the people who survived was a young man named Idris. Idris was a descendant of Amergin, the last High King of Lyonesse. One hundred years before Lyonesse sank, Amergin had been killed, and the Druid theocracy had ruled in his place. But Amergin's wife had escaped to the Danans with her infant son. The Danans were the magic people who lived high in the mountains. For five generations the Danans kept the descendants of Amergin in secrecy. And Idris was the last of that line.

"Now, the Four Treasures of the Lady Don—the Cauldron, the Sword, the Spear, and the Stone—were saved from the destruction of Lyonesse, although the Lady Don herself was killed. Llyr, the first Dreamer, gathered these Treasures and brought them to Idris. And Idris was tested. The Sword turned, the Cauldron spun, the Spear glowed, and the Stone cried out that Idris was High King.

"Then Idris, Llyr, Penduran, Math, and Govannon took counsel together, and they decided that they would fight the Coranians and push them from our land. And so began many years of struggle.

"Llyr made the testing devices, and they began to seek out others that had special gifts. Penduran taught and trained people with clairvoyance. Math did the same for the telepaths, and Govannon trained the psychokinetics. The clairvoyants were called Dewin, and they became our physicians. The telepaths were called Bards, and became our poets and our lawgivers. The psychokinetics were named Druids, and they became our scientists and philosophers. But Llyr was the only Dreamer, the Walker-between-the-Worlds, and one who could walk through the walls of time.

"Our ancestors built Caer Dathyl, an impregnable fortress in the mountains of Eryi. And Idris led his warriors in battle after battle against the hated Coranians and each time the Kymri won. For Idris was the High King and this meant he could gather the power of those with the gifts. He gathered the power of the Dewin and scouted out the enemy's movements from many leagues away. He gathered the power of the Bards, and used it to speak with wolves and eagles that attacked the enemy at his order. He gathered the power of the Druids and raised fog and wind and rain to confound the enemy.

"And finally, after twenty years of constant battle, we had won. The land was ours. So our ancestors gathered in Gwytheryn, the land in the middle of Kymru. They built Cadair Idris, the Hall of the High King. They built Caer Duir for the

Druids, Neuadd Gorsedd for the Bards, and Y Ty Dewin for the Dewin.

"By this time Idris, who had married Elen of the Roads, was the father of four children. So he divided Kymru into four parts. To Pryderi, his eldest son, he gave the land of Prydyn to rule. To Rhys, his second son, he gave Rheged. Ederynion went to his youngest son, Edern. And Gwynedd was given to Gwynledyr, his daughter. And Idris set Gwytheryn aside for himself and his wife, and for the Druids, Bards, and Dewin. And he gave Caer Dathyl to Llyr to be the home of the Dreamers. And that is the story of how Kymru came to be our land."

He glanced down again; hoping to see that Arthur was at last asleep. But the boy was as wide-awake as ever.

"Tell me about Lyonesse, Uncle Gwydion," Arthur begged.

"That story is far too long. You should be asleep."

"But I'm not sleepy."

"Hmm. Well, I won't tell you about Lyonesse. Not tonight. But I'll sing you a song about it. Listen, and I will sing what Math, the first Master Bard, wrote in mourning for his lost land.

There are three springs
Under the mountain of gifts.
Farewell to Slievegallion, to Aileach
And to Bri-heith, home of the lost Danans.
Your laughter is stilled; your joy is gone.

There is a citadel
Under the wave of the ocean.
Farewell to beautiful Temair,
White city of High Kings,

140

You are broken, crushed beneath the waves.

*There are four fountains
In the land of roses.
Falias and Murius, Gorias and Finias
I remember your proud Lords and Ladies,
And hear the echoes of your dying song.*

*There is a place of defense
Under the oceans wave.
My heart calls for Lyonesse,
But I hear no answer.
I weep forever for what is no more.*

The night was still when Gwydion finished singing. As the last words died away he glanced down at his nephew. Arthur had fallen asleep at last, listening to the tune of ancient sorrow.

Meirgdydd, Disglair Wythnos—late afternoon

THEY RODE INTO Dinas Emrys late in the afternoon. The small village clung tenaciously to the side of the mountain, like a man desperately clinging to life. Twelve primitive but snug thatched huts were perched on both sides of the road. Each hut had a small garden plot and a byre for sheep. A few cows, a small flock of hens, a well, and a very tiny grove of alder trees completed the settlement.

The mountains surrounded the village, not so much protecting it as ignoring it. The mountains in the distance rose blue and majestic purple in the waning light of the late afternoon sun. The closer mountains showed bare, dark rock, sporadically patched with carpets of green clover and overlaid with silver-blue ribbons of sparking streams.

Gwydion stopped the horse at the last tiny hut at the north end of the village. The rickety wood door opened, and Myrrdin stood in the doorway, waiting to welcome them.

Unbidden, Gwydion saw in his mind a picture of Myrrdin as he had last seen him in his quarters at Y Ty Dewin. He remembered the books, the tapestries and carpets, the beautiful tables of shining oak, the white, stone walls bathed in the light of a cheerful fire. Myrrdin didn't belong in a place like Dinas Emrys. And, of course, neither did Arthur, the heir of Idris, the future High King of Kymru.

But Myrrdin was smiling as Gwydion handed Arthur down into the former Ardewin's still strong arms. "Hello, Arthur. Do you remember me?"

Arthur nodded. "Great-uncle Myrrdin, the Ardewin."

"Just Uncle Myrrdin, now. You are a clever child." Myrrdin put Arthur down and turned to Gwydion. "Get down off that horse and come see our new house!"

"New?" Gwydion snorted. "This house was old before even you were born."

"Thanks for reminding me how long ago that was. And I'll thank you to keep a civil tongue in your head. Arthur and I have a fine house and a very fine flock of sheep." Myrrdin looked down at Arthur. "Perhaps you would care to see the sheep later?" Arthur nodded, his eyes shining shyly at Myrrdin.

"Now," Myrrdin said, taking Arthur's hand, "let me show you the place. You'll like it. And we certainly don't care what Gwydion thinks, do we? We can very well do without his opinion." Arthur giggled as they went inside.

The floor was of smooth wood, and the walls showed fresh plaster. A large fireplace occupied the far wall, and the stone hearth sported a few iron pots and pans and a small iron pot bubbled on a spit over the cheerfully cracking fire. A split oak table and bench occupied another wall. Two narrow mattresses stuffed with goose feathers were laid against the next wall, covered with colorful woolen blankets. Herbs were strung across the low ceiling to dry.

Incongruously, a large oak chest stood next to the door. It was carved with details of exotic flowers, trees, and animals. Gwydion recognized it from Myrrdin's chambers at Y Ty Dewin. Myrrdin saw Gwydion looking at the chest and smiled. "My father made it for me, many, many years ago. He was the Archdruid, Arthur, so he was very busy, but he loved to work with wood whenever he got the chance. I found that I simply couldn't bear to part with it."

Myrrdin went to the chest and opened the heavy lid. One whole side was crammed with books. There was a space for Myrrdin's clothes, as well as some clothes for Arthur that Gwydion had purchased and sent on ahead. There were two cups made of silver and inlaid with pearls. There was a basic torque of silver, one pearl dangling from it. It was the kind of torque that every Dewin wore, for Myrrdin had left the elaborate Ardewin's Torque behind at Y Ty Dewin for Cynan to wear. But even wearing this simpler torque would be denied him here. He must be just an old shepherd living with his grand nephew. Of course, eventually the people of Dinas Emrys would piece together that Myrrdin was much more than that—if they hadn't already. But that was to be expected in a small village. The people of Dinas Emrys held aloof from strangers. They would discuss Myrrdin, but only among themselves. After a time, when they had accepted him, they wouldn't even do that much.

Gwydion didn't bother to tell Myrrdin that he should not put either his torque or the rich cups in such an easily accessible place, because Myrrdin already knew that full well. Gwydion knew that soon, when Myrrdin had been able to come to better terms with this new life, his uncle would hide away these items in a safer place.

The fire crackled cheerfully, keeping the hut warm as dusk descended over the mountains. After Gwydion had stabled Elise they settled down at the table. A small cupboard yielded ale for Gwydion and Myrrdin and fresh ewes' milk for Arthur. Myrrdin occasionally stirred the boiling pot of soup over the fire. The smell was delicious.

"We'll eat soon, Arthur," Myrrdin smiled. "I'll bet that while you were on the road with your Uncle Gwydion you didn't get a hot meal."

Arthur gave a small, hesitant smile. "Uncle Gwydion doesn't like to cook," he volunteered.

"So he says, Arthur, so he says. But the truth is that he doesn't know how!"

Gwydion replied in mock indignation, "I do so!"

"Ha!" At this Myrrdin ladled the soup out into small hollowed-out loaves of bread. All three of them fell to the delicious dinner with a will. After they had sipped the last drop, they ate the bread and Myrrdin set out a wheel of rich cheese.

Arthur's eyelids began to droop and he gave a jaw-splitting yawn. "Time for bed, boyo," Myrrdin said gently, and scooped the boy up, laying him gently down on one of the feather mattresses. Myrrdin drew the woolen blanket up to under Arthur's chin, and kissed him on the forehead. "Good night."

"Uncle Myrrdin?" Arthur said, his words slurred with sleep.

"Yes?"

"When will my Da come?"

"I'm not sure, Arthur. As soon as it is safe."

Arthur considered this information. "He won't forget me, will he?"

"Never," Myrrdin said firmly. "Not even for a moment." With that reassurance, Arthur fell fast asleep.

Myrrdin rose from the floor by Arthur's side and made his way slowly back to the table. He picked up his mug of ale and took several swallows. "Was it bad?" he asked.

"Yes," Gwydion relied quietly as he stared into the crackling fire. "I promised Uthyr I would bring him here, one day. And I will. But not for many years, I think. Most people will believe that Arthur died, of course. But there will be some that won't. And those are the ones who will be watching Uthyr's and my movements very carefully for some time to come. It will be long and long before either of us come to Dinas Emrys."

The two men fell silent for a time. Finally, Gwydion spoke again, "What about you? How did you leave things at Y Ty Dewin?"

"As well as could possibly be expected. Cynan was quite reluctant to take my place. He felt that he wasn't the right man for the job. And, of course, he's right. But I can trust Elstar to keep Cynan from total disaster."

"Cynan's not stupid."

"No. But he's shy and easily intimidated. Fortunately, Elstar's not." Myrrdin shook his head. "Of course, she's the one who really made it tricky for me to leave. She wanted to examine me, to determine the nature of my incurable illness. Of course I dosed myself secretly with a few very nasty concoctions so that I would seem to be suitably ill." Myrrdin

145

shuddered. "I'm glad that part is over. And when she was firmly convinced that I was ill, she was equally firmly convinced that going off alone to die was the wrong thing to do. In the end I simply slipped out at night, when I was sure everyone was asleep. I knew better than to fog the vision of the Dewin when they looked for me the next day, so I settled for the one where we gently encourage people not to look too closely, that there is nothing there to be interested in."

Gwydion nodded. He had often used those masking techniques for his own movements. It did not do to use them too much, as they were very draining. But they came in handy sometimes.

"You are certain, then, Uncle, that you were not followed?"

"Positive. No one has any idea where I have gone. And, by the way, that's a very sorry flock of sheep I found waiting for me here. Where on Earth did you buy them? It will take me years to make them profitable."

Gwydion smiled. "Consider it a challenge."

Myrrdin snorted. "A challenge, he says. How long will you stay?"

"I'll be leaving for Caer Dathyl tomorrow morning."

"What are your plans?"

"My plans are to stay put at Caer Dathyl and raise Cariadas until she is tested and goes away to school. I'm going to see to it that she has a happy childhood, with a father who's always there."

"You'd better get some sleep, then, if you're leaving in the morning. Sorry I don't have a bed to offer, but, as you see, we are not equipped for visitors."

"Just a blanket in front of the fire is fine for me. I'd never ask you to give up your featherbed," Gwydion said grinning.

"Old bones, Gwydion. I have old, tired bones."

"Only when it suits you, Uncle. I'll bet if that sweet Neuad were here you'd feel just a bit younger."

Myrrdin scowled and threw a blanket at Gwydion. "Go to sleep," he growled as he blew out the candles and crawled into bed.

Gwydion wrapped the blanket around him and settled down on the floor before the hearth.

Gwydion watched the firelight dart and flicker among the shadows. He felt odd and disjointed, the way he always felt when he knew that an important dream was waiting for him. Idly he wondered what the dream would be as his eyes closed and he fell into a deep sleep. As he fell the Otherworld reached out for him, wrapped him in firelight, cloaked him in shadow, and took him away to hear the echoes of time within time, to walk through the walls between the worlds.

HE WAS A black raven with blood-red eyes. He surveyed the smoking battlefield below him. Bodies littered the landscape and he fluttered down to rest in the branches of a weeping willow tree, drawn here by the smell of death.

He saw a woman with her victorious warriors behind her standing on the bank of the river that bounded the battlefield to the east. She stared at the rushing waters and wept soundlessly, tears streaming down her beautiful face, with a look of regret even in her victory.

Unable to bear the grief on her face, he launched himself into the air with a cry and instantly found himself on the fringes of another battlefield beside a dark forest. He came to rest in the branches of a newly planted aspen tree that surrounded a freshly turned grave. Stones were piled to one side, waiting to be placed on top of the grave when it was filled. A league or so away a huge bonfire burned, fueled by the bodies of the dead warriors that had fallen in battle that day. He heard the harsh sound of a man weeping and the sound tore at his heart.

Again he shot up into the air, unable to bear the sounds of grief. And again he found himself at the scene of yet another battle. Bodies littered the plain, their blood soaking into the rich earth. Patches of Druid's Fire still burned blue and orange above the ground. Two men wept in each other's arms as they surveyed the smoking battlefield.

Their wracking sobs grated on Gwydion's senses, and the smell of death clung to him. So, for the third time he flew, trying to get away from the stench of grief and sorrow.

And again he was not successful. He found himself alighting on a yew tree that had been freshly planted over a newly dug barrow. This battlefield was the worst of all. There were dozens of fires set to consume the dead warriors' bodies. The men in the victorious army wept without ceasing as they gathered the bodies and fed them to the flames. Smoke stained the sky above the battleground. A man, his tunic and trousers dirty and bloodied, his head bowed and his shoulders shaking with grief, knelt next to the fresh barrow, his hand resting lightly upon the newly turned earth. The man lifted his grief-stricken face and shouted his raw sorrow to the uncaring, smoky sky.

Gwydion, laying before the pallet in the tiny hut in Dinas Emrys wept in his sleep, wept for the grief and sorrow he had seen in these places of death, wept until he could weep no more and the tears dried on his drawn, sleeping face. Wept for their sorrow—and for his own.

Three days later word reached the man that Arthur of Gwynedd was dead. He would have liked to believe that for he had his suspicions about the boy from the start.

Still, it could be true. And the fact that Myrrdin had announced an incurable illness and subsequently disappeared could also be true.

But he could not be sure. So he would watch the Dreamer carefully. Watch him until the Dreamer thought he was no longer watched.

And then the man would watch some more.

Part 2
The Dreamer

Alas for one who gives love to another
If it be not cherished;
It is better for a person to be cast aside
Unless he is loved as he loves.

The Song of Fand

Chapter Seven

Caer Dathyl
Kingdom of
Gwynedd, Kymru
Helygen Mis, 494

Meirgdydd, Lleihau Wythnos—late evening

The fortress of Caer Dathyl brooded in solitary splendor at the summit of Mynydd Addien. Proud and silent, the keep rose up like a fist out of the snowy mountain itself. The light of the waning moon glittered over the snow-covered walls. A single, round tower arched out of the stone walls, like the head of an eagle when it sights its prey. This was the Awenyddion's Tower, the tower where the Dreamers dreamed their dreams and suffered their nightmares.

Gwydion sat by the hearth in his study on the second floor of the Tower, sipping wine out of a golden goblet studded with opals, staring into the flames of the crackling fire. The firelight played harshly off Gwydion's handsome face, carving deep lines around his stern mouth and brow. His keen gray eyes glittered like ice, and the dark hair at his temples and within his closely cut beard was touched here and there with silver.

The restless flames tossed light and shadow over the round

chamber, illuminating portions of the room one moment, wrapping them in darkness the next. The room had no windows, for it was completely lined with row on row of bookshelves that stretched from floor to ceiling, broken only by the study door, the stairway to the upper-level sleeping chamber, and the small fireplace. The round, low ceiling was hung with clusters of small, silvery globes representing all the constellations that glittered in the sky over Kymru. The door to the study was carved to represent the four phases of the moon, each outlined in glowing silver—Disglair for the full moon and Lleihau for the waning, Tywyllu for the dark of the moon and Cynyddu for the waxing.

Large wooden chairs brooded silently at each end of the long table in the center of the room. The table was covered with books—some open, some stacked high, others hanging precariously near the edge where Gwydion had thrown them in exasperation after repeatedly failing to ascertain the whereabouts of Caladfwlch, the sword of the High Kings of Kymru.

Again and again he would remind himself that, when the time was right, the Shining Ones would put the proper clues in his path. But this thought always failed to comfort him. He was tired of being a pawn in the hands of the gods who made him wait and wait and wait while he inured himself at Caer Dathyl, trusting no one, reading his books, living with his nightmares.

He had read every book in this library—and every book in the three colleges—that pertained to Bran's movements just after the murder of High King Lleu. By now Gwydion felt that he as an authority on Bran the Fifth Dreamer. But this brought him no closer to understanding exactly what Bran had done with the sword.

Bran had found Lleu dying on the battlefield at the shores of Llyn Mwyngil. At that time Lleu still had Caladfwlch. Although it was known that Bran had spoken to the dying High King, it was not known what the two men said to each other. All anyone knew about the location of the sword was that it was no longer there by the time his murderers returned the next day to inter Lleu in Galor Carreg.

When Bloudewedd, Lleu's wife, and Gorwys, Bloudewedd's lover had murdered Lleu and taken over Cadair Idris, they had also taken the other Great Ones prisoner. They put Arywen, the Archdruid, Taliesin, the Master Bard and Mannawyddan, the Ardewin into the cells located beneath the throne room. They had collared the three Great Ones with *enaid-dals*, and the necklaces had effectively cut off their ability to use their gifts to free themselves. Bloudewedd and Gorwys had thought themselves safe.

But the next morning they had awakened to find that the Great Ones were gone. For Bran had freed them, fueling Gwydion's suspicions that there was more than one way into Cadair Idris. Worse still for Bloudewedd and Gorwys, they discovered that the Four Treasures were missing also. These Four Treasures—the Spear of Fire, the Stone of Water, the Sword of Air, and the Cauldron of Earth—were the implements needed to make a new High King, and their loss was a blow to Gorwys.

The four Great Ones each went to rouse the four kingdoms. Arywen went to Queen Siwan of Prydyn. The Queen was more than willing to march on Cadair Idris, for Gorwys was her husband, and Bloudewedd was her own sister. Taliesin went to Gwynedd and enlisted the aid of King Meilir. He, too, was eager to avenge Lleu, for his Queen was Lleu's younger sister. Mannawyddan went to Ederynion and returned with King Llywelyn. And Bran went to Rheged where it was easy to convince King Peredur, Arywen's longtime lover, to lend his aid. At the appointed time these Great Ones returned to Gwytheryn at the head of an army.

Gorwys, knowing they could not win, nonetheless marched with his tiny following from Cadair Idris to meet them on the plains of Gwytheryn. After a battle that lasted mere moments, Gorwys was captured. Bloudewedd opened the Doors of Cadair Idris and flew to stand with her lover.

The two were brought before the four Rulers, and the four Great Ones. There, Bran pronounced their doom. Bloudewedd was not to be allowed to die. Her spirit was to be infused in the Doors of Cadair Idris, thus allowing the previous spirit, that of Gilveathy the Traitor, to be released. Gorwys, too, was not to be allowed to go to the Land of Summer. Instead, Bran set his spirit to guard the shores of Kymru, charging him to rise and ride the length and breadth of Kymru to warn the Kymri should danger approach.

King Llywelyn alone dared to protest such measures, saying that death was punishment enough without binding the spirit beyond death. But Bran answered quite gently that he had promised Lleu he would not kill the High King's murderers. He had smiled softly when he said it, but even Llywelyn did not dare to question Bran's decision further.

The Rulers then asked Bran the location of the Treasures. Surely, they said, they could now be returned to Cadair Idris. But the four Great Ones shook their heads, saying only that the Treasures were safer where they were. And Bran proclaimed that the Doors to Cadair Idris were to remain closed and none would be allowed to enter there unless they came with the

Four Treasures in their hands.

The four Great Ones then took Lleu's Torque that Gorwys had worn and removed the pearl, the sapphire, the emerald and the opal. They had the Master Smith make rings for each jewel and gave them to the Rulers as thanks for their support. The pearl went to King Llywelyn and the sapphire to King Meilir. The emerald was given to Queen Siwan and the opal to King Peredur.

And in all that information there was not one clue to the location of the sword.

Gwydion had even traced Bran's later years, hoping to find something. Ten years afterward, Bran's mistress Princess Regan of Ederynion and their son were involved in a plot to murder King Llywelyn. Bran was forced to sentence the two to their deaths. Taliesin, Arywen, and Mannawyddan all died before Bran. In every case Bran visited them on their death-beds. He insisted on being left alone with each of them just moments before the end. When Bran died in Caer Dathyl his daughter, Dremas, at his insistence, was left alone with him just before he died. But what was said or done in those last few moments remained a mystery.

Yes, Gwydion was an authority on Bran. Unfortunately, it didn't seem to get him any closer to the information he was seeking.

Gwydion sighed as he sipped his wine. If only he wasn't cut off from the ones he loved. If only he could see Uthyr, talk to Myrrdin, be with Amatheon, spend time with Cariadas, his loneliness would not be so hard to bear.

But he could do none of those things. Not now.

He had seen his older brother rarely in the last eight years since taking Arthur away. Ygraine, still so bitter, would never even acknowledge Gwydion's presence in the few times he had journeyed to her court. Her cold, midnight eyes would look right through him, as though he was beneath her notice. She never even allowed him to speak to her daughter, Morrigan.

Like her mother, Morrigan had dark eyes and auburn hair. Her tiny features were a pitch-perfect replica of Ygraine. But the warmth in her eyes, her ready smile—these things she had inherited from her father. In those times when Gwydion had allowed himself to go to Tegeingl, he had watched Morrigan watching him in fascination, torn between her father's love for Gwydion and her mother's hatred, contenting herself with an occasional shy smile when she thought her mother wasn't looking.

But it wasn't Ygraine's hatred that made Gwydion stay away from Tegeingl. It was Uthyr himself that stopped Gwydion. For when he looked in his brother's eyes the complete absence of reproach broke Gwydion's heart. It shamed him that his brother gave him so much, and he had given Uthyr nothing at all, except pain.

Nor could he see Myrrdin although his uncle was only one day's ride away. For Gwydion did not even dare to ride through Dinas Emrys, did not even dare to Wind-Speak to Myrrdin. He occasionally felt he was being watched. What the watcher—or watchers—hoped to gain was not clear. He could not be sure that they had completely believed the story of Arthur's death. And, if not, he did not dare risk drawing their gaze to the one place he most wanted them to avoid.

He rarely saw his younger brother now, for Amatheon was still with Hetwin Silver-Brow in Rheged. Occasionally Amatheon would get leaves from his duties to visit Caer Dathyl. But those times were few and far between.

On six occasions in the past eight years, the Archdruid, Cathbad had visited Gwydion and made the tedious journey to Caer Dathyl. Gwydion was grateful for the visits and always sincerely welcomed Cathbad. When Gwydion was a boy, Cathbad had been the Druid at the court of Gwynedd and he had always been kind to Gwydion when they had met at Caer Gwynt. Cathbad was good company—wise and serene, as well as always ready with a good story or two to wile away the hours.

Though Gwydion did not truly believe Cathbad had ulterior motives for his visits his innate caution always came to the fore. He was very careful never to mention his nightmares, never to breathe a word of the true state of affairs, never to so much as hint that a High King had been born to Kymru.

He was less sure about Anieron's motive. The Master Bard was always appallingly well informed and he, too, would occasionally come to Caer Dathyl. Although Anieron had never even bothered to hint that he had questions, Gwydion sometimes worried that Anieron did not ask him anything because the Master Bard already knew everything there was to know.

He frowned, staring into the fire. The flames reminded him of the red-gold hair of his daughter, Cariadas. He missed her so much. She had been tested four years ago and he had seen what he had expected—that Cariadas would be the next Dreamer of Kymru. She was nine years old now, and studying clairvoyance at Y Ty Dewin. She would remain there for the next two years and after that she would be sent to the Bards to learn telepathy, then to the Druids to learn psychokinesis. Then she would return to Caer Dathyl and learn precognition from Gwydion himself.

Maybe her dreams would be better than his had been. He

hoped they would be, for her sake.

But now he must find a way to keep his promise and allow Uthyr to see his son again. Although he knew he was still being watched, he had thought of a way he could elude these potential spies, and still keep his promise.

He frowned, thinking of how best to get a message to Uthyr. He dared not relay a telepathic message, however innocuous, for it would have to filter through to Susanna, Uthyr's Bard. Though Susanna had been one of the people that had helped him to spirit Arthur away, he did not completely trust her. First, she was a Bard and he did not trust Anieron. Second, she was a woman. And there was no telling what a woman might do. Women were so unreasonable. He should know—he lived with Dinaswyn and Arianrod, two of the most unreasonable women in Kymru.

His aunt, Dinaswyn, had never gotten over being supplanted. It wasn't his fault that he had become Dreamer so early in his life, leaving her feeling displaced and useless. He had done all he could to lessen the sting but she was not the Dreamer any more, and he could not pretend that she was. He had no idea why the Shining Ones had chosen to send the dreams to him, but he was hardly in a position to argue with them. It was just like a woman, he thought sourly, to blame something on a man that wasn't his fault.

Arianrod, his cousin and sometime lover, was a far worse problem. She still lived at Caer Dathyl at Dinaswyn's insistence, although often she would travel to other courts, seeking new men, seeking diversion, seeking things that she was not perhaps even aware she was looking for. But she always returned to Caer Dathyl, and to Gwydion's bed.

And that was the problem.

He always told himself that when she returned he would end it. But when he saw her again he always succumbed to the temptation to take refuge from his pain and loneliness, in her glorious body. He knew that it was wrong, because he did not love her. He could not, he thought, truly love any woman. For to do so he would have to trust them first and that was impossible. He knew that he was using Arianrod, and the knowledge made him wince inwardly, ashamed.

Yet she, too, played a part in the wrong. She knew that he did not love her. And he did not think she had ever loved him. He often wondered why it was then that she would not just let him go.

Arianrod had returned to Caer Dathyl just a few days ago. So far, Gwydion had been able to avoid her—no mean feat in a fortress this size. But this would not last. She was sure to try to force a confrontation. And this time his mind was made up.

He twisted his thoughts away from Arianrod. For now he had to think of a way to get a message to Uthyr. And he had to be careful. Ah. Of course. Dinaswyn was the key. He Wind-Spoke to her. *"Dinaswyn?"*

"Coming," she replied quickly. A shade too quickly, he thought. She must have been hoping for such a summons.

He heard light footsteps on the stairs, and then Dinaswyn opened his study door. The passing years had contented themselves with bleaching the color from her face and hair, for while her skin was unlined, her hair now shone silver in the firelight. Her gray eyes, cool and watchful, surveyed him calmly. She was wearing a long, white robe, and her feet were bare.

"Found what you were looking for?" Dinaswyn inquired in a cool tone, gesturing to the book-laden table.

"No," he said, just as coolly. "Did you expect me to?"

"As I don't know what you are looking for, I hardly know what to expect."

Yes, he thought, trust Dinaswyn to pry. "I'm not sure myself, really," he lied. "I'll know it when I see it."

Her gray eyes hardened. "I see." Gwydion thought she probably did indeed.

"Dinaswyn, I wondered if you might do me a favor."

"Tell me how I may serve you, my dearest nephew."

Gwydion sighed inwardly. All conversations with her were like this. "Will you take a letter to Uthyr at Tegeingl for me?" he said mildly.

"That's it? A letter?" she asked in surprise. "Why?"

"Because I miss him," Gwydion said shortly.

"Gwydion, you never do things for sentiment's sake."

"Will you take it or not?" he asked impatiently.

"I will," she replied crisply. "When?"

"You leave tomorrow."

"The weather is a little difficult for traveling, Gwydion. You do know that it's winter, don't you?" she asked with some asperity.

Gwydion grinned. "I'll back you against a blizzard any day."

For the first time in a long time Dinaswyn laughed. Gwydion was surprised at how pleased he was to hear that sound. "I suggest, my dear aunt that you think of a good excuse to be in Tegeingl just now," he went on.

She frowned thoughtfully. "The Calan Morynion celebration is coming up in a few weeks time. As the most important woman there, I would lead the festival. Everyone at Tegeingl would say that I had really come to push myself to the forefront of the celebration, assuming it was the pride of a crotchety old woman shunted into the background before her time that brings me there."

"I like it," Gwydion said decisively.

"You should. It has the merit of being true," she said with a bitter smile.

"There's more to you than that."

She cocked her head at him. "Too smart for your own good, or for mine. Do me one favor in return."

"What?" he asked warily.

"When the time comes, when the test is truly upon us, don't forget me. Use me. Promise." Her gray eyes blazed and her voice held an urgency that he had never heard from her before. "Help me to make my life mean something. And my death."

"I promise that I will give you a task," Gwydion replied steadily. "But I will not let it lead to your death."

"That's my business, Gwydion," she replied cool as ever. It was enough to make Gwydion think he had imagined the fire he had seen in his aunt's eyes just a moment ago. "Write your letter then, nephew," she continued. "I leave tomorrow."

She turned and made to leave the room. But she stopped at the doorway, her hand on the door handle. Without turning around she said, "Good night, Gwydion. I wish you interesting dreams."

GWYDION FORCED HIMSELF to relax and sip his wine. He glanced at the stairs that led up to his sleeping chamber. Soon he must go up those stairs to sleep, possibly to dream.

But for now his task must be to keep his promise to his brother. As the first step, he must write a letter to Uthyr that only his brother would understand. Finding ink and parchment buried under a mound of books, he sat at the table and began to write.

My dearest brother:

How long it has been since I have last seen you. The years seem to fly by too swiftly, leaving a cold trail of unfulfilled promises behind.

I often find myself remembering that terrible storm that frightened us so when we were children. And I remember so clearly that evening by the birch tree under the waning moon. How I wish that we could go back to that time together.

Blessing to you, brother, from

Gwydion

That should do it, he thought. He was quite sure that in a month and a half, in the month of Bedwen, the month of the birch, in the week of Lleihau, the waning moon, Uthyr would meet him at the blasted oak in Coed Dulas. That same oak which had been struck by lightning during a storm long, long ago, while he and Uthyr had watched with horrified eyes, on the day that Uthyr had saved Gwydion's life.

He again perused the stairs that headed upward toward the bedchamber. Time to dream, he thought, as he folded up the letter, sealing it with wax from the candle. When he was done, he extinguished it. The dying fire glowed feebly, and the shadows multiplied.

He mounted the steps to the sleeping chamber. In the middle of the chamber lay a simple pallet, and next to it a small brazier burned. The roof was clear glass, allowing Gwydion to look up at the stars that wheeled overhead and at the waning moon. He discarded his robe and lay down naked on the pallet. He gazed at the stars that filled the winter night, trying to calm his breathing and clear his mind.

His gaze rested on the constellation of Ystwyth. It wound

like a river of molten silver, flowing through the night sky. As his eyes followed the winding road of the huge constellation he thought of the twists and turns and winding paths he took to ensure that he did what was required of him. He wondered if it would ever be enough. In musing about these things, he fell into a troubled sleep.

HE WAS ALONE in a tiny clearing within a dark wood. The trees hovered threateningly over him, their limbs blocking out the sky. Here and there bright beams of sunlight laboriously made their way through the branches, splashing small bits of light at his feet. The twisted trunks cast black, silent shadows that stained the ground, doing their best to obliterate the little sunlight that got through their heavy guard. The forest was utterly silent. No birds sang and no small animals rustled through the undergrowth.

He was naked and he shivered, for the air was cold beneath the trees. He lifted his hands to call fire to warm him, but nothing happened. Frantically he tried to Wind-Ride, to send his spirit up over the trees in an effort to find his way out of this dark prison. But his spirit remained fettered to his chilled body. He tried to Mind-Speak, calling out with his mind for help to anyone who might be close enough to hear. But he could not. Even his mind-voice was trapped. All his powers had deserted him, and he stood naked and defenseless under the brooding, malevolent trees.

Suddenly a streak of silver light shot down from the sky and into the forest itself. The silver light transformed, coalescing into the form of a dragon. The forest was silent as the dragon looked at him with large, green eyes. Sunlight dappled her silver scales, and he saw that around her sinuous neck hung a silver torque with a pendant of luminous pearl.

"Come," she said, speaking directly to his tired mind. Wearily, he managed to scramble onto her back. She shot from the ground and up through the trees.

And then they were out into the clean, crisp air, hovering far above the forest. He saw the dark forest beneath him, spreading like a stain on the green land. Ahead of him he saw a lake, glinting deep blue in the shining warm light of day.

Gently she landed by the lake and he dismounted, looking up at her. She lowered her head and gave him a mighty shove dumping him in the cool, clear water. He came up sputtering and he heard her laughter in his head, like the sound of silver bells. He grinned then, sharing in her laughter. He swam with delight, diving to the bottom of the lake and shooting to the surface to breathe the clean air. He cavorted in the water, feeling a joy he had never felt before. At last he made his way to the shore.

The dragon was gone. In her place was a man in Dreamer's robes of black and red. The man's long, auburn hair was clasped at the nape of his neck with a band of opals. His gray eyes, so like Gwydion's own, shone silver.

Gwydion's breath caught in his throat, for he knew this man. Bran ap Iweridd, the Dreamer to High King Lleu, held a book in his hands. The book had a binding of purple and gold and Bran held the tome out to Gwydion. Gwydion reached out, knowing that the book held the clue he had so desperately sought. But as his hands touched the book the scene melted, the book faded. He saw the brief image of an alder tree, silhouetted against a waxing moon. And then everything went dark.

HE WOKE ON his pallet with a start. It was night outside and he could tell that only a few moments had passed since he had fallen asleep. Cursing himself for a fool—for he recognized the book—he jumped up and hastily donned his robe, rushing down the steps to his study.

He located the book instantly. It was an innocuous book, a brief history of Kymru written for schoolchildren. But as the book was written when Bran himself was a child, and ended with the death of High King Macsen, Gwydion had rarely given it a second glance. Now he cradled the book in his hands, sitting by the hearth. He gestured absently and every candle in the room lit up. He opened the book but stopped, for he felt a bump in the binding, something that should not have been there.

He set the book down on the hearth, its cover open. Gingerly he gave the binding a twist. The parchment that was glued to the leather of the back cover split slightly to uncover a differently colored parchment beneath. Hardly daring to breathe, Gwydion gently pulled out the second parchment.

The handwriting was somewhat faded, but Gwydion had no trouble deciphering the message.

I gave a secret to my daughter,
So secret that she did not know.
And to her grandson she did give it,
A secret those Dreamers did not know.
And to his granddaughter he did give it,
This secret that they did not know,
In her granddaughter lies the secret,
A secret that she does not know.

Of course. Bran had planted in his daughter's mind a clue, a piece of subconscious information she had carried without being aware of it. And that information had been passed down from generation to generation through a process that only those of the House of Llyr possessed. The question was who was it in this generation that, all unknowingly, carried Bran's clue to the location of the sword?

He located and pulled out the Book of the Blood, the charts that traced the bloodlines of the House of Llyr. Referencing the poem, he saw that Bran had given the message to his daughter, Dremas, the next Dreamer. And she had passed it on to her grandson, Amatheon, the Eighth Dreamer. He, in turn, had passed it on to his granddaughter, Darun, the Tenth Dreamer. Darun had two granddaughters still alive. One was Arianrod, who was here in Caer Dathyl right now. He hoped with all his heart that she was the one who held Bran's message, for the other granddaughter was Rhiannon ur Hefeydd. And Rhiannon had disappeared from the face of Kymru years ago, and since then there had not been the slightest whisper of her whereabouts.

Even the fact that the animal in his dream was a silver dragon did not reveal which of these two women held Bran's message. Although the silver dragon was the emblem for the Dewin, it was a creature that accurately described both women.

It galled him that his quest for the sword should be dependent upon a woman. But that it should be dependent upon those two women galled him even more. For Arianrod was vain and selfish, and Rhiannon was childish and irresponsible. Rhiannon had fallen in love with the King of Prydyn, and refused to accept the task of Ardewin, the task for which she had been born, later disappearing in a fit of pique and taking her infant daughter with her.

He hoped he was not going to have to search the length and breadth of Kymru for her. The last dream image of the waxing moon and the alder tree clearly told him that he must begin the search for the sword by the fourth week of Ysgawen Mis, the month of the alder tree. It was now winter, and Ysgawen Mis was in the fall, but that would barely be enough time if he must accomplish the task of finding Rhiannon—a task at which all of King Rhoram's men had failed eleven years ago.

He sighed. He had successfully avoided Arianrod until now. But this would not get any better for waiting. He would have to test her now, tonight, and hope that she was the one.

HE DESCENDED THE stairs of the tower with Druid's Fire cupped in his hand to light the way. At the first level he turned left down the dark, rounded corridor. He passed Dinaswyn's rooms. No light shown beneath the door as he crept silently by. He came to the door of Arianrod's chambers and stopped. Light glowed beneath the door. He hoped she was alone. It would be awkward to get her attention if she had a man with her.

He knocked and within a few moments the door opened. The chamber, shaped like an arc, was lit with dozens of candles. On the far wall was a large, four-poster featherbed, with a headboard rounded to fit against the wall. Hangings of sheer, rose-colored silk wafted around the bed, drifting to the polished oak floor. Her rose silk bedcover shimmered in the candlelight, reflected in the ornate mirror that adorned the wall over the headboard. Large wardrobes covered another wall, filled, Gwydion knew, with countless gowns, presents from her many lovers. A large dressing table and chair were against the last wall, and the table was covered with small glass bottles and carelessly strewn jewels.

Arianrod herself glowed in the candlelight like a precious

gem. Her honey-blond hair, thick and wavy, hung like a shimmering curtain down to her thighs. It was the kind of hair that any man would ache to run his hands through. And Gwydion had, often enough.

Over her high cheekbones, her almond-shaped amber eyes glinted at him beneath dark eyebrows. Light glimmered off her night robe of ivory-colored velvet, open low in the front to reveal that she wore nothing underneath. A necklace of beaded amber encircled her slim neck and long, golden earrings hung from her delicate ears. Her lily-scented perfume wafted toward him.

"Gwydion," she said in her honeyed tone, and her wide, full mouth smiled lazily. "Still awake? You work too hard, *cariad.*"

He wondered if he should just go ahead, submit to temptation, and take her now without any further talk. Get it done, so he could get rid of her and move on to more important things.

He mused about what she had really wanted from him in the beginning, many years ago. He understood that she had wanted him for a lover because he was the Dreamer, one of the most powerful men in Kymru. Arianrod craved power for the security she thought it would bring, craved it to replace all that she had lost as a child when her parents had sailed away for Corania, never to return.

"You've been avoiding me," she said flatly when he did not answer her.

"I have, yes."

"Why?"

"Arianrod, we have more important things to talk about."

"Such as?"

"Such as a dream I had."

169

"Ah, and you need me for something. Of course, why else would you be here? After all, using people is what you do best."

Oh, she always knew just where to put the knife. And never hesitated to use it. And knew just when to twist it. Just like his mother.

He ignored the jibe, as he had learned to do long ago. "I dreamed of Bran. He planted a clue, a subconscious memory into his descendants. You are one of the two women who might hold that clue."

"And the other?"

"Is Rhiannon ur Hefeydd."

"Rhiannon! That fool," Arianrod said contemptuously. "You won't find that she holds anything important. Go ahead, then, Gwydion, search for the memory."

She crossed the room and settled herself on the chair before the dressing table.

He came to stand before her and gently placed his hands on either side of her head. "Close your eyes," he said quietly and she did so. "You are on a plain covered with wildflowers. Overhead the sky is clear, the golden sun spills down. A stream of clear, cool water runs across the plain, forming a pool at your feet."

As he spoke soothingly, Arianrod's head began to droop and her breathing slowed. He continued. "Before you is a rowan tree, with open branches that reach to the sky. It is covered with knots of tiny white flowers. Clusters of red berries glow within the branches. You approach the tree, for this is the tree of the House of Llyr, your House. You stretch out your hand to touch the bark and find that your hand sinks into the tree itself. You step forward, entering the hollow trunk. You descend down, down into the earth until you reach the roots of the tree.

"And there you see a well, filled with cool water. You stretch out your hand and cup the water in your palm. You drink. And as you drink, what do you see?"

He waited, but Arianrod said nothing. Her breathing was slow and even. He lifted her hand and let it go. It stayed in the air, as it should. He sighed. Arianrod did not hold the memory he sought, for it was obvious that she saw nothing, that she had no message for him. He brought her back slowly, having her climb the trunk of the tree and back to the plain.

"Wake up," he commanded, his hands still cradling her head.

Arianrod started awake, her eyelids fluttering. "Well?" she asked expectantly. "What did I say?"

"Nothing," he said shortly. "You do not hold the memory."

Her eyes glinted. "I see," she said. "So, you must find Rhiannon ur Hefeydd. Well, that will be interesting. Maybe you can get her to fall in love with you. Then you can use her any way you want."

"I didn't ask to have to find her," Gwydion said, stung.

"But you must, surely, look forward to using her," she taunted. "Since you are done with me."

"Arianrod—"

"Come now, Gwydion. You and I, we understand each other. Don't we?"

"I understand you. I'm not at all sure you can return the compliment."

"Oh, but I can. I know what you are. And what you want."

"No you don't."

"I believe that I do. What's the matter, Gwydion," she

went on with a smile. "Afraid I'll stab you in your bath?"

At this his clenched his hands into fists, to keep himself from striking her. No one talked about that. No one reminded him of what happened all those years ago. Swiftly he leapt toward her and grabbed her wrist. His face was drained of all color, twisted with pain. His gray eyes blazed. "Never speak of him to me again. Do you understand?" He shook her. "Do you understand?"

She laughed, for she did not fear him. Enraged, he lifted his hand to strike her, but caught himself. He had never struck a woman in his life, and he would not do so now. He rushed from the room and stumbled down the hall to his tower. He mounted the stairs, shaking. He made his way into the study and slowly sank into his chair. Unbidden, the memories flooded over him. Unwillingly, fighting every step of the way, he thought of his father, whom he had loved. And he thought of his mother and what she had done to them both.

HOW MANY TIMES when Gwydion was a young boy had he seen his father? He could count the times on one hand. For whenever Awst would come home to Caer Dathl he only stayed a few days before Celemon's anger, her emotional outbursts, her jealousy drove her husband away again.

Gwydion clearly remembered the time when he was only six years old. He hadn't seen his father for over a year. Waking up early, he roused his younger brother, and the two of them made their way to the kitchens to see if the cook would give them a little something before breakfast. They had stumbled into the busy kitchen, eyes heavy with sleep. Awst had been there, sitting on the hearth. They hurled themselves into their father's waiting arms, shouting for joy. Gwydion remembered the feel of his father's strong arms about him, the love and pride and joy in his father's face. Gwydion had felt safe, loved, and truly happy.

But only for a moment. For then Celemon had come down and everything had changed in an instant. Awst had reached out to hug her, and she had put her arm up to hold him off. She had begun to rant at him for staying away for so long, demanding to know if he had been with Queen Rathtyen in Tegeingl. He did not love them, she had screamed. He had two fine boys right here in Caer Dathyl, but he spent all his time with Uthyr, his son by the Queen. Within the hour Awst had left, driven away by his wife's recriminations.

Soon after this, Gwydion, who had been tested and found to be the next Dreamer, had been sent to Y Ty Dewin to learn the ways of the clairvoyant Dewin. Amatheon had joined him there a few years later, for his brother was Dewin. Gwydion had spent four years there before going on to Neuadd Gorsedd to learn telepathy from the Bards, and later to Caer Duir to learn psychokinesis from the Druids.

During those years he and Amatheon would see each other when they could. And their father visited quite often, at whatever college Gwydion had been living in at the time. Sometimes Awst would take them both to Tegeingl. There they met Queen Rathtyen, who was not the horrible woman their mother had told them about. The Queen had been kind to them both. And her son, Uthyr, had also been especially kind to young Gwydion, who was shy and awkward, soon becoming a hero in his half brother's eyes. Gwydion avoided going home to Caer Dathyl whenever he could, preferring to spend his holidays in Tegeingl with his father and brother, or at Y Ty Dewin, with his uncle, Myrrdin.

But then the day came when he was twenty years old and it was time to return to Caer Dathyl to complete his training with Dinaswyn. When he returned, he was greeted with reproaches from his mother for staying away so long. But Gwydion was no longer a helpless child and he defended himself. They had screamed and shouted until Dinaswyn had put an end to it by sending Celemon to her rooms and Gwydion to the garden.

For three years Gwydion trained with Dinaswyn in Caer Dathyl. He no longer suffered his mother's rages in silence, and the two fought regularly. Occasionally Amatheon, now a journeyman Dewin, would get leave to visit Caer Dathyl. Gwydion was always glad to see Amatheon, and grateful to his brother for coming, for he knew Amatheon only did so because of his love for Gwydion.

In those three years his father did not come once. Until one day Gwydion awoke to find his father sitting serenely by his pallet. The two men spent the entire day together. His father had been proud of him, he said, proud to have sired such a fine man. And Gwydion had glowed under his father's praise.

Now, thirteen years later, sitting by his lonely fire, Gwydion squeezed his eyes shut tightly. His breathing ragged, he tried to stop the remembering. But the memories came, crashing against his last defenses like ravening beasts, tearing the fragile peace of forgetfulness that he had built, oh so painfully, to shreds.

He remembered that Celemon had come down from her rooms that day. She had been smiling. She had drawn Awst's bath, she had said. And she had held out her hand to her husband, saying she would help him bathe. She had kissed Gwydion gently and reminded him to change for dinner. She

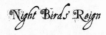

had tucked her hand into the crook of Awst's arm and led him, laughing, into the house.

But when dinner was served, only Gwydion and Dinaswyn were there to eat it. He remembered how they had sat at the table until long after dinner was done. How the steward had come to them, worried because the door to Awst's chamber was locked, and his knocking had brought no answer. How they had gone then to Awst's room and knocked on the door. How the silence had frightened Gwydion. How he, now in a panic, had used psychokinesis to unlock the door that had been bolted from the inside. How in the large, copper tub set in front of the fireplace he had seen them. How the firelight had flickered over the blood-red water.

He remembered the look on Awst's face—the look of surprise that was frozen there in that moment when his wife murdered him. And the smile on Celemon's dead face that must have been there when she stepped into the bloody water, slashed her wrists, and arranged herself in her dead husband's arms.

GWYDION REMEMBERED IT all. And remembering began to weep as the firelight turned his tears to blood in the Awenyddion's Tower in the fortress of Caer Dathyl, which stood in proud and lonely silence at the top of the world.

Chapter Eight

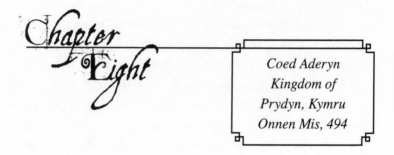

Calan Morynion, Disglair Wythnos—late afternoon

Rhiannon ur Hefeydd var Indeg swore as she stubbed her toe on a tree root and almost fell face down into the snow. She felt awkward trying to keep her balance while carrying a dead rabbit in one hand and a spray of snowdrops in the other. Taking a tighter grip on the snare around the rabbit's neck, she pushed onward through the snowdrifts.

She felt irritated and unsettled, out of sorts today. And she knew why. Today was Calan Morynion; the festival that honored Nantsovelta, the goddess of the Moon and Lady of the Waters, the goddess most revered by the Dewin. And that was the problem. Although Rhiannon was herself Dewin, she had turned her back on that part of herself long ago. The festival evoked far too much for her to enjoy it.

Today was also her name day. Today she was thirty-five years old and, as time went by in the quiet forest of Coed Aderyn, she tended more and more to dread the anniversary of her birth. It always reminded her that time was passing.

She suspected—she knew—that she was wasting the life she had been given.

Worse still, in the past few weeks she had begun to feel uneasy. Someone, somewhere, was thinking quite hard about her these days. The feeling was nebulous, not like the time when she first came to the woods. Eleven years ago all of Kymru had been looking for her. How irritating it had been to hear her name Spoken on the Wind over and over by telepaths up and down Kymru. It created such a din that she had headaches for months, even after they had stopped calling for her.

But this was different. It was as though someone was looking for her quietly, so as not to alarm her. Stalking her, perhaps.

Pushing these unsettling thoughts away, she continued to make her way between the dense trees to her home. She had told Gwen to stay inside while she was gone, but Rhiannon had little hope that her daughter would do as she was told.

Although the wood was silent, and she knew she was alone here, Rhiannon moved quietly for it was now her second nature. That had been hard to learn at the beginning, when she had first come here, bringing her child and her broken heart with her. They had almost starved that first winter. She had been forced to learn how to walk the woods quietly, to stalk and kill the wild animals in order to keep herself and Gwen alive. She had done it, for when the choice was learn or die, learning came quickly.

Once or twice a year, as need demanded, she visited the tiny village of Dillys to the west, just at the edge of the wood. There she would trade rabbit and deerskins for grain and other necessities. In the first years she had always made the journey with her heart in her throat, knowing that her description was being circulated and fearful that she would be recognized. But they never so much as blinked when they saw her and the baby. Of course, the people of Dillys, like those of other tiny villages, were closed-mouthed with outsiders.

Her doeskin boots, which she had patiently waterproofed by rubbing candle wax into them, made no sound as she glided across the snow. Her leather tunic and trousers were white; blending in with the snow-covered landscape. Her white winter wool cloak was hooded and lined with rabbit fur. The hood covered her long, black hair, which was tightly braided to her scalp. Her skin was tanned, and her large green eyes were fringed with long, ink-black lashes. Her snub nose was red with cold.

As she neared her home she automatically scanned the sky. But she could see no smoke rising from the fire she knew burned in the hearth. She smiled a little, for she was proud of her hard work. Realizing that even the dullest traveler would wonder about smoke rising from a lone hill, she had patiently hollowed out a fissure in the cave where she lived and set the hearth into the side of the cave itself. The smoke was drawn out through the fissure and into the series of connecting caves that went far back into the earth.

The opening to the cave under the hill was covered by a shimmering waterfall, which fed into a tiny pool. Even in winter the waterfall did not freeze, and the pool was never fully covered with ice. She made her way around the pool and climbed the wet rocks, slipping behind the waterfall and entering the hidden cave.

She stepped carefully, for the entrance was always slightly wet from the spray of water. Her eyes, dazzled by the snow, took a moment to adjust to the dim interior. She made her way

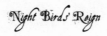

to the small table in the middle of the chamber and placed her burdens down on the rough wooden surface. The fire crackled merrily, and Gwen had lit the candles. She returned to the entrance and drew the heavy woolen curtain across it so that nobody would be able to see the glow of the fire.

As she looked around the chamber, the rough walls, covered with rock crystal, glittered in the light of the fire. Rushes covered the floor. The firelight played off the walls and the wooden shelves that she had built. One shelf, to the left of the entrance, contained a few books. A telyn, the small harp that had belonged to her father, stood silently next to the books. The tiny harp was covered with dust, for Rhiannon had not touched it in years. When her father died he had left her that harp, and her first instinct had been to smash it to pieces. But the beauty of the instrument always stopped her. So it sat mute, year after year, but still in one piece.

To the immediate right of the entrance were two stacked sleeping pallets. Next to these was another wooden shelf, which held a large golden bowl, an ivory-backed hand mirror, and a silver comb, the only gifts from Rhoram she had taken with her that long-ago night. In the middle of the rough wall, a small, intricately carved trunk squatted, its dark, satiny surface reflecting the fire's cheerful glow.

All was as it should have been, except for one thing. Her daughter was nowhere in sight. Rhiannon sighed in exasperation. She knew where Gwen was—exploring the caves. Over and over she had explained to Gwen how dangerous that was. Gwen could get lost, or the caves could collapse. But Gwen obviously felt that her mother was exaggerating these dangers, for she never paid the slightest bit of attention.

Rhiannon heard the sound of running feet, and Gwen

burst into the chamber through the opening in the far wall of the cave. She had a single candle tightly clutched in her tiny hands—at eleven years old she was small for her age. Her long blond hair was uncombed, and her delicate features were smudged with dirt. Her large blue eyes held her usual look of unfettered innocence. She wore an old blue gown, and doe-skin boots covered her little feet.

"You misjudged the time, I take it," Rhiannon said dryly, covering her relief that Gwen was unharmed.

Gwen's blue eyes widened in hurt surprise as she tried to hold off the inevitable scolding. "What do you mean?" she asked in her high, piping voice.

"You know what I mean, Gwenhwyfar ur Rhoram. You were exploring the caves again."

"Oh, no," Gwen replied earnestly. "You see, I thought I heard a noise just a moment ago, and I stepped back there just a very few feet to see if I could find anything."

"Ah, of course. And did you?"

"No. I can't imagine what it was."

"All right, Gwen," Rhiannon said wearily. "Let's go over this again. What part of 'stay out of the caves' is confusing to you?"

"Oh, Mam, please. I want to. Please let me," Gwen pleaded. "The caves aren't really dangerous. You worry too much. If you're not worrying that I'm lost in the caves you're worrying that I've drowned in the pool. If you're so afraid of water, why are we living with a waterfall on our doorstep?"

"I'm not afraid of water," Rhiannon said quickly. "And don't change the subject. You stay out of those caves, understand?"

Gwen nodded sullenly, her blue eyes filling with tears. She sat dejectedly at the table, her golden head bowed as she pretended to nonchalantly pick at her fingernails. But her hands were trembling slightly.

Rhiannon gazed at her daughter, and her heart softened. She struggled to be reasonable, for Gwen was her daughter and she loved her. But because she loved Gwen she was terribly afraid. She tried to clamp down on her apprehensions.

"All right, Gwen," she said quietly. "Let's make a pact here and now."

Gwen raised her head, her blue eyes still swimming with tears. "What's the pact?"

Rhiannon held up her hand, ticking down points on her fingers. "One: you may explore the caves."

Gwen leapt up, her face shining.

"Wait," Rhiannon said sharply. "There's a great deal more."

Apprehensively, Gwen sat down again.

"Two: you may explore, providing you Wind-Ride to me every few hours, showing me exactly where you are and what you are doing. Three: you must be proficient in Wind-Riding before you go into the caves again, and that means practice."

Gwen made a face, for she hated to practice. Practicing required stillness and concentration—neither of which appealed to her.

"Four—in exchange for the privilege of exploring the caves you will stay out of the pool unless I am with you. Now, is all that clear?"

Gwen nodded and rushed over to her mother to clasp her around the neck with her slender arms. "Yes, Mam. Let's practice now." Her blue eyes were alight with anticipation. Never had she been so eager.

"All right. Get the things, please." Gwen scurried over to the trunk and rummaged through the chest, returning with her hands full, and dumping the contents on the table. Rhiannon picked up her Dewin's torque. A single pearl dangled from a silver-encrusted pentagon, and she clasped the torque around her neck. Next, she picked up her plain silver band and slipped it on her finger.

Gwen lifted up the crystal, etched with the triskale—three wavy lines radiating from the center and cutting the round, milky white crystal into three equal parts. The crystal spun in the air from its silver chain as Gwen held it out to catch the light.

"Sit," Rhiannon said, holding out her hand for the triskale.

Obedient, for once, Gwen handed the crystal over and sat cross-legged on the floor, looking up expectantly.

"Now. Tell me of the gifts."

"Those with the gifts are called Y Dawnus, the gifted. There are four kinds of gifts—clairvoyance, telepathy, psychokinesis, and prophecy," she rendered in a singsong voice. "The Dewin are clairvoyants. They can Wind-Ride, sending their awareness to see things far away. They can Life-Read to learn the nature of another's illness. Dewin are the physicians of Kymru. They know herb lore, and treatments for the diseases of both men and animals."

"Good. Go on. What of the Bards?"

"The Bards are telepaths. They can Wind-Speak, communicating with other Bards. Bards can Far-Sense, which is to communicate with animals, in a limited way. The Bards are the musicians of Kymru. They track genealogies and therefore declare matters of inheritance when in dispute. They are the repositories of the law," Gwen quoted.

"Yes. Go on. The Druids."

"The Druids are psychokinetic. They can Shape-Move,

which is to move objects around at will. They can Fire-Weave, which is to start fires. With the help of the High King a group of Druids can control the weather. This is called Storm-Bringing. The Druids lead our religious rituals. They are our philosophers and astronomers."

"Go on."

"Lastly, there is the Dreamer. The Dreamer has all the gifts of the Y Dawnus as well as the gift of Dream-Speaking, which is prophecy. The Dreamer can also Time-Walk, which is to look into the past. The Dreamer is the Walker-between-the-Worlds."

"Excellent. Now, tell me of the combination of gifts."

Gwen took another deep breath and concentrated. "Sometimes a person, if he is of the House of Llyr, can have two gifts. Of these two gifts, one is always clairvoyance. Therefore, they are always Dewin. But they must be trained in using their other gift that could be either telepathy or psychokinesis. Only the Dreamer has all four gifts. No one ever has three."

"Excellent. Now, we will Wind-Ride. Are you ready?"

Gwen nodded her eyes wide with anticipation.

"We begin with the Body of Light. Close your eyes. Focus all your awareness to the soles of your feet. Imagine that they are filled with light." After a moment, she went on, "Now, imagine that the tops of your feet are light." Following Rhiannon's steady voice, Gwen continued to imagine her body of light.

Rhiannon then picked up the chain of the triskale and dangled it in front of Gwen's closed eyelids. "Open your eyes," she said, "Focus on the triskale. Breathe deeply."

Gwen, in her trance-like state, opened her eyes and gazed hazily at the dangling crystal. "Visualize your energy in the triskale," Rhiannon continued. "It begins to glow with your inner-light. The lines are radiating outward to all that is around you." Suddenly, the crystal began to glow, pulsing with white brilliance.

"Now, Gwen. Wind-Ride." Rhiannon turned her back to Gwen and waited. Then slowly, hazy at first, a picture began to form in her mind's eye of a young girl with golden hair, sitting cross-legged on the floor of a cave.

"Very, very good, Gwen," she said, turning back to her daughter. "Now, draw back your energy from the crystal. See that it dims as you bring the radiance back into yourself. Close your eyes. Your energy is returning to you. You are filled with strength, with the radiance of Nantsovelta. Thank the goddess, then open your eyes."

"I thank Nantsovelta, Lady of the Waters, for my gift," Gwen said dreamily then opened her eyes. "It worked!" she shouted.

"Indeed it did," Rhiannon smiled.

"But I've been trying to do this for so long and it never worked before!"

"You never had such a good reason to make it work before," Rhiannon said dryly.

Gwen frowned. "But I've seen you use the gift, and it never takes this long. You don't even use the triskale—you just do it. Why can't I do it like that?"

"You can. It's only a matter of practice. With clairvoyance or telepathy the person must be in a relaxed state. Visualizing the Body of Light and using the triskale are means of relaxing you. With practice you can relax your mind in seconds, without the use of anything else. The important thing is to learn control. A highly emotional state, like rage or fear or even joy can release the gifts, but the person has no control."

"Psychokinetics use a different way, don't they?"

"Yes. The Druid must be in a state of intense concentration—not relaxation."

"And that's why you can't teach me how to use it."

"Yes, that's why. I don't know anything about how that is achieved."

"Then how will I learn if you don't know?"

How indeed, Rhiannon thought. The knowledge that she had made a prison for her daughter came crashing in on her. So she spoke more sharply than she intended, "We'll talk about it at another time."

Rhiannon abruptly got up from the table and moved to the entrance, pushing aside the curtain and gazing through the gentle waterfall into the night. Beyond the waterfall she could see the full, silver moon rising over the forest. Seen through the curtain of water the moon wavered and rippled across her eyes. Nantsovelta, Lady of the Waters, goddess of the Moon, don't judge me too harshly, she begged. I'll put it right. Just give me time.

Taking a careful breath, she turned back to face Gwen who stood forlornly by the table, fingering the snowdrops that were scattered there. "It's time to celebrate Calan Morynion," Rhiannon said.

Gwen fixed a spray of snowdrops behind her ear. "Brush your hair first," Rhiannon said. Sighing, Gwen plucked the sprig out and went to get the comb. Rhiannon unbound her black hair from its tight braid. "Let me use the comb when you're done," she called, as she picked up the large golden bowl from the shelf and set it on the table. She placed three candles in the middle of the bowl, fixing them to the prongs set at the bottom. She set eight candles around the outer rim

185

and filled the bowl to the brim with water, scattering the delicate, white snowdrops. The tiny white flowers, the first flowers of spring, floated gently on the surface of the water.

Gwen handed her the comb, then went to the hearth. As Rhiannon combed her hair Gwen scraped the burning coals off to one side, then laid the branches of an ash tree into the fire pit. They both fixed sprays of snowdrops in their hair and stood by the table, looking down into the golden bowl.

"This is the Wheel of the Year before us," Rhiannon chanted. "One candle for each of the eight festivals in which we honor the Shining Ones." As Gwen lit each candle, Rhiannon named them. "Alban Awyr, Calan Llachar, Alban Haf, Calan Olau, Alban Nerth, Calan Gaef, Alban Nos, and Calan Morynion, which we celebrate tonight."

When the eight outer candles were lit, Gwen lit one of the three inner candles. "Great Goddess of the Moon, Lady of the Waters, we honor you," Rhiannon said.

As Gwen lit the second candle, Rhiannon went on, "Nantsovelta of the Pearls, Lady of the Swans, we honor you." As the third candle was lit, she said, "Silver Queen of the Night, the Bride of Day, we honor you.

"Let the Shining Ones be honored as they gather for the wedding of the Sun and the Moon. Mabon, King of Fire, Bridegroom to the Moon. Taran, King of the Winds and Modron, Great Mother of All. Annwyn, Lord of Chaos and Aertan, Weaver of Fate. The Protectors, Cerridwen, Queen of the Wood and Cerrunnos, Master of the Hunt. Y Rhyfelwr, Agrona and Camulos, the Warrior Twins. Sirona, Lady of the Stars and Grannos, Star of the North and Healer."

"We honor you," Gwen said in a solemn tone.

"With water are we refreshed and cleansed. With fire are

we purified. Blessings on the marriage of fire and water," Rhiannon said, gesturing to the candles floating in the bowl. Then they chanted together,

O silver flame of the night,
Enlighten the whole land.
Chief of maidens,
Chief of finest women.
Dark the bitter winter,
Cutting in its sharpness.
But Nantsovelta's mantle
Brings spring to Kymru."

Then they each picked up a candle from the bowl and went to the pile of unlit ash wood in the fire pit. "Now let the Bridegroom, Mabon of the Fires, come to claim his Bride." They lit the fire with the candles and the wood began to blaze, bathing the room in its cheerful glow.

They stood for a moment, watching the fire. If there had been others here, it would now be a time for music and dancing around a huge bonfire in the sacred grove. But many years ago Rhiannon had condemned them both to solitude, and so they celebrated alone.

"Oh, Mam," Gwen said excitedly, "I have a present for you."

"A present?"

"It's your name day."

"Oh. You remembered," Rhiannon said flatly. Gwen's face fell and Rhiannon was instantly repentant. She went on gently, "Thank you, Gwen. That's very thoughtful."

Gwen smiled tentatively, as Rhiannon put her arms around her daughter and hugged her. "Wait right here," Gwen said as she scurried off into the storeroom.

Gwen ran back in, holding something behind her back.

"Close your eyes and hold out your hands," she said.

Rhiannon did as she was told, and Gwen gently placed something in her hands. It was a bracelet, intricately woven with thin strips of leather. From the band a tiny, wooden heart dangled. It was made of ash wood, and polished to dazzling whiteness. Gwen pointed to the heart, "So you always have my love with you, wherever you are."

Rhiannon's eyes filled with tears and her throat was tight. "I'll wear it always. Help me put it on."

Gwen tied the strip of leather around her mother's slender wrist. "It's not too bad. It took me four tries to get it right."

"It's perfect," Rhiannon laughed and hugged Gwen again, holding her daughter close to her heart. And she thought in despair that the time was coming soon when she would have to send Gwen away from Coed Aderyn, back into the world beyond the wood, alone. That fact, now squarely faced, set her heart to beating wildly with the loss and sorrow and pain that she knew would come. And set her to pleading hopelessly and silently that she would be given be more time—just one more year, she begged—before she would have to endure a broken heart, again.

LATER, AFTER THEY had eaten, Rhiannon sent Gwen to bed. Gwen protested, but only halfheartedly and more out of habit, for her eyelids drooped noticeably.

"No arguments, Gwenhwyfar. It's been a big day. And you must be well-rested for more practicing tomorrow."

Sighing, Gwen kissed Rhiannon's cheek. "Night, Mam," she said, her words slurred with exhaustion.

Rhiannon helped Gwen to undress then settled her into the pallet, tenderly covering her daughter with a woolen blanket.

Rhiannon kissed Gwen's forehead, then made her way back to the bench before the fire. Even before she sat down she could tell by Gwen's breathing that the child was fast asleep.

Rhiannon tried to settle down in front of the fire but she was too restless. She felt it again—that feeling that someone was thinking of her. Thinking very hard. Perhaps actually beginning to look for her. She sensed an indomitable will. She shivered, for that will felt carved of ice, or stone—implacable, commanding, pitiless. He, or she, would never give up, never stop looking, and never leave her be.

She shivered again, and told herself that these thoughts were ridiculous. She was going into a panic over nothing at all. Nevertheless, she didn't feel like sitting still. Rising, she wrapped herself into her white woolen cloak and left the cave.

The cold night air was like a slap in the face. A few droplets from the waterfall splashed her as she went by and made her way down the rocks to stand by the pool. The full moon shone down brightly, turning the droplets in her hair to glittering diamonds, and turning the pool into molten silver.

Her doeskin boots made a crackling sound against the hard-packed snow. She stopped halfway around the pool, facing the waterfall. She gazed into the pool, her eyes tracing the path of the moon as it ran across the surface of the water.

Rhiannon stood silently by the pond. She remembered how she had first come to find this place, the year before she had been forced to go on with her life alone, with no one's love to sustain her. For after her aunt had died, she had always been alone.

RHIANNON'S MOTHER, INDEG UR DREMAS, was a woman of the House of Llyr, daughter of the tenth Dreamer of Kymru.

Indeg was Dewin, and she had passed the gift of clairvoyance to her daughter.

Rhiannon's father, Hefeydd ap Con, was a Bard of humble background. He passed the gift of telepathy to his daughter. It was the only thing he had ever given her.

Rhiannon was born in the town of Geneur, in Prydyn, her father's home. Indeg had refused to give birth to her daughter at Caer Dathyl, for her family had not been kind to Hefeydd, and she had loved him. After hours of labor, Indeg had finally brought forth a girl. And in that moment her life's blood had gushed out of her in a flood, and she died.

Hefeydd had gone mad with grief. He refused to see his tiny daughter. He spent hours next to Indeg's body, holding her cold hand, pleading for her to come back to him.

Finally, they had forced Hefeydd away from Indeg's lifeless shell, and sent her body back to her mother at Caer Dathyl. But Darun would not see Hefeydd to offer comfort, nor did she take any interest in her granddaughter. Hefeydd returned to Neuadd Gorsedd, for he too had no interest in the newborn baby girl. It fell to Llawen, Hefeydd's sister, to bring up this unwanted child.

Many years later Rhiannon came to understand that her Aunt Llawen had not been a beautiful woman. She was plain and plump with brown hair and muddy hazel eyes. But to Rhiannon her aunt was beautiful, for Llawen knew how to love. And that love had shone through her in everything she said or did. Llawen's love for her husband, Dudod, for her son, Elidyr, and for her niece, Rhiannon, permeated their home, making the simple house seem a palace.

Uncle Dudod, the brother of the Master Bard, was a traveling Bard, kind and charming and restless. Her aunt used to say that Dudod could charm the birds from the trees, and Rhiannon believed her.

The times when Dudod was home were the best of all. He would slyly appear from nowhere, simply walking into the house as though he did it every day. His green eyes would dance with joy, and Llawen would always drop what she was doing and throw herself into his outstretched arms. And they would kiss—a kiss that would often go on too long for the patience of Elidyr and Rhiannon. Then Dudod would grab his son, swinging him high in the air. He would pick up Rhiannon ever so gently, kiss her on the forehead, and tell her what a pretty child she was.

And always Rhiannon would ask if her father were coming home. Had her uncle seen him? Had her father asked for her? And always Dudod would say that perhaps Hefeydd would be along momentarily. He would say that Hefeydd was very busy, for being a Bard was hard, hard work. He would say that Hefeydd thought about her all the time and loved her dearly. And when her face fell Llawen would take her into her arms and stroke her dark hair and whisper, "Never mind, *cariad*. Never mind."

When Rhiannon was five years old her cousin Elidyr was sent to Neuadd Gorsedd to learn to be a Bard. Elidyr would be trained as heir to his uncle Anieron. One day Elidyr would be the Master Bard.

Rhiannon cried then, for Elidyr had been kind to her. But Llawen promised that they would go to Neuadd Gorsedd to see him one day. Rhiannon dried her tears for she knew that she could trust Llawen. So she waited confidently for the day when they would take their journey.

She thought that perhaps her father would be there. And

he would take her into his arms and kiss her and tell her how proud he was to have such a wonderful daughter. She spent a year spinning these dreams out of nothing, until the day that Llawen told her that the time had come for their visit. Rhiannon begged for a new dress to wear. "So my Da will think I'm pretty," she said, her eyes shining with the memory of her daydreams. "And then he'll love me." And Llawen, her eyes sad and wise, agreed that Rhiannon must indeed have a new dress.

At last they began their journey, traveling on horseback with Uncle Dudod. After a few days they came to Coed Aderyn, the wood on the border of Prydyn and Gwytheryn. They stopped to eat at a tiny pool, fed by a gentle waterfall. And Rhiannon, exploring, discovered a cave hidden behind the flowing curtain of water. All three of them marveled at such a perfect little place tucked away in the quiet forest.

When they reached Neuadd Gorsedd, Elidyr himself came running down the steps, wearing his apprentice robe of white. His light brown eyes were filled with happiness as he threw himself into his mother's arms. And then he picked Rhiannon up and manfully negotiated the huge stone steps that led into the college.

Rhiannon whispered, "Is Da here? I wore a new dress."

"He's not here," Elidyr answered in dismay. "He left yesterday."

"But—but did he know we were coming?"

Although Elidyr was only eight years old, he knew better than to tell her the truth. "No," he lied. "I guess someone forgot to tell him."

And though she tried not to, Rhiannon began to weep, tears trickling down her tiny cheeks. "But I wore a new dress," she whispered, forlornly.

Elidyr looked around in panic at his father, and Dudod took Rhiannon into his strong arms. "Come, let's go meet your Uncle Anieron." And Dudod kissed her tears away and Rhiannon wished passionately, hopelessly, that her father might come to love her one-day. Wished passionately, hopelessly that one day a man would come into her life that would love her.

IN THE COLD winter night, Rhiannon, remembering, knelt down by the still pool. She stared at the water, dark where the moon did not shine, bright where the moon's path cut through. Light and dark rippled across her eyes. Shadow and brightness, one and the same, she thought. One and the same.

Slowly, with a trembling hand she reached out, her palm hovering over the shimmering water. And, oh gods, oh gods, she thought that the fear would kill her, slay her in the snow and leave her lifeless body by the pool. And slowly, slowly she dipped her hand into the dark, into the light, and the cold made her hand tingle in shock as she remembered the day when she had begun to fear the water. The last occasion she had witnessed the living face of the only mother she had ever known.

The day that her life changed forever began just like any other day. Llawen and Rhiannon were eating breakfast when Dudod walked in from a month-long absence, as casually as though he had never left. Llawen shrieked and flung her arms around him. It was then, that Rhiannon noticed the stranger. He stood uncertainly in the doorway. He tried to smile, but the expression seemed ill suited to his sober face. He was not old, but there were sharp furrows on either side of his mouth and deep lines above his brows. He was thin and his scanty hair was dark. His eyes were the brown of freshly turned earth—earth that had been cut and scarred by the blade of the uncaring plow.

Llawen, at last releasing Dudod, caught sight of the man in the doorway. "Hefeydd," she breathed. "Oh, Hefeydd," and she went to him and held him close, tears streaming down her cheeks. Slowly, awkwardly, the man put his arms around Llawen. And Rhiannon knew that her Da had come to her at last. Dudod picked Rhiannon up and kissed her, but she had eyes only for her father.

Dudod carried her to the man. "This is Rhiannon," he said. "And this," Dudod went on as he looked down at her, "is Hefeydd ap Con, your father."

Rhiannon launched herself at him, grasping his neck in a stranglehold. "Da," she whispered, burying her face in his shoulder. But after just a few moments Hefeydd set her down on her feet, grabbing her thin arms, pulling them firmly away from his neck.

"Rhiannon," he said, and stared at her as though memorizing her face to carry away with him. "Daughter." He was silent for a long time and his silence seemed to freeze everyone in place. "Your eyes are your mother's," he said at last, his voice strained. "I must, I must—" he broke off, looking around in confusion.

"See to the horses," Dudod finished for him.

"Yes," Hefeydd said in a grateful voice. "I must see to the horses. Excuse me."

Rhiannon stood where he had left her, paralyzed with bewilderment. "He doesn't like me," she said in astonishment.

"Oh, but he does," Dudod said heartily. "Why, he came

all the way here from Neuadd Gorsedd just to see you."

But Rhiannon turned to Llawen for the truth. And sadly, Llawen shook her head. "Give him time to know you, child. He doesn't know you well enough to love you."

This struck Rhiannon as perfectly sensible, so she took heart and vowed to be very, very good so that he would come to love her.

Hefeydd returned and the four of them sat down for a late breakfast. Dudod spoke almost continuously, saying that he had bullied the Bards to letting Hefeydd come to visit. "He's very, very busy, you see," Dudod said confidently to Rhiannon. "Very busy indeed. But I made them let him come, because he wanted to see you so much."

Meanwhile, Hefeydd said scarcely a word. His movements were slow and careful. Llawen, too, said very little, merely pressing her brother to eat more. And Hefeydd and Rhiannon stole quick glances at one another when each thought the other wasn't looking. It was Dudod who suggested that they go to the lake to catch fish for supper. They walked to the small lake at the edge of the forest, not far from the house. The day was clear and warm with a slight, gentle breeze, and the lake rippled as the wind danced across its shining surface.

Dudod helped Rhiannon bait her hook, while Llawen and Hefeydd began to cast expertly as they stood on the rocky shore. Dudod warned Rhiannon to step carefully among the rocks, for they were wet and slippery. Then Llawen caught a fish, and Hefeydd caught another. Dudod, his strong hands placed over Rhiannon's tiny ones, helped Rhiannon reel in a fish, too. Llawen exclaimed over the fine catch as she helped Rhiannon to bait her hook again.

"A fine supper we shall have," Dudod said cheerfully.

"Indeed we will—after you clean the fish," Llawen shot back.

"Me?" he said innocently.

"Yes, indeed you. And I'll fry them up with dill weed and we'll have a fine feast. But I'm short on the dill." Her eyes cut to Hefeydd. "Why don't you two men go pick some dill weed for me?"

"But I want to fish," Dudod protested.

But Hefeydd, grateful for a reprieve, smiled shyly at his sister. "Come on, Dudod. Let's do as she says. You know how she is when she gets an idea in her head. Especially one that will make us work."

"But why do I have to go," whined Dudod, in a parody of a spoiled child.

"Because Hefeydd doesn't know where dill grows around here," Llawen said. "Bards," she continued as she turned to Rhiannon, "can be so slow. You have to explain everything to them." Rhiannon stifled a giggle at the mock outrage on Dudod's face.

Dudod laughed and kissed his wife. The two men picked their way carefully across the rocks, and disappeared into the woods.

Llawen and Rhiannon fished in silence for some time. The afternoon was hot, and the tension and excitement of the morning were catching up to Rhiannon, making her lids droop. When she almost dropped the pole into the water during a jaw-breaking yawn, Llawen said gently, "You're all worn out. Why don't you go lie down under that nice tree over there? And I'll wake you in a little while. Get along with you now." Llawen kissed her on the forehead, and told her to mind her way over the rocks.

Picking her way carefully, Rhiannon finally reached the green grass at the edge of the wood and lay down under a tree. Bright blue cornflowers dotted the grass and a white butterfly fluttered past. Lemon yellow globeflowers bent their heads slightly in the breeze. She picked some globe-flowers and lazily wove them into a garland. Then, her lids so heavy that they felt as though they were made of stone, she fell fast asleep.

They never knew what had happened—not exactly. Per-haps Llawen had slipped on a rock while pulling in a fish. Or perhaps she had thrown a cast too far, too fast. However it happened, she had fallen and hit her head on a rock, knock-ing herself unconscious and sending herself tumbling into the water. Unable to help herself, she had drowned.

Rhiannon, waking up somewhat later, sat up sleepily. But her aunt was not in sight. Thinking that Llawen had somehow left her behind, she ran to the rocks and saw her aunt's lifeless body floating in the lake.

Terrified, Rhiannon crawled over the rocks, slipping and sliding in her panicked haste. She neared the water's edge. "Wake up, Aunt Llawen, please wake up," she screamed. She reached out, but the body bobbed away. She screamed again, screamed for help, screamed for someone to find them, screamed for her aunt to wake up. She knew she should wade in after the body, but she couldn't swim and the lake was deep. And she was very afraid. In her panic she saw the water as an animal, waiting patiently for prey. Waiting for a little girl to wade in and then it would close in around her, drag her down to die away from the light. She sobbed again in terror as the sun beat down pitilessly on the bright shining surface of the water.

And then she heard them, scrambling over the rocks, Dudod shouting his wife's name in despair. He plunged into the water, towing his wife to shore, and Hefeydd grabbed her and they carried her to the grass, laying her down gently. Dudod turned her on her stomach and began to push just below her ribcage. He pushed and pushed but nothing happened. They turned her over again and Dudod put his mouth over hers and tried to breathe life into her dead lungs. The water glowed like a gemstone in the sun, as the two men tried to bring her back to life. But it was too late.

Dudod cradled Llawen in his arms, his body shaking with sobs, rocking her back and forth. And then Hefeydd looked at Rhiannon, his wide, brown eyes shocked and dull. "Where were you?" he asked, his voice cold and flat.

"I was sleeping," Rhiannon wept. "I'm sorry, I'm so sorry."

And then Hefeydd's brown eyes came alive, glittering with hatred as he stared at his tiny daughter. He reached out and grabbed her shoulders, shaking her. "You killed her. You killed her, too," he screamed. "Is there anyone I love you will not murder? What have you done? What have you done?"

RHIANNON, TWENTY-EIGHT YEARS later, kneeling by a pool on a cold winter night, gasped, snatching her hand out of the cold, silent water. "It wasn't my fault," she whispered, her breath coming harsh and fast. "I'm sorry, I'm sorry, I'm sorry," she wept, curled into a tight ball, rocking back and forth in misery next to the gleaming water. "I'm sorry," she whispered. "So sorry."

Chapter Nine

Dinas Emrys
Kingdom of
Gwynedd, Kymru
Bedwen Mis, 494

Llundydd, Lleihau Wythnos—late afternoon

The peddler and his guard toiled up the last incline on the road to the mountain village of Dinas Emrys. One look at the peddler was enough to make anyone wonder if it was really necessary for him to have a guard, as it was questionable that the man had anything worth stealing.

The peddler's gray, threadbare cloak was patched here and there with incongruously colored cloth—blue, yellow, red, and a small pink patch at the hem. The threads used to sew the patches were mismatched and sewn with long crooked stitches. Most of the peddler's face was hidden within the large hood of his cloak, allowing only a glimpse of a short gray beard and a pointed nose. The man's dry gray hair hung lank and lifeless around his shoulders beneath the hood. His doeskin boots had a hole in the toe.

The scruffy man-at-arms wasn't in any better shape. His leather tunic and trousers were worn and they too were patched where the leather had eroded. His tunic was spotted

199

and stained but the long, wicked dagger he carried looked both clean and sharp. His face was stubbled with the beginnings of a garnet-tinged beard, and his eyes were dark. He walked with a slouch and his leather boots were scruffy and worn. Perhaps his chief occupation was to guard the horse—a fine-looking animal, no doubt stolen. The horse was loaded down with packs containing the peddler's cheap wares.

It was late afternoon and the air was turning chilly, as it always did in early spring in the high mountains. The shadows had gathered, darkening the surrounding mountains as the sun began its slow descent. Flocks of sheep dotted the hillsides here and there. Urged on by their masters, they began moving slowly down the mountains to rest the night in the village byres. Occasionally dogs barked commands to their woolly charges. Smoke rose from the chimneys of the tiny huts, and a few women were gathered by the well, snatching a chance for a quick gossip before returning to their labors.

As the peddler and his guard neared the village, they could be heard arguing and snipping at each other. "I told you it was a ridiculous idea to come here," the guard said.

"And I told you, this is on the way to Caer Dathyl," the peddler replied, irritably.

"Oh, that's right. You think the great Gwydion ap Awst himself will buy a few pots and pans from you."

"Very funny. You know perfectly well that I have some nice cloth for sale."

"Oh, yes. Maybe he'll buy a length of that red stuff to make a new gown."

"He's got those two women living there, doesn't he? Dinaswyn, the old Dreamer, and that Arianrod. He'd buy presents for them, just to shut them up, I'd bet."

"Ha! You just want to get a look at that Arianrod. I hear she's worth looking at, but I doubt she'll think the same of you."

"This is business," the peddler said, airily. "I don't mix business with pleasure."

"Only because you never get the chance. And how do you know that Gwydion's even going to be there to buy anything from you?"

"He's almost always there, you moron."

The guard scowled, his dark eyes darting to and fro over the interested women at the well, the small huts, and a few scrawny chickens. "Good thing you brought me along to guard all the money you'll make in this place."

"You're always complaining. You get enough to eat, don't you?"

"Only when I'm doing the cooking."

By this time quite a crowd had gathered to hear the two men argue, the crowd growing as the men returned with the sheep. Fascinated, they started at the peddler and the guard, turning their eyes from one to the other to follow the argument.

"Look," the peddler said, exasperated, "the deal was you guard my horse and I feed you. I've kept my end of the bargain."

"Sure, if you call that oatmeal you make food."

"What do you call it, then?"

"Slop. Not even fit for the horse." A few men snickered.

"Fine," the peddler retorted. "Tonight we'll stay in some-one's house. Happy?"

"Only when I'm done traveling with you."

"Oh yes," the peddler sneered. "You had something better to do. You could have taken that offer from the King you told me about. You know, when he wanted you to lead his warband, but you said that he didn't pay well enough."

"He doesn't."

"Ha! The closest you ever got to King Uthyr was when you were hauled up for drunkenness."

The peddler glanced around and seemed to notice for the first time that the entire village watched them. Suddenly his manner changed and he began to address the crowd, his gestures florid and his voice smooth. "Ahem. Ladies and gentleman. A good day to you all."

"I was never hauled up for—" the guard started.

The peddler punched him in the arm, hard. "Shut up, you idiot. Can't you see I'm working?" The guard rubbed his arm and gave the peddler a dark look, but subsided.

"Ahem," the peddler went on. "As I was saying, my fine lord and ladies, a good evening to you all. How pleased I am to be guesting here in such a fine village." He gestured expansively at the huts as the crowd looked at him blankly. "Indeed. Nestled here in these beautiful mountains like a pearl nestles within its oyster." Still, there was no response as the crowd stared back at the peddler as though he had lost his mind.

"Ahem," he went on, clearing his throat. "Yes. A jewel of a place this is. For within such surroundings beautiful women do reside, hidden away like treasures, gleaming like gold and precious gems." He gestured to the stout, plain women by the well, who stared back in astonishment. "And what do such pearls, such treasures, deserve from the men who love them? Why, ribbons, of course, to vie with the brightness of their hair." He drew tangled lengths of ribbons from his pack, holding them up with a flourish. "Any man with a sweetheart would buy a ribbon for her hair. And, truly, a man who cared for his wife would buy her pots and pans to cook his dinner in. Fair receptacles for the fruits of her labor." He opened another pack, spreading the pots on a hastily set length of cloth.

The women began to eye the goods speculatively. The older ones eyed the tins, the younger ones eyed the ribbons. And the men eyed the women, warily.

The peddler's eyes picked out a young, fresh-faced girl. He picked up a length of blue ribbon and held it up to her fair hair. "Oh, indeed. Blue to match your eyes, my dear. A man would be mad not to have his eye on you—and mad not to purchase such a pretty trifle for such a pretty girl." The girl blushed, peering up at the peddler shyly.

A young man pushed his way through the crowd, holding a short length of undyed wool cloth. "This for the blue ribbon," he said, turning bright red, but standing his ground. The young girl blushed even more and looked fixedly at the ground.

The peddler deftly took the cloth and squinted at the close weave. He smiled. "Indeed, young sir. So be it. A ribbon for your lady fair," as he gravely presented the ribbon to the young man.

"You're overcharging," the guard said very quietly into the peddler's ear.

The peddler replied through his fixed smile, his lips barely moving, "You're taking all the fun out of this."

"Be fair with these people—or I'll pull all your teeth out," the guard replied, also smiling and giving the peddler a slap on the back that nearly sent him sprawling.

The peddler laughed as though the guard had said some-thing witty then picked up a red ribbon. "Ah, young sir," he called to the young man, "your fine cloth has brought you two ribbons." The young man came back to retrieve the second ribbon then went to the girl, shyly handing her the rib-bons. The girl drew them through her work roughened hands wonderingly and, finally daring to look up at the young man, smiled softly.

Then the village women began to seriously inspect the pots and pans and slowly the stock began to disappear, replaced by lengths of undyed wool, wheels of cheese, a wooden comb or two. The peddler smiled in satisfaction as the loot mounted up when an old man made his way through the crowd. His beard was long and gray and his robe was of plain, gray cloth. Sheepskin boots were wrapped around his feet and he carried a stout walking stick. His dark eyes flashed for a moment then subsided.

"What's going on here?" the old man asked.

The peddler bowed. "I am a merchant, good sir, on my way to Caer Dathyl when I stopped in this lovely village, nestled in these mountains like a pearl in an oyster—"

"Selling shoddy wares," the old man broke in. "Down on your luck, eh?"

The peddler drew himself up haughtily. Although his face was still hooded, his eyes could be seen to gleam deep within the hood. "I assure you, good sir—"

"And who is this? Leader of your illustrious warband?" the old man continued, jerking his stick at the now scowling guard.

"Are you insulting me?" the guard demanded, his hand on his knife.

"I? Insult you? No indeed. It must be insult enough to be forced to endure this peddler's company."

"I don't have to take that from you, old man," the peddler said angrily. The guard came to stand by the peddler, his hand still firmly on his dagger.

There was a commotion in the back of the crowd as a boy burst through to stand protectively in front of the old man.

The boy's hair was sandy, darkening to auburn. He had large, dark eyes set in a thin, tanned face. He was lanky and awkward as though he did not yet know what to do yet with his hands and feet. "Are you threatening my uncle?" the boy asked belligerently.

The guard turned ashen. He swallowed convulsively, looking at the boy as though seeing a ghost. Quickly, the peddler turned to the guard. "Stop staring," he hissed. The guard blinked at the force in the peddler's voice then set his face in stern lines. The peddler, reassured, stepped back.

"Your uncle, young sir, has questioned the value of my wares. We were merely discussing matters."

The boy looked uncertainly at his uncle, at the peddler, at the guard. "Well," he said in a passable imitation of a growl, "you'd better not threaten him that's all."

"I am well guarded, as you see," the old man said, smiling.

"You are indeed," the guard said, his voice somewhat hoarse. He cleared his throat. "And so, I might add, is this fine peddler. There is an accusation to be settled."

"Indeed," said the peddler smoothly. "And I have a way to settle it. You, my fine elderly fellow, shall put us up for the night. I hereby invoke the law of hospitality."

The old man's dark eyes flashed in outrage. "What? You dare—"

"In return," the peddler went on, "you may cook my dinner in one of these shining, new pots. And, if you agree that my wares are sound, as I am sure you will, we can discuss price in the morning."

The peddler waited, his head cocked arrogantly. The guard said nothing, keeping his eyes stubbornly off the boy.

"Outrageous." the boy said flatly. "We refuse."

The old man put a gentle hand on the boy's shoulder. "I'm afraid we can't. The law of hospitality forbids it. Very well," he said turning to the peddler, "but you will do the cooking."

The guard groaned. "Please don't make me eat his cooking again." The peddler shot the guard a poisonous look.

Involuntarily, the old man smiled then hastily put on a frown. "We'll discuss this further, in private," he said shortly. "Come."

The peddler hastily packed up his goods while the guard held the horse's reins. They followed the old man and the boy to the last hut at the edge of the village.

The old man jerked open the wooden door and motioned everyone inside with a curt gesture. "We'll take care of your horse in a minute," the old man said irritably. "Get inside." The peddler tied the horse's reins to the post beside the door then entered the little house. When they were all inside the old man slammed the door and bolted it. The boy stood suspiciously by the door, as though ready to run off for help at the slightest sign of trouble from their unwanted guests.

The peddler's eyes traveled over the cozy room, over the low-beamed ceiling hung with drying herbs, over the fire burning cheerily in the hearth, over the boy standing anxiously by the door. Then his eyes came to rest on the old man who was grinning. "Nice place you have here, Myrrdin," the peddler said.

"Thank you, Gwydion," the old man replied casually. "Arthur and I like it."

"Gwydion?" Arthur cried in astonishment. "Uncle Gwydion?"

"None other," the peddler replied, as he pulled off his hood and his gray wig.

"But your beard's gray!" Arthur exclaimed.

"Oh, that's just flour, it will wash off."

"What are you doing here?" Arthur demanded.

"Visiting." Gwydion glanced at the guard, who stood motionless by the hearth. The guard hadn't left off staring at Arthur, drinking in the sight like a man who is dying of thirst drinks in cool, clear water.

"Do you remember, Arthur, eight years ago when I brought you here? I made a promise then," Gwydion said gently.

Arthur nodded slowly, his eyes going to the guard who stood so silently.

"And the promise was?" Gwydion prompted.

"That you would bring my Da to see me one day," Arthur whispered.

"Yes. And so I have." Slowly Arthur and the guard came to stand before each other. The guard's eyes were misted as he uncertainly held out his arms.

"Da?" Arthur whispered. "Oh, Da." As he hurled himself into Uthyr's arms, he began to weep.

Uthyr held his son close to his heart, tears streaming down his drawn face. After a few moments he grasped Arthur's thin shoulders and drew back slightly to look at his son. He spoke to Myrrdin, but his eyes did not leave Arthur's face. "You've done well, Myrrdin. Thank you. Thank you for bringing up my son." He stopped for a moment, unable to go on. "My son," he repeated. "My boy." And then they were again holding each other close.

"Perhaps," Myrrdin said gently to Arthur, "you would care to show your father our fine flock of sheep. And perhaps he would care to take a little walk with you."

"Would you like to?" Arthur asked Uthyr, a little uncertainly, dashing his sleeve across his eyes.

"Oh, yes. You must show me everything, tell me everything of how you live." Uthyr said, smiling through his own tears.

Arthur smiled back and took Uthyr's hand. "We'll be back for supper," he called over his shoulder, pulling Uthyr out of the back door.

After they were gone, Myrrdin turned to Gwydion. His face was drawn with both sadness and joy. "Will you be able to bring Uthyr back here again?"

Gwydion shook his head. "No. It was risky enough as it was."

"So, what have you been doing for the past eight years?" Myrrdin asked.

"Sitting," Gwydion replied shortly. "Sitting in Caer Dathyl, refusing to go anywhere near this place. Once a year I attend the graduation ceremonies, and that is all."

"Still being watched, eh?"

"Not so closely, I believe. I sent Dinaswyn off to Tegeingl last month with a letter for Uthyr, telling him when and where to meet me. Then Arianrod and I had some problems, and she left in a huff. When the time came to meet Uthyr, I slipped out of Caer Dathyl in the dead of the night, appropriately blurring my image. Nobody saw."

"But if someone's watching Caer Dathyl they'll know you're not there."

"No," Gwydion shook his head. "The steward has orders to light my rooms every night. They'll think I'm still there. And with both Dinaswyn and Arianrod leaving, they might have chosen to follow their movements, just in case."

"How did Uthyr get away without being followed?"

"He said he was going on a hunting expedition with Cai. They left Tegeingl alone and made sure they weren't followed.

Cai's waiting for Uthyr in Coed Dulas and, hopefully, hunting up a storm."

"How long can you stay here?"

"For tonight only. Then I must go. Uthyr will meet up with Cai and return to Tegeingl loaded with the spoils of the hunt."

"Well," said Myrrdin brightly, "How about that new pot? I need to make dinner. You had best take care of the horse."

Gwydion led his horse to the small stable. There was no sign of Arthur and Uthyr. He hurriedly curried and watered his horse, anxious to return to the house for a long talk with his uncle. But Elise was in a bad mood, sliding out from under the brush, stepping on Gwydion's foot once or twice, dribbling water onto Gwydion's sleeve. Elise did not like to be left alone in the stable, with no one to talk to.

"Try talking to the sheep," Gwydion advised. But sheep, it seemed, were too stupid for decent conversations. "Next time I'll tell Myrrdin to get a horse for you to play with," Gwydion said sarcastically. Offended, Elise ignored him and began chewing nonchalantly on the hay. Gwydion shrugged and opened the pack to produce a new cast iron pot for Myrrdin. When he returned to the house he said, "It's a real bargain. As far as Uthyr's concerned you can keep it as long as I'm not the one who does the cooking."

"Well, make yourself useful and cut up some bread and cheese," Myrrdin said, gesturing to the two brown loaves and the wheel of creamy cheese on the table. As Gwydion began to slice, Myrrdin filled the pot with water and began to toss in various vegetables and herbs.

"Tell me about Arthur," Gwydion said as they worked.

"He's a good lad. Smart. Works hard. Takes good care of me."

"Any problems?"

"Everyone's got problems."

"You're hedging. Out with it."

"Well," Myrrdin said thoughtfully, "he's shy."

"Shy? Bursting in on the crowd like that, ready to defend you against all comers?"

"Cowardice and shyness are two different things. He thought I was in danger."

"Can't you fix that? What are people going to think of a High King who's shy?"

"It's more complicated than that, Gwydion. He's shy because he prefers not to let others get to know him, or to get close to others. And that's because he thinks it will be less painful for him when they are taken away from him. It's what happened with his mother and father. They were taken away."

Gwydion said nothing, but he began to slice the bread savagely. "I didn't have a choice," he muttered.

"I didn't say you did," Myrrdin went on serenely. "But you can't separate a boy from his parents at such a young age and not expect an effect of some kind."

"Such as?"

"Well, he doesn't trust many people."

Gwydion sighed. "All right. What else?"

"Um, he hates you."

"He can join the crowd," Gwydion replied flatly.

"He sees all this as your fault. You took him from his parents."

"To protect him. To make him High King."

"Oh, but he doesn't want to be High King."

Gwydion stopped slicing bread and stared at his uncle. "Doesn't want to?" he repeated blankly.

"No. Certainly not."

"Let me get this straight. Arthur is shy and slow to trust. He hates me and he doesn't want to be High King. Fine. I can deal with all that, one way or another. But will he do as he's told?"

"Depends on who's doing the telling. Will he do as you tell him? Probably not. Will he do as I tell him? Perhaps. But that's the thing. Don't tell him. Explain, don't demand. He's highly intelligent. He won't follow what you say just because you say it, but he might if you explain why and if he agrees you have good reason."

"Oh, great. That makes everything just perfect."

"Gwydion, all I'm saying is that you can't treat him as a tool. I know that's how you think of him. That's how you think of everyone. But you can't do that. Not with him. It will get you nowhere."

"Uncle, I don't want to get anywhere. If it were my decision, I never would have taken him away in the first place. If it were my decision, I would live a life where I could go to sleep and not fear my dreams. But it's not, and it never has been and it never will be. I've got the burden, the duty, to do what I must, use who I can. And I tell you that I will use Arthur as a tool—with or without his cooperation." Gwydion clutched the bread knife tightly, his eyes glittering.

"You'll be making a mistake."

"He doesn't have to like it," Gwydion said grimly. "He just has to do it."

"I want you to remember someone," Myrrdin said quietly. "Someone from long ago. Once there was a boy. He was shy and awkward. It was hard for him to trust others. He knew he would grow up to shoulder a burden he didn't want. Do you remember that boy?"

Gwydion said nothing, merely looking down at his suddenly clenched hands.

"And all that boy really wanted was to love and trust someone. He just wanted someone to help him. Someone to be kind to him, to show him how to bear his burden. Someone to keep him from being so alone. Do you remember?"

"Yes," Gwydion said slowly.

"Yes, of course you do. Remember that boy when you look at Arthur. Remember he bears a burden, as you did. And be kind to him."

"Tell me about Rhiannon ur Hefeydd," Gwydion said abruptly.

Myrrdin was startled. "Why do you want to know about her?"

"I had a dream."

"Tell me," Myrrdin said quietly.

So Gwydion told his uncle everything, ending with, "She holds the clue to the sword's whereabouts. I tell you it turns my stomach to think of having to even speak with such an impossible woman."

"Well," Myrrdin said slowly, not quite masking his delight, "as I recall, Rhiannon had absolutely no use for men. Until she met King Rhoram, that is. If I know her, she now despises men more than ever." Gleefully, Myrrdin looked over at Gwydion. "But I'm sure that you can change her mind. A nice man like you."

"You're enjoying this aren't you?" Gwydion said sourly.

"Gwydion, she's as impossible as you are."

"She doesn't have to like me. She can hate me, for all I care. But I need her."

"Oh, I'm sure it will work out. You can talk about how terrible women are and she can tell you how men are pigs. You'll keep each other amused."

"Are you laughing at me, perhaps?"

"Oh, gods, yes. I love this." Myrrdin seemed truly delighted. "Oh, I'd give anything to be a fly on the wall at that first meeting."

"I'm thrilled to give you some amusement," Gwydion said sourly. "Perhaps you could see your way clear to helping me find her. If it's not too much to ask."

"That's going to be a problem," Myrrdin mused. "No one's done it yet. Still . . . I wouldn't put it past Dudod to know her exact whereabouts."

"Do you really think he knows?"

"I'm not sure. But it would be just like him to guess and never say a word."

"I'll get it out of him," Gwydion said grimly.

"I doubt it," Myrrdin replied. "I think you'll just have to begin the hunt on your own. Maybe eventually Dudod will take pity on you."

"Tell me about her. Maybe I can figure it out for myself."

"All right. Just keep quiet and I'll tell you everything I can remember."

Obediently, Gwydion sat on the hearth and kept quiet. Myrrdin sank onto a stool in front of the fire, occasionally stirring the simmering stew. Then he began to speak quietly, lost in his reminiscences.

"I first saw her when she was just a little lass of seven. She was a pretty child, with wide, green eyes and black hair. Her aunt, Llawen, Dudod's wife, had recently died, drowned in a lake while little Rhiannon was sleeping. I don't think she ever got over that.

"Rhiannon's father, Hefeydd, never liked the child, never even saw her until the day that Llawen was drowned. He lost his head that day. Accused the child of killing everyone he loved. Sad, that was, and horrible for the child. Dudod said that she just seemed to close up within herself that day.

"Just a month after that Dudod brought her to Y Ty Dewin. She was clairvoyant and telepathic, you see. At that time I had just become Ardewin. I was busy with my new duties, and didn't make the time I should have to watch over her.

"She slipped into the life at the college as best she could. She was quiet and shy, never making any trouble. But soon I began to hear that she was disappearing for a few days at a time. She always turned up eventually, never saying a word of where she had been. I discovered that she was slipping off to Neuadd Gorsedd in the hopes of finding her father, who was a teacher there. But he always refused to see her. Finally, after about a year she stopped going. I never tried to stop her. I kept hoping that one day Hefeydd would consent to see her. But he didn't, and she gave up.

"When she was seventeen she graduated to journeyman. She was still shy and awkward, and felt herself to be plain—although in truth, she wasn't. She had the most extraordinary eyes. But she was frightened to death of men, and used no arts to attract them. When she returned five years later to graduate as Dewin she had gained some outward confidence but she was still somewhat shy. On the outside she was tougher than ever. And more frightened.

"The day of the graduation, Rhoram was there. He was only the heir to Prydyn then, for his father was still alive. Rhiannon was alluring that day, for she was happy and excited, and she forgot to think that she was plain. Well, you know how Rhoram looks at women. You know how much he likes them. He can make them feel at a glance as though they were the most desirable women in the world. And I saw it happen. She fell in love. He stared at her through the entire ceremony.

"Up until that moment I had planned to send Rhiannon to Rhoram's court as the Dewin there. But I changed my mind right in the middle of the ceremony, after I saw what was happening. She was too young, too untried to understand that a man like Rhoram would only want her for a short time. You know Rhoram. There's no harm in him but he's not the faithful kind. I could see what would happen to her in Rhoram's court. So I assigned her to another post. To protect her.

"Just after the ceremony word came from Neuadd Gorsedd that Hefeydd was dying and that he had asked to see his daughter. But Rhiannon refused to go. That night Hefeydd died, and the next day a Bard came from Neuadd Gorsedd bearing Hefeydd's harp. He had left it for her. She took it, stowed it in her saddlebags and left for her new post in Brycheiniog, without a good-bye to anyone.

"Well, she was gone, and I thought I had arranged things so cleverly by sending her out of danger. But I reckoned without Dinaswyn. Unfortunately, the bloodlines of the House of Llyr dictated that Rhiannon should have a child by Rhoram. Believe me, I argued with Dinaswyn long and hard about that. But there was no stopping her. I knew it would be a disaster.

"I tried to help by sending word to Rhiannon that after she became pregnant she was to begin training as my heir. I wanted her to understand that there was a future for her as Ardewin of Kymru when it was over with Rhoram, as I knew it would be, one day.

"Well, she went to Rhoram's court, as Dinaswyn ordered her to. Rhoram was King by then and his wife had recently died. And you know what happened then. I think Rhoram truly meant to marry her, as he said he would. I really do. But Rhoram wasn't a one-woman man. Eventually he fell in love with someone else. When Rhiannon found out she left Arberth with the baby. And she hasn't been seen since."

Myrrdin sighed. "I realize now that I should have gone to Arberth myself, before she discovered that Rhoram had tired of her. I should have been there to remind her that there was life after the death of love."

THE TWO MEN were silent for some time. Gwydion was disgusted with Rhiannon and her behavior. Her story had given him no feeling for her pain, only contempt. Did she think she should have been happy? No one was happy. She had thought that love would last and had been angry when it failed. When did love ever last? Love was of no use to anyone. It clouded the mind, it weakened a man. He had done without for many years, and he hadn't run away like a spoiled child. He had stayed in the world and faced up to his duty.

"Where did she grow up?" Gwydion asked suddenly, breaking the silence.

"Geneur. It's the chief town of cantref Gwarthaf, in Prydyn."

"She would know the area well, then?"

"Probably. But when she first disappeared, Rhoram searched that area thoroughly. Are you open to suggestions?"

"From you, yes."

"You should go to Neuadd Gorsedd. Speak to Anieron. Dudod's his brother, and if Dudod really does know anything, maybe Anieron can convince him to speak."

"I'd rather stay out of Anieron's way. I never know what he's up to."

Myrrdin shrugged. "I don't share your suspicions of Anieron. But if you want to find Rhiannon you're going to need his help. No way around that."

"True enough," Gwydion admitted.

"While you're there, talk to Elidyr. He's Dudod's son and Anieron's heir. Before he was sent to Neuadd Gorsedd he and Rhiannon both lived with Llawen. When she used to slip away to Neuadd Gorsedd she would talk to Elidyr. He might know something."

"All right."

"You should probably consider stopping by Caer Duir, also," Myrrdin went on. "Cathbad knows a great deal and might have some good advice for you. And, Gwydion, one last word that I am sure you will ignore. When you find her, go easy. Her life has been very difficult. Try charm. If you've got any."

"Why, Uncle, you know that women love me," Gwydion laughed bitterly.

"Not that kind of charm," Myrrdin said sharply. "I'm just suggesting you try to understand her. If you need her, it would be foolish to antagonize her."

"I'll do my best, Uncle."

"That's just what I'm afraid of," Myrrdin muttered under his breath.

UTHYR AND HIS son walked slowly up the mountainside beneath the gathering dusk. The moon had not yet risen, and they picked their way up carefully to rest upon an outcropping of rock halfway up the rough hillside. From their vantage point, they could see the fitful lights emanating from the tiny village. One by one, the stars began to come out. In the gathering gloom Uthyr could just make out Arthur's young, fresh face.

"So every day I take the sheep up the hillside. And I have to be careful with them because sheep are very stupid, you know. They can get themselves in the stupidest situations. I remember one time . . ." Arthur hadn't stopped talking the entire time, but Uthyr was content. Just to hear his son's voice was enough for him, after listening to the silence in his heart for so many years.

When Arthur had first been taken away Uthyr had buried his own grief to keep his wife from going mad. Night after night he had held her as she wept. Day after day he had comforted her by his very presence, his calm demeanor. He had rarely left her side for months. The responsibility of holding Ygraine together had helped him through that terrible time when he felt as though his right arm had been torn away from his body. As a man with a missing arm feels the phantom pain from a limb that is no longer there, so he had sometimes thought he heard Arthur's bright laughter from far away. He had sometimes thought, while riding home to Caer Gwynt after a day of hunting, how pleasant it was going to be to take Arthur hunting when the boy was old enough. He sometimes woke in the middle of the night, wondering if Arthur was warm enough and almost getting out of bed to go to his son's empty chamber to see. But then he would remember that Arthur was no longer there.

Just as he thought she would, Ygraine clung to Morrigan, the child they had left, hardly letting her out of her sight. But his precocious daughter seemed to instinctively understand her mother's need and had done her best to fill the empty place in her parents' hearts.

"So he had caught himself in a thorn bush. Stuck fast, he was, and bleating like his throat was being cut," Arthur was saying. "But he saw me and he knew I would fix everything. So he quieted right down and let me help him."

"Do you truly like being a shepherd?" Uthyr asked. And, oh, how it galled him that his son, his only son, lived in a hut and herded sheep. Arthur should have grown up in Caer Gwynt. He should have had a fine horse, and fine riding leathers, and a chance to learn the ways of a warrior. But Uthyr let none of this show in his voice.

"Oh, yes," Arthur answered. "Every day I am up in the mountains, with no other person around for miles. And the hills are quiet and you can feel the wind on your face. And the crocuses bloom up in the meadows. And there are streams and tiny waterfalls running through the mountains. And no one bothers you. It's all very peaceful."

"You like solitude?"

"Yes," said Arthur brightly. "Don't you?"

"I don't get much of it, really. There are always people around."

"How do you stand it?"

"Well, you see, that's something that every Ruler must get used to. One day, when you're High King—"

Arthur's face, barely discernible in the fading light became still. Uthyr stopped and gazed at his son in surprise. "That's not something you want, is it?" he said gently.

Arthur said nothing, sitting as though made of stone. "Arthur, I'm your father," Uthyr went on. "And I love you. You must know that. You can tell me things—things that are hard to say. And I'll listen. You mustn't think I won't understand."

After a moment, Arthur said clearly, "I'm not going to be High King. I've made up my mind. I want to be left alone. I just want to stay here in the mountains, forever."

"Why?" Uthyr asked quietly.

"I . . . I don't know anything about how to fight a war. I don't know anything about being wise and—and kingly. I'm just a shepherd."

"But you can learn," Uthyr pointed out. "So that's not really it, is it?"

Arthur swallowed and stared down at his feet, unwilling to meet his father's eyes. "Tell me the truth," Uthyr said softly.

"It's—it's too big for me. High King. It's too big. I can't. I'm not strong enough. I'll fail."

"And if you stay here and herd sheep, you won't have to try. And then you won't fail. Is that it?"

"Yes," Arthur said frantically. "I won't try. I won't. No one can make me—not even Uncle Gwydion. No one."

The two sat in silence for a long time. The stars wheeled brightly overhead; their shining patterns piercing the dark, velvet sky. "Myrrdin taught you the stars, didn't he?" Uthyr said suddenly. Startled, Arthur nodded. "Look there, then." Uthyr went on. "Do you see the constellation of Taran?"

Again Arthur nodded as he looked up at the sky. Uthyr continued, "Taran, King of the Winds, who represents the element of air, is honored especially in Gwynedd. You know that Caer Gwynt, our citadel in Tegeingl, means House of the Winds?"

Again, Arthur nodded.

"On the great doors to Caer Gwynt, there is a hawk. Now,

the hawk is a fine hunting bird, but I think the finest hunting bird is an eagle. Here in the mountains you must see many eagles. So you know what they are like. They are proud, fierce, and beautiful in their freedom. If captured they pine away and die, for they cannot bear chains.

"You are like an eagle, my son: proud in your solitude, fierce in defiance of your fate, beautiful in your need for freedom. But the eagle is able to soar because of the air beneath his wings. He flies the sky because he can ride the winds of Taran from here to the ends of the Earth. Because this is how he was made."

Uthyr paused and grasped Arthur's hands tightly in his own. "I sent you away when you were a child to ensure that you would grow up to be like the eagle—noble, ferocious, able to ride the sky on the wind. All this you can be. But there is a price to be paid for everything. Nothing is free. The price I paid to keep you alive was to sever myself from you. I pay the price in heart's blood because I love you so. And I will never stop loving you. Whether you are a High King or a shepherd. I ask one thing of you. When the time comes, weigh the price carefully. Because there is no wind for an eagle who breaks his wings. He is bound to the earth forever.

"You were born to be High King. I felt it even when you were in the womb, and I would put my hand on your mother's belly, and know what you were meant to be. So I tell you this, to turn away from what you were meant to be is to break your wings, to be earthbound forever. I would not want that anguish for you."

Arthur said nothing, but Uthyr noticed that his mouth was set in a stubborn line. He knew he had not convinced his son, for the aversion was too deep. But he hoped that a seed

221

had been planted that would one day bear fruit in his son's lonely soul.

"How is Mam?" Arthur asked, turning the conversation away from him.

"She is well. She asked me to tell you that she loves you dearly. And she made this for you." Uthyr reached into his tunic and pulled out a woolen scarf of sapphire blue. "She told me to tell you to wear it whenever it was a chilly night. She also said to drink chamomile tea in the winter, to keep from catching cold." Uthyr smiled. "Your mother is convinced that you can't take care of yourself. But that's not personal—she thinks the same thing about me."

Wonderingly, Arthur took the scarf and wrapped it around his throat. "It's perfect. So soft and warm. Please tell her . . ." Arthur paused, for his voice was in danger of breaking. "Please tell her that I am most grateful. And please tell her that I love her."

"I will."

"Will you come back? Will she come to see me?"

"I won't be back. And she can't come. Gwydion says it's too dangerous."

"Gwydion," Arthur spat, leaping up from the rocks. "I hate him! I hate him! He took me away. He wants to use me. He doesn't care what I want."

"Arthur, Gwydion is my brother. I love and trust him."

"Well I don't."

"Yes," Uthyr said dryly. "I can see that."

Slowly, Arthur sat down again. "I'm—I'm sorry I upset you."

"You'd be surprised how many people feel that way about Gwydion," Uthyr said mildly. "I wish I had a gold coin for every time someone told me that. I'd be a rich man."

"Then why do you defend him? Why do you trust him?"

"Because I know him. Not many people do. They think they do, but they don't. It's funny, but you remind me of him, a little."

"Me?" Arthur was clearly appalled.

"Oh, yes. If he had his way he's stay in the mountains, too. He loves the solitude. But he can't do that, because he's the Dreamer. And he dreams things that make his blood run cold. He didn't want to be the Dreamer, didn't want the burden. But he had to be. It's what he was born for, after all."

The night was quiet and cold, and neither said anything for an extended period. "You—you aren't disappointed in me, are you?" Arthur asked anxiously.

"No! Never. You must never, ever think otherwise. Come, I'm sure our dinner's ready by now."

As the two walked down the hillside and neared the tiny house, Arthur asked, "But if I don't become High King, if I refuse, will you still love me?"

Uthyr stopped and turned to face his son. "I will love you until the day I die, and beyond. Whether you are a High King or a shepherd, I will love you forever. Just remember that I only ever asked one thing of you. When the time comes for your final choice weigh the price carefully. There is a price for broken wings."

Chapter Ten

Addiendydd, Tywyllu, Wythnos—late afternoon

As Gwydion approached Caer Duir, the college of the Druids, he heaved a sigh of relief. He had been almost nine days on the road from Dinas Emrys, and he was weary.

The three-story, round keep of black stone reared up before him as he dismounted his horse at the bottom of the stairs. He looked up at the golden doors, bathed in the light of the late afternoon sun. On the left door, etched in emeralds was the sign for the oak tree, the tree most revered by the Druids. On the right door, outlined in emeralds, was the constellation of Modron the Mother.

To the west was a tall, slim observation tower that was used by the Druids to study the stars. A man exited the tower and walked swiftly toward Gwydion. The figure became recognizable as he neared.

Gwydion's cousin Aergol, Dinaswyn's son, had dark hair, clasped at the nape of his neck with a band of emeralds and gold. He was dressed in a brown robe trimmed with green. His dark eyes, as always, were opaque, not giving a hint as to what he was really thinking. Aergol was only a year younger than Gwydion, and the two of them had both lived in Caer Dathyl until Gwydion was sent off to school. Yet, for all that, Gwydion could not really say that he knew Aergol very well. For Aergol had in full measure his mother's reserve. His father's too, for King Custennin of Ederynion had been a somewhat cool and detached man.

"Welcome, Dreamer," Aergol said formally when he was near enough.

Gwydion nodded. "Aergol," he said, pleasantly enough. "How is Sinend?"

Gwydion's inquiry of Aergol's daughter and heir brought a spark of warmth to Aergol's demeanor. "She is quite well, Gwydion. I thank you for asking."

"And Menw?" Gwydion pressed on. Aergol's son by one of his fellow Druids was just a few years younger than his half sister, Sinend, and was reputed to be a fine boy.

"Very well," Aergol said with a smile. "Come, you must be weary. You have come, I assume, to see Cathbad?"

"I am and I have," Gwydion said as he handed the reins of his horse to the apprentice that had come over at Aergol's gesture. He followed Aergol up the steps and through the doors. Aergol turned right and began to ascend the stairs to the second level. At the top of the stairs he turned right again and led Gwydion to a small, pleasant room.

The arch-shaped chamber had a square window in the center of the far, rounded wall. A bed with a woolen spread of azure and green stood against the left wall, while a tiny wardrobe stood against the right. A small table was set beneath

225

the window. On the table was a pitcher of wine and a golden goblet chased with emeralds. The floor of black stone was dotted here and there with rugs woven in shades of green.

With a sigh Gwydion put his saddlebags on the bed.

"Would you like to rest a while before seeing Cathbad?" Aergol asked.

"No," Gwydion said. "I think a quick visit now would be better. I'll have a quick wash before dinner."

"As you wish," Aergol said quietly. "Come with me, then."

They returned to the corridor and turned left, passing the stairs. They came to a massive door of oak and Aergol knocked lightly then opened it.

A massive hearth covered the curved, opposite wall. All across the remaining walls hung tapestries of black, worked in silver, each showing a different portion of the night sky above Kymru. Just below the tapestries, which hung halfway down the wall, were massive oak tables, all covered with papers, books, and scientific instruments.

The highly polished floor of black stone was covered with huge carpets woven in green and brown, showing the many fruits of the earth—apple trees and vines, plum trees and wildflowers. Jeweled vessels of gold and emerald were strewn throughout the room—bowls and cups, combs and necklaces, plates and pitchers.

Cathbad sat in a massive oak chair set before the hearth. He was dressed in a rich robe of green with brown trim. Around his neck was the massive Archdruid's Torque of gold and emeralds, clasped at the center with a square inside a circle. Cathbad's hair was a thick, silvery gray and his eyes were dark.

When Aergol ushered Gwydion in Cathbad rose with a

smile on his benevolent face. "Gwydion!" he exclaimed and moved forward to embrace Gwydion. "You are well?"

Gwydion returned Cathbad's embrace. "I am well, Archdruid," he replied.

Cathbad gestured for Gwydion to sit. "Be sure you have a place set next to me at the table tonight for Gwydion," he said to his heir.

Aergol nodded and left the room, closing the door behind him.

"Well, now, Gwydion, to what do I owe the pleasure of this visit?" Cathbad asked with a genial smile. "And how long can you stay?"

"Just tonight, I'm afraid," Gwydion said. "I must leave in the morning for Neuadd Gorsedd."

"To visit Anieron?" Cathbad guessed. "Be careful, Gwydion, of Anieron, unless you want him to know your thoughts themselves before you even have them."

"How do you mean?" Gwydion asked, startled.

"Well, you know how he is. If there is anything happening in Kymru he doesn't know about—often even before it happens—then I'd be surprised."

Gwydion would, too, which was why he had some concerns about talking to Anieron. But there was no way around it. He would never be able to find Rhiannon without Anieron's help.

"I must go to him. For the same reason I come to you. I must find Rhiannon ur Hefeydd. And I must do it before Ysgawen Mis."

Cathbad's silver brows shot up. "That is quite a task, Gwydion, considering that we've been looking for her for eleven years."

"I know," Gwydion said tiredly. "But it must be done."

"Tell me why."

When Gwydion hesitated, Cathbad shrugged. "Well, of course you don't need to. I simply thought—"

"You are right," Gwydion said with a sheepish smile. "And it's not that I don't trust you."

"Yes," Cathbad said, his mouth twitching. "I can see that."

Gwydion laughed. "Very well! I must find Rhiannon because she holds the key to a clue left by Bran many years ago. A clue to the location of Caladfwlch."

"The sword of the High Kings? Why, that means . . ." Cathbad's voice trailed off as he understood Gwydion's message. "I see. A High King for Kymru."

"Yes. And I must find Rhiannon. She alone knows the clue to the sword's whereabouts. And without the sword—"

"The High King can't fully utilize his powers," Cathbad finished.

"That's right," Gwydion agreed.

"I wish I could help, Gwydion," Cathbad said. "But I have no idea where to begin to look for her. But I feel certain that Anieron knows something."

"That's what I'm afraid of," Gwydion said.

Alban Awyr, Cynyddu Wythnos—late morning

As GWYDION DREW closer to Neuadd Gorsedd, the college of the Bards, he saw that it seemed to be in an unusual state of activity. Apprentices in plain, white robes scurried in and out of the huge, triangle-shaped three-level building. The light reflected off the blue-hued stones and the huge silver doors. On the left side of the door two crossed lines had been carved, the symbol of the birch tree, the tree sacred to Taran, King of

228

the Winds. The right door was studded with sapphires that outlined the shape of that god's constellation. The sapphires danced before his eyes as he dismounted and looked upon the stone steps that approached the doors.

Elidyr, the Master Bard's heir, came hurrying down the steps to greet him. Elidyr was a pleasant looking man with sandy hair and light brown eyes. "Gwydion," he said, smiling, "what a delightful surprise."

Somehow, Gwydion doubted that his arrival was a surprise, nor was he certain it was delightful. "What's everyone running around for?" he asked, as he removed his saddlebag from Elise's back. An apprentice came scurrying up to take his horse.

"Preparations for the festival," Elidyr replied as they mounted the steps leading up to the keep. "It's Alban Awyr today, remember?"

"Sorry. I just lost track of time. How's your wife?"

"Elstar is well, thanks. As a matter of fact, she got leave from her duties at Y Ty Dewin and she's riding over today for the festival."

They passed through the sapphire studded doors and entered the main corridor that led to the Great Hall. The corridor was dim to Gwydion's sun-blinded eyes, and the cool air revived him enough to make him realize how tired he was. He walked very slowly. "How's Elstar coping these days?" he asked.

"Well, switching from Myrrdin to Cynan was difficult at first. You know Cynan—kind to a fault, not really made for leadership. But it's worked out all right. Elstar's just got a little more responsibility than an heir normally would. By the way, Elstar's bringing another guest with her that I think you'll be interested in seeing."

"Who?"

"Don't want to ruin the surprise. Come on, I'll take you to Anieron."

Perhaps Elstar was bringing Dudod with her, Gwydion thought. Now that's the man he would really like to see. Slowly he followed Elidyr up the winding stairs to the second story. "Is your father here?" Gwydion asked casually.

"No. Dudod's traveling. Anieron likes to use him to keep track of things, you know. And my Da loves to travel."

"Speaking of traveling, is there a place I could rest for a few minutes before I see Anieron? I'm all done in."

"Of course. I should have realized. I'll take you right to your room. Do you want a bath first?"

"Just a quick wash with a bucket of water would be fine for now. Do you have a few moments to talk?"

"I'll make the time. Here we are," Elidyr said as he opened the door to a small but pleasant chamber. The triangular window faced east, with a view of the huge birch grove where the festivals were celebrated.

Within the chamber a narrow bed was pushed against one wall. Small rugs in blue and white dotted the white stone floor. A narrow oak wardrobe stood next to a small table that held a basin and pitcher. Gwydion was grateful to see that the pitcher was full. He poured the water into the basin and splashed his face, drying it with a towel that lay next to the basin. Meanwhile, Elidyr poured wine into two blue glass goblets from a silver decanter that stood on a small table next to the door.

Gwydion took a small sip of the wine. His brows shot up. "Good stuff! Is this from Prydyn?"

"Straight from King Rhoram himself. Anieron said you'd be along soon, and he thought you might like it."

"And how," Gwydion asked carefully, "did Anieron know I'd be here?"

"You'll have to ask him that yourself. But he probably won't answer you."

"I sometimes think that man knows everything there is to know about everything," Gwydion said lightly, disguising how disturbed he was. "Tell me, have you heard from your cousin Rhiannon lately?"

Elidyr stared at Gwydion in surprise. "Rhiannon? No, have you?"

"Of course not. But I am looking for her."

"Why?"

"I had a dream," Gwydion said shortly. It was all that the Dreamer had to say to anyone to ensure full cooperation. Well, almost anyone. He had a hunch that Anieron would probably be another matter. But not Elidyr, of that he was sure.

"If you're asking do I know where she is, the answer is no. No one does." Elidyr frowned. "Except—"

"Except maybe your father?"

Elidyr shot Gwydion a sharp look. "Possibly. But I doubt you'll find her. She'd sense you were coming and run."

"Would she? Maybe she's ready to be found."

"You don't know her," Elidyr said shortly.

"Tell me about her. What's she like?"

"I can tell you what she was like. What she might be like now, I wouldn't even be able to guess." Elidyr paused, then sat down on the hearth. "Rhiannon was anxious to please, and naturally kind-hearted. It made her easily hurt, her tender heart."

"I hadn't heard she was that tender," Gwydion said shortly.

"Oh, but she was. That was the problem. When she gave her heart to Rhoram, and when he mangled it—as anyone but her expected him to do—she had no defenses."

"I heard from Myrrdin she had quite a few defenses."

Elidyr waved his hand in a dismissive gesture. "Surface only. Not even skin deep. A hard shell, certainly, but a thin one."

"With you, perhaps."

"Oh, yes, perhaps just with me. I loved her like a sister, you know."

"Did you?" Gwydion had his own opinion about that, seeing the look in Elidyr's eyes when he spoke of his cousin. "I understand she'd come here to try to see her father."

"As much as she could that first year she was at Y Ty Dewin. She was only seven years old and would walk all the way here. She'd show up, usually in the middle of the night, and Wind-Speak to wake me up. I'd sneak out of the dorm and let her in. We'd raid the kitchen, then try to get Hefeydd to open his door and talk to her."

"And did he?"

"Never. I used to beg her not to try. But she insisted. She always said that if he could just see her, he'd know what a good girl she was, and he'd love her. But after a while she realized it was useless and she stopped coming."

Elidyr got up restlessly and went to look out the window. Without turning around he continued, "I can't tell you what it was like to see her fight that losing battle. She'd show up exhausted, dirty, blisters on her feet. And when Hefeydd refused to see her, she would weep. I'd hold her until she stopped crying. If my Da were here, I'd take her to him. And he'd take her back to Y Ty Dewin in the morning. If Dudod wasn't here, she'd sleep in his empty room. Anieron always knew that she was there—you know how he is—and he'd send her back in the morning with some other Bard who could be spared."

"How often did she come here?"

"Every week," Elidyr said tonelessly. "Every week for one entire year. I was so glad when she stopped coming. I missed her, but I was glad."

"For her sake," Gwydion said.

"Yes, for her sake," Elidyr repeated.

"But not for yours."

Still staring out the window, Elidyr said, almost dreamily, "I loved her, you see. But I never told her. Wouldn't have mattered anyway, I suppose. She didn't love me, probably never would have.

"But sometimes, I think that if I had told Rhiannon that I loved her, maybe she wouldn't have fallen in love with Rhoram. And she wouldn't have been hurt so badly; she wouldn't have run away, she would have become Ardewin one day, instead of Elstar. Maybe I could have saved her, if I had tried." Elidyr trailed off and there was silence.

Abruptly, Gwydion said, "It was her choice to run away, to play the coward."

"Coward? Is that how you see her?"

"Don't you?"

"You don't understand anything." Elidyr said flatly. "She was a brave little girl, and a brave woman. And she gave herself away to a careless man."

"She ran away," Gwydion insisted, just as flatly. "Ran and hid like a child when things didn't go her way."

"Oh, and you haven't done that yourself in your own way?"

Elidyr asked, his voice heavy with contempt.

Gwydion opened his mouth to say that of course he had never run from tragedy, to say that he had never been a coward. Yet his denials of cowardice died in his throat.

"Rest," Elidyr said quietly, his brown eyes cool. "I'll be back in an hour to take you to Anieron." With that, Elidyr was gone, leaving Gwydion to the silence.

WHEN ELIDYR RETURNED an hour later, Gwydion coolly intimated that he was ready. Elidyr said nothing, merely motioning for Gwydion to follow him down the corridor. Elidyr knocked on Anieron's door, waited a moment then opened it.

Anieron's room where he received visitors was large. An oak table stood in the middle of the room with an ornate wooden chair behind it. Rows and rows of bookshelves jostled for place against the walls covered with large parchments containing the genealogical tables of the four royal houses of Kymru, as well as the House of Llyr.

A large, glass-fronted shelf held musical instruments— harps, pipes, and drums of all shapes and sizes. The floor was covered with a tapestry-like carpet woven to show blue nightingales, the symbolic animal of the Bards, in flight on a plain, white background.

A fireplace occupied most of the far wall where a fire burned cheerfully. Before the hearth two chairs stood, both cushioned in the white and blue of the Bards. A small table stood between the chairs, holding a silver decanter and blue-tinted goblets.

Anieron rose from his chair before the hearth. He was a tall man, and, although in his mid-sixties, he did not stoop.

He wore a robe of blue and the ornate Master Bard's torque of sapphires studded over a triangle of silver. His hair was a distinguished gray and he was clean-shaven. His green eyes were alert and piercing. He had a genial smile and a razor-sharp mind. Anieron radiated charm, as did his brother, Dudod. Unlike Dudod, however, he also radiated a sense of power.

Anieron smiled. "Ah, Gwydion, how very good to see you. Please sit down." Anieron motioned to one of the chairs before the hearth. Elidyr withdrew, not even waiting for Anieron's dismissal.

Still smiling, Anieron poured wine into one of the goblets and handed it to Gwydion. Then he sat down again in the other chair. Casually, he put his feet on the hearth and crossed his ankles. "To what do we owe the honor of your visit, Gwydion?"

"Why bother to ask? Don't you already know everything?" As soon as the words were out of his mouth Gwydion realized he had made a mistake by showing his irritation. He tried to mask it by casually sipping his wine, but it was too late for that.

"Do I detect a note of censure in your voice?" Anieron inquired softly. "Is that any way to talk to an old man?" Anieron still smiled, but his green eyes were cool.

Gwydion cursed himself for a fool. "Sorry," he said with a smile. "To tell you the truth—"

"Yes, let's try that, shall we?" Anieron interjected smoothly.

Gwydion took another sip of wine and tried to get a hold of himself. He had been very rattled by the news that Anieron had known he was coming. "To tell you the truth, Anieron," Gwydion repeated, "I've come here for your help." There, he thought, that should appease the old man.

But Anieron, his eyes cool as ever merely asked, "With what?"

"I'm looking for Rhiannon ur Hefeydd. I need to find her."

Anieron leaned back and took another sip of wine. "Why?"

"I had a dream."

Anieron waited with a look of polite attention of his face. "And?"

"And what?"

"And what was the dream?"

Gwydion took another sip. He had suspected that Anieron would choose to question him. There seemed to be nothing for it than to give Anieron a somewhat edited version of his need. Anieron would find out one way or another, if he didn't know already.

"The Shining Ones sent me a dream. In it Bran the Dreamer indicated that I must find Rhiannon ur Hefeydd. She carries a memory, a clue, passed down subconsciously through his descendants."

"A clue to what?"

Gwydion took a deep breath. "A clue to the location of the High King's sword."

He watched as Anieron, so dreadfully quick, pieced together the clues.

"Ah," Anieron said. "So, Kymru is to have a High King again. Of course."

Gwydion waited for Anieron to ask him who the High King was to be. But Anieron did not ask. Which only worried Gwydion more. No doubt that meant Anieron didn't need to ask, because he already knew.

"In truth, Gwydion," Anieron went on, "I don't know where Rhiannon is, but—"

"But you know someone who does," Gwydion finished for him.

"I believe so."

"Dudod."

"Yes."

"Where is he?"

"Traveling. I'll get in touch with him and see if I can persuade him to talk. I make no promises."

"I ask for none," Gwydion said. "But I thank you for your help."

Anieron smiled genially and sipped his wine. But did not answer.

GWYDION HAD BEEN back in his room for only a few moments when he heard a knock on the door. Elidyr poked his head in. "Visitor for you," he said, his face expressionless.

"Who in the world—" Gwydion started, but got no further. A young girl ran in and leapt into his arms. Gwydion laughed with delight and hugged his daughter close. "Cariadas! What are you doing here?"

Smiling, Elidyr left, shutting the door softly behind him as Cariadas replied, "I came over with Elstar and her son, Llywelyn. And when I got here, they told me that you had shown up. Oh, Da, I'm so happy to see you!"

"Let's take a look at you, my girl," Gwydion said as he stepped back to gaze at his daughter. Cariadas was now almost ten years old and her face contained the promise of beauty. She had his gray eyes and her mother's red-gold hair. At the moment her thick hair had come out of its careless braid and fallen down her back in tangled waves. She was slender and her skin was fair. She wore a plain Dewin apprentice robe of gray, bound at the waist with a leather belt. She was a sunny-tempered child and her delighted grin was infectious. Gwydion found himself smiling, as he hadn't done for some time.

"You look beautiful," Gwydion said. Oh, they changed so quickly when they were young. Since she was sent away to Y Ty Dewin at the age of seven he had only been able to see her briefly when she returned to Caer Dathyl for a few months during the end of each school year.

"You look tired," she said critically. "Are you getting your rest?"

"Some, thank you," he replied, amused at her concern.

"You really need someone to look after you. You know that?"

"You remind me of your mother when you talk like that."

"Ouch," Cariadas winced, for she knew how Gwydion had felt about Isalyn.

"It's all right," Gwydion said gently. "I was only teasing."

"No you weren't," Cariadas replied. "But never mind. I've been put in my place, as I deserved. At least, that's what Elstar always says!" She grinned at him and Gwydion laughed and hugged her again.

As they settled down on the edge of the narrow bed for a long talk Gwydion asked, "How are things at Y Ty Dewin?"

"Good. I love it there. Cynan is very kind to me—but he's kind to everyone. Elstar is a little stricter. She's worried I'll think too much of myself."

"Hard to believe," Gwydion said.

She lightly swatted his arm, "How can you say that when you know that I am full of humility?"

"Full of something, anyway," he murmured. "How are the lessons?"

"Oh, they're fun. I'm very good at Wind-Riding and I'm getting the hang of Life-Reading. I really am."

"Cariadas, I must tell you something in the strictest confidence."

"Da, everything you do is in the strictest confidence," she said, laughing.

"This is important, daughter."

Cariadas stopped smiling and turned to him, her little face serious. "Tell me."

"I will be doing a great deal of traveling this year. I'm not sure when I can be back to see you."

"Where you are going?" she asked anxiously.

"I cannot be specific."

"But Da, why can't you tell me where you are going?"

"Cariadas, if I could tell you more I would."

"You act like you don't trust me," she accused.

"I do trust you. But what you don't know no one can make you tell."

"Oh, Da," she sighed, giving in, "you make me so mad, sometimes."

"I have that effect on a lot of people," Gwydion replied dryly.

She smiled. "But I love you anyway."

"That's an effect I don't usually have."

"Well you could," she said, "if you took the trouble to be nice to people."

"Thank you," he said gravely. "I'll try to remember your advice. So, do you want me to escort you to the festival tonight?"

"Oh, yes. That will keep that nasty Llywelyn out of my face."

"Oh, ho. Already you begin to break hearts."

"He doesn't have one to break. Why, he's only four years older than I am and he's always criticizing me: 'Wash your face'; 'Your dress is torn'; 'Climbing trees at your age, how juvenile'; and on and on."

Gwydion said, highly amused, "Perhaps I should give Llywelyn some advice on how to handle women."

"No one needs advice from you on that subject," she laughed. Before Gwydion could ask her what she meant, she jumped up. "I promised Elstar I'd let her get me ready for the festival. She says that a future Dreamer must look her dignified best on important occasions." She made a face, swiftly kissed him, and was gone.

THE WAXING MOON had risen by the time the inhabitants of Neuadd Gorsedd had gathered in the sacred grove. The silver light of the moon glowed off the white trunks of the birch trees.

The clearing in the middle of the grove was filled with over a hundred Bards, journeymen and apprentices, all carrying birch branches and waiting for Anieron to arrive and begin the celebration. A huge bonfire made with birch wood was burning in the middle of the clearing. A stone altar stood at the western end. A golden bowl full of seeds and a silver goblet of wine were laid on top of the stone. Eight unlit torches had been placed around the altar.

Gwydion stood with Cariadas near the altar proper. Gwydion was dressed in a formal red robe with black velvet trim. He wore the Dreamer's Torque of opals and gold around his neck and his shoulder length black hair was bound back with a black ribbon. Cariadas wore a gown of red and the underskirt, showing just below the hem, was black. Her hair had been elaborately braided and tied off with red and black ribbons.

The night was silent, without even the slightest breeze to stir the branches of the trees. Overhead the stars glittered coldly. Anieron entered the clearing with Elidyr behind him. The Master Bard wore a cloak made of songbird feather—thrushes, sparrows, wrens, robins, and bluebirds. He carried a birch branch hung with dozens of tiny silver bells. As he stepped up to the altar, he shook the branch. The clear, ringing sound carried through the grove and up into the silent trees.

In his deep, powerful voice, Anieron began the festival. He gestured to the eight unlit torches. "This is the Wheel of the Year before us. One torch for each of the eight festivals when we honor the Shining Ones."

As he gestured and named each one, Elidyr lit the torches. "Calan Llachar," Anieron intoned, "Alban Haf, Calan Olau, Alban Nerth, Calan Gaef, Alban Nos, Calan Morynion, and Alban Awyr, which we celebrate tonight."

Again, Anieron shook the branch and the bells sang. "We gather here to honor Taran, King of the Winds, who woke the Great Mother from her enchanted sleep that the earth might be fruitful."

"We honor him," the crowd murmured softly, the sound of hundreds of hushed voices was like that of a rushing wind.

Anieron continued, "Let the Shining Ones be honored as they gather to watch the Great Awakening. Mabon, King of Fire. Nantsovelta, Lady of the Waters. Annwyn, Lord of Chaos. Aertan, Weaver of Fate. Cerridwen, Queen of the Wood. Cerrunnos, Master of the Hunt. Y Rhyfelwr, Agrona and Camulos, the Warrior Twins. Sirona, Lady of the Stars. Grannos, Star of the North and Healer."

Again, the crowd intoned as one; "We honor the Shining Ones."

In the sudden silence the clear, piping voice of Cynfar, the youngest son of Elidyr and Elstar, sounded like the bells themselves as he spoke his part in the ritual. "Why do we mourn? Why are we afraid?"

Anieron answered, "We mourn because Modron, the Great Mother, cannot be found. We are afraid because the spring cannot come."

"How can Modron be found?" the boy continued. "How can Spring begin?"

"Behold," Anieron said solemnly, "Taran, King of the Winds, is searching for Modron, his beloved. He sends the winds to look the world over. And, at last, Modron is found. She sleeps in the sacred grove and cannot awake. The winds bring this news to Taran, and he flies to her. See how the winds rustle the trees of the grove, and the leaves speak with the wind." Anieron shook his branch of bells. "See how the sounds of the air have awakened Modron." Strangely, just at that moment, a slight breeze began. It gently shook the birch trees that began to sway slightly. The rustling of the trees sounded a mournful sigh.

Gwydion felt a faint prickling on the nape of his neck. Something was wrong here. He could feel it. Something was terribly wrong. That breeze . . .

He gazed searchingly at Anieron, but the old man's face was bland as he tossed the seeds from the bowl onto the ground, then poured wine over the seeds. "The Earth has awakened and spring has come! Blessed be to Taran, King of the Winds."

"Blessed be to Taran!" the crowd shouted. The breeze blew harder; turning into a steady wind that tossed the branches wildly. The birch fire flickered, dancing on the wind. Gwydion looked around but he saw no concern on anyone else's face.

"Strange about the wind, don't you think?" he murmured to Cariadas.

She looked at him blankly. "What wind?"

Gwydion's breath caught in his throat as he realized that he was seeing something that no one else was seeing. Then he looked again at Anieron's face, and he knew that the Master Bard was seeing it also.

Anieron began the Alban Awyr song, and the crowd joined in gleefully.

Spring returns, the air rings with the songs of the birds.
The blameless nightingale, the pure-toned thrush,
The soaring wood lark, the swift blackbird.
The birds sing a golden course of fame and glory
In the countless woodland halls. Spring returns!

After the song was over, the Bards began to dance around the fire. Some began to tell the first stories in the great storytelling contest that would go on all night. Gwydion looked around for Anieron and saw him disappearing into the trees. Swiftly, Gwydion took off after him. Coming out of the grove he saw Anieron standing alone, looking to the northwest, toward Gwynedd.

The wind began to blow even harder, whipping Gwydion's robe and flattening the long grass in wild patterns. Gwydion grabbed Anieron's arm. "The wind—"

"Taran's Wind," Anieron said dreamily, not taking his eyes off the northwest.

"What's happening?" Gwydion asked frantically.

"Can't you feel it? There's a storm over Gwynedd. Taran of the Winds himself rides the sky tonight."

243

ALONE IN THE tiny cottage, Myrrdin paced restlessly. The fierce wind shook the house. The storm had seemed to come up out of nowhere. One moment Myrrdin had been waiting for Arthur's return so they could celebrate Alban Awyr together. Then the next, the storm had begun. There was no rain, no lightning, and no clouds, only the wind—shrieking, moaning, and wildly clawing at the earth.

Arthur really should have been back by now with the sheep. Myrrdin went to the back door thinking, for the hundredth time, that he had heard Arthur returning. He looked out and saw that the sheep had indeed come back. They bawled anxiously, huddled next to the closed byre door. With a sigh of relief Myrrdin slipped out the back door, struggling against the wind to shut it firmly behind him. The night sky was clear, and the waxing moon had risen, spilling its silvery beams over the harsh mountainside. Yes, the sky was clear. No storm clouds, but the wind blew more fiercely than ever.

He struggled against it to open the byre gate and the sheep hurried inside. But Arthur was not there. More worried than ever, Myrrdin counted the sheep as they crowded into the tiny stable. "Seven, eight, nine," he counted to himself. "Fifteen, sixteen, seventeen." Where in the world was Arthur? "Twenty-four, twenty-five, twenty-six." Twenty-six. But he and Arthur owned twenty-seven sheep. One sheep missing. Myrrdin guessed what had happened. One ewe had wandered off, and Arthur had gone looking for her. And he had not found her, or he would have returned with the flock himself.

Cursing, Myrrdin decided to Wind-Ride. He was desperately worried now. To be caught up in those mountains during a windstorm at night was dangerous indeed. The heavy wind was strong enough to tumble even a grown man off his feet and over a cliff. And Arthur was not a grown man—he was just a boy.

Myrrdin took a deep breath and tried to calm his wildly beating heart. As his pulse began to slow, he closed his eyes and his inner essence departed his body and flew from the byre up into the night sky, going higher and higher up the mountain in a desperate search for the missing boy.

ARTHUR SHIFTED HIS grip on the ewe as he struggled to bring her down the mountain. The wind whipped at his cloak and tugged at the blue scarf his mother had made for him. Hastily he wrapped the scarf closer around his neck with his free hand. It would never do to lose it. He thought of that scarf as his talisman, this gift from the mother he could barely remember.

He sighed, but merely in exasperation, for he was too young to think he could be in mortal danger. The wind tugged even harder at him. He had to get down the mountain to Myrrdin as soon as possible. He knew that Myrrdin would be worried sick by now, riddled with anxiety. A fierce gust almost pushed him off his feet and he stumbled. The terrified ewe struggled and Arthur almost lost his grip on her.

He looked up anxiously at the sky. Strange that the night was clear during a windstorm such as this. He struggled on down the mountain as best he could when a particularly strong gale blew him off his feet. He lost hold of the ewe and helplessly rolled toward the edge of the cliff. He reached out to grab something, anything to hold him, but his desperate grasping fingers encountered nothing but wind.

As he rolled toward the edge he realized that he was tumbling toward his death. A chaotic thought flashed through his horrified mind—his Uncle Gwydion was sure to be annoyed that a useful tool had been destroyed. Then the edge of the cliff loomed up to meet his terrified eyes as the wind took him for its own.

MYRRDIN'S SPIRIT SCOURED the mountains anxiously. In this form he could not be buffeted by the wind, not while his physical body remained safe in the byre. But he could see no sign of Arthur. The meadow grasses flattened and straightened in wild patterns. The wind whipped around the rocks, moaning in agony like a demented thing.

Suddenly, Myrrdin saw something at the edge of his vision. A scarf was tangled in a low, scruffy bush at the edge of a precipice. It fluttered mournfully in the gleeful wind. In horror, Myrrdin's spirit recoiled, rushed down the mountain, and slammed itself back into his waiting body.

Myrrdin opened his eyes and took off out of the byre at a dead run.

ARTHUR HUNG HELPLESSLY in mid-air, anchored to the Earth only by his desperate one-handed grip on a low, scruffy thorn bush. His blue scarf tangled in the bush at the edge of the cliff, fluttered madly. His body twisted in the merciless wind. The wind keened in his cringing ears with triumph. It snarled, it snapped, it tugged at his weakening grip. He closed his eyes and refused to look down. He already knew that the mangled body of the ewe lay far, far below. He sobbed in terror and knew that he couldn't hold on much longer. His grip was slipping. His body was chill and frozen by the harsh wind.

He was doing to die. He knew it. He couldn't hold on.

Just then, he looked up at his hand that was slowly slipping away from the bush.

And a gnarled old hand came out of nowhere and grasped his.

"Myrrdin," Arthur gasped.

Slowly, ever so slowly Myrrdin pulled Arthur back up to the cliff edge. The wind howled more fiercely than ever cheated of its prey. At last Arthur lay on the ground, anchored by Myrrdin's steady hands. As Arthur struggled to his feet he grasped the scarf still tangled in the bush and yanked it free.

The two made their way down the mountain, bracing each other against the now weakening wind. For the wind, knowing it had lost its prize was giving up and slinking away, to wait, perhaps, in some dark place for the chance to try again, one day.

	Cadair Idris, Gwytheryn and Arberth, Kingdom of Prydyn, Kymru Gwernan Mis, 494

Llundydd, Disglair Wythnos—late afternoon

Gwydion stayed for some weeks in Gwytheryn. He spent a few more days in Neuadd Gorsedd, then backtracked to Y Ty Dewin to spend the rest of the time with Cariadas. As a matter of form he told the Ardewin, his uncle Cynan that he was looking for Rhiannon. But he had not expected Cynan to be of any help, so he was not disappointed when that was indeed the case.

He had finally left Y Ty Dewin two days ago and now he rode easily through the tall grasses that covered the deserted plain where Cadair Idris stood. Cold and empty, the mountain waited silently for the High King to return.

Gwydion halted his horse at the bottom of the eight stone stairs that led up to the doors. Once bright and shining, the stairs were now dull and dirty. Rockrose had twined this way and that through cracks in the broken steps, the red flowers like spots of blood scattered carelessly on an abandoned carcass.

Slowly he mounted the stairs, the breeze sobbing in his

ears, his eyes on the huge iron, jewel-encrusted Doors that barred the way into the mountain. At his approach a humming began, building in intensity as the jewels on the Doors glowed increasingly brighter. The voice of the Guardian of the Doors blended with the mournful breeze and echoed off the shuttered mountain. "Who comes to Drwys Idris?" the disembodied voice asked. "Who demands entry to Cadair Idris, the Hall of the High King of Kymru?"

"It is I, Gwydion ap Awst. But I do not demand entry."

"The halls are silent. The throne is empty. We await the coming of the King. Without the Treasures you may not enter here."

Silence settled over the mountain like a pall broken only by the moaning of the wind. Gwydion waited patiently. At last she asked, "Why have you come, Gwydion?"

"I was near the mountain and had an urge to visit on my way to Arberth."

"And what is in Arberth?"

"Clues, I hope, to the whereabouts of Rhiannon ur Hefeydd. I must find her, as she holds the key to the location of Caladfwlch."

"Ah," said Bloudewedd. "So it is time to find the sword."

"Do you know anything of it?" he asked hopefully.

"I do not," Bloudewedd replied shortly. "Bran recovered the sword from Lleu on the shores of Llyn Mwyngil. And it has not been seen since."

"All I can hope, then, is that Rhiannon's clue will be sufficient."

"But it will not be," Bloudewedd said crisply.

"What?" he sputtered. "What do you mean?"

"Bran had left me a message for you, when he infused my

spirit into these Doors."

"A message?" Gwydion repeated, astonished. "And it is?"

"That if you wish to find the sword, you must seek guidance from those who once wore it."

"From the High Kings themselves? But they are . . ." He trailed off, turning to look at the silent stones of Galor Carreg, the burial mounds of the High King's of Kymru. "Oh," he said quietly. "I see."

"Yes," said Bloudewedd quietly. "I believe that you do."

THE SUN SLOWLY sank past the horizon and the moon rose, full and glorious. From somewhere across the plain a wolf howled mournfully.

Gwydion sat on the ground in front of the burial chamber itself, surrounded by the silent and dark massive standing stones that guarded the dead. The entrance to the chamber was a pit of darkness, only the fringes of the opening lit by the silvery moon.

Gwydion had dug a shallow pit before the entrance in the shape of a figure eight, the symbol for infinity, the sign of Annwyn, Lord of Chaos. He had snapped off portions of the yew and hazel trees that were planted on either side of the entrance and filled the shallow pit with the wood. The yew was Annwyn's tree and the hazel belonged to Aertan, the Weaver of Fate, Annwyn's mate. These two ruled Gwlad Yr Haf, the Land of Summer, the place where souls journeyed at their physical death to await rebirth.

It would be Annwyn and Aertan that would allow the souls of the dead High Kings to return for a brief time tonight. If, of course, he could persuade them.

He had already laid out before him a on clean cloth a piece

of bread, a small, wooden cup full of wine, a tiny mound of salt, and a piece of honeycomb he had been lucky enough to get from a nearby hive earlier in the afternoon.

He stood now; knowing the time had come. He raised his hands and called Druid's Fire. Fire instantly filled the shallow pit, licking at the pieces of yew and hazel.

"I, Gwydion ap Awst, the Twelfth Dreamer of Kymru, call on Annwyn, Lord of Chaos and on Aertan, Weaver of Fate. I beg a boon."

He fell silent, listening. A very slight breeze stirred the grasses surrounding the stones.

"I ask that the souls of the High King's of Kymru—Idris, Macsen, and Lleu Silver-Hand be released from the Summer Land and allowed to come to me tonight. They have a message for me that I must hear for the good of Kymru."

Again, Gwydion paused. A cold wind whipped around him, seeming to come from the ground itself. The yew and hazel trees nodded slightly in the sudden breeze.

"I invite the dead to feast with me. I give them grain, for the element of fire." He picked up the piece of bread and flung it into his Druid's Fire. The fire flared orange. "I give you wine, for the element of water." He flung the contents of the tiny cup onto the fire and it flickered with a blue sheen. "I give you salt, for the element of earth." He flung the salt into the flames, and it flickered with a green cast. "And I give you honeycomb, for the element of air." He cast the piece of honeycomb into the fire, and it glowed whitely.

Gwydion now stood quietly before the darkened entrance and waited. He had done everything he could do. He only hoped that it was enough.

The darkness that pooled to the tomb's entrance stirred. A

figure stepped forth, glowing slightly in the night, followed by two others. The three shadowy ghosts came to a halt before Gwydion on the other side of the fire pit.

He recognized each one from his dreams. Dark-haired and silver-eyed Idris, the first High King. Bluff honey-blond Macsen, the second High King. And finally, golden Lleu with his hand of silver, the last High King of Kymru.

"You have called us," Idris spoke in a hollow voice, "and we have come."

"We have come as Bran had known we would," Macsen sighed.

"We have come to give you that which will help you find what you seek," Lleu said.

"Listen well, Dreamer, for this is what you want," Idris said. "It is called the Battle of the Trees, and it was written by Taliesin for you."

The three of them recited as one:

On winter's first day
Shall the trees
Face the Guardians.

On winter's first day
Shall the trees
Do battle.

The alder tree, loyal and patient,
Formed the van.
The aspen-wood, quickly moving,
Was valiant against the enemy.
The hawthorn, with pain at its hand,
Fought on the flanks.

Hazel-tree did not go aside a foot
It would fight with the center.

And when it was over
The trees covered the beloved dead,
And transformed the Y Dawnus,
From their faded state,
Until the two were one,
In strength and purpose,
And raised up that which they had sought.

On winter's first day,
The one who is loved shall die.
And tears will overwhelm
The lonely heart.

Gwydion bowed formally. "I thank you, High Kings, for your message. May I ask a few questions of you?"

Idris nodded. "Though we may not be able to answer fully, we will tell you what we can."

"The Captains of the Rulers of the four kingdoms are the ones referred to in this poem. For one of their titles is that of the tree for that kingdom. Thus the alder tree is for Cai, the Captain of Gwynedd. And the aspen is for Angharad, the Captain of Ederynion. The hawthorn is for Trystan, the Captain of Rheged, and the hazel is for Achren, the Captain of Prydyn."

"That is so, Dreamer," Macsen said. "These are some of those who are required to join you in the search for the sword."

"And the Y Dawnus spoken of? Who besides myself must accompany us?"

"The one you seek."

"Rhiannon?" Gwydion asked. "She must go with us?"

Lleu nodded. "She holds another piece of the puzzle, as you have dreamed. But she has a larger part to play."

Gwydion nodded his head, although everything within him protested this.

"You shall be joined by one other, who we cannot name," Idris went on. "He shall come to you, although he will not know why."

"Is there anything else you can tell me?" Gwydion asked thoughtfully. "Who is the one who shall die?"

"We cannot say," Lleu replied softly. "But be assured that the soul of that one shall dwell among the dead in the Summer Land in joy and peace."

"Do not fail, Dreamer, in this quest," Idris said sternly. "For without the sword a High King cannot forge the powers of the Y Dawnus into a weapon against the enemy. And this is a weapon that the Kymri must have."

"For the enemy is coming," Macsen said.

"Coming for you all," Lleu said.

Meirgdydd, Disglair Wythnos—late afternoon

TWO DAYS LATER, as he was riding by Coed Aderyn, his horse began to slow. "What are you doing?" Gwydion asked. Elise tossed his head and snorted.

Oh, yes, they were nearing a wood. "Thank you," Gwydion said politely. He had mentioned to Elise that he wanted to go slowly through any wood for he thought it likely Rhiannon would be hiding in one. Forests were, after all, the best hiding places.

His plan was simple. Ride through and Wind-Speak for Rhiannon. She was a telepath as well as a clairvoyant, and she would not only hear him, she would be able to respond. Of course she would be warned that she was being looked for. But there was also a chance that she would answer. She might be very tired of hiding and need only an excuse to come out—an excuse that would allow her to keep her dignity. Although her dignity was not of the slightest importance to him, he assumed it would be of importance to her. If she did not answer, and was warned, that would be all right, too. For she might run again, and she would be less careful in her panic. She might even be careless enough to allow her trail to be followed.

And so he began to call, casting his Wind-Speech as far as he could. *"Rhiannon ur Hefeydd. It is the Dreamer who calls you. I have dreamed of you. In the name of the Shining Ones I charge you to return to the world, for a mighty task awaits you."* A bit pompous, he thought. But it got the point across. And offered a challenge that she might respond to.

He halted Elise, and waited. But there was no answer. Slowly, he rode on.

RHIANNON WAS HUNTING when she heard the call. The words echoed in her head, and the stag she had been stalking bounded away before she could bring it down. Curse the Dreamer, she raged. She ran for cover beneath a twisted hedge. If he were Wind-Speaking, perhaps he would be Wind-Riding as well. He might see her.

Fuming, and, she had to admit, frightened, she crouched down. Delicately, she began to Wind-Ride, hoping to spot him. If she were careful, he would sense nothing. She would be careful. It was what she was best at, after all.

She pulled her awareness from her body, and her spirit

rose up to hover over the trees. She felt his presence some miles to the south. Silently she flew toward him and, within moments, she caught sight of him.

He had a short, dark beard that he was absentmindedly scratching as he rode. She wondered irritably why he grew that thing if it itched. His gray eyes were alert, but they did not see her as she hovered at the very edge of his awareness.

She studied his face. It was stern and cold, set within the harsh cast of his ruthless will. Yet he was handsome, she'd give him that. And she was sure he could be charming, if he chose to be. Just long enough, no doubt, to trap his prey.

She pondered what he would do if she answered. He seemed to be calling in a general way, perhaps not really even expecting a reply. She would love to shock him.

She almost did. She almost answered, almost told him what she thought of his ridiculous, pompous message. But at the last moment, her native caution stopped her.

What in the world had she been thinking? She must be mad. Come out of hiding after all these years? Never. One day she would send Gwenhwyfar back into the world, because she had to. But she, personally, would not go. Not for all the mighty tasks, not for all the Shining Ones. Not for anything.

Slowly, delicately, she withdrew back into her own body. And remained hidden under the brush until Gwydion was far, far away.

Gwyntdydd, Cynyddu Wythnos—early evening

THREE WEEKS LATER, just as dusk was descending, Gwydion reached the city of Arberth, the capital of the Kingdom of Prydyn. The countryside outside of the gates to the city was given over to acre upon acre of grapevines. It was spring so the vines were barely budding.

The city walls were rectangular, with the longer western side perched on the very top of the ragged cliffs leading down to the sea. As he neared the eastern side of the city he could faintly hear the sound of the surf pounding the shore to the west, creating a ceaseless, wordless harmony to the far-off, lonely cry of the gulls.

As the city watchmen took their places, torches were just being lit in the circular towers that rose from the four corners of the city walls. As he rode up to the gate the two men who were just closing it for the night stopped and let Gwydion ride through. He had put on the Dreamer's Torque a league or so back so that people would be sure to recognize him. That recognition would get him through the city gates and the gates of Caer Tir, the King's fortress, with no questions asked. He nodded absently to the two men, but did not stop.

He continued down the main road, riding by Nemed Collen, the sacred grove of hazel trees. The grove was dark and silent. The twisted branches of the trees were wrapped tightly together, as though for protection.

Elise cantered down the almost deserted road, for most people had already gone to their homes for the evening meal. All along the road the torches were being lit. Gwydion fidgeted in the saddle. He was uncomfortable returning to Arberth, and didn't want to stay here any longer than he had to. The last time he came here was for Isalyn's funeral. It was hard to believe that she had died nine years ago. It felt like longer than that. Memories of her were hazy and distant, for he avoided thinking of Isalyn whenever possible. He hadn't loved her and she had known it—known it and resented it and clung to him in spite of it.

257

Elise's hooves clicked sharply on the cobbled road. The city was quiet and he could clearly hear the seagull's mournful cries as they settled in for the night. He rode up to Caer Tir just as the doors, made of iron covered with gold leaf, were closing for the night. The huge head of a snarling wolf, the symbol of Prydyn, was carved on the doors. Outlined in black onyx with emerald eyes, the wolf seemed to glare at him.

The doorkeeper stopped as he was closing the doors, staring at Gwydion. Slowly, the man smiled. "Gwydion ap Awst. I knew you'd show up again, one day."

Gwydion grinned. "Right as always, Tallwch."

Tallwch hadn't changed much since the last time Gwydion has seen him, nine years ago. He had brown hair, cut ruthlessly short and steady brown eyes. His face had, perhaps, a few more lines, but otherwise he looked much the same. Tallwch had been Gwydion's friend during those months he had been forced to stay here with Isalyn. As the gatekeeper, he had seen Gwydion come and go on his many trips out to the countryside to get away. The two men had struck up a casual friendship, for Gwydion had seen the sympathy in the man's eyes, though they never spoke of it. Often Gwydion and Tallwch and Dafydd Penfro, Rhoram's counselor, would stay up far into the night playing tarbell, swapping stories, drinking wine. He had never seen a man for holding his liquor like Tallwch ap Nwyfre.

"What are you doing here?" Tallwch asked.

"Can't you guess, since you're so clever?"

"Ho, ho," Tallwch said flatly. "You always were a funny man."

"Where is everyone?"

"Most folks are in the Great Hall. Come on, we'll stable

your horse and go on in. Unless you want a bath first."

"You saying I need one?"

"Wouldn't hurt." Tallwch looked at Gwydion critically. "But then, it probably wouldn't help, either."

"It's nice to have friends."

They led Elise to the stables, which were just to the right of the gates. Gwydion made sure that the horse was comfortable in his stall before he grabbed his saddlebags. As they crossed the cobbled courtyard in front of the Great Hall, Tallwch took the saddlebags from him and hailed a passing servant. "Boyo, take this to the guest house, would you?" he asked, relinquishing the bags.

Dusk had deepened into night. Dimly, he heard the sound of merriment from within the Great Hall, penetrating the thick stone walls and heavy oak doors. "Sounds like a party," Gwydion commented.

"Just mealtime, like always. Rhoram likes it noisy. It keeps him from having to talk to the Queen."

Gwydion stopped and stared at Tallwch. "When did this start?"

"Not long after they were married. Truth is, he never got over losing Rhiannon."

"Losing her? I thought he had tired of her?"

"So did he. Well, we all make mistakes don't we? Ready to go in?"

"As I'll ever be," Gwydion said. The noise from the hall was rising in volume. Tallwch opened the door and they entered into the Great Hall of Caer Tir.

The din assaulted his ears fiercely. The hall was filled to the brim with laughing, shouting men and women. Uthyr's hall was casual, too, but never as chaotic as this.

Table after table filled the hall, set up for the evening meal. People sat at the long benches or on the tables themselves, and even (in a few cases) underneath them. Bright banners hung the walls. Over the fireplace hung a huge banner of a wolf's head, worked in black on a green background and fringed with gold.

In the corner to his left, Gwydion saw a wrestling match in progress. Two men grappled with each other to the shouts of the crowd gathered round them. A fire roared in the huge fireplace in front of which people played pipes and harps, laughing and singing, although Gwydion couldn't imagine how they could hear themselves above the din. Directly in front of him a dice game was in progress. He peered through the crowd, trying to locate people he knew.

Over on the dais at the far right of the hall he saw Queen Efa sitting at the King's table. She was a slender, petite woman with dark red hair and large brown eyes. Her gown was autumn green, embroidered lavishly with emeralds and gold thread. The man sitting next to her was her brother, Erfin ap Nudd, the Lord of Ceredigion. The two sat in splendid isolation as they chatted amicably together.

Gwydion peered ahead of him and recognized the woman who was shooting dice with such skill. It was Achren ur Canhustyr, Captain of Rhoram's *teulu*, the PenCollen of Prydyn. This was one of the people that Gwydion now knew would help in the search for the sword.

Achren's black hair was braided tightly back from her face and her dark eyes were sparkling with mirth. Her wide mouth was stretched in a grin at the continuous complaints of her companions that the dice were loaded. Gwydion had not seen her in some time, but the passing years seemed to have touched her lightly. Her slender, strong body, dressed now in black riding leathers, looked in as good a shape as ever. Her habit of eyeing everyone in sight, of always knowing what was going on around her, of seeming to have eyes in the back of her head, had also not changed. As she threw the dice she spotted Gwydion through the crowd, although he had only been standing there for a few brief moments.

Instantly she handed the dice to another warrior and was by his side. "Gwydion ap Awst. What a surprise," she said calmly.

"I wouldn't think so, Achren. Your people are too well trained for that. I assume you heard I was coming about a league away."

"Two leagues," she grinned, but the smile did not reach her dark eyes.

"Where's Rhoram?" he asked.

Achren jerked her thumb at the crowd grouped around the wrestlers. And there he was, in the forefront, laughing and calling out bets (and insults, as the spirit moved him). His clothes were rich—a black tunic over an emerald undershirt. His breeches were black and tucked into long, black boots. The King's Torque of gold, studded with emeralds, hung around his neck. He wore an emerald ring on his right hand. He was smiling, but Gwydion was shocked by his appearance. His sunken blue eyes glittered like a man with a high fever. His movements were sharp and restless. His skin was stretched tightly over his prominent cheekbones, and the tendons on his hands stood out far too sharply.

"Is he ill?" Gwydion gasped.

"In a manner of speaking," Achren said dryly, but Gwydion saw the fear in her eyes. "I do so hope you keep that question to yourself."

"What's wrong with him?"

Achren jerked her thumb to the spot where Queen Efa sat.

"Oh. Well." He remembered something Tallwch had recently said to him. "We all make mistakes, don't we?" he said inanely.

Achren, her eyes cool and hard looked him up and down, and her wide mouth quirked. "Very astute. Homespun wisdom is the best, isn't it?"

He had forgotten that Achren's tongue was sharp when she was annoyed. Remembering that Achren and Rhiannon had been good friends once, Gwydion said abruptly, "I'm looking for Rhiannon ur Hefeydd. What can you tell me?"

"Why?"

"I had a dream. She must be found."

Achren studied him thoughtfully. "After the meal we'll talk, if you wish."

"Yes," he said, "let's talk later." He studied Rhoram for a moment longer. "I guess I'd better go say hello. Who's that lad standing next to him?"

"Geriant."

"Little Geriant?"

"Not so little anymore, is he?" Achren asked.

Geriant was Rhoram's oldest child by his first wife, Queen Christina of Ederynion. At seventeen, he was no longer a boy, but a young man. Like his father, he had golden hair and deep blue eyes. Unlike his father, he looked healthy, happy, and strong.

"Come on then," Achren said. "I'll take you to him." She began pushing her way though the crowd. Gwydion looked around for Tallwch and saw him standing with the musicians at the fireplace. Tallwch raised his goblet and nodded to Gwydion.

He followed Achren. As they came up to the King the wrestling match ended. Rhoram had called a draw and his warriors shouted and complained. "I said a draw," Rhoram shouted. "I can't wait any longer—I'm famished." The crowd moaned and hissed. Rhoram laughed. Then he saw Gwydion.

The laughter died and was replaced with a genuine smile of welcome. For a brief moment, Gwydion saw a glimpse of the man Rhoram had been long ago.

"Gwydion. Gwydion," Rhoram said, coming up to him and slinging his arm around Gwydion's shoulders, giving him a brief hug. "You are welcome here."

Rhoram turned to face the crowd. "This is my honored guest, Gwydion ap Awst, who has come to visit his old friend." Rhoram grinned, "He's the Dreamer, so get out of his way, or he'll have a dream about you!" The crowd began catcalling bets as to which unfortunate would be the first to figure in Gwydion's ominous dreams.

"Gwydion, do you remember my son?" Rhoram stretched out his hand and motioned Geriant to his side. The young man smiled and bowed his head slightly.

"I remember, you," Gwydion said smiling, "but not as being quite so tall!"

Geriant grinned. "It's been a while then!"

"It has indeed." He turned to Rhoram. "He makes me feel so old."

"We are old, Gwydion," Rhoram said quietly.

"Come on, Rhoram," Achren said sharply. "Efa's ready to scream. Time to eat."

"Efa's always ready to scream," Rhoram muttered, but he followed Achren though the crowd toward the dais motioning for Gwydion to follow.

As they neared the fireplace, Rhoram stretched out his hand and a beautiful young girl came running to him. She clasped his hand and kissed his cheek lightly. "Gwydion, you remember my daughter, Sanon." Like her father and brother, Sanon had golden hair. But her eyes were dark. She looked to be about fourteen years old. "This is Gwydion ap Awst, my dear, the Dreamer," Rhoram explained. "It's been quite some time since you've seen him."

Sanon's eyes widened, their pleasant light replaced by a young girl's instant infatuation as she took in his handsome face and air of authority. She blushed and curtsied slightly.

"Come, my treasure," Rhoram said pretending he hadn't noticed Sanon's reaction. "It's time to eat." He motioned for Sanon to precede them. Rhoram kept pace next to Gwydion. Softly he said to Gwydion, keeping the smile plastered on his face, "Touch her and you're dead."

"I wouldn't dream of it," Gwydion said sincerely.

"Good. Let's keep it that way, shall we?"

They reached the King's table, now almost full as Rhoram's chief officers took their places. "Efa, you remember Gwydion ap Awst," Rhoram said in a neutral tone.

The Queen smiled brilliantly. "Indeed I do remember you, Gwydion. It's been years. How is Cariadas?"

"Perfect," Gwydion answered smiling.

"Yes. I'm sure Cariadas is as charming as her mother," she said. Gwydion remembered that Efa and Isalyn had disliked each other intensely. She went on, "Of course you remember my brother, Erfin."

"Can't say as I do," Gwydion said smoothly. "Was he here when I was?" Actually, Gwydion remembered Erfin quite well—well enough to want to irk him.

Like his sister, Erfin had fiery red hair, and his eyes were brown. But while Efa's eyes were large and beautiful, Erfin's were small, almost shifty. Erfin forced himself to smile and nod pleasantly, but he was indeed annoyed, as Gwydion had intended.

Rhoram, smothering a smile, motioned for Gwydion to take a seat to his left, while Dafydd Penfro, Rhoram's counselor, sat on Gwydion's other side.

"Gwydion," Dafydd exclaimed. "It's good to see you, man." Dafydd Penfro was shrewd, highly intelligent, and devoted to the Rulers of Prydyn. He had been Gwydion's friend during that terrible time when he had stayed in Arberth against his will. Gwydion smiled with genuine pleasure. "Good to see you, too, Dafydd!"

"But not good to be back here, is it?" Dafydd's eyes were keen as he sat down.

"No," Gwydion said shortly. "Not good at all."

"Well, now, Tallwch and I will take good care of you. See if we don't."

At the end of the table, Ellywen, Rhoram's Druid, sat in cool, self-imposed isolation. She nodded distantly to Gwydion when she saw him staring at her. Achren, who sat a few places over, was laughing with Geriant, but her eyes were wary. Sanon was stealing glances at Gwydion whenever she thought he wasn't looking.

Up and down the hall people were taking their places at the tables. When the hall was relatively quiet, Ellywen stood up and solemnly intoned the evening prayer.

The peace of lights,
The peace of joys,
The peace of souls,

Be with you.

"Awen," the people responded in unison, momentarily subdued. Ellywen had a delightful way of making a blessing sound like a curse.

Servants began to bring in heaping platters from the kitchen. Steaming potatoes, still in their jackets, slabs of venison flavored with sage, great wheels of rich yellow cheese, and crusty loaves of bread were brought to their table. Gwydion loaded his plate, for he had been on the road a long time.

When the meal was done, and the goblets filled, he sat back in his chair, anticipating the nature of the evening's entertainment. He assumed it would be a continuation of the earlier part of the evening—wrestling, dice, and music. Unfortunately—or fortunately, depending on how you looked at it—it was Achren who took it upon herself to provide the night's merriment. Years afterward, he was never sure exactly why she had done it. To enrage Efa, certainly. To jolt Rhoram, definitely. To irritate Gwydion, possibly. Perhaps all of the above.

"Gwydion is looking for Rhiannon ur Hefeydd," she said in a penetrating tone. "Anybody have any ideas?"

Gwydion choked on his wine. Efa stiffened and dug her nails into the arms of her chair. And Rhoram slowly lowered his goblet set it gently on the table. He turned to Achren. "What did you say?"

"I said, Gwydion's looking for Rhiannon," Achren answered calmly, as though she had said nothing of great importance.

Blankly, Rhoram turned to Gwydion. "Why?"

"A dream I had told me to find her," Gwydion said between gritted teeth.

"Why ask here? Why ask us?" Rhoram's voice rose until he was almost shouting. "Do you think I know anything? Do you think that if I knew where to look I'd still be sitting on my backside in this gods-forsaken hall?"

"A miracle," said Achren, her voice cutting through the air like a dagger. "It actually speaks. Just like it was alive."

In fury, Rhoram turned to her, his once dead eyes glittering with rage. "You dare to mock me?"

"It even talks," Achren went on, her tone was full of inexpressible contempt, "like it has a backbone. This is truly amazing. I wonder how it's done?"

Rhoram threw his goblet at her, but she ducked. The goblet crashed against the far wall and rolled away. Everyone in the hall froze, staring at Rhoram. "You will pay for this, Achren. I promise you," Rhoram said, his tone deadly.

"It speaks," Achren repeated calmly. "Like a King. Finally. After all these years."

Rhoram, quick as thought, grasped a knife from one of the empty platters. He leapt across the table, grabbed Achren by the arm and twisted her around, until his dagger was at her throat.

"What, Achren, do you think the payment should be for mocking me? You're death, perhaps?" Rhoram asked, coldly, clearly, implacably.

"If I die, Rhoram," she said calmly, as though she did not have a knife at her throat, "it will be payment enough just to know that Prydyn has its King again."

For a long moment, it hung in the balance—Achren's life and Rhoram's living death. In the end, what happened in that moment was forever burned into Gwydion's memory. For he saw the King of Prydyn choose to return to life.

Rhoram's blue eyes began to glitter. Color returned to his face. He released Achren, spinning her away from him. She straightened then faced him, her head high.

In a carrying tone Rhoram said, "Achren ur Canhustyr, Captain of my *teulu*, PenCollen of Prydyn, you forget your place. I shall remind you. Tomorrow, at dawn, you will lead my warriors in a hunt. And you will bring back to me the heads of five wild boars. Five, mark you. I will accept nothing less. You will bring them to me by noon, tomorrow. Or you will leave Prydyn and never return."

Rhoram turned to Gwydion, "Come with me, Gwydion ap Awst, we have business to conduct." Then he firmly strode out of the now silent hall.

Gwydion followed swiftly. He looked back behind him as he went out the door. He saw that Achren was smiling with genuine pleasure, and that Queen Efa was looking at her husband's Captain as though wishing her dead.

GWYDION HURRIED AFTER Rhoram, who marched down the steps of the Hall and suddenly stopped by the well in the deserted courtyard. Rhoram lowered the bucket into the well and pulled it up brimming with cold, clear water. Then, without further ado, he plunged his face into the water and came up again, gasping. "Gods that's cold," he said, wiping his face with his sleeve.

"What are you doing?" Gwydion asked in bewilderment.

"Waking up," Rhoram replied. "Waking up after years and years." He began to hum a little tune, still mopping at his wet face.

"Rhoram, what are you talking about?"

"I'm talking about what Achren did. What did you think I was talking about?"

"What exactly did she do?"

Rhoram's smiled faded. His eyes were very blue and very serious. "She made me see myself and I didn't like what I saw." Rhoram returned to the hall steps and sat down, motioning for Gwydion to sit down beside him. The ceaseless song of the crickets could be heard in the distance. Overhead the stars gleamed impossibly bright in the night sky.

"Eleven years ago," Rhoram said quietly, "I lost the woman I loved. The woman I still love. But I didn't know it, not until it was too late. I made a horrible mistake. A mistake I can't fix. And I let that mistake tear me to pieces. And that was the worst part. People make mistakes, you see, and live with them the best they know how. But my best wasn't very good. Achren made me see that tonight. And so," Rhoram went on, his voice firm, "from now on I shall do better."

Gwydion hardened cynic that he was, believed that Rhoram would, indeed, do better. He had a fleeting thought that he hadn't done any better than Rhoram had in living with the past. That thought flashed through his mind, and then was gone. "Can you talk about her?" he asked.

"All you want. But truly, I don't know anything."

"Tell me, Rhoram, what if you saw her again? What if she came back to you? What would you do?"

Rhoram was silent for a long time. Finally he said, "She won't come back to me, Gwydion. She'll never trust me enough to give her heart to me a second time. Believe this, for I know her. Once trust is broken, it's gone for good."

"Rhoram," Gwydion said abruptly. "I need something."

"It is yours, Dreamer, if I can make it so."

"I need you to send Achren to Caer Dathyl. She must be there by Suldydd, Cynyddu Wythnos, in Ysgawen Mis."

"Because?" Rhoram asked, his brows raised.

269

"I'd rather not say."

Rhoram looked at Gwydion for a long moment. "Very well," he said. "Come," he went on lightly. "Let's go back inside. I feel a need to play."

"Play?"

"The harp. I'm very good at that."

"What about Efa?" Gwydion said suddenly.

"What about her? We'll go on together, as always. She has what she wants. She's the Queen."

"And you?"

"Ah, well. I'm the King. And there are some beautiful ladies in my court, don't you think? I get by." Rhoram grinned and stood up, reaching down a hand to help Gwydion to his feet. He stood there for a moment, looking at Gwydion. Then he said quietly, "If you find her, tell her I miss her and hope to see her again. And tell her I'd like to see my daughter, very much."

Gwydion nodded. "Anything else?"

Rhoram shook his head. "I think not. It's better that way."

As they mounted the steps, Gwydion said quietly, "It's good to see you again, Rhoram."

When they reentered the hall the crowd was silent, listening intently to Sanon as she stood before the hearth, singing in a clear, sweet voice. Rhoram made his way through the crowd, picking up a harp that was sitting on one of the tables. He sat on the hearth, and played the tune to Sanon's song. Sanon smiled at her father and kept singing.

What evil genius, Gwydion wondered, had prompted her to sing that song? She was singing of Cuchulainn, one of the kings of lost Lyonesse and of his doomed love affair. Cuchulainn had fallen under the enchantment of Fand, one of the Danans, the magic folk of that realm. Cuchulainn's wife, Emer, had found out about the affair, catching the lovers together. Sanon was now singing Emer's words to Cuchulainn.

What is red is beautiful,
What is new is bright,
What's tall is fair,
What's familiar is stale.
The unknown is honored,
The known is neglected.
We lived in harmony once,
And could do so again,
If only I still pleased you.

Gwydion eyed Rhoram as he calmly played the harp, shocked that the King had not even winced at the words. For one moment, Sanon almost faltered, but Rhoram's smile encouraged her to go on. Gwydion made his way to where he saw Dafydd standing against the wall. "Where's Efa?" Gwydion asked softly.

"She left as soon as Sanon started singing."

"She's still alive, then."

"Right. If Efa had taken a swing at Achren, as she had wanted to, she wouldn't be," Dafydd grinned.

"Where is Achren?"

Dafydd jerked his head over to the dais. "Over there."

"Thanks." As Gwydion made his way toward Achren, Sanon was finishing up her song. King Cuchulainn had decided to stay with his wife, and Fand, the enchantress, was leaving.

It is I who will go on a journey,
Though I like our adventure best.
Alas for one who gives love to another
If it be not cherished;

271

It is better for a person to be cast aside
Unless he is loved as he loves.

Gwydion sat down on the empty chair next to Achren. She turned her head slightly to look at him out of the corner of her eye, but said nothing.

"Rhoram looks much better, don't you think?" he asked.

"Better than I'll look tomorrow after hunting down five wild boars," she said dryly.

"It worked," Gwydion replied.

Achren smiled slowly. "Yes. It did."

"When was the last time you saw Rhiannon?" he asked suddenly.

Her dark eyes became distant with memory. "The night she left. I was on guard duty that night, near the outer gates of the city, when I saw her riding up. She had Gwen in a sling around her neck."

"So she rode up to the gates," Gwydion prompted. "What did she say?"

"Why, nothing. We looked at each other for a moment, then I opened the gates, and she rode out."

"And that was it? Nothing else?"

"She stopped and smiled at me after she rode through. Tears were streaming down her face. But she smiled at me. And she waved good-bye."

"And so you just let her leave."

"She was my friend," Achren said simply. "And it was what she wanted. That was good enough for me."

Chapter Twelve

Alban Haf—late afternoon

Thirty days later, weary and travel-stained, Gwydion arrived outside the gates of Llwynarth, the capital city of the Kingdom of Rheged.

He had left Arberth soon after his arrival, spending only a few days with Rhoram, withstanding the melting looks directed at him by Rhoram's daughter and enjoying the spectacle of Achren ur Canhustyr returning muddied, exhausted, but triumphant, with the heads of five wild boars (and a few extra scars).

Despite his growing anxiety that he would never find Rhiannon, his trip across Rheged fed something in him. Rheged was renowned for its honey, its beeswax candles, its superb mead and ale, its golden wheat. The land itself seemed to be made of fire—wheat fields glistening under the hot sun, rich honey glowing with an inner light. Gwydion was the Dreamer and, as such, he owed his primary allegiance to Mabon of the Sun, the Lord of Fire. And Rheged was Mabon's land.

Yet he did not expect to find any answers here to his most pressing problem—where to find Rhiannon. For here in King Urien's court there were none who had known her well. Still, this trip throughout Kymru was giving him the chance to re-connect with all the Rulers of this land. Since it had recently become clear that he needed Kymru's Captains at his side, it was as well that he had already determined to visit each Ruler. He needed the support of all of them both now and in the un-certain future. So he reconciled himself to this long journey, in hopes that it would bear fruit at a later time.

The gates of the Llwynarth were still open for it was only late afternoon and people were still going in and out of the city. Many of the people were from the outlying areas around the city, coming in to celebrate Alban Haf, the festival of Modron, the Great Mother, which would take place later tonight.

Llwynarth was built in the shape of a circle. Four watch-towers stood equidistant from each other around the circular stone walls. The stones had a golden cast to them, caus-ing the walls to glow in the late afternoon sun. As he rode through the southern gate he left the main road, passing Nemed Draenenwen, the sacred grove of hawthorn trees. As it was early summer, the trees were coated with clusters of delicate white flowers.

"You honor us, Dreamer, with your presence."

Gwydion recognized the call of Esyllt ur Maelwys, the King's Bard. *"How kind of you,"* he answered.

"I've orders from Anieron to help you in any way I can. Do you need anything?"

"I need to see Urien and Ellirri."

"I'll send Trystan to escort you," Esyllt replied.

Of course she would send Trystan. Trystan ap Nap was the

Captain of King Urien's *teulu*—and Esyllt's lover. Everyone knew that. Everyone except, perhaps, March, Esyllt's husband.

"*Thank you Esyllt,*" Gwydion said. "*Remember me to March, won't you?*"

"*Yes,*" she replied shortly, and then the contact was broken. Apparently she and March were still married. He wondered why. In Kymru a couple could be divorced if they declared their marriage over by mutual consent, at any one of the eight festivals. If Esyllt didn't love her husband, why didn't she divorce him? And if she did love her husband, why did she keep Trystan as her lover?

He rode by Crug Mawr, the burial place of the Rulers of Rheged. The stones stood dark and silent—an incongruous note on this beautiful summer afternoon.

Gwydion was looking forward to spending some time with King Urien and Queen Ellirri. King Urien was a generous, good-natured, talented warrior, not overly clever or subtle. Subtlety came from his Queen, Ellirri of Gwynedd. She was full sister to Madoc and half sister to Uthyr. Gwydion had known Ellirri since childhood and he remembered her well—and fondly—from his visits to Tegeingl as a boy.

At last he reached the gate of Caer Erias, the King's fortress. The gate was iron covered with gold leaf. On it was carved a rearing stallion, his mane flying in the wind, outlined in shimmering opals. The horse's opal eyes glowed as Gwydion rode through the open gate.

There, true to Esyllt's word, stood Trystan, the Captain of Urien's warband, the PenDraenenwen of Rheged. Trystan was broad shouldered and muscular, standing just under six feet. He had brown hair and green eyes which shown with intelligence and humor. Trystan smiled and held Elise's bridal as Gwydion dismounted. "Ho, Gwydion. How long have you been on the road, man?"

"Thirty days," Gwydion said wearily, as he slid down from the saddle. "Where are Urien and Ellirri?"

"In the ystafell. But you're not going there yet."

"I'm not?"

"You," Trystan said emphatically, "need a bath. And a change of clothing. Come on, it won't take you long. They will still be there when you're done."

Too tired to argue, Gwydion acquiesced and turned back to Elise to unbuckle his saddlebags.

But Trystan had already done so, and given Elise's reins to a waiting groom. Taking Gwydion's arm, he led him past the stables and over to the bathhouse. He handed Gwydion his bags, then nodded to the door. "Bathe. Change."

"Yes, Mam," Gwydion grinned. "Anything else?"

"Yes. Wash your mouth out with soap while you're at it," Trystan said, grinning in his turn.

After his bath, Gwydion changed into more formal clothes, knowing that after the meal they would celebrate the festival. He put on his black robe with red trim and clasped the Dreamer's Torque of opal and gold around his neck. Instead of tying his black hair back with a leather strip as he usually did, he used a golden ring studded with opals.

He was ready when Trystan reentered the bathhouse. Trystan nodded, "Better. Now you look more like the Dreamer and less like something the cat dragged in."

"Thanks," Gwydion said dryly. "Are Urien and Ellirri ready to see me now?"

"Yes. Leave your bags here. I'll get someone to take them to your room."

Gwydion followed Trystan out of the bathhouse. The men and women of Urien's *teulu* had halted their afternoon practice and were making their way back to their quarters under the ceaseless prodding of Teleri ur Brysethach, Trystan's lieutenant. Teleri was a tiny woman, no more than five feet tall. She had dark brown hair, cut short to frame her face and fine, gray-green eyes. She eyed Gwydion and Trystan as they made their way across the courtyard, but did not speak to them, absorbed in her task.

Gwydion followed Trystan through the door to the ystafell, the Ruler's private chambers. The ystafell was a large, two-story building, set across the courtyard from the *teulu's* quarters. The main room on the lower floor of the ystafell was furnished formally, for this was where Urien and Ellirri usually received visitors on state business. Two large, canopied chairs, cushioned in red and white stood in the center of the room. The floor was covered with a cream-colored carpet woven with a dizzying array of red, circular patterns. The right wall was covered with a large tapestry of a rearing stallion, worked in gold and opal.

As they mounted the stairs the sounds of a wrestling match reached Gwydion's ears. Trystan and Gwydion came to a halt in the first doorway at the top of the stairs. The room was bright and airy with a large hearth and a thick carpet of cream and red. At the moment the carpet appeared to be littered with bodies.

King Urien, his large face flushed with exertion and laughter was lying on his back grappling with his eldest son, Elphin. "No, lad, like this," Urien instructed and, quite suddenly, Elphin was on his back with Urien looming over him.

King Urien had brown, sun-streaked hair and velvety

brown eyes that seemed small in the expanse of his large, good-natured face. He was tall and broad and as strong as an ox. His eldest son, Elphin, would look exactly like him in ten years. Elphin was only nineteen years old now, and his skin was not yet weather-roughened like his father's. He was muscular, but not yet as broad.

"Owein," Elphin cried out between bouts of laughter, "Help me!"

At his call Elphin's younger brother, Owein, a lad of seventeen years, launched himself into the fray, landing on his father's back and knocking him to one side. Owein had reddish brown hair and his mother's deep blue eyes. His leap was accomplished in swift, competent silence, the strength in his leap belaying his slender build.

Urien roared as Owein pinned him to the floor and Elphin, now released, sprang up to continue the match. "Two against one, eh?" Urien cried.

"I'll help you, Da," fifteen-year-old Rhiwallon called out and the match was on. Elphin and Owein fought against Urien and Rhiwallon. The fight was over in the blink of an eye. For Owein instantly flipped young Rhiwallon onto his back just as Urien did the same to Elphin. Urien and Owein glanced at each other, and burst out laughing.

"No fair, no fair," thirteen-year-old Enid shouted as she ran into the room. She stopped in front of her father and brothers and put her hands on her hips. "You didn't wait for me." Enid had her mother's red-gold hair and blue eyes.

And then Queen Ellirri entered the room. She was a tall, slender woman. Her heart-shaped face was framed with a cloud of reddish gold hair and her eyes were sharp sapphire blue. She was dressed in a cream-colored gown, with an underskirt of rich, deep red. A necklace of opals encircled her slender neck, and her hair was braided into a crown at the top of her head. Opals were scattered throughout her hair.

"No fighting now, Enid. You've just gotten dressed up," she said, her voice calm and cool. "And you boys—you are supposed to be dressed up by now, too. Festival tonight, remember?"

Reluctantly the boys straggled to their feet. Ellirri smiled at them and the three smiled back. "Very handsome, all of you. But your manners," she shook her head.

"What's wrong with our manners, Mam?" Elphin asked.

"Well for starters you are ignoring your guest," she said, nodding to Gwydion who still stood in the doorway.

"Gwydion!" Urien roared, coming to his feet. "How are you, man?" he asked, giving Gwydion a hearty slap on the back that nearly felled him.

Gwydion straightened up and noticed that four pairs of awestruck eyes were staring at him. "The Dreamer," Owein breathed. "You are welcome here," he continued, bowing. He poked Elphin in the ribs. Elphin started, and then he too bowed. Rhiwallon also bowed and Enid, at a pinch from Owein, overcame her momentary paralysis and curtsied.

"All right, everyone. Boys, go get changed. Enid, dear, please go see the steward and tell her to set another place at the high table." The children scattered to do Ellirri's bidding. "Trystan," she continued, "thank you for bringing Gwydion here." Trystan, recognizing a dismissal when he heard one, grinned and promptly left.

"You should change too, Urien, dear. I'll take Gwydion to our rooms. Join us as soon as you can, won't you?"

Urien smiled at his lovely wife and kissed her hand. "Your

wish is my command, as always."

Ellirri smiled and softly patted his rough cheek. Then she turned to Gwydion. Delicately she put her hand on his arm. "You are welcome, here, Gwydion. Come."

He followed her across the hall to her room. The chamber was bright and cheerful. The furniture—wardrobes, chairs, and tables—was carved from light oak wood. Her huge, canopied bed was covered with a taupe-colored spread, worked in gold thread. The floor was covered here and there with small rugs, woven in red and cream. Golden vases that held masses of bright, red roses were scattered throughout the room.

She gestured Gwydion into a chair before the hearth. She sat on a chair next to him, and turned her fine, blue eyes upon him, smiling warmly. "Tell me all the news, Gwydion. How is Uthyr?" The two had been very close growing up. She had been far closer to her half brother, Uthyr, than to her full brother, Madoc.

"I haven't seen much of him lately. I don't get to Tegeingl at all any more."

"I hope there's no trouble between you two."

"No trouble. But I am not very welcome at Uthyr's court just the same."

"Ah, yes, Ygraine. Charming as always, I'm sure," Ellirri said, smiling.

Gwydion smiled back. "Indeed. But last I saw Uthyr he was well." He didn't mention, of course, that the last time he saw his brother he had been disguised as a scruffy man-at-arms.

"I'm glad he is well. I hope he is happy," she said doubtfully. "I doubt he has ever gotten over Arthur's death. Now, Gwydion, my dear, I am so glad to see you, but why have you come?"

"What makes you think I have a special reason?" Gwydion asked.

"My dear Gwydion, you never, ever do anything without two or more motives up your sleeve. You forget, I've known you a long time."

Urien entered the room, sparing Gwydion a reply. He was dressed in a red tunic and breeches, with a beige-colored undershirt. He wore the Ruler's Torque of gold, studded with opals, around his thick neck. An opal ring glittered from his right hand and a large opal dangled from his right ear. His short brown hair was freshly combed and his ruddy face glowed.

"Well, Gwydion," he said in his usual bluff tone, "What's up?" He turned toward Ellirri. "Has he said yet?"

"Not just yet, dear. Here, sit down." She gestured to another chair but Urien took a place at the edge of the hearth. "Chair's too little, I'd break it," he grinned. "Now," he turned to Gwydion, "tell us."

"I'm looking for Rhiannon ur Hefeydd."

"Oh, that gal that ran off a while back?" Urien asked.

"The same."

"Well, she didn't come here. Is that it?"

Ellirri said gently, "Perhaps Gwydion will tell us why he is looking for her."

"I had a dream," Gwydion said shortly.

"See?" Urien said, turning to his wife. "That's all he ever says. Waste of time asking him anything. You know that. Plays his own game. Always did."

Unaccountably, Gwydion flushed. Urien's analysis of Gwydion's constant evasions embarrassed him, perhaps most of all because Urien had said it without rancor.

"I'm sorry, Gwydion. But we have learned nothing here about her. Perhaps in Prydyn they know more," Ellirri said.

"I just came from Prydyn, actually."

"Oh! How is Rhoram?" Ellirri seemed to know something about how Rhoram usually was, for she asked the question with some trepidation.

"Better. He was doing quite well when I left."

"Was he?" She turned to her husband. "I believe it might be well for Elphin to visit there now."

"For what?" Urien asked in surprise.

"To meet Sanon, of course. Rhoram's daughter."

"Planning an alliance?" Gwydion asked.

"If they like each other," Ellirri replied serenely. "I think I'll send Owein with him as well. It would be good for him to travel a little."

"Do as you think best, my dear," Urien said.

"I need Trystan," Gwydion said, somewhat abruptly.

"When?" Ellirri asked, her brows raised.

"He must come to Caer Dathyl by Suldydd, in Cynyddu Wythnos, Ysgawen Mis."

"Why?" Urien asked curiously.

"I cannot tell you. Not now."

Urien and Ellirri exchanged glances. Urien shrugged and Ellirri turned back to Gwydion.

"As you wish, Gwydion, dear," she said calmly. "He will be there."

"So," Urien said, turning to Gwydion, "you've looked in Prydyn for this Rhiannon. And now here. Sorry we can't help you. Where next?"

"I thought I'd go to Dinmael and talk to Queen Olwen."

Ellirri and Urien exchanged a quick glance. Softly, Ellirri

said, "I'm not sure that's such a good idea, Gwydion."

Gwydion was startled. "Why not?" He was pretty sure that Olwen would never actually like him, but he thought she had gotten over what happened between them long ago.

"Well, you see—" Ellirri broke off, blushing hotly.

"What my wife's trying to say is that you won't be welcomed there," Urien said bluntly. "Because Olwen's a dumb, stubborn bitch."

"What my husband's trying to say, Gwydion, is that Queen Olwen is a bit angry with you," Ellirri broke in.

Gwydion sighed. Getting the story out of these two was like pulling teeth. Again, he asked, "But why?"

"Kilwch's death," Urien said succinctly.

Kilwch had been Queen Olwen's husband and Urien's brother. He had died while swimming in the ocean two years ago when a treacherous undertow had swept him away.

Gwydion gritted his teeth. "And still, I am in the dark. What have I got to do with Kilwch's death? Surely she doesn't think that I had anything to do with it?"

"That's just the problem," Urien rumbled. "She's angry because you let it happen. She says you must have dreamed of it, but did nothing. She says you wanted Kilwch to die, because you were jealous. She says you perch yourself in Caer Dathyl like some poisonous spider and spin your webs all over Kymru. She says—"

"I think Gwydion gets the gist of it, dear," Ellirri interrupted.

"But, but, that's ridiculous," Gwydion sputtered. "Even if I had dreamed Kilwch's death I couldn't have prevented it, no matter what I did. Surely she knows that."

"Hard to tell what she really knows, Gwydion," Urien

said. "I tell you Olwen's become unhinged by my brother's death. She's a cold, hard woman—like her sister, Ygraine—who never forgets an injury. At least, that's what I say. Ellirri here, though, says it's more complicated than that. She's probably right. She knows things like that."

Gwydion turned to Ellirri. "Well?" he asked. "What do you think?"

"I think," Ellirri said quietly, "that Kilwch was a good husband—kind, and loving. Olwen undervalued him every day of their marriage, and I think she's regretted that since the day he died. And so, she has to blame someone. And that someone is you."

"She'll have to stand in line then," Gwydion said lightly. "There are a lot of people ahead of her who blame me for their problems." Although he smiled when he said it, Ellirri laid her hand on his arm in silent sympathy. Her kindness caught him off guard and, for a moment, his throat tightened. He cleared his throat. "Well, I'll just have to deal with her the best I can. I need to go there."

"Good luck," Urien said cheerfully. "You'll need it."

THE GREAT HALL that night was warm with light and cheerful laughter. The fire glowed in the huge fireplace, turning the banner above it of a horse, outlined in opals and gold, into a shape of living flame.

The King's table on the dais was a large one in order to accommodate his family and the chief officers of his court. Gwydion sat now at Uthyr's right and on Gwydion's right sat Sabrina ur Dadweir, Urien's Druid. She was a raven-haired, blue-eyed beauty. If she had shown the slightest interest in him, Gwydion would have gladly reciprocated—for the night, anyway. But she did not. They chatted amicably together, but that was all.

Young Owein sat next to Sabrina. Owein was quiet, but though he rarely spoke he listened attentively to everyone. Bledri sat on Owein's right and the boy's occasional glances at the King's Dewin spoke volumes of dislike.

Just now Bledri was regaling young Enid with an amusing story. Enid hung breathlessly on his every word with a young girl's infatuation shining in her blue eyes.

Breaking off in the middle of his story to Enid, Bledri leaned forward across the table and turned toward Gwydion. The gray eyes in his handsome face were alight with mischief. "Tell me, Gwydion ap Awst, do you know the story of Cadwallon and Caradoc?"

"I do," Gwydion replied mildly, wondering what Bledri was up to. Cadwallon and Caradoc had been twins, the sons of the first King of Rheged. The younger twin's jealousy of his older brother had almost ruined the kingdom.

"An old and far too familiar tale, don't you think?" Bledri said smiling, but his eyes cut to Owein on his left. "Two brothers, and the younger madly jealous of the older. Jealous enough of his older brother to want to kill him and take his place as King." Bledri shook his head in mock dismay. "Such a shame. What happens to brotherly love in such a situation, eh? Oh, but I am forgetting. Perhaps Owein could tell us about that."

Owein stiffened, his eyes shooting daggers at the smiling Bledri. Sabrina, too, had stiffened at Bledri's taunt, and even Enid's smile faded.

"What do you mean by that?" Owein said sharply.

"Why, nothing to be upset about," Bledri said smoothly.

"Your elder brother is heir, and we all know you love your brother. But such a situation can be difficult. I thought that perhaps you could tell us how you yourself avoid feelings of rancor. For we know you do, don't we?"

Owein flushed and his hand darted to his dagger. Suddenly, Sabrina said artlessly, "Oh. That reminds me of something that I heard the other day. It seems that there was this wise woman who had a cat . . ." She launched into a long and rambling tale about a mischievous feline who had drunk an untended potion made by his mistress, rendering the cat invisible. By the time she was done the tension had eased, although Bledri still had a sardonic smile on his handsome face.

"Owein," Urien called out from farther down the table.

"Yes, Da?" Owein answered his voice calm, though his face was still flushed.

"Better start packing, boy," Urien said cheerfully.

"Where am I going?"

Ellirri leaned forward and announced, "Elphin and Owein—Trystan will be taking you to Arberth to visit King Rhoram's court."

Across the table Esyllt, the King's Bard, frowned. "Madam," she said in her low, musical tones, "I think I should go, too." Trystan's eyes brightened, and March, Esyllt's husband, looked up quickly. He said nothing, but protest was visible in every line of his stocky, heavy frame.

"I think not, Esyllt," Ellirri replied. Although the comment was made gently, it was obvious that the matter was not open to further discussion.

But Esyllt tried again, anyway. "But madam, I think that—"

"I'm sure you do, my dear," Ellirri interjected smoothly.

"Nevertheless you shall stay here. Sabrina, I believe it is time to begin the festival."

Sabrina nodded and rose. Her blue eyes glistened momentarily as she took in Esyllt's flushed face, March's relief, and Trystan's disappointed scowl.

As the folk in the Great Hall began to file out behind Sabrina, Gwydion caught Ellirri's arm. "What was that all about?" he whispered, nodding to Esyllt who was leaving arm in arm with her husband. Trystan followed closely behind, his face tight.

"Trystan needs to concentrate on protecting my sons, Gwydion," Ellirri said sharply. "With Esyllt along he'd have eyes for no one but her."

"I don't get it. Why doesn't she just divorce March? Trystan's in love with her and she's in love with him."

"Are you so sure about that? I'm not. And neither, I think, is Trystan."

"Women," Gwydion spat, putting a world of scorn into the word. "They get hold of a man and ruin them, if they can."

"Don't be foolish," Ellirri said sharply. "You forget. For every woman who treats a man like a dog, there is a man who will let her."

GWYDION STOOD NEXT to Ellirri and Trystan in Nemed Draenenwen, the sacred grove of hawthorn trees. Many hundreds of folk from the city were gathered here to celebrate Alban Haf, the festival honoring Modron, the Great Mother.

Trystan stood on Gwydion's right, while Esyllt stood some paces away, next to her husband. Trystan shot glance after glance at Esyllt, as though waiting for something, but she stood quietly, not daring to raise her eyes.

The moon was full shining through the delicate white flowers that covered the trees. An unlit bonfire of holly and oak was laid out in the middle of the grove. A stone altar stood at the eastern end of the clearing. Two golden bowls studded with opals, one full of grains and another filled with sprigs of vervain, were laid on top of the stone. Eight unlit torches had been placed around the altar where Sabrina now stood. Lifting her hands, she began the ritual.

"This is the Wheel of the Year before us. One torch for each of the eight festivals in which we honor the Shining Ones," she intoned solemnly. As she pointed to each torch, they in turn burst into flame. "Calan Olau, Alban Nerth, Calan Gaef, Alban Nos, Calan Morynion, Alban Awyr, Calan Llachar, and Alban Haf, which we celebrate tonight. We gather here to honor Modron, the Great Mother of All. She who gives life to all, she who gives us the Earth's bounty."

As one the crowd responded, "We honor her."

"Let the Shining Ones be honored as they gather to watch the great battle of the champions. Taran, King of the Winds and Mabon, King of Fire. Nantsovelta, Lady of the Waters. Annwyn, Lord of Chaos and Aertan, Weaver of Fate. Cerridwen, Queen of the Wood and Cerrunnos, Master of the Hunt. Y Rhyfelwr, Agrona and Camulos, the Warrior Twins. Sirona, Lady of the Stars and Grannos, Star of the North and Healer."

Again, the crowd responded, "We honor the Shining Ones."

Enid, her face flushed with pride, began her part in the festival. "Why is this the longest day of the year?" she asked.

Sabrina answered, "This is the day when Mabon, King of Fire, Lord of the Sun, tarries in his journey across the sky to watch the champions of Modron and Aertan fight to unleash the bounty of the Earth."

"Why do they fight?" Enid continued.

"Behold, Modron struggles to bring forth the fruits of the land. She seeks to give birth to the bounty of summer. But she must have vervain to aid her in the birthing. So she sends to Gwlad Yr Haf for the herb, but Aertan, the Weaver of Fate, commands Modron to choose a champion to win the vervain from her."

Enid asked, "Who are the champions that fight for the vervain?"

Sabrina answered, "Modron chooses the Holly King as her champion."

At these words a man entered the grove. He was dressed in red and green and carried a branch of holly. He bowed to the assembly.

"And Aertan chooses the Oak King for the fight," Sabrina continued.

Another man entered, dressed in green and gold, carrying a branch of oak. The two men faced each other, theatrically brandishing their branches. Sabrina went on, "The bounty of the Earth hangs in the balance. The champions begin."

The Holly King and the Oak King fought each other, clashing their branches together in a stylized manner. Then, with a flourish, the Holly King struck the oak branch out of the Oak King's hands. A great shout went up from the crowd and the Holly King lifted his branch over his head in victory.

"Celynnen is victorious!" the Holly King shouted. "The Holly has won! Let the bounty of the Earth come forth."

Sabrina tossed the grains in the golden bowl over the laughing, shouting crowd. "Let vervain, that which Modron has won for us, be given to all." She threw sprigs of vervain, and, as each person caught them, they fastened the sprigs onto their clothing.

Sabrina shouted, "Let the Dance of the Wheel begin!"

Four men and four women each took a torch from around the altar and danced toward the unlit bonfire. They touched the torches to the holly and oak wood and the fire blazed up, bathing the crowd in its golden light. And then they all began to sing,

Quiet is the tall fine wood,
Which the whistle of the wind will not stir.
Green is the plumage of the sheltering wood.
Golden are the growing fields.
Good is the warmth of the grass.
Swarms of bees hum in the sunlight.
Fair white birds fly on high. The days are long,
We dance for joy, at Modron's bounty.

Urien was dancing with his laughing wife around the bonfire. Bledri was partnering young Enid, and Elphin was dancing with Esyllt. Gwydion glanced at Trystan standing beside him. Trystan's face was tight with anger as he watched Esyllt.

Sabrina came up to where he and Trystan stood and Gwydion opened his mouth to ask her to partner him, forgetting that he hated to dance. But instead, she grabbed Trystan's hand and drew him into the circle around the fire, giving him no chance to protest.

She was laughing and smiling up into Trystan's stern face. But though Trystan danced with her, all his attention was on Esyllt, as she danced with Elphin on the other side of the fire. Gwydion looked around and saw March, Esyllt's husband, taking in Trystan's scowling face. March smiled sourly to himself and quietly left the grove.

MEANWHILE, MANY LEAGUES away in Prydyn, Rhiannon returned to the cave beneath the waterfall, her hands full of vervain to use in celebrating the festival of Alban Haf. But Gwen was not there.

Rhiannon muttered angrily to herself. No doubt the child was still exploring the caves. She went to the back of the cave, to the fissure through which Gwen would always go exploring. "Gwenhwyfar," she called. But there was no answer.

For a moment she considered Wind-Riding through the caves in an effort to locate her daughter. But she was tired. She would wait a little longer. She turned to the cold hearth where a fire should have been burning. Shaking her head in exasperation, she lit the fire herself, and began preparing the evening meal.

GWEN FOUND HERSELF in the most beautiful cave she had ever seen. She lifted her torch high, awestruck. The torchlight glittered off crystal-covered walls. It seemed as though the cave itself was on fire. Oh, if only she could bring her mother here to see this. Suddenly, it struck her. It was late. She should have been back by now, but she had lost track of time. Her mother would be angry. Maybe if she ran back the whole way she would get home before her mother did.

Quickly she turned and started to run. Although she had traveled far, she knew her location and ran confidently through the dizzying series of caves, competently skirting the occasional ruts that lay in her path.

But she was running too fast. She tripped over a stone and her torch went flying. She landed heavily, all her breath knocked out of her by her fall. She sat up and tried to get her breath back. Suddenly, she was aware of how dark it was. What had happened to her torch? It must have been extinguished when she fell.

She froze where she sat, trying to orient herself. How far away from home was she? How could she find her way back? When she went exploring she left a trail of tiny white stones in her wake. But without the torch, how could she see them?

If only she knew how to call fire. Psychokinesis was one of her gifts, but she still did not know how to use it. But her other gift was clairvoyance. She could use that gift to Wind-Ride to her mother, and Rhiannon would find her and help her get home.

But the dark pressed in on her so. She tried to be calm. She must be calm, for how else could she Wind-Ride to her mother? How else could she get home if her mother did not find her?

Slowly, she got to her feet. She forced herself to breathe deeply. Calm. She must be calm. And she would be calm—if only she didn't have the feeling that there were things in the dark that were ready to reach out and grab her, pull her down. Dirt would clog her lungs; she would never breathe the air again. She would die here and hidden horrors would feed on her bones.

Suddenly she began to cry in her panic. "Mam," she sobbed. "Mam." Her mother would never find her. She would be trapped here under the Earth forever and ever. The dark would take her and feed on her. She would never get out of here.

She must get home! In panic, she started to run, sobbing as she ran. But she had only run a few yards when the earth crumbled beneath her feet, and she began to fall. She clutched wildly at the air to stop her fall, but it was no use. As she slid down to the bottom of the pit, she screamed in fear and despair. And then the earth covered her and she knew no more.

RHIANNON WAS TRULY worried now. Gwen should have been back long ago. She lit one of the torches and made her way back to the fissure. On an impulse she grabbed a length of rope. Taking a deep breath, she ventured into the heart of the earth.

As she walked the torchlight played on the walls, chasing the shadows round and round. She called out Gwen's name, but could hear only echoes.

Gwen had told her once that she never got lost, because she always marked her way with tiny white stones she carried in her pocket. Rhiannon followed the stones that were laid out on the floor every few feet through the bevy of caves.

"Gwen," she called again. "Gwen, Gwen," the echoes mocked her. Cautiously, she made her way around a pit in the cave floor and continued on her way.

And then she heard it. She stopped where she was and listened. There it was again. A sob. Weirdly distorted by the echoes she could not tell where it was coming from. She went on, following the stones. And the sound came closer. "Gwen," she called again. Quickly now she followed the sound until she came to another pit. Sinking to the ground beside it, she lowered her torch. And saw her daughter's beloved, dirt-streaked face far below.

"Mam, Mam," Gwen sobbed, extending her arms for her mother.

"Yes, yes. I'm here," she said in her most soothing tones. "Hush, little one. I'll soon have you out."

She worked quickly; tying the rope around a tall, heavy stone, testing to be sure the stone would bear the weight. She threw the other end of the rope down to her daughter. "Tie this around you, under your arms."

Still sobbing, Gwen did as she was told, and Rhiannon pulled hard at the rope. Hand over hand she pulled her daughter up from the pit. At last, Gwen was out. Rhiannon held her as Gwen sobbed hysterically.

"I fell. The torch went out. And I couldn't find the way. So I ran and I fell into the pit. And the dirt covered me and I couldn't breathe. And I clawed my way out until I could breathe, but I couldn't get out of the pit. I thought I would die there. I thought you would never come."

Rhiannon held Gwen and gently stroked her hair. "All right, little one. It's all right. I'm here now." She helped Gwen to her feet, untied the rope, and grabbed the torch. "Let's get back home. We'll clean you up and eat, and you'll feel better."

They slowly made their way back through the caves, Gwen holding tightly to her mother's hand. "And next time you go exploring you'll take two torches, just in case." Rhiannon said soothingly. "It won't happen again."

"No," Gwen sobbed. "Never again, because I'll never come back. I won't ever be trapped again."

"Gwen, you love the caves!"

"No," Gwen repeated. "Never, never again."

Chapter
Thirteen

Meirgdydd, Lleihau Wythnos—early afternoon

Gwydion stayed in Rheged for another three weeks, spending his time with Urien and Ellirri and their children. He had never been a part of a happy family before, and he found himself fascinated. He sat with them in the evenings as Elphin helped Rhiwallon make a new bow; as Queen Ellirri assisted Enid in stitching a new dress; as Owein carved tiny wooden stags and boars and horses for gifts that he presented to his family. One evening Owein even carved a raven, the symbol of the Dreamers, and gave it to Gwydion.

At last he forced himself to leave and resumed his journey, traveling north. When he passed into Ederynion the landscape changed. Ederynion was a country of forests and sea and fog. The kingdom produced paper from those extensive forests, prized throughout Kymru for its fineness. But more importantly, Ederynion was known for its beautiful glass works. The sandy beaches provided the fine sand to make glass goblets and beakers, glass windows, and delicate glass bottles for perfume.

As he rode he often mused on just what kind of reception he could expect in Dinmael, the Queen's capital. Years ago he and Olwen had met at the graduation ceremonies at Neuadd Gorsedd. Olwen had been there to represent her father. Gwydion had been finishing up his studies at the college, preparing to journey back to Caer Dathyl to continue under Dinaswyn's tutelage. The two had become lovers. He recalled that Olwen had been insatiable, a passionate and stirring bedroom partner.

It had been a glorious few days. But that was all it had been. She had actually expected him to return with her to Ederynion. But he was destined to be the Dreamer, and, while he would have been pleased to continue as Olwen's sometime lover, he refused to go with her. Olwen had been used to having her own way in all things and they had parted badly. But that had been almost twenty years ago. It astonished him that she could hold on to a grudge for so long. You almost had to admire such tenacity, he thought.

As he neared Dinmael the salty air blew fresh against his face and he heard the pounding of the waves against the rocks. Dinmael was at the northern tip of a peninsula, surrounded by the sea to the east and north.

The city itself was built in the shape of a pentagon to honor Nantsovelta, Queen of the Moon and Lady of the Waters. He rode through the southern gate and passed Nemed Aethnen, the sacred grove. Tomorrow the festival of Calan Olau, to honor Mabon of the Sun, would be celebrated there. The aspen trees shivered as he rode by. He rode past Ty Meirw, the brooding standing stones under which the Rulers of Ederynion were buried.

Soon, too soon to suit him in his present mood, he rode up to the gate of the Queen's fortress. The iron gate was covered in silver. A graceful white swan, outlined in pearls, was carved into the doors. Her wings were outstretched and her emerald eyes glittered balefully at him as he rode through.

A tall, slender woman with an unmistakable air of command halted him as soon as he was through the gate. Angharad, Queen Olwen's Captain, the PenAethnen of Ederynion, wore sea green breeches tucked into white boots and a white undershirt beneath a sea green tunic. Her flaming red hair was braided into a crown at the top of her head. Her cheekbones were high and proud beneath light green eyes.

"Gwydion ap Awst, Dreamer of Kymru," she said, her voice low and musical. "I bid you welcome to Dinmael on behalf of Olwen ur Custennin, Queen of Ederynion."

"You are very formal, Angharad," Gwydion replied, smiling. "Is this how you greet your friends?"

"No," she said steadily. She refused to meet his gaze and crisply signaled for a groom to take his horse and for another servant to take his saddlebags. "You are to come with me. The Queen awaits you in her chambers." Angharad turned then, signaling for Gwydion to follow.

"Angharad, what is this? What's happened here?"

In a low voice, she continued, "Do as I bid you, Gwydion. I am under orders. Follow me and ask no more questions. I will come to you and explain when I can." She marched off stiffly, Gwydion following.

As they came to the door of the ystafell, Angharad ushered him inside. When he first entered the room he was momentarily blinded, for the room was dim and the afternoon sun was bright outside. As his eyes adjusted, he noted that there was a bright green banner on the wall to his right, show-ing a white swan with outstretched wings stitched in silver and pearls. The thick carpet beneath his feet was woven of strips of sea green and white. Open cabinets lined the walls, filled with delicate glass works—colored goblets, plates rimmed with silver, graceful beakers, tiny bottles studded with jewels.

In a straight back chair before the hearth sat a young girl, no more than sixteen years of age. She had auburn hair and deep blue eyes. She wore a gown of sea green and around her throat she wore a silver chain with a single pearl dangling from it. This, without a doubt, was Elen ur Olwen, the Queen's daughter and heir.

Queen Olwen sat stiffly upright in a chair canopied in white and sea green, stitched with pearls. Olwen wore a gown of white. There were pearls in her rich, auburn hair, woven within a net of sea green ribbons. Around her neck she wore the royal Torque of Ederynion—an imposing necklace of silver and pearls. A large pearl ring glowed softly on her right hand. Her amber eyes studied him coldly.

A man stood in the dim shadows behind the Queen's chair. He had a proud and haughty face with dark brown hair and glittering brown eyes. Gwydion thought he looked familiar, but could not instantly place the man. Angharad had taken up a position next to Gwydion, between him and the door.

For a moment all was silent as Gwydion waited for Olwen to speak. At last she spoke her voice cold and hard. "Gwydion ap Awst, Dreamer of Kymru, what is your business here?"

No welcome, no gesture to sit down, no offer of food or drink. And he was tired. Remembering that Olwen despised familiarity, Gwydion smiled brilliantly and replied with feigned enthusiasm. "Ah, Olwen. I came because I knew I would find warmth and solace here in your presence. I could not stay away, for I longed for another glimpse of your kind and beautiful face. It has been too long."

Next to him a choked sound, quickly cut off, told him what Angharad thought of his inane speech. He went on blithely, "And I heard how beautiful young Elen herself had become, the very image of her mother. And I see now that it is true." He gave Elen a languishing glance and a graceful bow that made her sit up more stiffly than ever—and brought a touch of color to her pale face.

"Do you take the Queen for a fool?" the man behind Olwen's chair hissed.

"Ah, you have the advantage of me, I fear," Gwydion said in a jocular tone. "I cannot place you. But it's so hard to see you, hiding behind the Queen."

"Oh, gods," Angharad whispered so only Gwydion could hear. "You've done it now." And young Elen, surprisingly, smothered a smile behind her hand.

The man stepped out from behind the chair and stood in front of Gwydion. He wore a robe of sea green trimmed in silver, which proclaimed him to be Dewin. "I am Llwyd Cilcoed, brother of Alun Cilcoed, the Lord of Arystli."

"Ah, yes," Gwydion said. "I recall you, now, for one of the graduation ceremonies I attended at Y Ty Dewin. You were but a journeyman, then."

"Now I am the Dewin to Rheidden Arwy, the Gwarda of commote Caerinion."

"Oh," Gwydion said politely. "Why aren't you there then?"

Again, there was another choked sound from Angharad. But the Queen had not moved. Her face remained impassive and remote. "Gwydion ap Awst," Olwen spoke again. "I have asked you a question. Why are you here?"

"Have I come at a bad time?" he asked innocently.

Olwen rose slowly, like a snake uncoiling. Tall and proud she stood before him, pining him with her gaze. "You are not welcome here in my country. Did you not know this?"

"I did not," he lied promptly. "For what reason?"

"My husband is dead," she said flatly. "You saw his death in your dreams but you did nothing."

"There was nothing I could do, Olwen," he said mildly. "I do not choose my dreams. And the dreams I have are unchangeable."

"You lie!"

"Someone has lied to you," he said calmly, his eyes flickering to Llwyd Cilcoed, "if they told you I could have prevented his death. I could not."

"And I say you lie," she hissed. "I say you killed him. Out of spite."

"Out of spite for what?"

"He was my husband."

"Olwen," he said wearily, for he tired of this game, "if I had wanted that job, I would have taken it some time ago. But I didn't, did I?"

The Queen flushed in rage. "You are to leave my country, now."

In truth, he knew it would be best to leave Dinmael. But Gwydion did not like being told what to do. "I am the Dreamer," he said calmly but implacably. "And the festival of Calan Olau, which honors Mabon of the Sun, is tomorrow. I claim my right as Dreamer to lead the festival."

Olwen opened her mouth to refuse permission. But she obviously thought better of it, for under the law, Gwydion did have the right. Finally, between gritted teeth, she said, "You will stay and lead the festival. Then you are to go. Is that understood?"

Gwydion bowed. "Very well."

"Angharad," Olwen continued, "you will see to it that the Dreamer stays out of my sight until the festival. Then you will see to it that he leaves immediately afterward."

"I will, my Queen," Angharad bowed.

"Go now," Olwen ordered Gwydion. She turned away and took her place on her chair. "Why are you still here?" she asked Gwydion as she seated herself.

Gwydion opened his mouth for a reply that would have done him no credit, but Angharad caught his arm and dragged him from the room, slamming the door behind her.

"You idiot," she fumed, as they crossed the courtyard. "Go to the guest house. The steward has assigned a special room for you, at my request. There will be a guard outside your door. Stay there until I come." She signaled to a warrior, who joined them. "This is Emrys ap Naw. He is my lieutenant. And your guard." She turned to the young man, who was looking at Angharad with worship in his eyes, worship that she apparently did not see. "Take him to his room. And make sure he stays there."

THE ROOM WAS small and the furnishings were plain. There were no windows.

A narrow bed with a plain, brown woolen blanket stood in the far, left corner of the room. A large, oak wardrobe was wedged into the corner next to the door. The floor was bare.

Although Gwydion could use his psychokinesis and other gifts to leave this room whenever he truly wished, he stayed here. He wanted to hear what Angharad would have to say to him. So he waited as patiently as he could.

A scraping sound coming from the wardrobe alerted him that he would soon have company. He had noticed the secret catch in the back of the wardrobe hours ago. The door of the wardrobe opened and Angharad entered, followed by a man and a woman.

The man was of medium height with brown hair, lightly powered gray at the temples. He had a genial smile and blue eyes. He was dressed in blue and white and wore the Bard's torque.

The woman had long, dark brown hair that hung loosely about her shoulders. She wore the formal robe of the Dewin, sea green trimmed with silver, and her Dewin's torque. Her light brown eyes were wary as she regarded him.

The Bard took a seat nonchalantly on the bed, and patted the place beside him. "Sit here, my dear," he said to the woman. "It's safe—I'm old enough to be your father."

The woman smiled. "Except that my father's not so handsome," she teased, as she settled herself next to him. Angharad took up a position next to the door.

"I believe you know everyone here?" Angharad said dryly.

Gwydion bowed, "Talhearn ap Coleas, the Queen's Bard and Regan ur Corfil, the Queen's Dewin. Or, the Queen's official Dewin at any rate. I fear you have competition. I met him this afternoon."

"Gwydion ap Awst," Regan asked frowning, "why have you come here?"

"Everyone keeps asking me that," he complained. "But I have some questions for you. Such as why the Queen's Bard, Dewin, and Captain have to sneak into my room to speak to me. Why there is a guard outside my door. That sort of thing."

"Gwydion," Angharad said wearily, "You heard the Queen's command. You are to stay out of her sight until the festival. You are the one who insisted on staying."

"You've seen Llwyd Cilcoed. I assume you noticed the kind of hold he has over the Queen?" Talhearn asked.

"Ah, yes. I did notice, thank you."

"Llwyd Cilcoed is making things difficult here for everyone," Regan said. "As the Queen's lover, he has some power, but it's not enough for him. He seeks to undermine Olwen's trust in each of us that he may be the only one to hold sway with her. But the Master Bard has told Talhearn, and I have been told by my Ardewin to give you whatever aid you need in your task. Thus we must speak to you, but only in private, so that Llwyd Cilcoed does not get wind of it and misrepresent us to Olwen."

"Don't make a mistake, here, Gwydion," Angharad warned. "These two, as well as Iago, our Druid, will support you in any way they can. But they will not go against Olwen's express orders. Nor will I. We are loyal to our Queen—not to you."

"By the way," Talhearn said curiously, before Gwydion could respond, "What exactly is your task?"

Gwydion sighed. "I'm looking for Rhiannon ur Hefeydd."

"Have you tried asking Dudod?" Talhearn asked.

"Anieron has sent for him. Do you really think he knows?"

"Oh, yes. The only trick will be in persuading Dudod to tell you."

"I'm hoping that Anieron's taking care of that. I also need Olwen to lend me your aid, Angharad."

"Aid with what?" she asked, suspiciously.

"I cannot say at this time."

"She'll never agree," Regan said.

"I think she will," Gwydion replied confidently.

"Gwydion," Angharad said abruptly, "Is there nothing that will get you to leave?"

"Angharad, I won't be hustled out of Dinmael and that's that."

Regan turned to Angharad. "Is he always this stupid?" she asked.

"He's a man, Regan. They are all that stupid," Angharad replied.

"Does this mean you don't want to stay the night?" Gwydion inquired innocently.

"Ha, ha," Angharad said flatly.

"I'm beginning to think you don't like me anymore. There was a time—"

"Now you listen to me, Gwydion ap Awst. You will stay here until the festival tomorrow night. You are not to leave this room unless I am with you." Angharad jerked her head at Talhearn and Regan. "Come on."

As they piled into the wardrobe and out through the hidden door, Gwydion halted Angharad. "You sure you won't stay?" he asked with a grin.

"Good night," she said flatly, but Gwydion thought he saw her hide a smile.

Calan Olau—evening

THE NEXT EVENING Angharad returned to take him to the festival. Silently she motioned for him to follow. Her lieutenant, Emrys, fell in behind him. As they walked out of the gates and down the road to the grove, Regan and Talhearn, each carrying a torch, joined them, one on each side of Gwydion. It was Tywyllu, the week of the new moon, so the night was especially dark and the stars shone overhead like diamonds, cold and hard.

They were silent as they walked. Like ghosts, like shadows, they made their way through the aspen trees into the huge clearing in the center of the grove.

The clearing was full, with hundreds of people waiting to celebrate the festival. An unlit bonfire made of rowan wood was laid out in the center. At the north end stood a large stone altar, on its surface a silver platter holding a loaf of bread and a small mother-of-pearl bowl filled with grain. Around the altar eight unlit torches were set in brackets.

As Gwydion made his way to the altar he saw that Iago, the Queen's Druid, was standing behind it, waiting for him. Iago was dressed in the Druid's robe of dark brown trimmed in green. His long, black hair was held at the nape of his neck by a golden ring. His huge, dark eyes glittered as he looked at Gwydion. Solemnly, he drew back and let Gwydion take his place behind the altar.

Off to one side the Queen stood magnificently attired in sea green and pearls. Her face was cold and unyielding. Llwyd Cilcoed stood next to her, a sneer on his face.

On the Queen's left her daughter, Elen, stood. Dressed in a white gown Elen shone like a luminous candle. Her auburn hair was woven with sea green ribbons and pearls dangled from her delicate ears. A younger boy, about fourteen years old, stood protectively behind Elen. Gwydion knew that this was Lludd, Elen's younger brother. The boy was tall and broad for his age, and stoicism sat ill on his good-natured features.

Angharad, Emrys, Regan and Talhearn had taken up places near the altar and Gwydion lifted his hands and gestured to the unlit torches. "This is the Wheel of the Year before us," he intoned. "One torch for each of the eight festivals when we honor the Shining Ones." As he pointed to each torch it burst into flame. "Alban Nerth, Calan Gaef, Alban Nos, Calan Morynion, Alban Awyr, Calan Llachar, Alban Haf, and Calan Olau, which we celebrate tonight."

After the torches were lit Gwydion continued, "We gather here to honor Mabon of the Sun, King of Fire, who brings the harvest to Kymru."

As one the crowd chanted, "We honor him."

"Let the Shining Ones be honored as they gather honor the giver of the harvest," Gwydion said. "Taran, King of the Winds and Modron, Great Mother of All. Nantsovelta, Lady of the Waters. Annwyn, Lord of Chaos and Aertan, Weaver of Fate. Cerridwen, Queen of the Wood and Cerrunnos, Master of the Hunt. Y Rhyfelwr, Agrona and Camulos, the Warrior Twins. Sirona, Lady of the Stars and Grannos, Star of the North and Healer."

"We honor the Shining Ones," the crowd responded.

Lludd stepped forward to speak his part in the ritual. "Why do we gather here?"

Gwydion replied, "We gather to honor Mabon. For behold, he has gone to the depths of Gwlad Yr Haf and returns with the harvest in his hands."

Then Gwydion began the chant, "In the long night of the year—"

"The land was bare and cold," the crowd intoned.

"In the dawn of the year—" Gwydion continued.

"Buds burst upon the trees, shoots sprouted from the

ground," they replied.

"In the noon of the year—"

"Flowers bloomed, grain grew, the land was fruitful."

"Now is the time of harvest. Ripened fruit falls into our hands. The golden wheat falls beneath the scythe. For Mabon has returned victorious," Gwydion finished.

He raised the bowl of grain and cried, "Behold, the grain that Mabon has given." He came out from behind the altar, followed closely by Iago, and made his way to the unlit fire of rowan wood.

Iago lit the wood with Druid's Fire and Gwydion tossed the grain into the fire and said, "The light of Mabon, King of Fire, shines on us at night. The light of Mabon, Lord of the Sun, shines on us by day."

Returning to the altar, Gwydion held up the loaf of bread. As he did so, loaves were distributed throughout the grove. When everyone had a piece of bread, Gwydion said, "From Mabon comes our bread." He tore off a piece and ate it, gesturing for the people to do the same. "All hail Mabon!" he cried.

Around the blazing fire people began to dance, singing the ritual song.

Greetings to you, sun of the seasons,
As you travel the skies on high,
With your strong steps on the wing of the heights,
Victorious hero, bringer of harvest.
Sweet acorns cover the woods,
The hard ground is covered with heavy fruit.
Grain has ripened golden.
Greetings to Mabon, bringer of the harvest.

Gwydion turned to Iago, to thank him for his aid in the ritual. His back was to the surrounding trees, so he was completely unprepared for what came next.

Iago gave a shout and pushed Gwydion to the ground. Out of the corner of his eye Gwydion saw the flash of firelight on a knife that flew from the trees toward the place where he had been standing a moment before. With a gesture Iago Shape-Moved the knife, stopping it in mid-air, causing it to fall harmlessly to the ground.

Gwydion, lying prone on the ground, suddenly seemed to be surrounded. Prince Lludd, Princess Elen, Talhearn, and Regan clustered around him to offer further protection from peril. Angharad and Emrys plunged into the trees after the assassin.

Iago reached down and helped Gwydion to his feet.

"My thanks, Iago," Gwydion said shakily. "You saved my life."

"My Archdruid has given me orders to give you any aid I can," Iago said modestly. "I am glad to have been of service to you."

"Well done, Iago," Princess Elen said with a smile.

Iago flushed, but did not reply. But his heart in his eyes as he looked at the young and beautiful heir of Ederynion.

At that moment Olwen, followed closely by Llwyd, imperiously made her way up to Gwydion. The people around him fell silent.

"What happened here?" the Queen demanded.

"Someone tried to kill the Dreamer," Talhearn said. "Tried to kill him in our own sacred grove."

"Angharad and Emrys went after him," Elen volunteered. "I hope that they catch him."

In this hope Elen was not disappointed. For just then Angharad and Emrys returned to the grove, each holding the arm of a man. The man's clothing was nondescript—brown riding leathers and well-worn boots, one with a crack on the heel. Blood dripped slowly from a minor head wound. He had long, greasy hair and a bushy beard.

"Who are you?" Olwen demanded.

But the man refused to answer, simply staring at the Queen. His eyes shifted to Gwydion, and narrowed when he saw the Dreamer was unharmed.

"That's right," Gwydion said softly. "The knife you threw was deflected by the Druid. You have failed your master."

"What is your cenedl?" Olwen demanded. "Who are your kinsmen?"

"My kinsmen know nothing of this," the man said. "And I will not tell you who they are."

"You will tell me," Olwen said, her tone deadly. "Believe that."

"I do believe that I would if I were alive," the man said with a grimace. "But I will not be."

"Stop him!" Gwydion cried as the man broke free of Emrys's grasp. The man brought his hand to his mouth and swallowed something. Angharad and Emrys took him in a fresh hold, Angharad forcing the man to his knees.

"What did you take?" Gwydion demanded as he knelt beside the man. "Tell me!"

"I will tell you," the man rasped. "Because it is too late to help me. It was pennyroyal."

"How much?"

"All that I have. I am a dead man, Dreamer. You will get nothing from me."

"You would kill yourself rather than betray your employer?"

"It was in the terms. I do not make promises I cannot

309

keep." The man gasped and clutched his belly.

Regan also knelt beside the man and put her hand on his forehead. She shook her head. "He's right. He's a dead man."

Even as she said that, the man stiffened and cried out. Then he went limp and slumped to the ground. Angharad gestured and four warriors picked up the would-be assassin's body and left the grove.

"Take him back to the fortress, Angharad," Olwen said coldly, gesturing to Gwydion.

"Yes, my Queen," Angharad bowed.

Olwen turned to Gwydion. "Tomorrow you will be gone from my city. See to it that you make for the border as quickly as possible. I want you out of my kingdom."

Gwydion held up his hand. "My safety, Olwen," he said coldly, "was in your hands. Yet I almost died tonight while under your protection."

Olwen flushed but did not answer, for she knew the truth of that statement.

"You owe me a boon."

"Name it," she said between gritted teeth.

"Your Captain, the PenAethnen, must journey to Caer Dathyl. She must be there by Suldydd, Cynyddu Wythnos, Ysgawen Mis."

"Very well," Olwen said stiffly.

Llwyd Cilcoed's face darkened. "My love, surely you don't mean to do as he wishes."

"It is the law," Olwen said shortly. "The safety of the Dreamer as my guest was compromised. He is within his rights to ask me for a boon. Go now, Gwydion ap Awst. I trust we will not meet again." So saying she stalked off, with Llwyd close behind.

"Come, Gwydion," Angharad said sternly. "You've caused enough trouble for one evening."

Gwydion bowed to Iago. "My thanks for saving my life. If there is anything I can do in return, you may call on me."

Iago, Angharad, Emrys, and Talhearn escorted Gwydion back to the fortress.

When they returned to him room, Angharad said, "I'm locking you in for the night, Gwydion. Both Emrys and I will be right outside your door. Iago, keep an eye on that secret entrance from Gwydion's room. Have Talhearn stay up with you to watch. I don't think there is another assassin here, but it's better to be safe than sorry."

"Yes, Angharad," Iago said. "Good night, Gwydion."

"Good night, Iago. And thank you."

Angharad left, with Emrys right behind her. Gwydion got up from the bed and sat in front of the fire. Disdaining the chair, he huddled upon the hearth, watching the crackling flames. He held his hand out to the fire and did not flinch. For he had taught himself not to do that long ago.

He was psychokinetic and therefore could Fire-Weave, and he often did this elaborately, making a game of it. A necessary game, for, he thought bitterly, how people would laugh at him if they ever found out that the great Dreamer was afraid of fire.

He thought back then, remembering it all as if it had just happened yesterday, instead of years ago. He thought of the last time he almost died—the time when he would have died, if not for Uthyr.

GWYDION AP AWST, the future Dreamer of Kymru, rode nervously on his pony. He was a solemn boy of six years, thin and frail. He despaired of ever becoming as strong and handsome as his father. Awst rode next to him now, laughing and calling out greetings to the people he knew, as they rode down the streets of Tegeingl. They were very close to the fortress of Queen Rathtyen. Gwydion was so nervous he could barely swallow.

He had never met the Queen. And, he had never been out of Caer Dathyl on a trip with his father. His mother had always made sure of that. Of course, his mother had objected strenuously when Awst came to Caer Dathyl to take Gwydion away on this trip. But for once, his mother's objections hadn't done any good. Awst had been determined to have his way. Best of all, Gwydion had Awst all to himself, for Amatheon had been far too young to make the trip.

Gwydion worshipped his father, and had been euphoric at the prospect of traveling with him. But he was less happy about their destination. He didn't think that he wanted to meet Queen Rathtyen. His mother had told him that the Queen was a wicked woman, that she had stolen Gwydion's father and that was why Awst never came home. She even said that Awst and the Queen had a son—a boy named Uthyr that Awst loved more than he loved Gwydion or Amatheon. His mother even said that the Queen loved Uthyr more than her legitimate children by her husband, King Rhodri, and that was why she made Uthyr her heir instead of her other son, Madoc.

But on their trip Awst had explained very gently that his mother was mistaken. He had explained that he and the Queen were very good friends. It was true that he and the Queen had a son, but Awst loved all his sons equally. It was true that Uthyr was her heir, and that was indeed unusual. But Uthyr had been tested and was not Y Dawnus, and he was the firstborn son of the Queen. The will of the Shining Ones was to be accepted, not questioned.

But Gwydion was frightened now. What if his mother was right? What if Awst did love this other son more? Then what would he do? The gates of the Queen's fortress seemed to loom over the small, frightened boy. The sapphire eyes of the fierce hawk carved upon the closed gates glittered ominously at him.

Slowly, the gates swung open. A woman with rich reddish brown hair and kind blue eyes came forward. She was dressed in a gown of blue and a silver torque, studded with sapphires, hung around her slender neck. The woman smiled into Gwydion's apprehensive eyes, and all his fears seemed to vanish in that instant.

She came up to his pony, followed by many people, but Gwydion had eyes only for her. "Welcome, Gwydion ap Awst, to Tegeingl," she said in a rich, melodious voice.

Quickly Gwydion slid off his pony and bowed. Smiling, she held out her hands to him and raised him to his feet. "I am Rathtyen and I am so glad to meet you at last."

Gwydion gulped audibly. This was the Queen! The Queen herself had greeted him as an honored guest. And he knew then beyond all doubt that all his mother's harsh words about the Queen were lies.

Rathtyen turned to Awst, who had dismounted by then, and the two embraced. She then gestured to the man who stood a small distance behind her. The man was tall, with reddish golden hair and a stiff expression. "This is my husband, Rhodri. And this," she gestured to a young boy, "is my oldest son, Uthyr."

The two boys studied each other. Uthyr was taller and

broader than Gwydion, for he was two years older. He had reddish brown hair and dark eyes. 'You are welcome here, brother," Uthyr said formally. "Do you like to ride?" he went on in a friendly tone.

Shyly, Gwydion nodded.

"I like riding, too. I have a new pony. But he's not as fine as yours," Uthyr said cheerfully.

Gwydion smiled tentatively at his half brother and an answering grin lit up Uthyr's face. And that was the beginning for them of a bond that only death would break.

For the next few days the boys were inseparable. Gwydion met Madoc, the son of the Queen and her husband, Rhodri, but he did not like the boy. There was something sly about him. Madoc was only five and his little sister, Ellirri, was just three. Uthyr was unfailingly kind and patient with Ellirri, and the little girl worshipped her brother, following him everywhere.

The day Ellirri was left behind at the fortress with Madoc she cried and cried. For she was too young to take part in the hunting party. In truth, so was Gwydion, but Awst refused to leave him behind. So they set out—Awst, the Queen, King Rhodri, Uthyr, Gwydion, and many warriors from the Queen's *teulu*. It was a real hunting trip and they would camp out in the forest of Coed Dulas for the night.

They had left early in the morning and reached their campsite by mid-afternoon. In the tumult of setting up camp, Gwydion and Uthyr were able to slip away. They played that they were mighty hunters, stalking their prey through the forest. So intent were they on their game that they strayed far away from camp.

In the middle of stalking through a thicket, Gwydion suddenly said, "Wait a minute. Are we lost?"

"Lost? Of course not," Uthyr replied cheerfully.

"But I don't hear any of the others."

Uthyr stood still and listened hard. From far away they heard the muted roll of thunder. "Uh oh," Uthyr muttered. "Storm. We'd better get back."

"But which way?"

"This way." Uthyr said, with feigned confidence, and they set off. The afternoon grew darker and through the trees they saw storm clouds piling up over the forest.

"We're lost aren't we?" Gwydion finally asked, fighting to keep his voice from trembling.

"Yes," Uthyr replied seriously. "We are. But don't worry. I'll take care of you."

"I'm—I'm not scared."

"Oh, I know that," Uthyr said. He took Gwydion's thin, cold hand into his large, warm one. "Come on. Let's keep walking."

Overhead, thunder rolled and flashes of lightning split the sky. After each flash they were momentarily blinded, and had to halt until they could see again. The wild wind whipped the trees in a manic frenzy. But it did not rain.

Gwydion was horribly frightened. He was lost, and the storm was so fierce. And he was only six years old. At each flash of lightning, at each roll of thunder, he hunched his thin shoulders, and held more tightly to Uthyr's hand.

They took what shelter they could beneath a large, spreading oak tree. Panting, they stopped to get their breath back. A flash of lighting, so bright they had to close their eyes, hit the tree cracking through the air like a whip. With a huge, tearing sound the tree split, and half of it came crashing down. Uthyr jumped out of the way, still holding Gwydion's hand.

But Gwydion did not move fast enough and, as the tree fell, he was trapped beneath the heavy branches. The tree was on fire, blazing up like a torch. Gwydion, blinded by the smoke, and baked by the heat sobbed in terror beneath the branches that pinned him.

And then Uthyr let go of his hand.

But Uthyr did not run. Instead, he grasped the burning trunk and, straining with all his might, he lifted it slightly, just enough to allow Gwydion to crawl out.

Gwydion scrambled away from the tree on his hands and knees, and Uthyr dropped the burning branches, nursing his scorched hands. Gwydion felt a horrible heat, a burning, and a blistering on his back. He leapt up to run but Uthyr, with a cry, jumped on him, beating out the flames that were consuming him.

And then, suddenly, oh blessed relief, their father was there. And the Queen and many others, besides. Awst grabbed both of his sons, hauling them far away from the burning tree. He held them close and hugged them fiercely with tears of relief flowing down his white, drawn face.

"Uthyr," Gwydion sobbed. "Uthyr saved me. I was trapped. The fire—"

"Yes, yes," Awst soothed. "It's all over. You're all right now."

"It burns, Da. It burns," Gwydion moaned.

"I know, I know," Awst replied. "Hush now. You're going to be all right."

"It burns, it burns."

SOMEONE WAS SHAKING him awake. He opened his eyes and blinked, recognizing the face of the man standing over him. It was Dudod, Rhiannon's uncle. His face was lined with weariness. His green eyes were shadowed and subdued.

"Have you come to help me then?" Gwydion slurred, still half asleep.

Dudod smiled sadly. "I have come to take you to her. And may the gods forgive me for what I do."

Chapter Fourteen

Gwaithdydd, Disglair Wythnos—early evening

Gwydion and Dudod left Dinmael early the next morning. Their hasty parting did not seem to break any hearts. Angharad was clearly glad to see him go. Olwen was, for her, ecstatic—she almost smiled.

Dudod had said they were making for Coed Aderyn. "But I went to Coed Aderyn," Gwydion protested. "On my way to Arberth. And I called out to her. But there was no answer."

"No," Dudod replied shortly. "I'm sure there wasn't. But that's where she is, all the same."

They traveled steadily for the next fifteen days. Dudod was silent and withdrawn. During the day he rode ahead of Gwydion, cutting off all chances for conversation. At night Dudod demanded they stop at the nearest farmhouse or village, where they played and sang for their hosts in return for meals and shelter.

On the fifteenth evening, Dudod, reining in his horse, announced, "We're just a few miles away from Rhiannon's place. We'll just camp out tonight and be there first thing in the morning, before she's had a chance to leave the cave."

"She lives in a cave?" Gwydion asked in surprise.

"It's got a waterfall in front of the entrance. If you didn't know it was there you'd never find it."

"How did you find it then?" For the first time Dudod was in a mood to talk about Rhiannon, and Gwydion was quick to take advantage of it.

Dudod dismounted and looked solemnly at Gwydion. Suddenly, he smiled. "You've been very patient, lad. Much more patient than I thought you would be. We'll fix supper, then I'll tell you what you want to know. And give you some advice, which you will doubtless ignore."

Gwydion knew better than to reply. After they had eaten a meal—which Dudod had cooked—they settled down on a convenient log placed before the fire.

"How did you find out where she was?" Gwydion asked. "Did she contact you?"

"No. She doesn't even realize that I know where she is. Once, when Rhiannon was only a little girl, and when my wife was still alive, we traveled to Neuadd Gorsedd to see Elidyr. Rhiannon hoped to catch a glimpse of her father—a forlorn hope, as usual," Dudod said with bitterness. "Anyway, we stopped for an afternoon rest in Coed Aderyn by a tiny lake with a small waterfall. And Rhiannon went exploring and found a cave behind it. After Rhiannon disappeared, I remembered that place. I went there once, many years ago, to be sure. And she was there."

"Did she see you?"

Dudod gave Gwydion an affronted stare. "Are you mad? Nobody sees me if I don't want them to. I," he said with mock dignity, "am an accomplished sneak."

"I'm sure you are. All those years of knowing where she is, and you never let on. And now, I spend months going to every kingdom in Kymru, asking useless questions and getting saddle sores, and you knew where she was all along."

"Do I sense a bit of irritation?"

Gwydion thought about that seriously for a moment. "Actually, no. The trip was useful after all, even if I didn't discover her whereabouts for myself."

For some time the two men were silent, staring into the flames and lost in their own thoughts. At last, Gwydion said, "Years ago I asked you to tell me where Rhiannon was. And you pretended that you didn't know. What made you decide to take me to her now?"

"Anieron. My brother can be very persuasive. That's why he's the Master Bard."

"Anieron may have asked you to do this, but only you decide what you will do. So why did you?"

Dudod sighed. "It was time. For over eleven years Rhiannon has hidden herself and her daughter away. That can't go on forever, and I'm sure Rhiannon knows it. If nothing else, she must return Gwenhwyfar to the outside world. Her refusal to do so is ruining that child's life."

"I could point that out, I suppose." Gwydion mused.

"I wouldn't," Dudod said sharply. "You can't simply descend upon the woman and tell her what to do. You must be gentle. You must appeal to her higher instincts—not to her mistakes."

"But to point out her mistakes would have the merit of being true."

"The more truthful the accusation, the angrier we get.

Don't you know that?"

"So," Gwydion continued, "how do you suggest I handle Rhiannon?"

"Very carefully," Dudod warned. "No accusations. Be sure that you explain yourself. She won't respond to bullying, but she will respond to reason."

"You surprise me there," Gwydion said dryly. "I wouldn't have thought she would respond to reason."

"Why ever not?"

"Well, she's a woman, isn't she?"

Dudod looked at Gwydion for a long time. Finally, he spoke, "Indeed she is. I fear, however, that your experience with a limited number of women has led you astray. They are not all so emotional and irrational."

"You could have fooled me."

"Yes, I imagine you can be easily fooled into seeing only what you expect to see," Dudod said shortly.

"You don't think much of me, do you?"

"You guessed."

Gwydion shrugged. He was used to that. His mind turned instead to the important question on how best to handle Rhiannon. Perhaps he could appeal to her sense of duty. Except that she didn't appear to have any. Yet something Myrrdin had said could help. "Myrrdin says that Rhiannon and I are a great deal alike," he repeated absently.

"Myrrdin is a wise old man. But I am wiser still. I won't even bother to ask you when you talked to him last."

Swiftly, Gwydion raised his keen gray eyes to Dudod's glittering green ones. "Why bother to ask what you already know?"

"Why indeed?"

Meirgdydd, Disglair Wythnos—early morning

DUDOD ROUSED GWYDION early the next morning. After a hasty breakfast they rode into the forest of closely packed trees and lush undergrowth. After a few leagues they reached a large clearing. The forest floor was dotted with wildflowers of glistening white, bright red, deep blue, and lemony yellow. A small waterfall played lightly over a rocky slope and fed into a blue, jewel-like pond. The sunlight turned the drops into tiny diamonds. The water bubbled exuberantly in the bright, clear, summer morning.

"Let me go first," Dudod said in a low tone. He dismounted and, walking up near the waterfall, gave a shout. For a moment nothing happened. Then Rhiannon, dressed in a plain black gown, appeared suddenly from behind the waterfall. With a cry, she hurled herself into Dudod's arms.

As Gwydion worked his way closer, leaving his horse behind the trees, he saw that her long, wavy black hair was unbound, falling below her waist. She was slender and her feet were bare. Her back was to Gwydion as she clung to Dudod and he could not see her face, buried as it was in Dudod's shoulder.

Tears were running down Dudod's face as he gently held Rhiannon to him. "Child," he whispered. "Niece. I missed you so."

"Uncle Dudod, I can't believe you're here. How did you find me?" she wept.

"I knew you'd come back here."

"And you never told anyone," Rhiannon marveled.

"Oh, well, not until very recently."

Rhiannon stepped back from Dudod's arms. "What do

you mean?" she asked sharply. "Who have you told?"

"Ah," he replied, trying to sound casual. "Just one person."

"Who?"

Behind her, Gwydion cleared his throat. As she whipped around, he bowed low. "Gwydion ap Awst, Dreamer of Kymru. And I know how to keep secrets, too, never fear."

She stared at him, the tears of joy drying on her face. Her green eyes were enormous. She had a snub nose, a pointed chin, and, at the moment, a most forbidding expression.

"Why have you done this to me, Uncle?"

"That will take some time to explain. Perhaps we may go up to the cave and sit and talk for a while."

"Yes," Rhiannon said shortly. "Let's do that. By all means, please share the hospitality of one you have betrayed."

"Rhiannon," Dudod pleaded, "just calm down."

"Calm down?" she asked, her voice rising. "You bring that—that schemer to my home, and you tell me to calm down?"

"Yes I do," Dudod replied with some heat. "We have come a long way to speak to you, and with very good reasons. Do you think I would have done this unless I judged it to be of the greatest importance?"

Rhiannon studied Dudod, ignoring Gwydion completely. "I'll be the judge of what's important." She turned back to the waterfall without another word.

They followed her over the rocks and slipped behind the gentle waterfall. Parting a woolen curtain, she led them into her cave. A fire crackled atop the hearth, over which a pot of water steeped in herbs was boiling.

To the left of the entrance were books and a small harp resting upon wooden shelves. "That's Hefeydd's harp," Dudod said in surprise.

"Yes," Rhiannon said shortly.

"Don't play it much, do you?" Gwydion said, taking in the dust that covered the beautiful instrument.

"No." She gestured for them to sit at the table and made her way to the back of the cave that was hidden in shadow. "Gwenhwyfar," she called. "You can come out now."

Slowly, a young girl with long, blond hair came out of the shadows. She had widely spaced blue eyes and wore a plain gown of brown cloth. She, too, was barefoot. Shyly she smiled at Dudod. "Great-uncle Dudod?"

Dudod nodded, smiled, and held out his arms. Without hesitation, Gwen launched herself into Dudod's embrace. "Mam talks about you sometimes. I have always wanted to meet you. Did you bring your harp?"

Dudod laughed. "I did indeed. Why don't we go out by the pond, and I'll play some songs for you? Would you like that?"

Rhiannon cocked a sardonic brow at Dudod. "Leaving me alone with the Dreamer? Thanks a lot."

Gwen looked over at Gwydion. Pulling her dignity about her, she said, "We do not know each other."

"I am Gwydion ap Awst var Celemon, Dreamer of Kymru," he bowed.

"I am Gwenhwyfar ur Rhoram var Rhiannon, Princess of Prydyn. I am also clairvoyant and psychokinetic."

"Are you now?" Gwydion said with interest. "Can you Fire-Weave?"

Gwen glanced at Rhiannon, who was standing stiffly by the hearth. "Um, not yet," she replied.

"But you can Wind-Ride? And Life-Read?" he asked.

"I Wind-Ride very well. And Life-Read a little."

"Ah. But the psychokinetic abilities—not quite familiar with them yet?"

"Mam doesn't have them, so she can't teach me."

"Would you like to learn?"

"Oh, yes," Gwen replied, her eyes shining.

"Well, perhaps I can arrange something."

"Perhaps you could leave the arrangement of my daughter's education to me," Rhiannon said sharply.

Dudod rose and took Gwen's hand. "Well, you two have a great deal to talk about—"

"I wouldn't be too sure of that," Rhiannon broke in.

"So Gwenhwyfar and I will be on our way," Dudod continued smoothly. "Come, child."

Gwen hesitated, waiting for Rhiannon's response. Rhiannon reluctantly nodded at her daughter, and the two left the cave.

Rhiannon went to the hearth and poured two steaming cups of chamomile tea. She placed one in front of Gwydion and sat down at the table opposite him. Holding her mug with both hands, she took a few careful sips, frowning into her cup.

"I've been looking for you for a long time," Gwydion began.

"Have you?" she said in a disinterested tone.

"I have," he replied mildly, and supped his tea. He waited for Rhiannon to ask him the next, obvious question. But she did not. She drank her tea, ignoring him.

"I went a lot of places looking for you. One place I went to was Arberth."

Her eyes cut to him, her green gaze sharp. "And they didn't know anything there, did they?"

"No. But I talked to Rhoram. He gave me a message

for you."

Rhiannon's hands tightened on her cup until her knuckles were white. But her voice was cool. "Did he?"

"Yes. He said that he hoped to see you again. He said that he wanted to see his daughter, too, very much."

"Is he—is he well?" she asked hesitantly.

"He wasn't, no. But he seems to be better now."

"For having seen you?" Rhiannon laughed harshly.

"No." Talking to this woman was hard work. He felt as though every word he uttered could be turned into a trap, a snare. He took another sip of tea, wishing for something stronger. "It was something that Achren did. He had been very unhappy for a long time. It seems that Queen Efa didn't turn out to be all that he thought she was."

"I could have told him that," Rhiannon said.

"So Achren mocked him, you see. She mocked his—what shall I call it—his living death, the living death he fashioned out of his regret. And it woke him, brought him back to life." He was silent for a moment. "Perhaps the time for living death has passed for you also. Perhaps it is time for life for you as well."

Rhiannon sat back, eyeing him sardonically. "What a lovely sentiment. And how kind of you to be concerned. You have been looking for me, you say." The subject of Rhoram was apparently closed. "Why?"

Now for it. He took a deep breath. "You hold a memory. A clue."

"Do I?" she said flatly.

He spoke slowly, clearly, and firmly, as though to a child of erratic temperament. "Yes, you do."

"And?"

"And I must get it. It is a clue, handed down through certain descendants of Bran the Dreamer. It has come to rest in you, in your subconscious."

"I see."

Her palpable disinterest, her monosyllabic replies, stung him. But he attempted to keep calm. "And that is not all."

"No?"

"No," he said shortly. "The dead High Kings of Kymru themselves have told me that you must accompany the rest of us on a quest."

"The rest of us?"

"The captains of Kymru. Cai of Gwynedd; your friend Achren from Prydyn; Angharad of Ederynion; and Trystan from Rheged."

"And the quest is?"

"To retrieve Caladfwlch from wherever it now lies."

"The sword of the High Kings? To give, presumably, to the next High King of Kymru."

"Yes."

"So you want to hypnotize me to retrieve a memory. Then you want me to leave my home and my daughter and go with you on a quest for the sword. Is that correct?"

"Yes."

"Yes. So you see, I did understand you. Thank you for using little words so that I could do so."

"I'm just trying to explain," he said patiently, perhaps a little too patiently.

"You're treating me like a child, Dreamer," she said sharply. "But I am not."

The skepticism in his face was unmistakable. As soon as he had done that, he knew he had made a mistake. Her face continued to harden. Gwydion had not thought that possible.

In a dangerously calm tone, she went on, "And what, may I ask, do you suggest I do with my daughter while I go off with you?"

"How should I know? Why don't you take her to Y Ty Dewin? It's where she belongs, after all. She needs training. Training she can't get living in a cave. She's psychokinetic as well as clairvoyant. She—"

"And what right do you have to tell me what to do?"

"You asked me," he replied, his voice rising.

"It was a rhetorical question, idiot."

Idiot. This was enough. "Oh, that's typical. Just like a woman. Doesn't surprise me at all. Blame the man for what you started. Of course."

"Oh, I like that. Just like a man. Come in here demanding things from me. Saying I must do this, I must do that. Men always want something. And they never want to give anything in return."

"I'll be giving something in return, all right," he shot back. "I'll be enduring your childish temper tantrums."

"Oh no you won't. Because I'm not going anywhere with you."

"Of course you're not. What ever made me believe that you would think of anything other than yourself?"

"You're a fine one to talk. Since when does the Dreamer care about anyone else?"

His voice quiet and cold, he replied, "I've spent my entire life doing my duty to Kymru. I never think of myself."

"You never think of anyone else," she sneered. "Do you honestly think you can walk in here and get my consent to use me like you do everyone else?"

"At least you'd be of some use, now, wouldn't you?" he sneered in his turn.

"Leave me alone, do you hear me? All I want is to be left alone."

"There's nothing I would personally like better than that. Do you think I want to pull you kicking and screaming from your hole? Do you think I would drag myself all over Kymru looking for you if I could help it? Do you think I'm here because I long for the pleasure of your company? Don't make me laugh."

She jumped up. "You can't walk into my home and talk to me like that."

"Oh yes, I can," he said, rising to his feet. "You're nothing but a spoiled brat. You ran away. You secluded yourself for all these years when you should have been learning how to be the next Ardewin. You took your daughter away and condemned her to a life in hiding. Who do you think you are that you can do these things and still demand respect from anybody?"

"Get out," she screamed. "Get out."

"Oh, don't worry, I'm leaving. Just try to remember one thing, if there's any room left in your mind for anything but self-pity. If we cannot find the sword, Kymru is doomed. There will be blood on your conscience. If you have one, which I doubt."

"A fine one you are to talk about conscience. Even tucked away in Coed Aderyn, I hear gossip. You never even go to see your brother, to offer him comfort since the death of his son. You treat Dinaswyn as though she were a dilapidated old rag. And you made the mother of your child so miserable that she had to die just to stop the pain."

All the color drained from his face. "Congratulations," he

said steadily, his voice like the winter wind. "It takes a very talented woman to know just how to twist the knife into the guts of a stranger." And with that, he turned on his heel and was gone.

LATER THAT EVENING, after Gwen had gone to bed, Rhiannon settled down before the fire to think. All day, after Gwydion had left in a rage, taking Dudod with him, Rhiannon had been silent. She had spoken to Gwen in monosyllables, if at all, answering none of her daughter's anxious questions.

Rhiannon had changed into her riding leathers and gone hunting into the woods, unable to keep still. She had returned with the carcass of a fat summer deer slung over her shoulders, her knives tucked into her boots.

But no matter how busy she kept herself, Rhiannon could not stop herself from thinking.

Perhaps she had been too hasty. Somehow her conversation with Gwydion had gotten out of hand almost as soon as it had begun. Of course, she had been thrown off-balance by his very presence. It had been a shock. And before she had regained her equilibrium, Gwydion had begun his demands.

He had spoken to her as though she were a child. Then he had criticized her for the way she was raising her daughter—as though he was entitled to give his opinion. Then, crowning indignity, he had insulted her. Not once, but several times.

And yet, hadn't his statements about Gwen stung all the more because they were true?

But it was the last part of that hideous conversation that had shamed her the most. The part where she had hurt him as greatly as he had hurt her. She had meant to wound, to fight back. But she hadn't meant to hit quite so hard.

What had happened to her? Was she so soured by the years of feeling wronged by the world that her very soul had shriveled into something petty, something poisonous? Oh, she wasn't like that. She wasn't.

If only Rhoram had not turned from her. Even now she could not truly let him go, going over and over in her mind how it had been between them, from the glorious beginning to the humiliating end.

SHE HAD FIRST noticed Rhoram when she was just twenty-two years old, at the graduation ceremony at Y Ty Dewin. Effortlessly he had captured her heart during the ceremony. Captured her with his golden hair, his blue eyes, and his obvious admiration.

When Myrrdin had put the Dewin's torque around her neck that day, had framed her face with gentle hands, and had given her the post of Dewin to the Lady of Brycheiniog, Rhiannon was shocked. She had been so sure that Myrrdin was planning on sending her to the royal court of Arberth. And she had so much wanted to go, now that she had seen Rhoram. But she swallowed her disappointment, telling herself that it was not the first time she had failed to get what she wanted. And it would not be the last.

Later, during the celebration, Myrrdin had sought her out. "Child," he said gently, "I have just received word from Neuadd Gorsedd. Your father is dying, and begs that you come to him."

"No," she said, without a moment's hesitation. "I will not go."

"Think carefully. Do not do something you will regret later."

"I'll never regret it," she said fiercely. "Never."

"Oh, child, do you think I don't understand? Now is your chance for revenge on him for all the years he has slighted you. But he wishes to make amends with his last breath. Will you let him do this?"

"No."

"Then so be it. I will remind you of one thing. The Wheel turns, as it always does. What you do today will come back to haunt you. Someday, perhaps, a child of your own will feel that you have wronged them. And perhaps they will take revenge on you as you do today. Think one last time before you do this. Or it may be your turn, one day."

SHE HAD LEFT Y Ty Dewin the next day to go to Brycheiniog, in Prydyn. Marared ur Canhustyr who ruled the cantref was not an easy woman to serve, for she demanded the best from everyone. But she was fair and she even had a spark of humor to go with her sharp intelligence. So a year passed in Brycheiniog, as Rhiannon looked after the health of the folk of Tewdos, the chief city in the cantref where Marared had her home.

Early in her second year there Rhoram's wife, Christina, died of a fever in Arberth, and she began to dream dreams that she had no business having. For now Rhoram was free to marry again. These were foolish thoughts. She had only seen him once and had never even spoken to him. But she was young and foolish and she began to hope.

Soon after this Marared's sister, Achren, the Captain of Rhoram's *teulu*, came to visit. Achren was a striking woman with black hair, dark eyes, and a wicked smile. She and Marared laughed and laughed over Achren's stories of her amorous adventures. Adventures which did not, thank the gods, include Rhoram. Rhiannon, hungry for any word of Rhoram, listened breathlessly to Achren's stories of life in Arberth.

She discovered that Rhoram was charming, clever and—hard to bear—unfaithful. But she knew why. It was obvious to her that he simply hadn't found the right sort of woman. If he did, he would be faithful. She was sure of it.

Then one day a message came to her from Dinaswyn, the Dreamer. Dinaswyn's orders were to proceed to the court of Arberth, mate with Rhoram of Prydyn, and become pregnant. She was then to return to Y Ty Dewin to await the birth of the child and begin her instruction as Myrrdin's heir. She had been selected to be the next Ardewin of Kymru.

She could hardly believe her good fortune. A glittering future awaited her. At last she would have something that she longed for. To be Ardewin was an honor indeed.

And to be able to see Rhoram again! To be his lover and to make him happy—until the time came for her to go to Y Ty Dewin, of course. She would bear his child and such a thing would bind them together forever.

So she left Brycheiniog with a high heart and journeyed to Arberth. It was not until she entered the King's ystafell and looked into his eyes of brilliant blue that she understood that her life might become quite complicated indeed.

IN THE BEGINNING they were so happy. She lived in a golden world, warmed by Rhoram's love. His eyes followed her even in a crowded hall. No other woman existed for him except her.

Rhoram's children by Queen Christina—a son, Geriant, and a daughter, Sanon—loved Rhiannon and thought of her as their new mother. She spent hours with them teaching them to ride, picking wildflowers, fishing in the sea. Rhoram's sister,

Isalyn, was kind and the two women became friends. She and Achren also became good friends, the Caption teaching her some of the finer points of weaponry, improving her skill with a knife blade until Rhoram joked he didn't feel safe with the two of them around and armed.

All was very well, until the day she discovered she was pregnant. Somehow she had managed to forget that this was the reason she was with Rhoram in the first place. She had managed to forget that her duty was now to leave her lover, to go to Y Ty Dewin and begin her instruction for the important post of Ardewin.

When she told Rhoram, hesitantly, the news that she was pregnant and explained that she must return to Y Ty Dewin, he begged her to stay. He could not live without her. He loved her so much. Could she wait for just a while? Would she do that for him?

She allowed herself to be persuaded; saying that it was only for a while. But deep down she knew that she could never willingly tear herself away from him.

And then the messages began. Messages from Myrrdin begging for her return. Messages from Dinaswyn, demanding her compliance. But she stubbornly resisted. She was in love with the King and he with her. They made each other happy and that was right. Others just didn't understand. They were jealous of the love she had found.

She became pale and listless as her pregnancy advanced. She was terrified Rhoram would turn from her then. But he did not. He treated her more gently than ever. And he told her that, after the child was born, he would make her Queen of Prydyn.

In due course the child was born. They named her Gwenhwyfar and Rhoram was delighted with his tiny daughter.

And then Rhiannon began her long wait. She waited for Rhoram to keep his promise to marry her and make her Queen of Prydyn. But Rhoram, although he was as kind as ever, began to be distant. And Rhiannon began to be afraid.

"YOU DON'T LOVE me anymore, do you?" The question hung in the air for a moment before shattering the fragile peace of silence and pretense that existed between them.

Horrified, Rhiannon wished the words back the moment she uttered them. But it was too late. The words had been said and there was nothing that could change that.

So she waited for his answer. He laid down his pen and slowly turned to her. It broke her heart to see the caution in his eyes.

"Why do you ask that?" he asked carefully.

Too late to turn back, she went steadily on. "It is the truth, though, isn't it? Never mind why I ask it. I just don't understand why. What has happened?"

"Rhiannon. Stop. Don't do this. I do love you. I truly do."

The words she wanted so desperately to hear rang false, so terribly hollow, a death knell to all her hopes and dreams. And so the tears came. She wept with no sound, but the tears gathered and spilled over her white face, as blood from a gaping wound.

Rhoram, his sorrow and his guilt written so plainly on his weary face, looked everywhere else, looked at anything else in their sleeping chamber, except at her.

"It's Efa, isn't it? You're in love with her," she whispered. She had meant to accuse, to demand the truth, to shame him. But she knew before she started that she was beaten. And so the question came out as a strangled whisper, although she tried to make her voice steady.

"No. Truly, I am not," he said earnestly. But the obvious falsehood in his weak denial robbed the words of comfort.

"Do you want me to go?"

At last a reaction, a real one. He jumped as though stung. "Go? No. Oh, no. You mustn't go." In this she had finally heard the ring of truth. He was not ready for her to leave him. He didn't want her to go, but neither did he want her to stay. He didn't know what he wanted.

He came to her then, held her and kissed away her tears. He told her he loved her and that she mustn't go. That he could not bear to let her go. Not yet. These last two words he did not say, but she heard them clearly in his halting tones.

So as they made love she silently said farewell to Rhoram and to the peace and comfort she had known with him. That was all over now.

When he was spent and sleeping beside her, she intertwined with him as she had done so many times before, listening to his breathing, feeling the beat of his heart, and savoring the feel of his skin beneath her gentle fingers.

He stirred briefly as she got out of bed, but did not wake. Softly, swiftly, she gathered some clothes, and a few treasures—her Dewin's torque, an ivory-backed mirror and silver comb that he had given her, a golden bowl, her father's harp—making an untidy bundle. She got into her riding leathers, picked up her boots, and quietly crept from the room, looking one last time at his beloved face, so defenseless in sleep. So young. She had thought he was a man, but he was just a boy.

She made her way to the nursery where the children slept. She smoothed the blankets over young Geriant, and kissed little Sanon's forehead. And then she turned to the cradle where her own little daughter slept. Gwenhwyfar was only six months old and already a beauty with her soft down of blond hair and wide, blue eyes. Lighting a candle she held it near so she could see her daughter's face for one last time.

Her mind was made up now. She would leave Rhoram but not to take up her duties as the future Ardewin of Kymru. No, she was done with that. The world had nothing to offer her anymore. She would hide away, go to a beautiful place that she knew. She would leave the pain behind.

Deep down she knew that beneath her self-pity vengeance lay, frigid and unforgiving. She would make them all sorry. All. Rhoram and his faithlessness. Dinaswyn and her precious plans. Myrrdin who surely despised her for letting her father die alone. She would shut them out. All of them. Now and forever.

Except there was little Gwen sleeping in her cradle. A child who surely needed her mother.

Without stopping to think about what she was doing—for she knew if she hesitated she would not, could not, do it—she wrapped Gwen in her small, woolen blanket and picked her up. The child did not wake.

Clutching her bundle in one hand and her baby in the other, she carefully made her way out of the ystafell and into the courtyard.

She made her way to the stables where she saddled her horse and stuffed her belongings into the saddlebags she found there. She fashioned a sling out of the blanket and tied it around her neck to hold the baby.

Tallwch was at his post when he saw her riding across the courtyard toward him. He bowed, opened the gates to Caer

Tir and watched her go in silence, the glitter of tears in his wise eyes.

She rode through the dark and silent city to the outer gates. And there, Achren stood, alone. Like Tallwch, Achren said no word, but silently opened the gates. After she was out of the city that she had loved but which was now hateful to her, Rhiannon turned back to look at Achren. The tears spilled down her face so that it was difficult to make out her friend who stood so silently at the open gate. But she tried to smile. She lifted her hand in farewell and Achren saluted her and tried to smile in return. Then, slowly, Achren closed the gate. And the sound of the gate's closing found an echo within her as her own heart closed in sorrow, in pride, and, most of all, in cold, hard vengeance.

IN HER CAVE where vengeance had led her, Rhiannon dragged herself back from the past. The fire had died down to glowing coals. And she knew where she was. She was at a crossroads. A decision was being asked of her, and she did not want to make it. It pressed on her in the silence.

Quietly she stood and walked to the shelf where her father's harp stood. She stared at it for a long time. Slowly she reached a trembling hand toward the instrument. Gently, she stoked the frame of seasoned oak. Carefully, she picked it up and held it against her for a moment. Hesitantly, she moved toward the hearth and sat down, still cradling the harp in her hands.

Tentatively she began to turn the pegs, tightening the strings. They did not break. She plucked one string and to her astonishment it rang out in a clear, proud note.

One by one she tuned the strings. When all was in readiness, she hesitated for a long time. But then, as if impelled

by a force greater than herself, she softly began to play an air
that she had heard long ago, a song sung by Queen Deirdre of
Lyonesse, Deirdre of the Sorrows; a song of the glen where
she had lived with her lover, until the lover had been killed
by treachery.

Glen of the silent blue-eyed hawk,
Glen with rich bounty from every tree.
Glen sheltered by peaks on every side,
Glen of the blackberry, wild plum and apple.
Glen of the tangled branching yew,
Glen of mists and white-winged swans.
Glen of the clear brilliant sun,
Glen of the graceful women, perfect as pearls.

As she sang softly of this perfect place, a place that only
love could make she had a new thought, startling in its truth
and simplicity. Poor Da. He had found such a glen with Mam,
and then lost it when she died. Poor Da.

Her father had been a broken man. He had not been able
to bear the blows that life had dealt him. He had lost the only
thing that was dear to him and the loss had hollowed him until
he was nothing but an empty shell. It was not a father who had
rejected her, but a walking corpse—a body that had continued
to breathe long, long after its death.

In the end he knew. But she was too prideful, too stubborn, too set on revenge. Oh, Da, forgive me, she thought. I
didn't understand.

And as she forgave him she made the turning at the crossroads.

She sighed and set the harp back on the shelf. She knew
what she must do. She lifted the blanket that shut out the
waterfall and stepped out into the night. She swiftly made her

339

way down the slippery rocks and knelt by the pond. The full moon rode the sky proudly overhead. Nantsovelta, she prayed silently, give me the strength to do what I now must do.

It was the Lady of the Waters herself who saved Rhiannon's life that night. For at that moment she felt the sense of danger, of death lurking just behind. She raised her hand to her throat, and it was that which kept her alive. For her hand kept the descending garrote from instantly strangling her.

She struck at the figure that stood behind her kneeling body, aiming with her elbow into his groin. The man grunted and his hold on the garrote loosened slightly. She sprang up, pulling her knives from her boot tops and whirling to face her assailant.

He crouched in knife-fighting stance as he dropped the garrote and pulled a knife from his belt. They circled each other, each looking for an opening. He feinted and she leapt back. But she knew better than to let him follow it up and she feinted left while she kicked out with her right foot, catching him on the knee. He went down and she leapt on top of him, burying her knife in his chest.

Blood spilled from the wound, over her hands and onto the damp grass. "Who are you?" she panted. "Why did you try to kill me?"

She did not think he would answer, but he did. "For the clue you hold," he rasped. "For the memory from Bran."

"To keep me from helping the Dreamer. How did you know he did not get it today?"

"I saw him leave," the man gasped, "in a rage. He would not have been angry if you had given it to him."

"Who sent you? Who seeks to keep the Dreamer from finding the sword?"

But the man did not answer. Instead, he gave a sigh as blood bubbled from his lips. And he died.

She got to her feet, her other knife still clutched in her hand, the first knife buried in the dead man's chest. She would bury him tonight, in the woods. Gwen must not find out what had happened.

Tomorrow she and Gwen would start for Arberth. Gwen would be returned to her father before going on to Y Ty Dewin and then to Caer Duir for the training she needed to have. Rhoram would care for Gwen during this first, most difficult time of adjustment.

And she? She would not, could not, stay in Arberth. She would not, could not, take Gwen with her where she was going. For she had a task to complete. A payment to make for running away all those years ago.

She would journey to Caer Dathyl, to the Dreamer. She would give up the memory she held. She would do whatever she needed to do to find the sword.

She would run no more.

Arberth, Kingdom
of Prydyn and
Dinas Emrys and
Caer Dathyl,
Kingdom of
Gwynedd, Kymru
Gwinwydden and
Ysgawen Mis, 494

Addiendydd, Tywyllu Wythnos—early evening

Preparations to leave the forest took two weeks, for Rhiannon was not certain when she would return. Gwen would not come back. She did not tell her daughter that. She only said that they were going to see King Rhoram for an indefinite period of time.

She packed all the perishable food and sealed up the barrels of flour and meal. She altered one of her dresses for Gwen. She hauled out the old saddlebags and packed them full with their best clothes, her Dewin's torque, some things that Rhoram had given her long ago, and her Da's harp, carefully wrapped in a length of woolen blanket.

When all was ready they left the wood. They traveled for some days on foot to Cil, where they purchased horses. Rhiannon traded her golden bowl for two fine mounts and a few other items.

During their trip Rhiannon talked of Geriant and Sanon, Gwen's half brother and half sister, and how they had loved

Gwen when she was a baby. She spoke fondly of Achren, of Tallwch, of Dafydd Penfro. She spoke of Rhoram in glowing terms. She said next to nothing about Queen Efa, only that she had not known her well.

It was a fine summer evening when they reached Arberth. It was still light outside, for the sun would not set for another hour or so. There was time for Rhiannon and Gwen to visit the bathhouse before showing themselves at the gates of Caer Tir.

The bathhouse contained four bathing rooms, four steam rooms and a large common room. The floor was tiled in creamy sea green with a latticework of wood set between each tile. There were cupboards and shelves filled with towels, robes, and jars of creams and herbs.

After they had bathed Gwen sat as still as she could while Rhiannon combed out her long, blond hair, teasing the tangles out gently. As she smoothed her daughter's bright hair she marveled, "It's the exact shade of your father's."

"Do I look like him?" Gwen asked anxiously.

"You've his golden hair and blue eyes. Now, let's get you dressed."

Rhiannon pulled out a fine, blue gown and a long linen shift of lighter blue. Gwen put on the shift and Rhiannon threw the gown over her head and helped settle it into place. The light blue shift showed at the top of the laced bodice of the gown, and the tight-fitting sleeves of the shift showed beneath the looser sleeves and at the hem. The gown was embroidered with silver threads at the hem and neckline.

"You look very fine, my Gwen. Very, very fine."

"Do I?" Gwen asked anxiously.

"Missing something though. How about this?" She

clasped a necklace around Gwen's neck, a small sapphire, set in a circle of silver dangled from a thin silver chain.

"Your Da gave this to me the day you were born."

"Oh, you should wear it!"

"No, I wear my Dewin's torque. You wear this."

Rhiannon put on a fine, pearl-colored shift beneath a gown of emerald green. Tiny pearls dotted the hemline. Around her neck she clasped her Dewin's torque. Then she pulled out a lovely hair band of emeralds and pearls and set it over her hair.

"Oh, Mam," Gwen breathed. "You look beautiful."

As she examined herself in the mirror she thought that there might be something to that. The jade hue of her gown and the emeralds in her hair made her eyes appear greener than ever. Her long, wavy, black hair hung rich and full to her waist. The pearl color of the shift gave her skin a lustrous sheen.

She turned to Gwen, and was horrified to see tears in her daughter's eyes. "Oh, Mam," Gwen breathed, "I'm afraid." Having said it, the words began to tumble out, and the tears began to flow. "I'm afraid. There will be so many people there and I've never been around other people before. I'm afraid I'll do something stupid. And they will laugh at me. Maybe Da won't like me. Maybe—"

Rhiannon took Gwen into her arms and patted her, all the while speaking in soothing tones. "*Cariad*, I know you're scared. But you are Gwenhwyfar ur Rhoram var Rhiannon. You are a Child of the House of Llyr. That alone commands respect from all you meet. And remember, your Da is a good, kind man. He wants to see you more than anything in the world."

"How do you know?" Gwen asked tearfully.

"I know him," Rhiannon replied firmly.

"But it's been so long. Maybe he's changed."

"Some things never change. Now dry your eyes and take a deep breath."

"You'll stay right next to me, won't you? You won't leave me?"

"Of course I won't," she said without hesitation, pushing the truth to the back of her mind, so Gwen would not see it in her eyes.

THE GATES OF Caer Tir were still open, but the courtyard was nearly deserted, for most of the inhabitants of the fortress were gathered in the Great Hall. As they walked their horses through the gates Gwen stopped to stare at the snarling wolf's head, outlined in onyx with emerald eyes that was carved on the golden doors. She swallowed hard.

Suddenly a deep voice spoke, "Do not be afraid of the wolf, child. Those of the House of PenBlaid, the Head of the Wolf, know he is their ally—not their enemy."

Wildly, Gwen looked around as a man who stepped out of the shadows by the gate. He was of average height, with short, brown hair, and brown eyes. "Welcome back to Caer Tir, Rhiannon ur Hefeydd. Welcome back, Gwenhwyfar ur Rhoram var Rhiannon."

"Tallwch," Rhiannon said with a smile. She held out her hands and Tallwch took them and kissed them lightly.

"I knew you'd come back, one day," he said.

"Oh, you always did know everything."

"That is exactly what Gwydion ap Awst said to me when last he was here."

"Did he?" Rhiannon said coolly.

"He was looking for you. I take it he found you."

"He did indeed. Where is Rhoram?" Rhiannon asked before Tallwch could question her further.

"In the Great Hall. I suggest you allow me to announce you. It's better that way."

Offering one arm to Rhiannon and the other to Gwen, he rather grandly escorted them to the half-open doors of the hall. The noise was immense. There seemed to be a great deal of shouting, laughing, talking and singing.

"Is something special going on tonight?" Rhiannon asked curiously, while Gwen cringed with the assault on her ears.

"Oh, it's always like that."

"Since when?"

"Since Rhoram needed as much diversion as possible to prevent him from having to talk to the Queen."

Rhiannon, her heart beating uncomfortably fast, struggled to maintain her outer composure. Sternly she reminded herself of three things—Rhoram had a wife, Rhoram could not be trusted, and there had been an attempt on her life to prevent her from aiding Gwydion ap Awst.

The noise was beginning to quiet down. "We'll just wait until Ellywen gives the blessing. That will be the best time." Tallwch said calmly.

They edged toward the doors as they heard a woman's voice, cool and hard, reciting the evening prayer.

The peace of light,
The peace of joys
The peace of souls
Be with you.

"Awen," the crowd replied.

"Stay behind me," Tallwch said, leading them into the

now quiet hall.

The first person she saw was Rhoram, sitting at the table on the dais. His hair was still bright gold, and he was richly dressed in a tunic of emerald green. His long fingers toyed with his jeweled goblet, the emerald ring around his finger glittering. He was looking down into the cup and smiling faintly, as though the blessing amused him.

She saw Queen Efa sitting stiffly beside him. She wore a niam-lann, a circlet of gold around her forehead, a cluster of emeralds resting above her brow. She wore long, golden earrings and rings without number. Her dress was green and gold.

The table was full of those she knew—Sanon and Geriant, whom she barely recognized, so grown were they. Achren with her crooked smile. Dafydd Penfro, Rhoram's counselor. So many others she remembered.

Into the silence, Tallwch suddenly boomed, "Guests come to your Hall, great King. Noble guests of the House of Llyr."

Rhoram looked up. "Gwydion? He was just—" Rhoram stopped abruptly as Rhiannon and Gwen came forward to stand by Tallwch.

"These are your guests. Rhiannon ur Hefeydd var Indeg, Dewin of Kymru. Gwenhwyfar ur Rhoram var Rhiannon, Princess of Prydyn."

The hall fell silent as people froze in astonishment. Then Sanon and Geriant erupted from their chairs and rushed pell-mell down the length of the hall, throwing themselves into Rhiannon's open arms.

"You came back," Sanon whispered. Rhiannon kissed the top of her bright, golden head, and Geriant, grinning like a mad man, said nothing but hugged her tightly.

"I came back. And I brought your sister with me."

Gesturing to Gwen, who was standing behind her, she pulled her daughter forward.

"Gwenhwyfar, this is your sister, Sanon. And your brother, Geriant."

There were tears in Sanon's eyes and in Gwen's too, as Sanon gently hugged her.

"You are welcome here, sister," Geriant said with a smile.

Rhiannon looked up at the dais and saw Rhoram getting to his feet. Efa frantically clutched his arm, but he loosened her hold gently, almost absently.

Slowly, he made his way down the hall, never talking his glittering eyes from her. He was pale and his face was expressionless. For one horrible moment, Rhiannon was sure that she had miscalculated. Then she saw the welcome in his sapphire eyes.

Like a man who is fearful that he is only dreaming, he reached out his hand to caress her cheek. "Rhiannon. Rhiannon ur Hefeydd. You came back," he said slowly.

She nodded and started to speak. "For—for a while. I—" but no further words materialized. Her heart was beating so rapidly that she could not think. "I bring you a gift."

"A gift. A gift greater than you?"

"I bring you your daughter." She reached out and drew Gwen to her side.

"Gwenhwyfar." He looked down at her for a long time. "Oh, my child. How beautiful you are," and he drew her into a tender embrace. He closed his eyes briefly and when he opened them they had the sheen of tears. There were tears in Gwen's eyes as she clung to her father.

Finally, Rhoram drew back. "Thank you," he said to Rhiannon, his voice raw. "Thank you for my gift. The most wondrous gift I have ever received." He smiled at Gwen and reached out his hand to touch her bright hair. Then he turned his sapphire gaze back to Rhiannon.

He said nothing, drinking in the sight of her as a man who has been thirsty for long and long will drink a draught of clear, cool water. Then he smiled, then he grinned, and then he grabbed her and swung her around in wild abandon. Then Dafydd Penfro and Achren were there, demanding their turn to greet her.

After the tumult died down a little Rhoram said, "Come. You two shall sit at my table." He took her hand and then grabbed Gwen's hand and led them up to his table. People she knew called greetings to her. She flushed and smiled and returned their greetings as best she could.

As she neared the table Queen Efa stood stiffly. As though this happened every day Rhoram calmly said, "My dear, you remember Rhiannon ur Hefeydd?"

"I do indeed," Efa said, her voice cold. "You are welcome here in my hall."

In her hall. Oh, yes. Rhiannon donned a honeyed smile and said sweetly, "How kind of you. I hardly dared think I would find such a warm welcome here."

"Yes, strange isn't it?" Efa replied, with a smile as poisonously false as Rhiannon's own. "Come, we shall squeeze you both in somehow."

After some shifting Rhiannon and Gwen sat among the company. Efa was on Rhoram's right, but Rhiannon sat on his left. Gwen sat directly across from her father between Sanon and Geriant. The three young people had their heads together, talking swiftly. Where had Gwen been all this time? What was it like to live in a cave?

349

Queen Efa ate little and said less. But Dafydd Penfro, obedient to Rhoram's sharp look, was attentive to the Queen; and eventually even Efa relaxed a little.

Achren leaned forward and asked Gwen if she knew how to hunt. "Mam taught me some, and I'm pretty good with a spear," Gwen answered.

"Know anything about swords?" Achren asked.

"No."

"Want to learn?"

"Oh, yes," Gwen said, her face shining. "I'd love to."

"Achren," Efa said coolly, "I hardly think that this is a proper thing to teach an eleven-year-old girl."

"Why not? She should know how to defend herself, don't you think?" It was hard to tell just what Achren might have meant by that, but her dislike of the Queen was clear.

Rhoram stepped into the breach. "Sanon doesn't much care for it herself. But you and Geriant should have a fine old time. Achren taught him, too. And I have a few tricks to teach."

Achren snorted. "Nothing you didn't learn from me."

"Ha! You talk as though I never win when we duel."

"I let you win, sometimes, to cheer you, "Achren grinned.

"You see, daughter," Rhoram said to Gwen with a mock grimace, "an old man is not respected in his own house. It's terribly sad, isn't it?"

"You're not old," Gwen protested. "Or, well, not very, anyway."

Everyone laughed at that, for Gwen's qualifying statement was said with a great deal of earnestness. Gwen blushed, but the laughter was friendly, and she was not ashamed, only startled.

"I must talk to you," Rhiannon whispered urgently to

Rhoram under cover of the laughter. Rhoram acted as though he hadn't heard her. He leaned forward, "How about a song, Sanon? Maybe you and Gwen both know some of the same tunes?"

Sanon leapt up, grabbing Gwen's hand. "Come on. We'll think of something."

"Geriant, keep an eye on them will you?"

"Sure, Da," Geriant said good-naturedly, and ambled after the girls who had scampered over to the hearth.

Rhoram glanced at Dafydd Penfro. Rising, Dafydd offered his arm to the Queen. "Shall we get a good place for the show?" Efa nodded and reluctantly allowed him to lead her to a chair before the hearth.

"Come," Rhoram said to Rhiannon. They slipped out of the hall, stopping just outside the doors. They heard the sweet voices of Sanon and Gwen raised in song.

I have been a multitude of shapes
Before I assumed a constant form.
I have been a sword.
I have been a tear in the air.

Rhoram turned to her and took her hands in his. He kissed them gently. "How long will you stay?"

"I can't. I can't stay at all. I must go. Tonight." The words came with difficulty, but she said them. She had promised.

Rhoram stared at her. "Is it—is it something I have done? Have I made you uncomfortable here?"

She laughed, a little wildly. Uncomfortable? Oh, gods, he had no idea.

"What did Gwydion ap Awst say to you?" he demanded.

"He said he needed my help. So," she went on, taking a deep breath, "I go from here to Caer Dathyl to see him and take up my task. And I'm leaving Gwen here."

"Ah. And does Gwen know this?" Rhoram asked carefully.

Oh, Rhoram had always been so quick to understand her. How could she had forgotten that? "No."

"You should have told her."

"I couldn't find the words to explain." Within the Hall the song continued,

I have been the dullest of stars,
I have been a word among letters,
I have been a book in the making.
I have been the light of lanterns.

"Rhiannon," Rhoram said softly. "Look at me."

Hesitantly, she raised her eyes to his glittering, jewel-like gaze.

"Rhiannon, I must tell you two things. The first is that I still love you. I was a fool to let you go." Briefly, she closed her eyes at the words she had wanted to hear for so long. It was her daydream turned nightmare, for the words had come too late. She had already come to the crossroads and chosen her path.

He went on, "The second thing is that you mustn't fear me, *cariad*. I demand nothing from you. So tell me, for I am your friend now and always. Explain why you do this thing."

"Years ago," she began, hesitantly, "I refused to do my duty. I threw away the chance to become Ardewin."

"Because I begged you."

"Because I wanted to. And then, when things went wrong I ran away. I stole Gwen out of vengeance."

"You couldn't bear to part with your daughter. You loved her."

"I wronged her. I can't change that. But I can try to make

it right, by returning her to her real home. And I can repay my debt to Kymru. I refused my duty before. I won't do it again. Or there will be nothing left of me."

"Will you come back?"

"No." It was, perhaps, the hardest thing she had ever said.

"I see." He gave a bitter laugh. "I've dreamt of this moment for years. But like all dreams, it turns bitter when it comes true. You come back only to leave me again."

"Rhoram—"

"No, no. You don't understand. I'm not blaming you. I brought it on myself by letting you go so long ago."

I have been a sword in the grasp of a hand,
I have been a shield in battle.
I have been a string in a harp.
Disguised for nine years,
In water, in foam.

"Rhoram, how could I stay? You have a wife," she said sharply.

"So I do, so I do. If you want to call her that. Of course, she doesn't love me and never did. But she loves being the Queen."

"Rhoram, Rhoram. I beg you. Please don't do this to me. I can't stay."

"I know." He said nothing for a long time. He looked up at the sky and the full moon washed over his face. Finally, he turned to her. "Tell me then, what can I do to make it easier for you?"

Oh, truly she was the beloved of Rhoram ap Rhydderch. Who but one that loved her so would let her go her own way at the crossroads? "Take care of Gwen," she whispered.

"I will."

"I must say good-bye to her now."

"Won't you at least stay the night?"

"I can't." She swallowed hard. "If I do I will never leave."

"I wish—never mind, you know what I wish," he tried to smile but it died before it reached the corners of his mouth. Gently he framed her face with his hands. "Rhiannon ur Hefeydd, I claim a kiss from you before you go."

The wasted years fell away as their lips touched. All the passion, all the longing, all the terrible, wonderful love returned in full force. His arms tightened around her as she sank deeply into his kiss. A low moan escaped him, and she pulled herself away, gasping. His hands instantly dropped from her, and he stepped back. "I'm sorry," he offered hoarsely. "I didn't think it would be like that."

"Some things never change, do they?" she said breathlessly.

"No, they don't. I'll—I'll go get Gwen."

After he went back inside the hall she sat down on the steps. Her legs were shaking and her heart was choking her. How could she leave? But how could she not?

At last Rhoram returned, holding Gwen's hand. "Oh, Mam," she said, "did you hear me?"

Swiftly she pulled herself together and stood. "Yes, indeed," she said, her voice as steady as she could make it. "You have a beautiful voice. You and Sanon sound well together."

"Oh, she's wonderful. I'm going to love it here. How long can we stay?"

"I'm—I'm glad you like it here, little one. Because—" She stopped. Oh, what a coward I am, she thought. What a fool.

"Your Mam and I have had a long talk, Gwen. And we've come to an agreement we think you will like. You've lived with your Mam for a long time. And now, it's time to live with me," Rhoram said gently.

Gwen quickly turned to Rhiannon. "You're leaving me here? Why?"

"I must. I must go to the Dreamer. He has laid a task on me that I must do."

"You're deserting me?" Gwen's voice rose.

"No," Rhiannon said pleadingly. "I'm leaving you with your father."

"You planned this from the start," Gwen accused. "You knew it all along. Why didn't you tell me?"

"Gwen, don't take it this way, please. If I had a choice—"

"You have a choice! How can you do this? How can you leave me alone?"

"I wish I knew," Rhiannon whispered.

"I hate you! I hate you!" Gwen screamed.

Rhiannon flinched as Gwen began to sob. "I do. I do hate you. You don't care anything about me. You just leave me because I'm in the way."

She reached out to take Gwen in her arms but was pushed away. Rhoram put his arm around Gwen's shoulders as she sobbed and Rhiannon watched helplessly.

"I'll take care of her, Rhiannon. Do what you must do," he said softly.

Oh, gods. How could she leave them both, these two that she loved so much? But she must. She must. She turned and ran toward the stables, Gwen's sobs echoing in her ears.

Addiendydd, Tywyllu Wythnos—dusk
ONE MONTH LATER, Rhiannon arrived in the tiny village of Dinas Emrys, sick at heart and weary beyond endurance.

She reined in her mount by the village well, hauled up

the bucket, and watered her horse as the sun slowly sank behind the purple mountains. The people in the village were already at their evening meal, and the tiny square was deserted. She could hear faint laughter as families and friends gathered for the evening. The sound made her feel more lonesome than ever.

Her exit from Caer Tir had taken its toll on her. There were dark circles beneath her swollen eyes, for she slept poorly. She often thought she heard Gwen's sobs again in the dead of the night. The cries echoed within her and the misery she carried made her heart feel as heavy as stone.

She wondered now where she would spend the night. On this journey she had not dared to sleep alone in the wilds. So every night she had invoked the law of hospitality, and gone to a nearby house for shelter. In every place the people were kind, attentive to her needs, and unquestioning, as the law demanded. Grateful, she had repaid them in the only way she could—she had played her harp and sung for them.

But tonight she was doubtful that she should even stop here in this tiny village. She was almost at Caer Dathyl; indeed, she would be there tomorrow. She was half inclined to keep riding for another league or so and camp for the night. And even more than half inclined to turn her horse around and go back to Arberth. For the nearer she came to Caer Dathyl and Gwydion, the greater her misery became.

Sighing, she made to remount when someone touched her arm. She jumped and turned to confront a young boy perhaps thirteen years old. He had auburn hair and dark eyes. He was slender, slightly built, and deeply tanned.

"Your pardon," he said softly. "I didn't mean to startle you."

She took a deep breath. "It's all right," she said evenly.

"My Uncle offers you the hospitality of our house for the night."

She hesitated. "I thank your Uncle, but I am not staying the night here. Please tell him I am grateful but I cannot stay."

"He said that if you were to refuse I was to ask if Hefeydd's harp was being cared for properly now."

"How did—" She halted. "Who is your uncle?" she asked carefully.

"My Great-uncle, actually. Come. He is waiting."

In a daze she followed the boy. Who was he? There was an air about him—something that did not belong in this mountain village. And his Great-uncle—who in the world could that be? There were few people who knew about her father's harp. She thought of one person in particular. Oh, it couldn't be. It wasn't possible. For Myrrdin was dead. Wasn't he?

The boy led her to a tiny hut at the edge of the village. An old man stood in the doorway, looking out at her. "Rhiannon," the old man said tenderly.

"Myrrdin. Oh, Myrrdin." She threw herself into his waiting arms and he held her gently as she began to weep.

The boy stabled her horse and returned with her saddlebags in tow. Bashfully, he handed her a tiny square of linen to wipe her eyes, and Myrrdin helped her to a bench before the crackling fire.

"I'm sorry," she muttered, embarrassed. "I don't know what came over me."

"Oh, I think you do, child. Here, drink this." Gratefully, she took a mug of ale from his hand and drank. As she tried to calm herself, she looked closely at the boy who was stirring a kettle of soup that boiled over the fire. There was something about that boy. Something elusive, but familiar.

"Gwydion must have found you," Myrrdin said quietly. "Where is Gwenhwyfar?"

"Arberth." Her voice broke. She cleared her throat and went on. "I left her there with Rhoram."

"I see." She thought that he probably did. He always had. "And now you are going on to Caer Dathyl. Does Gwydion know you're coming?"

"I doubt it. When he and I met we—ah, had words. Have you spoken to him? Is he at Caer Dathyl?"

"He is at Caer Dathyl. And no, I have not spoken to him. We never speak. It is safer that way."

"I can't believe you are alive! What happened? Why the secrecy?"

"That is for Gwydion to say."

"Myrrdin, I have left my woods, left my daughter, left the man I love who begged me to stay—to come to Caer Dathyl and join Gwydion in doing what must be done. I can assure you that Gwydion ap Awst will tell me exactly what he is up to. He can tell me tomorrow or you can tell me tonight. Whichever you prefer. I prefer to know now."

"You two didn't hit it off, I take it."

"No. And you weren't surprised, I take it."

"Certainly not. I expected it." He thought for a moment then gestured for the boy to stand beside him. "This is Arthur. Arthur, this is Rhiannon ur Hefeydd, a woman of the House of Llyr. You have heard me speak of her."

Arthur gave a credible bow, all things considered. He was too bashful to look directly at her, staring instead at his feet.

Arthur, she thought. Now who in the world—of course. "Arthur ap Uthyr. Uthyr's son," she said incredulously. "Alive. He never died either. Myrrdin, you left Y Ty Dewin to raise

Uthyr's son in secret. How did Gwydion ever get you to do that? No, never mind." She was thinking out loud now, on the trail of a mystery. "And why hide him? Why pretend he was dead? Why unless he was in danger. In danger because he is more than the heir to Gwynedd. But he was tested. I heard that. Gwydion himself was there—" She stared at the boy, who lifted his eyes to hers and blushed. "Oh. Of course Gwydion was there. May I be one of the first to bend my knee to the future High King of Kymru?"

Myrrdin laughed heartily. "Oh, very good."

"And you Arthur? You don't seem very pleased," she said curiously, for his young face had become grim and set at Myrrdin's words.

"I'm not," he mumbled.

"Why?"

He looked up at her. His dark eyes set and stubborn. "I don't like being used. Uncle Gwydion does that to everyone who will let him. And I won't let him."

"Hmm. I said the same thing to Gwydion not very long ago."

"And what did he say?" Arthur asked eagerly.

"That I was selfish. That it wasn't his idea and if he had a choice he'd never lay eyes on me again."

"And will he?" Myrrdin asked intently.

She turned to him, looking into his dark eyes. He knew. He knew she had almost made up her mind to run back to Arberth and give herself up to an even more profound prison than the one she had constructed for herself all these years. "I don't know," she said finally.

"Will you play Hefeydd's harp for us?" Myrrdin asked gently.

"How did you know I had it?"

"Because you have changed, and changed a great deal or you wouldn't be here. And how could you have done that and yet left his harp behind?"

Arthur brought her saddlebags over to her. Under Myrrdin's gaze she retrieved the harp and unwrapped it. The smooth, satiny oak of the frame gleamed in the firelight.

"Play a song for me," Myrrdin said. "Play Taliesin's song of Cadair Idris."

Rhiannon stared at him in surprise. "Why that song?"

"I have a fancy for it. Come, indulge an old man."

Hesitantly, she played the sorrowful, opening chords. And then she sang,

The court of Lleu Lawrient lies
Stricken and silent beneath the sky.
The thorns and blighted thistles over
It all, and brambles now,
Where once was magnificence.
Harp and lordly feasts, all have passed away.
And the night birds now reign.

After she finished, the room was quiet. Arthur, his head bowed and his fists clenched, said nothing. Myrrdin stared into the fire. Rhiannon stilled the strings of the harp and sat silently, her eyes blinded by tears. At last, Myrrdin stirred and caught both their gazes with his suddenly stern and compelling eyes.

"Who asks what we want for ourselves? Does the Wheel of Life ask? Do the Shining Ones? Do the seasons wish to know if we are happy? I tell you that the night birds reign in Cadair Idris. I tell you that the court of the High King is no more. And I ask you, both of you, if this means anything to you. Anything at all."

Arthur paled, but he did not speak. Rhiannon answered, "I left my child. I left everything I hold dear. It means something to me."

"So you say. But you were almost ready to turn back. And I tell you that you cannot. You have left your woods. And tonight I have heard you play your father's harp. And so I know—you can't turn back. Because you've come too far."

"Myrrdin," she said, the words tumbling out, "I dread tomorrow. I dread seeing Gwydion again. Letting him hypnotize me, rooting around in my soul for his precious clue. I hate him. I do. How can I go anywhere with him? He already despises me. He'll gloat because he will think he has beaten me."

"Hate him then, if it makes you feel better. He'll care nothing for that. As for gloating, he would consider it a waste of time."

This was not the understanding and sympathy she sought. Offended, she said indignantly, "You treat it as if it was nothing important."

"It isn't," he said simply. "And you know it. Child, do you think our meeting was by chance? Do you think you would be led so far and allowed to turn back now? As for Arthur," he turned to look at the boy who gave him back stare for stare. "As for Arthur, his time hasn't come yet to decide."

"I have decided. I have told you," Arthur said stubbornly. "Over and over."

"Oh, so you have. So you have. I forget sometimes," Myrrdin said, smiling slyly at the boy.

Arthur unwillingly smiled back and shook his head. He turned to Rhiannon. "You see how it is? He never listens to a word I say."

"Don't worry about it. He does that to everybody. And he's set in his ways. He's very, very old, you know."

"Come, enough compliments for one night," Myrrdin said. "It's time to eat."

They ate and talked and even laughed a little, although Arthur was inclined to brood at first. Rhiannon spoke kindly to him and even teased him a bit so that, by the time the meal was through, they were friends. Arthur insisted that she take his bed, he could do very well by the fire, he said. He colored when he offered, and she thanked him kindly pretending not to notice his blush.

"Good night, child," Myrrdin said and gently kissed her forehead. "It has been a pleasure to see you after so many years. I know we shall meet again."

"I hope so."

"Oh, we shall. And perhaps you will play your harp for me again."

"Da's harp, you mean."

"No, it is your harp now. Good night, my dear."

Meriwydd, Tywyllu Wythnos—late afternoon

THE NEXT DAY Rhiannon arrived in Caer Dathyl. The late afternoon sun shone on the cold, gray stones of the fortress as she reined in her horse and dismounted. The fortress was built in the shape of a circle, with the round three-story Dreamer's tower jutting out defiantly toward the sky. She assumed that Gwydion was in the tower now, and, having seen her ride up was gloating over his victory.

She started up the stone steps to the huge, closed, golden doors of the fortress. The left-hand side was etched with the sign for the rowan, one vertical line slashed by two horizontal ones, all outlined in glittering opals. The right-hand side was covered with a glowing representation of the constellation of Mabon, also outlined in opals. Her heart in her throat, she raised her hand to knock.

But before she could do so, the doors opened slowly. It was not Gwydion, whom she had expected but rather Dinaswyn. Her face was proud and cold, as though carved from the same stone as Caer Dathyl itself. Her gray eyes, so like Gwydion's, glittered and her silvery hair was braided and wound about her head. She was wearing a plain gown of black with a linen shift beneath it of bright red.

"Welcome, Rhiannon ur Hefeydd var Indeg. Welcome to Caer Dathyl," Dinaswyn said in a cool voice. With a formal gesture, she held out a golden goblet jeweled with opals that flashed in the sunlight.

Rhiannon took the cup and sipped. "My thanks, Dinaswyn ur Morvryn var Gwenllian," she said, just as coldly.

"You wish to see Gwydion," Dinaswyn stated.

"I do," Rhiannon replied evenly.

"Then come with me." Well, Rhiannon had not expected a warm welcome from Dinaswyn—no one in his or her right mind ever expected that. She shrugged and followed the former Dreamer through the entrance hall and out into the central courtyard. In the center of the circular courtyard stood a grove of rowan trees forming yet another circle. The rowan trees were bright with clusters of red berries, and birds flew ceaselessly about them.

"He is in the grove," Dinaswyn said, her manner still cool and formal.

"Not in his Tower then?" she asked.

363

"Nemed Cerdinen, Rhiannon ur Hefeydd, is where he goes when his tasks weigh most heavily upon him, when his cares press heavily, when things are going ill for him."

"I see. And was that your habit, too, when you were Dreamer?"

"It was. Both Gwydion and I have spent much time in that grove, thanks to you."

"Ah. Still angry after all this time?"

"You were a fool, Rhiannon. You could have been Ardewin but you threw it away. You defied your fate."

"No, I defied you. Fate, it seems, has caught up to me at last." She wasn't going to be pushed around by Dinaswyn. If she took a humble line now, she'd never hear the end of it. So she lashed out on a sore spot with deadly accuracy. "And really, Dinaswyn," she went on, "you shouldn't hang on to your anger like that. It's bad for your health. And I'm sure Gwydion wouldn't want anything to happen to you—he relies on you so."

Dinaswyn stiffened. "More than he knows," she said quietly.

Rhiannon carefully searched Dinaswyn's cold face, and saw now what few people had ever bothered to see. She saw the ghost of a woman who had, perhaps, once loved and laughed; a woman who had, somehow, sustained a wound from which she had never recovered. Unaccountably, Rhiannon was seized with pity. Impulsively, she put a warm hand on Dinaswyn's arm in silent sympathy.

She had expected Dinaswyn to snatch her arm away. But Dinaswyn did not. Swiftly, she covered Rhiannon's hand with her own cold one. "Go to him," she said urgently. "He needs your help badly. He is tired and discouraged and angry with himself for failing with you. And, Rhiannon, please remember that what he has become isn't entirely his fault. Be patient."

"I can't promise that I will always succeed in that. But I promise to try."

Dinaswyn did not smile, that was not her way, but her cold, gray eyes warmed slightly. She nodded toward the bright rowan trees. "Go."

Rhiannon entered the tiny grove. In the middle of the circle of trees, on a carpet of green moss, Gwydion ap Awst sat brooding, his back to her. He wore a simple tunic and trousers of black and his knees were drawn up beneath his chin. His hands were clasped around them and his head was bent. He sighed as she came up behind him. Without turning around he said, in a weary tone, "Dinaswyn, I asked not to be disturbed."

"She neglected to mention that," Rhiannon said.

Swiftly, his head came up. For a moment he did not move, then he stood and turned around to face her. "Rhiannon ur Hefeydd. You came after all," he said slowly.

"Well," she said lightly, "I was in the area and I couldn't resist dropping by."

His gray eyes brightened and his mouth quirked slightly. "Were you now?"

"I was."

"Well, now that you're here, perhaps we could talk together like two civilized human beings."

"Well," she said dubiously, "we could try."

"Why don't you sit down?" He gestured for her to sit, and they sat on the green moss, facing each other.

"Why did you change your mind?" he asked, his silvery eyes keen.

"Someone tried to kill me."

His hands clenched into fists, but he did not move otherwise. "Tell me," he said quietly.

She told him of the attack, and of how she had hidden the body. "I didn't want Gwen to find out," she finished.

"Did you tell anyone? Rhoram, perhaps?"

"No. If I had told Rhoram he never would have let me leave Arberth."

"Hard enough for you to leave as it was, I imagine," Gwydion murmured.

She searched his face, looking for signs that he was mocking her, but he seemed to be quite serious. "It was," she said shortly.

"Then I am even more indebted to you for coming. There was an attempt on my life also."

"Where? When?"

"In Ederynion. At Mabon's festival."

"Before you came to find me."

"Yes. The man was killed. He took poison rather than give up the name of his master."

"And my would-be murderer told me nothing of who—only why," Rhiannon mused.

"The Captains of the four kingdoms will join us here in Caer Dathyl by tomorrow. They have their own roles to play, according to the poem given to me by the High Kings. But I, for one, will be very grateful for their expert protection. There is none better."

The afternoon sun poured through the rowan branches, pooling between them as they sat facing each other.

Gwydion's sharp gaze softened a little. "Rhiannon, I am glad you have come."

The intensity of his gaze made her drop her eyes. "I am

tired," she said abruptly, as she stood. "It has been a very long journey for me."

His tone was full of indifference as he replied, "Find Dinaswyn, then. She will show you to your room." He waved her away and turned slightly to stare at a bright patch of berries hanging from one of the trees.

She turned and left the grove. She did not look back. And so did not know that Gwydion turned back to look at her the moment she had turned away. He did not take his eyes from her until she was gone.

Part 3
The Search

On winter's first day
The one who is loved shall die,
And tears will overwhelm
The lonely heart.

> Taliesin
> *Fifth Master Bard*
> *Circa 275*

Chapter Sixteen

Caer Dathyl
Kingdom of
Gwynedd, Kymru
Ysgawen Mis, 494

Suldydd, Cynyddu Wythnos—early afternoon

The silence spun out as Gwydion and Rhiannon sat across from each other in the study of the Dreamer's Tower.

Gwydion was not at all surprised by the silence—he had expected it. After all, Rhiannon had lived in isolation with only her daughter for company for many years. She would not be adept at the art of conversation so soon after leaving her forest.

And he—well, he had not been one for conversation either these past years. Even as a child he had often kept his own counsel.

No, he was not at all surprised by the silence.

But he was surprised by how comfortable it was.

It seemed almost a companionable silence, one that was not filled with the anxiety to speak or the desire not to. And that made him very uncomfortable indeed.

The room was a cozy one, illuminated by the bright fire

370

that blazed on the hearth and by numerous candles placed in golden, branched candleholders. Floor to ceiling bookshelves covered the walls, broken only by the door to his sleeping chamber and the door leading to the lower levels. This door was carved with four silvery disks to represent the four phases of the moon. The ceiling was hung with clusters of small, silvery globes modeled on the constellations that wheeled in the sky above Kymru.

In anticipation of their guests six wooden chairs were placed around a long, wooden table in the center of the room. For now, both he and Rhiannon sat in cushioned chairs before the fire.

Gwydion glanced at Rhiannon, knowing that she would not notice his stare, for she was Wind-Riding.

He took the opportunity to study her in a leisurely fashion, which he would not have done if she had been paying attention. His gaze lingered on her beautiful emerald eyes, her high cheekbones, her slim neck, her full breasts, and her slender waist. If she hadn't been so patently dangerous he would have considered offering himself as a sexual partner. But she was dangerous. He knew it. He knew with every fiber of his being that to become involved with her would be like playing with fire. But fire was not to be toyed with. No, he would not toy with her, much as he might want to. And he did want to.

At last she stirred and her emerald eyes sharpened. Gwydion quickly looked away from her and into the fire.

"They are coming," she said, and though there were no windows for Gwydion to check the truth of her statement, he did not need to. For she was right. They were here, at last.

THE DOOR OPENED slowly, and Dinaswyn stood framed by

the doorway. "Your guests have arrived, Dreamer," she said formally, then stepped aside to gesture them in.

The first one through the door was Achren, King Rhoram's Captain. Her black hair was tightly braided to her scalp. Her black and green riding leathers were travel-stained. The badge of Prydyn, a black wolf on a field of green, glittered on her tunic. Her cloak was forest green wool. Her dark eyes were bright as she saw her old friend again. Rhiannon flew from her chair and embraced Achren.

"So," Achren said with a grin, "we meet again."

"So we do," Rhiannon answered dryly with a glance at Gwydion, "at the will of the Dreamer."

"Indeed," Achren said. "And I must say," she went on, turning to Gwydion, "this had better be good. I've been on the road for almost a month."

"As have I," Angharad said as she entered the room. Her tunic and trousers of white and sea green were dusty, but her green eyes were bright and alert. The badge of Ederynion, a white swan on a field of sea green, was sewn onto her tunic. Her molten red hair was bound in a braid that reached down to the small of her back, and her cloak was sea green. "And I agree with Achren," she went on, "this had indeed better be good."

"Rhiannon ur Hefeydd," Gwydion said formally, "this is Angharad ur Ednyved, the Captain of Queen Olwen of Ederynion."

Both Rhiannon and Angharad formally bowed to each other.

"So, you were indeed found," Angharad said, her brows raised.

"And persuaded to come to Caer Dathyl, like the rest of us," Trystan said as he entered. His dark brown hair was pulled back at the nape of his neck with a strip of red leather. His green eyes sparkled as he smiled. His red cloak and his leather tunic and trousers of red and white were clean but worn and the white horse on a field of red, the badge of Rheged was fastened to his tunic. "Like these ladies I came from a long way myself. Unlike them, my looks are diminished by my weariness."

"Very good, Trystan," Angharad said. "Flattery will get you almost anywhere."

"Almost," Trystan said, his hand on his heart. "You cut me to the quick."

"Somehow I doubt that," Angharad answered dryly.

"Very wise," Cai said the last one through the study door. His brown hair hung loose to his shoulders, and his sharp brown eyes were alert as he took in the entire room at a glance. He wore riding leathers of blue and brown and the badge of Gwynedd, a brown hawk on a field of blue, was fastened to his tunic. He had discarded his brown, woolen cloak and carried it over his arm.

"Rhiannon, this is Trystan ap Naf, Captain to King Urien of Rheged and Cai ap Cynyr, Captain to King Uthyr of Gwynedd."

The two men bowed to Rhiannon, then moved forward to the table at Gwydion's signal. Angharad and Achren also moved to the table, sitting opposite the two men. Rhiannon took her place at one end of the table while Gwydion turned to dismiss Dinaswyn. But Dinaswyn was too canny to remain for a dismissal and had already left.

"So," Gwydion said as he took his seat, "let us begin."

But Rhiannon interrupted him. "Actually, I'm curious about Alban Nerth. I suppose that most of you were on the road traveling during the festival."

He realized that she was right—they all needed some time to settle in, and talking of the Alban Nerth celebrations that took place just two weeks ago would help to do that. Alban Nerth specifically honored the warrior. All day warriors participated in games of strength and agility such as archery, spear throwing, and horseback riding. The three or four warriors that excelled at these games took part in one final contest: to be the first to shoot their arrow through an apple in mid-air.

"Actually, I did not have to leave Tegeingl until four days ago," Cai said. "So I was in the city for the festival."

"And no doubt won," Rhiannon smiled.

Cai grinned ruefully. "Actually, I didn't. I was one of the four to shoot for the apple, but another's arrow found it first."

"Uthyr's," Gwydion said with a certainty.

"Uthyr's indeed," Cai agreed. "The only person on Earth I am not ashamed to lose to."

"I was on the road," Achren volunteered. "Which means I missed my chance of winning this year against Rhoram. He won last year and I was disappointed not to be able to challenge him again."

"No doubt he won and put the arrow through the apple again this year, too," Rhiannon answered.

"No doubt," Achren said gloomily. "And no doubt I will hear about it every day until next Alban Nerth."

"But surely you won wherever you stopped for that day," Trystan said. "I know I did."

"Of course I did!" Achren exclaimed. "Do you think I don't know my business?"

"He didn't say that," Angharad jumped in. "He said—"

"I heard him," Achren replied shortly. "And since when

does Trystan need you to defend him?"

Both the women's hands flew to the daggers at their waists. Rhiannon swiftly got to her feet. "I think," Rhiannon said quietly, "that a brief rest might be in order. After all, you have both traveled far and are no doubt tired."

Angharad jerked her head at Rhiannon. "Who is she who thinks she knows so much about what does or does not wear out a Captain of Kymru?"

"She's a civilian," Achren answered. "She doesn't know any better. But she's a friend of mine, so don't be rude."

"I, rude?" Angharad asked in astonishment.

"Some might think so," Achren said with a grin.

"Come, come, ladies," Trystan said with a warm smile. "Let's begin again, shall we?"

"What's that about?" Achren asked with her brow quirked.

"He thinks he's charming," Angharad explained seriously.

"Ah, charming." Achren slowly stood up and leaned over the table toward Trystan. "Do not make the mistake of thinking I am a woman first," she said quietly. "For, above all, I am the Captain of Prydyn and if you annoy me with your insistence of calling me a 'lady' I will wipe the floor with you."

Trystan rose and planted his hands on the table, his smile gone. "And do not make the mistake of thinking that I won't hurt a woman," Trystan said. "If you annoy me further you will find that out for sure."

"Don't even think about it, Trystan," Angharad said, her green eyes flashing. "If you take her on you take me on as well."

Cai rose at that. "I hardly think that this is constructive," he began.

But the three other captains turned on him as one. "Shut up!" they exclaimed.

At that, Cai's face hardened and his brows drew together. In a dangerously quiet tone he said, "Do not even consider angering me. You would not want to see what happens if you do."

Finally, with a sigh, Gwydion rose, the last one of them to have remained seated. "While this has been very amusing, perhaps if you gave me a few moments of your precious time we could accomplish something." He did not raise his voice, yet they all slowly sank back into their seats nonetheless.

"Now," he said when they were all seated and the room was silent, "let me tell you—" But what he saw in the doorway halted him, and the words died on his lips. The others swiveled in their chairs to face the doorway, and Gwydion noted dimly that each of the Captains had their hands on their daggers. A formidable group indeed.

But the figure in the doorway raised his hands in mock surrender. "I give up," Amatheon said, pretending to cringe in fear.

"Amatheon!" Gwydion exploded. "What in the name of the Shining Ones are you doing here?"

"Interesting question," Amatheon said as he sauntered into the room. "One I would like an answer to as much as you." He bowed to Rhiannon and placed a kiss on her palm. "Welcome back, lady, to the land of the living." Something in his voice, in his eyes, apparently put Rhiannon at ease and she did not take offense. Instead, she smiled faintly.

But before she could speak Gwydion rapidly crossed the room to stand before his younger brother. Amatheon wore riding leathers of silvery gray and his dark hair was pulled back and secured at the nape of his neck with a silver clasp.

His Dewin's torque of silver and a single pearl glittered at his throat. His blue eyes were weary with travel but he smiled at his brother.

"Amatheon," Gwydion began his voice even but not concealing his anger, "what are you doing here?"

"I tell you, brother, I do not know. I know only that I had to come."

"And I know only that you have to go!" Gwydion exclaimed.

"Not smart, Gwydion," Rhiannon said.

Gwydion turned on her. If she was going to defend his brother—

"Even Amatheon does not know why he has come. If that is so, might he not have been called here by a power greater than you? There are powers greater than you, you know," she said in an acerbic tone. "Or have you forgotten that?"

"I have not forgotten that," Gwydion said between clenched teeth. "Very well, brother. Be seated."

Amatheon pulled a chair to the table next to Rhiannon and smiled at her in a way that Gwydion did not like at all. He remembered that the two of them had gone to Y Ty Dewin together and had once been good friends.

"As I was saying before I was interrupted," Gwydion said in a voice that would freeze fire, "let me tell you why I have asked you to come here. The Shining Ones have commanded me to find Caladfwlch, the sword of the High Kings of Kymru."

He braced himself for the inevitable questions. For it was obvious that the sword was needed only because there would be a High King to wield it. Of those in the room there were four that knew who that High King was: Gwydion himself; Rhiannon, for she had stopped at Myrrdin's hut and managed to piece together the truth; Amatheon, for he had been present ᴌne day of Arthur's birth; and Cai, who had aided Gwydion the night he had taken Arthur away. But the other three, Achren, Trystan and Angharad had no idea who that High King was and Gwydion was sure they would ask.

But they did not. He waited for them to, however, until Achren said, "No, Gwydion, I am not going to ask who the High King is."

"No point to that," Angharad chimed in.

"Because you won't tell us anyway," Trystan said.

"Which is just like you," said Cai, attempting to further conceal his knowledge.

"Well," Gwydion said, clearing his throat, "in that case, I'll just go on."

"Please do," Rhiannon invited him sweetly.

Gwydion scowled. "Some months ago I had a dream. And in that dream I saw a dragon, the symbol of the Dewin. And then I saw Bran, the Fifth Dreamer. Bran held out a book, and when I awoke I took that book and found in the lining a parchment that had been hidden there." Gwydion picked up the parchment and read:

> I gave a secret to my daughter,
> So secret that she did not know.
> And to her grandson she did give it,
> A secret those Dreamers did not know.
> And to his granddaughter he did give it,
> This secret that they did not know.
> In her granddaughter lies this secret,
> A secret that she does not know.

"And just what did that piece of nonsense mean?" Achren demanded.

"It meant that Bran had left a clue, a memory in the mind

of his daughter. And this unconscious memory was so powerful that she passed it to her grandson and so on, all unknow-
ing. As I traced the family tree I realized that the poem pointed to one of two women, Dewin in the twelfth generation of
Llyr—Arianrod or Rhiannon. Naturally I tested Arianrod, but
the memory was not in her."

"That must have made her well and truly mad," Angharad murmured. Rhiannon tried to hide her smile behind
her hands, but Gwydion saw it. He raised his brow but both
women looked at him in exaggerated innocence.

He went on. "So I knew I must find Rhiannon to get that
memory. I did not know, at that time, who else was needed to
accomplish the task of finding the sword. That understanding came later, as I stopped at Cadair Idris and spoke to the
Guardian of the Doors. She, too, had a message for me from
Bran given her when he bound her to the mountain. And the
message was that I must ask the guidance of the High Kings
themselves."

They were silent as Gwydion described his night at Galor
Carreg, the burial mounds of the High Kings. "At last they
came, and they gave me a poem. This is what they said:

On winter's first day
Shall the trees
Face the Guardians.

On winter's first day
Shall the trees
Do battle.

The alder tree, loyal and patient,
Formed the van.

The aspen-wood, quickly moving,
Was valiant against the enemy.
The hawthorn, with pain at its hand,
Fought on the flanks.
Hazel-tree did not go aside a foot
It would fight with the center.

And when it was over
The trees covered the beloved dead,
And transformed the Y Dawnus,
From their faded state,
Until the two were one,
In strength and purpose,
And raised up that which they had sought.

On winter's first day,
The one who is loved shall die.
And tears will overwhelm
The lonely heart.

"I knew then," Gwydion went on, "that I would need the four Captains of Kymru. For they are the trees referred to in the poem. Cai is PenGwernan, the head of the alder. And Angharad is PenAethnen, the head of the aspen. Trystan is PenDraenenwen, the head of the hawthorn, and Achren is Pen-Collen, the head of the hazel. And, somehow, you would all be vital to finding the sword."

"And the Y Dawnus identified in the next to the last stanza?" Cai prompted. "That would be?"

Gwydion had no intention of telling them that the High Kings had said another Y Dawnus was to come, compelled without knowing why. For he was acutely conscious of the song's last stanza—that one who is loved shall die. He was horribly afraid that he knew who that would be. "That would be Rhiannon and myself," he said, looking hard at Amatheon. "And no one else."

But Amatheon merely smiled and did not answer.

"My quest for Rhiannon was successful and she has agreed to help us," Gwydion said, inclining his head in Rhiannon's direction.

"And her message from Bran?" Achren asked.

"Has yet to be heard."

"Then how can you be sure she holds it?" Cai asked.

"Because she was almost killed to prevent her from sharing it," Gwydion said.

"Obviously you won the fight," Achren said to Rhiannon in a conversational tone.

Rhiannon nodded. "I used the move you taught me years ago."

"I told you it would work," Achren pointed out.

"So you did," Rhiannon said with a smile.

"Are you ready, Rhiannon?" Gwydion asked.

"I am."

"Amatheon," Gwydion said, "be prepared to write down what she says."

Amatheon picked up fresh parchment, ink and quill from the table and signaled to Gwydion that he was ready.

Gwydion left his chair and came to stand next to Rhiannon. "Face me," he commanded, and gently placed his hands on either side of her head. "You are on a plain with wildflowers at your feet," he began, his voice low and soothing. He guided her with his words across the plain into the rowan tree and to the well beneath the tree, the well of memory. "You stretch out your hand and cup the water in your palm. You drink." He took a deep breath for this was the moment. "As you drink, what do you see?"

"I see a man," Rhiannon answered, her voice dreamy. "He is dressed in black and opals. His smile welcomes me, but there is such sadness there I think my heart will break for him. Such sadness, such loss. And yet there is wisdom, payment for the grief, the sorrow he has endured."

"What is he saying to you?" Gwydion asked, his voice even. He motioned for Amatheon to write.

Seek Hard Gash
At the Battles of Betrayal.

Y Dawnus, joined together,
Guarded by alder and aspen,
By hawthorn and hazel,
Shall walk the corridors of time
And piece together
The broken circle.

Then shall the Guardians go
Horse and hawk,
Wolf and swan,
To their appointed places.

Thus will Trees and Y Dawnus,
Guardians and the dead
Meet together
On winter's first day.

Gwydion brought Rhiannon back slowly, having her ascend the tree trunk and taking her back to the plain. "Wake up," he commanded.

She opened her eyes. "Well?" she asked. "Did I have it? The message?"

"You did indeed," Gwydion answered and, nodding to Amatheon, he had his brother recite the poem.

"Hard Gash," Trystan mused. "Caladfwlch."

"Yes," Gwydion said. "To be sought at the Battles of Betrayal."

"Which are?" Cai asked.

"There are four," Rhiannon said quietly. "The first is the Battle of Naid Ronwen, Ronwen's Leap, where Queen Gwynledyr of Gwynedd killed her husband for his betrayal and where Ronwen, her husband's mistress, jumped to her death, taking her little girl with her."

"The second is the Battle of Galor Penduran, "Amatheon said, "Penduran's Sorrow, where King Pryderi led an army against his father, High King Idris, and killed Llyr, the first Dreamer."

"The third is the Battle of Duir Dan," Rhiannon continued, "Druid's Fire, where the twin brothers, King Caradoc of Ederynion and King Cadwallon of Rheged battled. They were finally stopped by their mother, who led an army of Druids to halt the battle."

"The last is the Battle of Ynad Bran, Bran's Justice, where he rightly condemned his mistress and son to death for their murder of King Llywelyn of Ederynion," Amatheon said. He looked back at the others. "Rhiannon and I had a history teacher at Y Ty Dewin who was very big on battles. We had to memorize everything about them."

"I see," Trystan said with mock gravity.

"So we must journey to each of these places," Angharad

said. "Naid Ronwen in Gwynedd, Ynad Bran in Ederynion, Duir Dan in Rheged, and Galor Penduran in Prydyn."

"These are the places I saw in my dream," Gwydion murmured, and wondered how he could not have realized this sooner. For this was the dream he had had the night he had given Arthur over to Myrrdin's care; the dream where, in raven's shape, he had visited the sites of these battles, tasting the grief of those who had participated in the campaigns. He periodically still had that dream, but was never able to deduce its meaning. The others were looking at him, and he shrugged. "Just a dream that I now understand," he said.

As one they stared down again at the poem that Amatheon had written out from Rhiannon's memory.

"What of the part about the Y Dawnus?" Trystan asked. "It says that they are joined together, guarded by what must be we Captains. Who does the Y Dawnus refer to?"

"Again, it must refer to Rhiannon and myself," Gwydion said in a tone that brooked no argument. But from this group, argument was to be expected.

"How can you be so sure?" Angharad asked. "Suppose you two are not the proper Y Dawnus?"

"We must be," Gwydion insisted. "For we are the two that have been brought together from Bran's messages to me."

"It does not say that here are only two," Rhiannon said.

Gwydion ignored her and braced himself for Amatheon to put in a word but his brother still remained curiously silent, merely frowning down at the poem.

"What does it mean to walk the corridors of time?" Trystan asked. "Isn't that something only the Dreamer can do?"

"Normally, yes," Gwydion admitted. "But somehow, in this case, I will only be able to do that with the help of another

Y Dawnus—and the Captains."

"How do you know it is you who will walk in the past?" Rhiannon put in. "It might be me."

"It is a Dreamer's gift," Gwydion said tightly. "Nobody else could possibly do it."

"I might just surprise you."

You already have, Gwydion thought. "The broken circle, now. I have no idea what that is."

"A message of some kind, I expect," Trystan said. "But what kind I do not know."

"I see we haven't much time," Rhiannon said. "It says here we must confront these Guardians on Calan Gaef, the first day of winter. That's only five weeks away."

"Indeed," Gwydion said. "We must hurry."

"Who are these Guardians?" Cai asked. "The horse and hawk, the wolf and the swan. These are the symbols of the four kingdoms. Could that mean our Rulers?"

"I think not," Gwydion said with a frown. "I think it refers to the animals themselves."

"Going to what appointed place?" Achren asked. "It says that the trees—which means us—shall bend them to our will. But what do they guard? The sword itself? Or a clue to its whereabouts?"

"Who can say at this point?" Amatheon put in. "No doubt it will become clear to us as we search."

"That is a search," Gwydion said sharply, "that you will not be taking part in."

"But I will, brother," Amatheon said quietly. "For why else was I called here?"

"I do not believe for one moment that you were 'called' here," Gwydion lied. For, in his heart, he thought that

385

Amatheon had indeed been compelled to come to Caer Dathyl as he had said. In his heart he knew that his brother was meant to accompany them. But how—in the name of all the gods—how could he possibly let his brother come? For the last stanza of Rhiannon's poem was burned into his brain:

One winter's first day,
The one who is loved shall die.
And tears will overwhelm
The lonely heart.

Was his heart not already lonely? And whose death would surely overwhelm him? Whose death if not Amatheon's? No, he could not let his brother come with them. He could not.

"You do not believe I was called here?" Amatheon asked incredulously. "You think that I am lying?"

"I did not say that—" Gwydion began.

"How could you believe that?" Amatheon went on, his blue eyes wide with shock and distress. "How could you?"

Gwydion floundered, for he did not mean to hurt Amatheon. But then he hardened his heart. He was going to save Amatheon's life, no matter what. Even at the expense of his brother's love. But he had reckoned without Rhiannon.

"He does believe you," Rhiannon calmly explained to Amatheon. "He's just afraid."

"Afraid of what?" Amatheon asked, astonished.

Rhiannon nodded down at the poem. "Of the last verse. The one that says someone will die." Her emerald gaze met and challenged Gwydion's silvery one. "He is afraid, Amatheon, that you will die if you come with us."

"I see," Amatheon said quietly. He rounded the table until he stood directly in front of Gwydion. "But if you do not let me come, I will follow anyway. So you see, you really have no choice. I'm sorry."

Gwydion clenched his fists in fury to keep himself from lashing out at his brother, so angry was he. Because he knew Amatheon would do that—he would follow. And perhaps be in more danger because of that.

"He was sent here, Gwydion," Rhiannon insisted. "You know that's true."

He knew, but he did not want to admit it, so he did not answer, merely staring at his brother, their gazes—silver and sapphire—challenging each other.

"He must go with us," Rhiannon continued. "There must be a reason he has come here now. The gods themselves require Amatheon's presence in this quest."

"You say that," Gwydion said, not taking his eyes from his brother, "because you do not understand. You say that because you do not believe that the last verse refers to him. You say that because you do not care for him as I do. You say that because he is not your brother."

"I say that because it is true," Rhiannon said, her voice cool. "And you know it."

The trouble was that he *did* know it. He knew it, and hated the knowledge.

"You must let him go," Rhiannon pressed. "You must."

Please, Mabon of the Sun, he begged silently. If there was one moment where you were pleased with your Dreamer, remember it. Remember it, and do not let this thing happen.

"Gwydion," Amatheon said quietly. "Brother. Why was I called if not to go?"

Then he had a thought. Perhaps, if he was very careful, if he was vigilant, he could see to it that Amatheon survived. Amatheon would not be in danger until the Guardians—the

387

hawk, the swan, the horse and the wolf—showed themselves. Until then, his brother would probably be safe. And then he thought of something else that might help. A deal he could make. Then they would see.

"Very well, brother," Gwydion said quietly. Amatheon's eyes began to sparkle. "But before you rejoice in your victory, hear me out."

With an effort Amatheon composed himself, and looked back solemnly.

"I will allow you to go with us only as far as Naid Ronwen, the first battlefield we must visit. If—and only if—your presence is required to see what we need to see, then you may accompany us to the other battlefields."

Amatheon nodded and opened his mouth to speak. But Gwydion raised his hand and Amatheon was silenced. "Furthermore," he went on, "you must leave us at my command."

"But—" Amatheon began.

"At my command. I require your promise."

The room was silent as Amatheon thought it over. It was a moment Gwydion would remember for years to come for it seemed to him that not only were the people in the room silent, all of Kymru was hushed and still, waiting to hear what Amatheon would decide.

At last, Amatheon agreed, "I promise."

"Then so be it," Gwydion said the words like ashes in his mouth. "Brother."

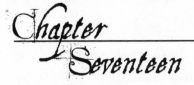

Chapter Seventeen

Commote Creuddyn
and Naid Ronwen
Kingdom of
Gwynedd, Kymru
Ysgawen and
Collen Mis, 494

Meriwydd, Cynyddu Wythnos—noon

After four days of traveling east they reached commote Creuddyn. To the south the forest of Coed Dulas shimmered in the distance, crowned with leaves of flame—the blazing scarlet of the rowan, the oak and the hawthorn and the shimmering gold of the aspen and the birch mingled in fiery harmony.

Cai thoughtfully scanned the horizon. They were nearing River Mawddoch, though they could not yet see it over the Earth's curve. Low-rocked walls divided portions of the gently swelling hills that stretched out before them. The walls were covered with yellow corydalis that crept through gaps in the stones. Shrubs of yellow bush cinquefoil dotted the ground and red snapdragons waved gently in the cool breeze.

"Who oversees this land?" Trystan asked, turning a little in his saddle to speak to Cai, who rode at the rear of the party.

"The Gwarda is Diadwa ur Trephin," Cai answered.

"Well-liked?" Achren asked from up ahead. "No trouble?"

"Fair-handed would be the most accurate description," Cai replied. "But in terms of trouble—well, Uthyr could tell you more about that."

"Meaning?" Angharad inquired.

"Meaning that she has been arguing with Uthyr for several years over a patch of land between Creuddyn and Uwch Dulas, the commote to the north. Seems she is convinced that the land belongs to Creuddyn, while the Gwarda of Uwch Dulas strongly disagrees."

"Why doesn't Uthyr just rule on it, then?" Amatheon asked curiously. "Stop the argument."

"He did," Cai said, with a grin. "But Diadwa didn't like the outcome. Uthyr gets a letter about that every week."

"She sounds painful," Gwydion said absently, but his eyes cut to Rhiannon, who rode beside him.

"I saw that look, Gwydion," Rhiannon said coldly. "Go ahead and say it—you won't be happy until you do."

"Say what?" Gwydion asked with wide-eyed innocence.

"Go ahead and say that she's painful because she's a woman. Go ahead and say that all women are."

"Why, Rhiannon, I'm surprised at you," Gwydion said. "How could you talk about your fellow women like that?"

"Want me to shoot him?" Achren asked Rhiannon, gesturing to the bow strapped to the side of her horse's saddle.

"We'd be happy to," Angharad put in, baring her teeth in a smile. "Just give the word."

"Company," Cai said, nodding toward the horizon.

A band of men sat motionless on their horses at the top of one of the distant hills. The man at the head of the pack lifted his arm and motioned the horsemen forward; the band galloped swiftly toward them.

"Thieves?" Trystan inquired calmly, loosening his bow as both Achren and Angharad did the same.

Cai rode up next to Gwydion at the head of the party and squinted ahead. "I think not. I believe they wear Diadwa's badge."

"I have no wish to be detained, Cai," Gwydion said shortly.

"No doubt. But detained we will be."

"We're in a hurry," Gwydion insisted.

"And Diadwa is one of Uthyr's Gwardas," Cai answered. "And must not be offended. Come, Gwydion, I know my own people. If we can avoid being sidetracked, we will. If not—" Cai shrugged. "Things could be worse."

"Don't be churlish, Gwydion," Rhiannon said sharply. "Besides, a regular bed would be a nice change. Since you won't let us invoke the Law of Hospitality and instead make us sleep on the cold ground every night—"

"We've just started our journey," Gwydion pointed out coolly. "A little early to complain, isn't it?"

"Gwydion," Amatheon put in, "I don't think Rhiannon was—"

"If you don't like it," Gwydion went on to Rhiannon, "you could always go back to your cave."

"Except for the fact that you need me here," Rhiannon pointed out.

"Unfortunately," Gwydion said.

Cai sighed. The journey was going to be very long indeed if these two kept at it like this. They had only been on the road for four days, but it felt like much longer.

The band of horsemen came to a halt in front of the party. There were about twenty men and women in the warband. They wore tunics of stiff leather and carried bows and arrows as well as short spears and small shields. The lead horseman urged his horse forward until he was just a few feet from Cai. The man bowed in his saddle.

"Cai ap Cynyr, PenGwernan of Gwynedd, I bid you welcome to commote Creuddyn in the name of Diadwa ur Trephin."

Cai, in turn, bowed in his saddle. "I thank you for your welcome, Berwyn ap Cyrenyr, Captain of the *teulu* of Diadwa the Fair."

"May we know the names of your companions?" Berwyn asked politely, as formality dictated. But Cai knew that it was not really a question.

"Of course," Cai said, and would have gone on to introduce his companions if Gwydion had not taken over.

"I," Gwydion said, "am Gwydion ap Awst, the Dreamer of Kymru. And we are on an errand of some urgency."

Berwyn bowed. "But of course, Dreamer," he said, still very polite. But his brown eyes were keen. "Nonetheless, I long to know your companions."

Cai cleared his throat. "Naturally," he said, giving Gwydion a warning glance. He quickly introduced the rest of them—Rhiannon and Amatheon, Trystan, Angharad and Achren.

"Such exalted company must receive the best that Creuddyn has to offer," Berwyn said, again all politeness. But they fully understood the underlying implacability of his tone.

Nonetheless, Gwydion tried to argue. "Captain, I must insist—"

"You are all welcome here today," Berwyn went on smoothly. "For this very afternoon we are celebrating the marriage of our Bard and his lovely lady. We already have a feast planned. Your presence will make the marriage ceremony and the feast even more special to our lady and the happy couple."

"Very well, Captain," Gwydion said, at last admitting defeat.

"We are greatly honored," Cai said formally. "Lead on."

LESS THAN AN hour later they rode up to the fortress of Diadwa ur Trephin. The huge wooden doors set into the large stone walls of the fort were flung wide open, and a great many finely dressed people were milling about the sizeable court-yard talking and laughing, eating and drinking, calling out cheerful greetings to each other.

Autumn flowers decked the courtyard: clusters of white alyssum and bright, yellow tansy; rose-purple fireweed and red and white snapdragons; white chamomile and yellow corydalis.

Berwyn and his men dismounted, motioning for Cai and his party to do the same. As they did so a small, slender woman in a rich gown of dark blue descended the steps lead-ing to the Great Hall. She had long, dark brown hair frosted with silvery strands and held back from her face by a band of blue cloth embroidered with silver and tiny sapphires.

"You are welcome here, Cai ap Cynyr," she said, her pow-erful, rich voice incongruous coming from such a tiny frame. "As are your companions." She inclined her head to the rest of the party. "We are particularly honored to have the Dreamer himself with us."

Gwydion cocked a brow at Cai. "The man who rode on ahead gave the word, no doubt," Cai said, answering Gwydi-on's unspoken question.

"Ah," Gwydion said, then turned back to Diadwa. "Lady Diadwa, we are honored to be your guests. I understand from your Captain that a wedding is due to take place here today."

"It is," Diadwa said proudly. "And a feast after. I beg you

to be my guests here. You are welcome to spend the night under my roof." True to the Laws of Hospitality, Diadwa did not ask them their business. Only the glint in her keen, gray eyes showed that she wished to.

"We would be honored," Gwydion replied.

Cai was relieved. After Rhiannon's comment about warm beds he was afraid Gwydion would stubbornly insist that they camp out again tonight.

"The wedding is for my Bard, Jonas ap Morgan to his lady, Canna, and begins within a few moments. Dreamer, do you care to officiate or shall my Druid perform the ceremony?"

"I defer to your Druid, Lady," Gwydion said politely.

Diadwa's smile told Cai that Gwydion had guessed rightly—that to take the place of the lady's Druid would not have been wise at this late hour. Marriages and other ceremonies were normally conducted by Druids and, although custom dictated that the Dreamer took precedence over them, in some cases it was best to leave the ceremonies to the local Druids.

A man in a robe of brown trimmed with green came down the steps of the Great Hall. Around his neck was a golden torque decorated with a single emerald. His smile was friendly but Cai noticed that the smile did not quite reach the man's steady, dark brown eyes.

"Ah, Glwys," Diadwa said. "Glwys, you know Cai, King Uthyr's Captain. And this is Gwydion the Dreamer." She named the other companions then gestured to Glwys. "This is Glwys ap Uchdryd, my Druid."

Glwys bowed, the smile still pasted to his face. "You are all welcome on this day. And the ceremony is about to begin." He gestured to the bottom of the steps. "Please stand there, to one side, if you will."

Amatheon nudged Rhiannon. "Maybe after this wedding is over I could have the Druid do ours. Interested?"

Rhiannon turned to Amatheon and batted her lashes. "My goodness, you are the third man this month to ask me that."

"But definitely the most attractive."

"Of course."

Behind them Gwydion scowled ferociously. Cai smiled to himself.

At the Druid's gesture, the rest of the folk in the courtyard grew quiet and came to gather around the steps, parting in the middle to leave an aisle for the couple to walk. Glwys took his place at the top of the steps and Diadwa followed him, standing off to one side.

At Glwys's nod, a man exited from the *teulu's* quarters. He wore a tunic and trousers of dark red and a crown of sweet alyssum around his brow. He was a small, slender man with unruly, sandy hair and pale green eyes. He carried an alder branch with large, saw-toothed leaves. He fairly brimmed with contentment as he tried to suppress a jaunty grin, but failed utterly as he made his way through the crowd and ascended the steps, coming to stand before Glwys.

Again the Druid nodded, and a woman exited from Diadwa's ystafell. She wore a gown of dark red, and her pale blond hair was crowned with a chaplet of red snapdragons. She carried a vine of ivy in her tiny hands and her smile, which she could not suppress, was sweet, turning her plain features into a face of beauty. Her fine amber eyes were alight, and she could not stop gazing at her intended husband as she, too, ascended the stairs and came to stand before the Druid.

Glwys took the ivy vine from her hands and loosely

bound the bride and groom's left hands together with the vine. Jonas and Canna clasped the alder branch as one with their right hands.

At the Druid's gesture, the two of them spoke: "As we are bound hand to hand, so we are bound heart to heart." Jonas's clear voice trembled, and Canna's was virtually inaudible. "In each turn of the Wheel I have looked for you. Blessed be to Aertan, who has guided us to find one another again. At every return may I find you. And may we meet again in Gwlad Yr Haf as the children of Annwyn, together forever."

Cai, remembering speaking these words to his wife, Nest, on their wedding day, swallowed hard, his heart full. For, never had he loved a woman as he loved his wife, never had he even thought to be so happy, even after over ten years of marriage. He was a lucky man and he knew it.

He glanced around at the others. Trystan's green eyes were dark with longing as he looked at the couple, no doubt thinking of Esyllt, who was married to another. Trystan would not, Cai thought, understand for some time why Esyllt refused to divorce her husband. Poor boyo, perhaps he would never understand and remain in thrall for the rest of his life. Cai hoped not, for he liked Trystan very much.

Achren looked up at the couple with an indulgent smile that seemed to say marriage was all very well and good for those with nothing better to do.

Angharad and Amatheon eyed each other through the ceremony, though only when the other wasn't looking and Cai bet himself that it would not be much longer before those two were sharing a bed.

Gwydion, on the other hand, seemed to be ignorant of that. He had no idea that his brother's interest was in Angharad, making the mistake of thinking that Amatheon was really interested in Rhiannon. Gwydion had clearly mistaken the tone of the teasing relationship Amatheon and Rhiannon had formed and was just as clearly jealous.

The Druid took the ivy vine and the alder branch from the couple and gently laid them on the stones at his feet. He then stretched out his hands over the heads of Jonas and Canna. "Blessed be to Cerridwen and Cerrunnos, the Protectors of Kymru, whose steadfast love and partnership protect us, their children. So too may you protect and cherish each other and your children."

Diadwa stepped forward and gave each of them a gold ring. The couple placed the rings on each other's fingers then spoke together. "I wed you now, with this symbol of the Great Wheel, of death into rebirth, of endings into beginnings. I pledge to keep faith with you now and in the lives to come."

Glwys raised his hands and turned the couple around to face the crowd. "I declare that these two are now husband and wife."

The crowd cheered, calling out congratulations, swiftly moving on to raucous comments that led Jonas to blush and Canna to giggle as each remark became more outrageous than the last.

Although he did not know why, Cai felt a momentary shiver as the bride and groom clasped hands and descended the stairs. It had something to do with how Jonas looked at Canna with his heart in his pale, green eyes, something to do with a weakness of character that Cai briefly sensed. For he perceived that Jonas was a man that would clearly put his bride before all else. He hoped that there would never come a time when Jonas would have to choose between Canna and his duty to Kymru. For in such a contest, Kymru would surely lose.

Suldydd, Disglair Wythnos—afternoon

THE NEXT DAY they arrived at Naid Ronwen on the shores of the River Mawddoch. The river, wide and deep sparkled beneath the afternoon sun and shimmered like a silvery, curved blade as it wound its way through the gentle hills.

They dismounted and made their way to the bank of the swiftly rushing river. Willows bent their spreading branches of bright yellow leaves over the water. Shrubs of moneywort sporting bright yellow cup-like flowers grew tenaciously on the banks. Wall germander with soft pink flowers sprawled on the shore. White mayweed still flowered in tufts here and there and bright yellow tansy grew in clusters. Thrushes sang in the willow trees, their liquid notes soaring into the crisp, cool air.

"It seems so peaceful here," Amatheon said softly, effortlessly responding to the magnificence of the golden afternoon. "Hard to believe what happened here."

"So long ago," Rhiannon agreed. "Yet still, one might think that the battle had left some mark. If not on the land than at least on the walls of time itself."

"We must hope that it did," Gwydion said, looking around him. "For if it did not than I do not know what we could possibly discover here."

"Tell us, then, Gwydion, exactly what happened," Trystan said, his green eyes keen as he surveyed the scene.

"Yes, we want to hear all about the Battle of Naid Ronwen," Achren agreed as she dismounted.

"Perhaps then we will know what to look for," Angharad said, her bright red hair glowing as she absently loosened it from its braid.

Amatheon stared mutely at her molten hair as she shook it out. As he did, Achren's generous mouth quirked in amusement, but she held her silence.

Angharad caught Amatheon's gaze on her and smiled slowly. Amatheon's blue eyes darkened and a flush came to his cheek, but he did not look away. He smiled back and would, perhaps, have spoken, if Gwydion, not noticing his brother's distraction, had not chosen that moment to speak.

"It is called Naid Ronwen, Ronwen's Leap, because it was here that Ronwen, the mistress of the King of Gwynedd, chose to take her life and the life of their daughter well over three hundred years ago. It was right at this spot, so legend says," Gwydion went on, gesturing to a rock that protruded from the bank and into the rushing water, "that she leapt.

"This is the story. Gwynledyr, daughter of High King Idris, was Queen of Gwynedd. And she chose Eadwulf, Prince of Corania, as her husband, to help seal the recent peace we had made with that land. In Eadwulf's retinue was a woman named Ronwen, the wife of one of his retainers. But she was also Eadwulf's mistress whom he had refused to give up on his marriage. After a time Queen Gwynledyr suspected her husband was being unfaithful to her. She insisted that Ronwen be dismissed, so Eadwulf pretended to send Ronwen back to Corania; but instead, he had her installed in a tiny house deep in the forest of Coed Dulas. There, Ronwen gave birth to a daughter, Sabra.

"By now the King and Queen had three children. One day Gwynledyr took her children with her to visit her father and mother in Gwytheryn. While she was gone, Eadwulf took it into his head that his chance had come to have both his mistress and the rule of Gwynedd. His head turned by his own courtiers, who do things very differently in Corania, he declared that a woman was unfit to rule. He had himself proclaimed King and chose Ronwen as his Queen, imprisoning Gwynledyr's chief officials.

"But Gwynledyr swiftly learned of her husband's perfidy through the Bardic network. Enraged, she returned to Gwynedd and raised a sizeable army. She came to Coed Dulas and had the love nest of Ronwen and Eadwulf put to the torch. She then marched on Tegeingl only to discover that her people had already ousted Eadwulf the day before. Eadwulf, Ronwen, Sabra, and their retainers had fled, but Gwynledyr, using her Dewin, readily located them heading east.

"She and her *teulu* pursued Eadwulf's men and brought them to bay here on the shores of River Mawddoch. Seeing them crest the hill, Eadwulf turned and ran, leaving Ronwen, Sabra, and his men behind. But Gwynledyr pursued him and drew her bow. The arrow flew across the hills to bury itself in Eadwulf's traitorous back.

"Gwynledyr's *teulu* descended on Eadwulf's band and killed them all to a man. But they spared Ronwen and Sabra, bringing them instead before Gwynledyr, who was waiting for them here on the banks. Gwynledyr had it in her mind to spare these two, thinking to send them back to Corania. But Ronwen unwisely taunted Gwynledyr, thinking, perhaps, that her life was already forfeit. She mocked the Queen, saying that Eadwulf was disgusted with Gwynledyr, always longing to be free of her and her embraces. In a rage, Gwynledyr ordered that Ronwen be killed, but said that Sabra would be spared.

"But Ronwen, mad with grief and fear grabbed seven

year-old Sabra in her arms and leapt into the river. Gwynledyr's men leapt after her but it was too late, for they had both
long since drowned."

"And what," Achren asked, "did the Coranians do at the
death of Eadwulf?"

Gwydion smiled. "At the news of his brother's death the
King of Corania sent Queen Gwynledyr a present of six cups
of silver and sapphire."

"Of course," Achren said gravely. "Brotherly love."

"Speaking of brotherly love," Amatheon began to Gwydion.

But Gwydion cut him off. "We will try it without you,
first, as I said before."

Amatheon opened his mouth to protest but stopped at the
look on Gwydion's face.

"Well?" Rhiannon asked, her arms folded. "Just how do
we do this?"

"We follow the instructions from your poem," Gwydion
said coolly. "To refresh your memory, it said:

Y Dawnus, joined together.
Guarded by alder and aspen,
By hawthorn and hazel,
Shall walk the corridors of time"

"WHICH MEANS?" RHIANNON pressed.

"Which means that you and I are to join hands and kneel,"
Gwydion answered, as he took her hands in his. Since Cai
was watching very closely, he saw that a faint flush came to
Rhiannon's cheeks, ebbing away swiftly. Even more interesting, a reddish cast also came to Gwydion's face, but it, too,
quickly faded. Cai smiled to himself.

"Now," Gwydion went on, his voice steady, "the captains

will please circle us."

Achren, Angharad, Trystan and Cai huddled around the two Y Dawnus, forming an outer circle, placing their hands on Rhiannon and Gwydion's shoulders. Rhiannon and Gwydion bowed their heads and waited.

The afternoon grew hushed—the birds stopped singing and even the sound of rushing water was muted. But beyond that, nothing happened. They stood there a while longer, concentrating as hard as they knew how. But still nothing.

"Gwydion," Amatheon said gently from outside the circle. "Brother."

Gwydion's head came up and his hands tightened on Rhiannon's. He stared at Amatheon with fear in his silvery eyes. But it was obvious that Gwydion would do what he knew must be done.

At last, he did. He nodded, letting go of one of Rhiannon's hands, gesturing for Amatheon to kneel on the bank beside them. Amatheon knelt and joined hands with them. Then the three of them again bowed their heads as Cai and the others placed their hands on them.

And then Cai stiffened as a force bore down on him, expelling all the air from his lungs and bringing a curtain of darkness over his eyes.

AT FIRST EVERYTHING was dark. Then a shining light spiraled through the darkness, illuminating what were clearly the banks of the River Mawddoch. But this time his companions were gone. There was no sound to any of the images he saw as they silently spun before him.

He saw a small party of men gathered around a woman and a little girl. The woman's mouth opened in a silent scream and she clutched the arm of a golden-haired man as she pointed to a band of horsemen clothed in blue and brown that were descending the clover-studded hills to the west.

But the golden-haired man shook himself loose from the woman's crazed hold, throwing her roughly to the ground, breaking from the knot of men, and running to the north as swiftly as he could. His blond hair streamed out behind him, his powerful legs pumping, his shoulders straining against his rich tunic of sapphire blue. Around his neck an ornate torque of sapphires glittered.

One person from the band of descending horsemen pealed off from the rest, going in pursuit of the running man. The pursuer was a woman, and her rich, auburn hair streamed out behind her as she grasped a bow and knocked an arrow to the string. With a fierce cry she let the arrow loose, and it flew across the plain to bury itself in the back of the running man.

He fell to the ground and lay there, moaning. The woman drew her horse up beside him and looked down, her face impassive, as the man struggled to rise. But he could not, for he was wounded too deeply. At last he raised himself to his knees and looked up at the woman. For a moment they stared at each other. There were tears on the man's handsome face but none on the woman's. The man nodded his head as though something had been proven beyond a doubt then fell forward, dead.

The woman dismounted and reached out to the dead man's neck, snapping off the massive torque of silver and sapphire and placing it around her own neck.

The woman remounted, turned her horse and sped to the knot of fighting men without a backward glance at the dead man on the plain. The fight on the shores was brief and fierce, and when the band of horsemen in blue and brown were done, there were none left standing of the group on the banks save the screaming woman and the little girl.

The woman on horseback dismounted and came to stand before the other woman and the little girl. The little girl was a beautiful child with hair of gold and tear-filled eyes of sky blue. The little girl's mother was also beautiful and she, too, was golden-haired. But her eyes were a hard, emerald green and her mouth was set in a sneer, as she looked at the auburn-haired woman with the sapphire torque.

The golden-haired woman's face was contorted as she called what were clearly deadly insults at the auburn-haired woman. The men that surrounded them both put their hands to their weapons but at a gesture from the auburn-haired woman they subsided.

The auburn-haired woman gestured at the little girl, offering something. But the golden-haired woman, a smile of triumph on her beautiful, mad face snatched up the child. She backed away from the men, her child in her arms, her back to the river. Step by step she retreated to the rock that overhung the water. The auburn-haired woman cautiously advanced, her hand outstretched, speaking what were perhaps soothing words.

But the golden-haired woman, with a triumphant look on her face, whirled away and leapt over the water, her screaming child in her arms. The two hit the water with a mighty splash. The auburn-haired woman gestured and a number of her warriors leapt into the water, clearly bent on saving the two. But the golden-haired women's head was swiftly drawn under the water. The men dove again and again, searching for the two, but came up empty-handed.

Then the scene changed. He could tell by the lengthening shadows that some hours had passed. But the auburn-haired woman still stood on the banks, looking into the water. On the plain behind her a bonfire burned, consuming the bodies of the men who had died that day. A smaller fire burned next to the larger one but the auburn-haired woman did not even turn around as the body of the golden-haired man was thrown into the roaring flames.

Someone hailed the woman and she turned from river. Five warriors came to her from the south. Four men carried the body of the golden-haired woman, while one man cradled the dead child in his arms. The auburn-haired woman wept at the sight, her hand reaching out to the little girl, grief etched on her beautiful face.

Again the scene changed. The fires were gone—indeed, Cai could not even tell where they had been, for clover once again grew thickly on the ground. A single horseman descended the hills toward the river. He wore a tunic and trousers of black. Around his neck a massive torque of gold and opals glittered with a fiery light. His hair was rich auburn and secured at the nape of his neck with an opal clasp.

The man dismounted at the riverbank and stood still for a moment, looking at the rock from which the woman had leapt. At last he turned and made his way to the willow tree closest to the rock. He took something from his saddlebag wrapped in a black cloth. He laid his hand on the tree and the bark split beneath his fingers, showing a shallow hollow within the trunk. The man placed the bundle in the tree then again laid his hand over the gap. The bark drew tightly together over the hollow, sewing itself up as though the fissure had never been.

The man nodded, satisfied, and turned to mount his horse.

But as he did, he stopped for a moment, and looked Cai full in the face. The man's silvery gray eyes bore into Cai with a power that Cai shivered to see. But the man smiled a sad and wise smile.

Then the darkness descended again, and Cai knew no more.

HE REGAINED CONSCIOUSNESS slowly. At first he could not understand why he was laying full length on the ground or why his companions were kneeling beside him, anxiously scanning his face as he opened his eyes.

"Are you all right?" Amatheon asked, his blue eyes dark with concern.

"I hope to be," Cai said hoarsely. He sat up, aided by Trystan and Gwydion. He did not feel that it was wise to rise to his feet just yet—not with his head splitting in two the way it was. In addition he felt a low ringing in his ears and his stomach was queasy.

"Just give me a few moments," he said hollowly, closing his eyes against the pain in his head.

"What did you see, Cai?" Achren asked, apparently too impatient to give him his few moments.

"Achren," Rhiannon pointed out, "Cai just asked for a few moments. I assumed he meant a few moments of silence."

Achren snorted. "Don't be such a baby, Cai."

Cai sighed. He liked Achren very much, in spite of the fact that she was tough as old boots and expected everyone else to be the same. "You'll understand better when it happens to you," Cai said, gingerly holding his head in his hands. He thought that his head might very well burst, but then the pain subsided to a dull ache. At last he lifted his head and eyed them all as they clustered around him.

"Can you talk yet?" Gwydion asked as he handed a dripping water skin to Cai.

Cai gratefully took a drink of cool water from the River Mawddoch.

"Here," Rhiannon said, handing him a small bottle of some unidentifiable liquid.

"What is it?" Cai asked even as he swallowed a portion of the contents.

"A tisane of feverfew. It will help your headache."

"If you have done playing doctor, Rhiannon," Gwydion said, "perhaps we can get on with it."

"I am a doctor," Rhiannon flared. "I don't know what you meaning by 'playing,' but—"

"Please," Cai begged, his head still aching. "Not now."

Rhiannon subsided with a flush on her cheeks, her green eyes hard as emeralds. Gwydion merely looked at her coolly then turned back to Cai.

"I saw the Battle of Naid Ronwen," Cai said quietly.

"Everything?" Angharad asked. "Even—"

Cai nodded. "Everything; even when Ronwen jumped into the river with Sabra in her arms. I saw Queen Gwynledyr come down from the hills with her warband. Eadwulf, coward that he was, he ran, leaving his companions behind. But Gwynledyr rode him down and killed him. She took her torque back, and rode away without a backward glance. And she wept when they brought back the bodies of Ronwen and Sabra. I saw it all."

"And what might that mean?" Trystan asked Gwydion. "What clue is there in that?"

"I don't know," Gwydion answered with a frown.

"Oh, that wasn't the clue," Cai said wearily. "It was what

I saw next."

"And what was that?" Achren asked impatiently.

"I saw a man ride up to the willow tree over there," Cai went on, pointing to the trees on the riverbank. "I think it was Bran—he wore the Dreamer's Torque."

"Ah," Gwydion said with satisfaction. "Of course. What did he do?"

"He took something from his saddlebag. I couldn't tell what, it was wrapped in cloth. Then he placed it in the tree trunk."

Amatheon had risen to his feet and was inspecting the tree Cai had indicated. "I don't see any kind of hole in this trunk," he said, baffled.

"He Shape-Moved," Cai said. "He opened the trunk then closed it when he was done."

Gwydion, the only one of them able to Shape-Move walked over to the willow tree. "About here?" he asked Cai, placing his hand on the trunk.

"A little lower down and to the left," Cai replied.

Gwydion placed his hand where Cai indicated, and the bark of the tree parted like water beneath the Dreamer's palm. He reached in to the trunk and grasped something, pulling it out into the light. Before he examined his find he again placed his hand on the trunk, then sealed up the fissure he had made.

He walked back to them, Amatheon by his side, as he gently held something in his hands. The cloth had disintegrated long ago and the thing he held flashed brightly in the sun. Cai rose to his feet with the rest of them, his headache subsiding, and joined the others as they crowded around Gwydion.

The thing Gwydion held in his hands was flat and made of bright, untarnished gold. It was formed in an arc, and sapphires winked on the rounded side. On the upper right-hand side the words "Seek the" glimmered, outlined in emeralds. On the lower, pointed portion of the arc was a cluster of pearls outlined with rubies in a second, tinier arc. Words were etched in the golden arc and they were silent as Gwydion read them out loud:

> *Death comes unannounced,*
> *Abruptly he may thwart you;*
> *No one knows his features,*
> *Nor the sound of his tread approaching.*

"Bran's words surely?" Rhiannon asked softly.

"No doubt written at High King Lleu's death," Gwydion said quietly. "How Bran suffered at the death of his friend."

"This must be a piece of the broken circle that the poem mentions," Trystan said.

"Then there are three more of these," Angharad put in.

"With a chance for a headache for the rest of you," Cai said, "at the other battlefields."

"We can only hope, then, that when we have assembled the full circle it will mean something to us in terms of the location of the sword," Amatheon said.

"I don't think you'll have to worry about that," Gwydion said absently as he gently held the arc in his hands. "We'll understand it, when the time comes."

MEANWHILE, FAR AWAY to the northwest, a hawk circled the sky above the mountains of Eryi. The huge bird rode the winds, occasionally emitting a fierce cry.

And then the call came, and the hawk almost dropped to the ground with the sheer force of it.

It was time. Time to go south, to journey to the special

place. He did not know who or what called him there. He did not yet know what he was to do there, once he reached it. But he knew he was born to do this, and so did not hesitate.

He circled the sky once, twice, three times. And then he flew south, the wind beneath his wings.

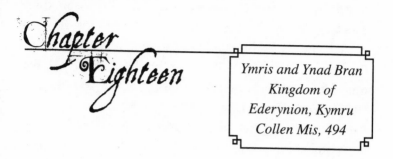

Chapter Eighteen

Addiendydd, Disglair Wythnos—early afternoon

Three days later they crossed the border into Ederynion and the following day they drew near to Ymris, the chief city in the cantref of Arystli.

And during those four days, Angharad and Gwydion had argued, and argued, then argued some more.

To the south loomed Coed Ddu, the Dark Forest, which stretched throughout most of the southern portion of cantref Arystli. Scarlet leaves of oak and rowan blazed in the distance, offset by evergreen firs and alders. Yellow birch and aspen dappled the forest with splashes of gold. Overhead the sky was clear, and there was a crisp breeze blowing that danced through the long, brown grasses of the plain that unfurled before them.

Angharad rode in front of the group with Gwydion the better to continue their "discussions." Rhiannon and Amatheon rode behind them, with Cai, Trystan, and Achren bringing up the rear of the party.

Angharad clenched her teeth and reminded herself that to lose her temper would be counterproductive. But she was precariously close to doing it anyway.

For Gwydion still refused to go just a few leagues out of their way to Ymris itself, claiming that they did not have the time. But Angharad continued to insist that they go to the city and acknowledge the Lord of Arystli, Alun Cilcoed. Angharad continued to point out that Queen Olwen herself, if she knew, would demand it.

"It would be in insult to one of Olwen's most important Lords," Angharad said again, for what seemed like the hundredth time, "to come so near and not pay our respects."

"We are not going out of our way to visit Alun Cilcoed of all people," Gwydion said flatly. "I wonder," he went on in an abstracted tone as he raised his eyes to the sky, "just how many times I am going to have to say that."

"I told you, he's nothing like his brother."

"Llwyd Cilcoed is a toad," Gwydion said, "and, no doubt, comes from a family of toads. When I was visiting Olwen, Llwyd was rude and overbearing."

"Now who does that remind me of?" Rhiannon put in with exaggerated innocence. "Let me see . . ."

"Ha, ha," Gwydion said tonelessly.

Rhiannon, Angharad knew, was on her side in this debate. Not because she thought visiting Alun Cilcoed was important, but because she never missed an opportunity to annoy Gwydion. Cai, Trystan, and Achren all sided with Gwydion, saying that Alun would not be insulted if he weren't even aware that they were in the area.

And Amatheon—well, Amatheon did not join into the debate at all. Angharad knew full well why. He was interested in her. He teased Rhiannon and paid her extravagant compliments, but he watched Angharad almost all the time. Yet he was also loyal to his brother and to Gwydion's wishes. So Amatheon kept his silence—unwilling to commit himself to either side in this ongoing debate.

"If anyone could tell me just what Olwen sees in that Llwyd Cilcoed I would be most grateful," Gwydion went on.

But Angharad would not answer him, though she knew exactly why Olwen was attracted to Llwyd Cilcoed. She wondered why no one else seemed to understand. For Llwyd bore a resemblance to Kilwch, Olwen's dead husband—the husband she had not valued until he was dead, the husband she had not known she loved until it was too late. Since he died Olwen looked for Kilwch in every man she saw, searching for a way to say how sorry she was. And she had found it in Llwyd Cilcoed.

This was something Angharad knew, but she would tell no one. For Olwen was both Angharad's Queen and her friend, and Angharad would not speak of private matters to others. Besides, Gwydion was only trying to distract her from the matter at hand. And she would not be distracted. She opened her mouth for another try, when help came in a manner she had not expected.

"I hear Alun Cilcoed is very rich," Rhiannon said idly.

"Yes, he is," Angharad replied, turning slightly in the saddle to glance back at Rhiannon. "Most of the trees we use in producing paper in Ederynion come from his forest of Coed Ddu. He has a large paper-production yard just outside the gates of Ymris. And you know how much in demand parchment from Ederynion always is."

"I suppose he must have a very large fortress, then,"

Rhiannon went on. Her green eyes were gleaming as she met Angharad's confused glance, then she cut her eyes to Amatheon, who was suddenly listening intently.

"Huge," Angharad replied, still wondering just what Rhiannon was getting at. Whatever it was, Trystan, Cai, and Achren seemed to have already understood it—they were all trying to hide their grins.

"Too bad, then, that we won't stop there. I hear Alun is known for his hospitality. Besides being able to sleep in a bed I have no doubt that he would supply us with privacy. Perhaps even giving each one of us our own sleeping chamber."

"Really?" Amatheon asked his blue eyes alight as he glanced up.

"Honestly, Rhiannon," Gwydion said absently as he carefully scanned the countryside, "you and your preoccupation with sleeping in a bed. I had no idea you were so fragile."

"And I had no idea you were so paranoid," Rhiannon replied sharply. "As if an occasional chance to sleep in a bed is hurting something. You know perfectly well that the Laws of Hospitality—"

"Are you really going to rant about that this entire trip?"

"I might," she said sweetly, baring her teeth in a smile.

Amatheon went on, as though nobody else had spoken. "Our own rooms?" he asked Angharad.

"I don't see why not," Angharad replied.

"Gwydion," Amatheon said eagerly, "I think it would be wise to stop and pay our respects to Alun Cilcoed. I really do."

Gwydion halted his horse and the rest followed suit. He eyed his brother suspiciously. "Now you want to stop to see Alun Cilcoed? I hardly think—"

Gwydion stopped. He looked at Amatheon's face. His

eyes cut to Rhiannon and he scowled, opening his mouth to say something that would, no doubt, have been rude. But then he halted again as he followed Rhiannon's gaze—for she was watching Angharad and Amatheon with a half smile on her face. Then it dawned on him. He glanced at Rhiannon who sat her horse with an air of innocence.

"Thank you, Rhiannon," he said shortly. "Thank you very much."

"I don't know what you're talking about," Rhiannon said airily.

"Yes you do," Gwydion insisted. But then he looked over again at Amatheon and his brother's hopeful, fresh face. He sighed. "All right, then. We stop and see Alun Cilcoed."

It took them less than two hours to come within eyeshot of the gates of Ymris. The city was large, almost as large as Queen Olwen's city of Dinmael and it appeared to be just as busy. The huge gates were open and people streamed in and out, for it was market day and folk from many leagues around had come to town to buy, to sell and to trade. The stone white-washed city walls gleamed under the clear sky.

Outside the walls was another much smaller stone enclosure. The gate of this structure was also opened wide and people were bustling in and out, some holding bundles in their hands.

Angharad nodded toward the smaller structure. "That is the paper mill. I suspect Alun Cilcoed is there right now."

"Then by all means, lead us on to the paper mill. I certainly didn't come this far out of our way to miss this," Gwydion said sourly.

"Gwydion, you are a sore loser," Rhiannon said tartly.

"As are you," he said swiftly. "Witness the cave I found

you in."

"You—" Rhiannon began, her green eyes hard and angry.

"Don't," Amatheon said, reaching over and touching Rhiannon's arm. His blue eyes were begging and, after a moment, Rhiannon nodded tightly and held her silence.

Angharad led the way as they rode in through the open gates into a huge courtyard. Wooden poles were set up through the yard. They served as a prop for a huge canvas tarp in the event of rain. But today it was clear, so the canvas remained rolled and stacked against one wall.

"How does this work?" Achren asked curiously.

"You've never seen paper being made?" Angharad asked in surprise.

"In Prydyn we make wine, not paper," Achren pointed out. "Know much about making wine?"

"Not much," Angharad admitted. She pointed to rows of huge, wooden tubs of water sitting to the left of the gate. "These tubs hold a mixture of linen, straw and wood. The metal pistons positioned above each tub are used to pound the mixture into a fine pulp. The pistons are powered by this team of oxen which circle the tubs."

"At least you don't use horses," Trystan said in relief. "That's not a job for those fine animals."

"Some mills do use horses, of course," Angharad said with a smile, "but never horses from your Rheged. Those horses would be far too fine for work such as this."

The team of oxen, led by a caller, circled the vats. The caller lifted his voice, cajoling the animals forward, calling them his beauties, his lovelies, entreating them in a singsong voice to follow him, which they did eagerly.

Angharad nodded to a group of men who were tilting one

416

of the tubs, pouring the contents into a huge vat. "The pulp is now fine enough to use the molds on."

Men and women, holding tray molds with fine, wire mesh on the base, dipped the molds into the vat and lifted them out again, allowing the water to drain out.

"They put the molds over there and leave them to drain out as much as possible. When they are dried they turn the tray over and deposit the contents on those pieces of felt. Then they put more pieces of felt over that, and add more parchment. Then they take the pile and put it on a press, to squeeze as much water as they can out of it." A woman lifted one of the piles and took it to the huge press, positioning it under a vise. A man pulled a few levers and the pile of felt and parchment was squeezed tightly as water slowly seeped out.

When that was complete the woman took the pile to another group of women. "They are hanging each sheet up to dry," Angharad said as the women hung the sheets over a huge line that stretched across one full side of the compound.

"What are they using to hang them on?" Amatheon asked.

"Human hair," she answered. "It's the only thing soft and fine enough."

"Then it's done?" Amatheon asked.

"Not yet. Then they take the dry sheets and dip them into those vats there," Angharad said, nodding her head to another portion of the courtyard.

"What's in them?" Rhiannon asked.

"Gelatin. Made from horse's hooves. After that they will hang the sheets up again until they dry."

"Then they are done," Gwydion said.

"Then they are done," Angharad agreed.

"And here, I do believe," Rhiannon said, "is the man we

417

came to see."

Alun Cilcoed, having caught sight of them, made his way through the press of people, tubs and oxen that crammed the courtyard. Alun had dark hair and intelligent brown eyes. He was tall, taller even than Gwydion and lean. He was dressed in a laced-up tunic and trousers of soft, tanned leather. His arms were bare, for he was not wearing a shirt beneath his tunic. The only ornament he wore was an armlet of gold on his upper right arm. His locks were tied back at the nape of his neck with a piece of leather. Although it was autumn, and the day was somewhat cool, Alun's forehead was beaded with sweat, for he was working alongside his people.

"Angharad ur Ednyved," Alun said formally, bowing low. "You are most welcome here. To what do we owe the honor of your visit?"

"To the fact that you have a large fortress," Angharad said dryly.

Alun's brows went up.

"I promised my companions that you would be able to provide a room for each of us for the night," Angharad explained, her lips twitching, although her tone was solemn.

Alun grinned and as he did Angharad noticed that her companions smiled, even Gwydion. "Then, by all means, you must join me tonight. We will feast together and you shall have the best my house can offer."

"And the sleeping arrangements?" Angharad asked pointedly.

"You shall each have a private chamber," Alun said grandly, "as that is clearly what you came for." He eyed them all then grinned again. "Whether you each stay the night in them is certainly up to you."

Angharad stretched luxuriously on the feather mattress. A fire burned cheerfully in the fireplace. A huge bearskin rug rested before the hearth. The bedstead was covered with a fine coverlet of sea green. A glass beaker full of red wine along with two glass goblets tinted a delicate green rested on the small, oak table next to the bed.

Angharad, having just visited the bathhouse, was clean and warm and wrapped in a guest robe of green velvet. Her red hair, still slightly damp from her bath, cascaded down her back as she slowly drew a comb through the shining strands.

The knock on her door did not startle her, for she knew who it was. But when she opened it, she discovered she was wrong.

"Gwydion!" she exclaimed.

Gwydion stood with his arms crossed and a scowl on his handsome face.

"What are you doing here?" she asked, more sharply than she had meant to. She definitely did not want Amatheon to see Gwydion at her door and get the wrong idea.

"I don't want to spend the night, if that is what you are worried about," he said shortly. "Don't be ridiculous."

"It is not a ridiculous assumption," she pointed out, stung. "After all, we've spent a few nights together before."

"True," Gwydion said a gleam in his silvery eyes. "But this journey is hardly the time or the place to continue such meetings."

"I didn't think it was," she said shortly.

"Didn't you?" he asked, his brows raised.

"You—"

"I meant Amatheon," Gwydion explained. "What are you trying to do, Angharad? Curious to compare brothers?"

419

She flushed, if only because part of her had been entertaining that notion. She lashed out, raising her hand to slap his face, but he caught her hand before she could.

"Don't even think about hitting me, Angharad," he said evenly.

"And don't even think about telling me what to do," she said between gritted teeth as she snatched her hand from his grasp. "What is this all about, anyway?" she asked in a calmer tone. "We are friends, Gwydion, who have been, on occasion, lovers. Since when do you care who I sleep with?"

"Since the man in question is my brother."

"And that matters because?" she asked, her brows raised.

"Because I think he might be in love with you."

Angharad's breath caught in her throat. She had not thought of that. Surely Gwydion was mistaken.

Gwydion, correctly interpreting her expression, went on, "I know what I'm taking about. I know my brother. What will you do, if I am right?"

"I don't know," she said honestly, after a moment of silence. "I really don't."

"Ah," he said, the scowl melting from his face. "I see."

"You see what?"

"I see that loving my brother back is not out of the question."

"How do you know that?" she asked brusquely.

"Because if it was out of the question you wouldn't still be contemplating sleeping with him tonight."

They were both silent for a moment. Then Gwydion went on, in a gentler tone. "What will you do, Angharad?"

"I really do not know," she said slowly. "But I can promise you, Gwydion, that I will be careful."

"Than that is enough, I suppose. Good night, Angharad,"

he said as he raised her hand to his lips and turned it over to kiss her palm. "I wish you a pleasant evening."

She watched him walk down the corridor and turn the corner. She stood for a moment in her doorway, thinking on what Gwydion had said.

She knew that the wisest thing she could do would be to turn away Amatheon at the door. She was the Captain of the warband of the Queen of Ederynion, and that was the most important thing in her life. Her experience of men indicated that they wanted to be the most important thing. That was why she had long ago decided that a permanent relationship was not for her, for she would not put up with a man who demanded that he be the center of her world.

She slowly shut the door and returned to the edge of the bed, picking up the comb again and absently running it through her hair. It would be best to send Amatheon away. She knew that now. She had no wish to hurt him, and no intention of becoming permanently involved.

She answered the door, her comb still in her hand. It was he. His blue eyes were alight with desire. Before she could even speak he reached out and caressed a thick, silken lock of fiery hair that cascaded over the front of her robe, drawing his breath in sharply as he did so.

"Amatheon," she whispered. And then she drew him into the chamber, her lips on his, closing the door behind him.

Meriwydd, Disglair Wythnos—early afternoon
THE PARTY DREW near to the gravesite in the bright afternoon. The mound lay just on the fringes of the forest, surrounded by delicate aspens whose golden autumn leaves shook and whispered in the slight breeze. Sweet white alyssum sprouted

through the stones of the mound, so thick that it seemed that the grave was covered with a delicate snowdrift.

Angharad made to dismount her horse but Amatheon was already there, lifting her from the saddle and setting her on the ground, his hands spanning her slim waist. The others tried to hide their grins, but Angharad didn't really mind that at all. She felt like grinning herself, for her night with Amatheon had been truly wonderful. He had been passionate, as his brother had been, but he had also been tender and loving, for his deepest feelings were involved. And this was as unlike Gwydion as could be. Their lovemaking had been the best she had ever had—and she had had many men. But never one like Amatheon.

"Thank you," Angharad said to Amatheon after he helped her down.

"Yes," Achren said, her generous mouth twitching, "if you hadn't helped her down she might have fallen."

Rhiannon laughed. "Her experience on a horse being so limited," she explained.

Amatheon, his eyes alight, smiled. "Tease me all you want to," he said cheerfully, "I can take it."

"You should," Cai said as he dismounted. "Since you can certainly dish it out."

Trystan, still on his horse, batted his lashes at Amatheon. "Maybe you could help me down too?"

Amatheon, a grin on his face, pulled Trystan from the saddle to the ground. Trystan rolled and instantly got to his feet with an answering grin. The two men squared off, each going into a wrestler's stance.

"I bet my saddle on Trystan," Achren said.

"Done," Cai replied promptly.

"Pardon me," Gwydion said acidly as he got down from his horse, "but does anyone happen to remember what we are doing here? I ask just out of curiosity."

"Oh, Gwydion," Rhiannon said as she, too, dismounted, "you're such a killjoy."

"Apparently someone's go to do it," Gwydion said shortly. He fixed Amatheon and Trystan with his silver eyes and the two men straightened up, an innocent look upon their faces.

"We weren't doing anything," Amatheon said ingenuously. "We were just waiting for you to get on with it."

"Than wait no more," Gwydion said.

"Tell us about this place," Cai said seriously. "What exactly happened here? And when?"

"It happened in the year 275," Rhiannon replied as Gwydion opened his mouth to answer. "Ten years after High King Lleu was murdered. It was called the Battle of Ynad Bran. Known as the fourth Battle of Betrayal."

Gwydion gave Rhiannon a hard look at her interruption and she smiled sweetly at him. "Perhaps," she said graciously, "you would care to take it from here?"

"I would," Gwydion said shortly.

But Angharad thought she saw the faintest gleam of humor in his eyes. It was a sight rarely seen, and it surprised her.

"It began in 260," Gwydion said as the others gathered around the grave. "That was the year when Sulia, the Queen of Ederynion, died; the year her husband, King Llywelyn, became unhinged by grief at her loss. King Llywelyn called his three daughters to him after the funeral. There was Regan, the eldest, mistress of Bran the Dreamer. There was Gwladas, the second daughter, wife to King Peredur of Rheged. And there was the youngest, Luched, who was not yet married."

Gwydion gazed down at the barrow as a slight breeze shook the aspens. "Regan and Gwladas, mindful of the riches they could still get from their father, spoke effusively of their love for him when he asked. But Luched was forthright and honest. She said that she loved her father as meat loves salt. Which is to say that they complement each other. But King Llywelyn took this to mean that she did not love him. In a rage, he exiled her from Ederynion, declaring that she was an untrue daughter.

"Luched traveled to Cadair Idris and told High King Lleu what her father had done. Lleu and Bran, along with many others, tried to get Llywelyn to change his mind, but he was adamant. Lleu offered Luched a place in Cadair Idris. After a very short time Dylan, Lleu's younger brother fell in love with Luched and, with Lleu's blessing, the two were married.

"In Ederynion King Llywelyn was becoming increasingly erratic. He became forgetful; sometimes thinking for days at a stretch that his wife was still alive and his mind began to wander more often. His advisors pled with Regan and Gwladas to help him, but they did nothing. The advisors begged Llywelyn to allow Luched to return, but he refused.

"Five years later Lleu was murdered," Gwydion went on. "Dylan and Luched left Cadair Idris and went to live at Caer Dathyl, at Bran's invitation. Regan was highly displeased by this and threatened to leave if Bran did not revoke his invitation. But Bran refused to change his mind and Regan left Caer Dathyl, taking their son, Cacamri, with her. Apparently, Bran, who had been disenchanted with her for some time, was relieved to see her go."

"And his son?" Trystan asked.

"Was more like his mother than his father," Gwydion replied. "So Bran did not object when she took him. He objected only when Regan wanted to take their daughter, Dremas, also. For Dremas was to be the next Dreamer, and Bran refused to let Regan take her. So Regan, along with her son, went to Ederynion and took over the government of that land, for by this time King Llywelyn was incapable of ruling in any effective way. She dismissed her father's Captain and installed a man of her own choosing. She got rid of all Llywelyn's advisors and replaced them with men and women loyal to her.

"She ruled in her father's name for five more years, until 275. That year her sister, Gwladas came to visit. Gwladas was not happy in her marriage. Regan played on her sister's unhappiness, seeking to get her cooperation in a scheme to murder their father. For Regan was tired of waiting for the rule of Ederynion to be wholly hers. If Gwladas would help her, Regan would make Gwladas her co-Ruler, and could leave her husband for good. Why Gwladas ever believed her sister, I'll never know."

"Her plan," Rhiannon clarified, "was to have Gwladas murder their father. And ensure that Gwladas alone took the blame."

"True," Gwydion continued. "The sisters arranged for Llywelyn to take part in a hunt. Cacamri prepared and gave to Gwladas a skin of wine laced with poison. During the hunt Gwladas gave it to Llywelyn to drink. Llywelyn fell very ill, but made it back to Dinmael before he collapsed. At last he repented of his treatment of Luched and sent word to her, via the Bardic network. Luched, Dylan and Bran came to Dinmael as quick as they could and arrived so swiftly that Llywelyn was still alive.

"It was there that Bran discovered the truth of the matter.

He caught Regan taking the Torque of Ederynion from her father's dying throat. Then he found the poisoned wineskin, and tricked Gwladas into confessing. Regan, Gwladas, and Cacamri fled, but not before Cacamri tried to stab his father. But Dylan saved Bran's life and the three murderers got away in the confusion, taking with them Regan's warriors as well as Gwladas's men."

"Was Bran wounded?" Achren asked.

"His lover and his son had just murdered the King of Ederynion," Trystan mused, "and his own son had tried to kill him. I'd say he was wounded."

"Yes," Gwydion agreed. "He was." He paused and the breeze chose that moment to shake the aspens again, and they shivered as though in sympathy with Bran's pain. "Bran, Dylan, Luched and her father's loyal warriors followed the three, and brought them to bay here, at the fringes of Coed Ddu. The *teulu's* fought through the afternoon as Luched led the battle against her sisters. She killed Mael, Regan's Captain, and that ended the battle. Regan, Gwladas, and Cacamri were brought before Luched, Dylan, and Bran for judgment."

"Bran would not plead for the lives of his lover and his son," Rhiannon said quietly.

"No, he would not," Gwydion said just as quietly. "It was Bran himself that upheld the law, for according to it, patricide is punishable by death. When Bran pronounced it, Gwladas and Cacamri pled with Bran to change his mind. But Bran was adamant, for it was indeed the law. So all three were condemned."

"How did he justify that?" Cai wondered.

"He said that the only way the punishment could be remitted was via a High King. And with Lleu dead, there was no

High King," Rhiannon said.

"I suppose you think him wrong," Gwydion said to Rhiannon, intently watching her face.

Surprised, she turned to him. "No, I don't," she said. "He was right. And how it must have hurt him to say it."

"I didn't think you would understand," Gwydion said, his voice low.

"Didn't you?" she replied.

The two eyed each other for a few moments. At last Gwydion held out his hand and she took it. Amatheon squeezed Angharad's hand, then stepped forward and joined hands with Gwydion and Rhiannon.

Achren, Cai, and Trystan surrounded the three Y Dawnus. Then they all turned to her, waiting for her to join them, to complete the circle, to receive the message that Bran had sent them from the past.

She stepped forward and joined them, gently laying her hands on Amatheon's shoulders. Suddenly darkness veiled her eyes, and she was falling, falling, falling into long ago.

A BRIGHT LIGHT almost blinded her after the darkness and she blinked rapidly, trying to focus. She was standing at the fringe of the forest, and the gravesite was gone, the spot unmarred and covered with green grass.

She raised her eyes and beheld a fierce battle taking place in front of her. Men with badges showing a silver swan on a field of sea green fought desperately with each other. Although they clearly gave out their battle cries, Angharad could hear nothing. Weapons clashed and rang, but all was silent as she watched.

Two women and a young man were standing in the center

427

of the field, the battle raging around them. The first woman was tall and slender, and her auburn hair had come loose from its braid and flowed down her slim shoulders. Around her neck was an ornate torque of silver and pearls. Her eyes were dark and cunning, and she stood imperiously, unafraid, a dagger gripped tightly in her hand. The second woman was heavier, with brown hair and her gray eyes were fearful and full of tears as she cringed away from the battle. The young man's hair was auburn and his eyes were gray, filled now with fierce battle-fever as he, too, crouched, ready to fight.

The second woman cried out then and pointed and Angharad followed her movement, although she could not hear what the woman said. She was pointing at a third woman who had stepped to the front of the opposing battle line. This woman also had auburn hair, but it was braided tightly and wound around her head. She had eyes of silvery gray and her expression was determined as she faced the warrior who had stepped up in front of her in challenge.

The two fought for only a few moments, and then the silver-eyed woman stepped forward, going under the warriors' guard and thrusting her sword into his chest. The man's back arched in agony and he fell, blood spurting from his wound.

Then, on either side of the woman, two men appeared. One had golden hair and a fierce expression. The other had long, auburn hair and cold, gray eyes. Around his neck he wore an ornate torque of opals and gold. He raised his hand and shouted something, pointing to the woman who wore the silver torque.

The warriors guarding the two women and the young man rose from their battle-crouch at the man's words. They were surrounded by the warriors led by the silver-eyed woman and surrendered their weapons.

The man with the opal necklace stepped forward past the warriors and stood in front of the three. The woman with the silver torque looked at the man with contempt, while the second woman sank to her knees. The young man stood frozen in fear.

The silver-eyed woman stepped up then and went straight to the woman with the torque. She pulled the torque from the woman's neck, her face implacable. The man with the golden torque spoke again, and the brown-haired woman collapsed in a huddle at his feet. The young man dropped to his knees, clearing pleading. But the man with the golden torque shook his head.

The woman whose neck was now bare simply looked at the man, her face twisted with hatred and pride. She spat at the man and the woman who now wore the torque gestured to one of her warriors. Swiftly the man stepped forward and plunged his blade into the woman's chest. She sank to her knees, both hands gripping the blade, never taking her eyes off the man with the golden torque. And the man watched implacably, unmoving as she died.

The man with the golden torque watched, did not move, did not speak, did not look away: even as tears gushed from the young man's eyes, even as the young man sank to his knees in supplication, even as a warrior stepped forward and speared the young man, even as the young man fell forward and died.

Then, at the silver-torqued woman's gesture another warrior plunged his blade into the brown-haired woman, and the three were dead. All the while the golden-torqued man stood, unmoving, his eyes glittering, his head held high.

Then the scene changed abruptly. The field was lush

and green, cleansed of the taint of battle. The gravesite was back, but the aspens were small, clearly newly planted. Alyssum had begun to grow between the stones, but the growth was sparse.

The man who had watched the deaths so stoically crossed the field on a golden horse. He halted the horse before the grave and dismounted, looking at the stones, his head bowed. Around his neck glittered a torque of gold and opals.

He turned and took something from the saddlebag that was wrapped in black cloth. He knelt down at the foot of the grave and stretched forth his hand. The earth parted slightly, forming a hole. In this cavity he placed whatever object he was carrying, then stepped back. At his gesture the earth mended itself, covering the hole.

He stood for a moment, looking down at the grave, his face still hidden from her. At last he raised his head and stared right at her as she stood at the foot of the grave. She saw that tears were streaming from his silvery eyes and down his grieving face. Yet he gave her a brief smile before the darkness took her again.

SHE OPENED HER eyes to see Amatheon bending anxiously over her.

"Relax, Amatheon," Gwydion was saying. "You know she'll be fine."

"Eventually," Angharad croaked.

Rhiannon handed her a small cup. "For the headache," she said.

Gratefully, Angharad drank. She looked up and caught Cai's sympathetic gaze. "Now I know what it was like for you," she whispered.

"Tell us," Gwydion said as Achren and Trystan helped Angharad to her feet.

"I saw the battle, of course," she said carefully. If she didn't do everything carefully just now her head would split in two. "Bran just looked at the three of them as they were executed. He never even turned his face away."

Achren raised her brow. "A cold bastard."

"I don't think so," Angharad replied. "The scene shifted, then, and Bran came back to stand before the grave. And he grieved. Who knew that a man could come to such grief as the grief I saw in his face and still live?"

"And what did he do with our message?" Gwydion asked softly, after a moment.

"He buried it, at the foot of the stones."

Gwydion went to stand before the grave. He stretched out his hand and the earth parted, just as Angharad had seen Bran do. Something glittered in the dirt, for the cloth that had covered it had long since rotted, and Gwydion reached down and picked it up.

Like the first piece they had found, this piece was gold and the curved arc of one side was rimmed with sapphires. On the lower left, lined in emeralds, were the letters "ovelta." A cluster of pearls outlined with rubies formed a second arc on the pointed portion. A poem was incised on the piece and Gwydion read it aloud:

Woe that I ever was born
And my father and mother reared me,
That I did not die with the milk of the breast
Before losing my heart's brother.

"Poor Bran," Amatheon said quietly. "He had been grieving for Lleu, still, even as this new grief came to him."

"Bran would always grieve for Lleu, I think," Gwydion said, "first and foremost."

"Forever," Angharad agreed.

FAR TO THE north, on the shores of Llyn Wiber, a swan glided over the cool, clean water. Her feathers gleamed whitely in the sunlight and the water sparkled and shone beneath the sun's golden rays.

And then the call came and the swan halted on the water, her head reared back in surprise.

It was time. Time to fly south, to journey to the special place. She did not know why she had to do this thing, only that it must be done, that the call could not be ignored.

She spread her huge wings and launched herself skyward with a cry of farewell to the other swans gathered there. She set her course south, and flew.

Chapter Nineteen

Meriwydd, Lleihau Wythnos—late morning

Trystan rode at the rear of the party, lost in thought, for he knew they were coming closer to Duir Dan and knew that the next part in this quest was in his hands.

They had crossed the border from Ederynion into Rheged earlier that morning and rode now across the smooth plain. The seemingly endless flat expanse was covered with long grass, some brown and withered, some so bright a green it was like spying a nest of precious, glowing emeralds. Haycocks dotted the plain, glistening in golden mounds. A slight wind blew, swooping down over them, stirring the grasses into patterns whose meanings were elusive, impenetrable.

Gwydion led the party, as always, flanked by Amatheon on his left and Cai on his right. Cai was regaling the two brothers with some story, apparently having to do with Uthyr and his latest hunting expedition. It seemed to involve a wild pig, a bet, and a great deal of mud. Gwydion was actually laughing; something he so rarely did that it still astonished

433

Trystan that the Dreamer even could.

Just ahead of him Angharad rode in the middle, with Achren on her left and Rhiannon on her right. Their conversation had to do with Amatheon and his skill in the art of love-making as compared to Gwydion's. As near as Trystan could tell, Angharad seemed to be saying that while Gwydion might have more finely honed skills, Amatheon was more enjoyable due to the fact that there was, according to Angharad, love involved—something conspicuously absent in Gwydion's bed.

It amused Trystan to notice that Rhiannon appeared to be contemptuous of Gwydion and his skills in that area, but she listened very closely all the same. Achren was clearly not minded to test Angharad's word in this, but she was curious nonetheless and asked a number of pointed questions that anyone less forthright than Angharad would undoubtedly have refused to answer.

Trystan sighed to himself, for all this talk reminded him of Esyllt, King Urien's Bard, the woman he had loved for what seemed now to be most of his life. He missed her, and even at this moment the memory of their many nights together stirred him. For she tempted him with her white arms, her silky light brown hair, her beautiful blue eyes, tempted him with her promises, with her low laughter, with her sweet kisses.

Yet promise after promise she had broken. Time after time she had given her word that she would divorce her husband, yet she never had, always drawing back from taking that final step, always pleading with him to understand, always telling him that she truly loved him, and him alone.

Trystan spied movement on the far western horizon. As he expected it was a herd of wild horses making their way through the tall grass. Herds of horses proliferated throughout

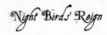

Rheged, but none were finer than those that roamed the plains of Maenor Deilo.

A fierce neigh drifted across the plain as the lead stallion reared and called out. The herd swirled and eddied restlessly as the stallion continued to call out. And that, Trystan thought later, was all the warning they received. Later he marveled that the horse had sensed what was to happen, that the stallion had done his best to alert them. At the time, however, there was very little time for reflection, for it was difficult to think clearly when fighting for your life.

The men seemed to spring out of the earth itself, although they had surely simply been hidden in the long grasses. They leapt up silently, daggers in their hands. There were at least fifteen of them, maybe more, and they seemed to come straight for Trystan, disdaining the others. The only reason he did not die in that first moment was because of Achren and Angharad.

For quicker than thought these two captains had their weapons out and began fighting the men off so swiftly, so impossibly, it took Trystan a moment to realize he wasn't dead. Rhiannon's shout alerted the others and Cai, Amatheon, and Gwydion turned their mounts and rode swiftly back to where Trystan and the three women fought.

Gwydion gestured and fire sprung up between Trystan and the man who was closest to him, forcing the man to back away. In that moment Rhiannon plunged her dagger into the man's neck and he fell. Another man leapt at Trystan, forcing him from the saddle as the two struggled. Trystan lost sight of what the others were doing as he rolled on the ground, fighting off this attacker. At least the others were drawing the men off him, for he only had the one man to contend with at the moment. Trystan drew his dagger as he rolled on top of his assailant and plunged the blade into the man's throat. Blood spilled over Trystan's hands. He rose to his feet, crouched in fighting position, just in time to meet another attacker.

Although he had only a second to take it all in, he clearly saw the entire battle. Achren and Angharad were fighting valiantly, their swords drawn, holding four of the men at bay. Cai was fighting three off at once, a dagger in his left hand and his sword in his right. Amatheon and Rhiannon held their own but they were not as experienced as the captains of Kymru were and Trystan knew they wouldn't last much longer. Gwydion laid about him with Druid's Fire, holding his dagger but not using it as much as he did the flames. But Trystan knew that calling fire was not easy, even for the Dreamer, and knew Gwydion could not continue much longer either. There were still eleven attackers on their feet and Trystan could see it would only be a matter of time before they were overwhelmed.

Hoof beats laced the edges of his awareness as he continued to fight. Had the herd come to help them, called, perhaps, by Gwydion or even Rhiannon? He would not take the risk of glimpsing around but he hoped that was what it was.

But it was not, for out of the corner of his eyes he saw ten mounted men riding to them from the west. This was, no doubt, more of the enemy and he knew they were done for. He spared a last thought for Esyllt, for his King and his Queen, and for their children whom he loved and would not see again.

It was the war cry that the lead rider gave out that changed everything. For Trystan knew that cry, knew that voice, knew that rider. He answered the cry with a like one, and realized that he would live through the morning after all.

For the rider was Cynedyr the Wild, son of Hetwin Silver-Brow, Lord of Gwinionydd. Cynedyr was one of Trystan's dearest friends, and one of Amatheon's, too, for Amatheon served in the court of Hetwin.

Cynedyr and his men fell on the attackers, mowing them down as a scythe mows through wheat. Within moments the attackers were dead. All but one, for Gwydion had cried out and pointed to one of the men, shouting that he was to be spared, and Cynedyr's men had obeyed instantly.

Cynedyr sprang from his horse and gave out a whoop at the sight of Trystan and Amatheon, who returned Cynedyr's call, pounding each other on the back in exuberant welcome.

"I see I came just in time," Cynedyr grinned as he eyed Trystan and his companions. "I may never forgive you for trying to have a party without me."

Trystan laughed. "It seems that the gods themselves invited you all the same. What do you here?"

"Why, I came to see the Gwarda, Eiddon ap Dalldef."

"For what purpose?" Trystan asked.

"To collect the galanas, the blood-price, his man owed to my Da," Cynedyr explained. "Two weeks ago, in Llwynarth, Eiddon's men and my men ended up engaged in a friendly brawl. But things were awry, and one of my men was killed. I came here and spoke to Eiddon's court yesterday. They were in agreement that the accused clan was in the wrong, and have granted the galanas I had asked for."

"And what did you ask for?"

"As this is Maenor Deilo; I of course asked for horses," Cynedyr replied, his eyes alight with glee.

"How many?"

"Four—three for me and one for the King, as his share of

the galanas. King Urien is looking for a new mare for Princess Enid. It was sheer luck that I was nearby at this moment," he went on, more soberly. "We were west of here, eyeing the herd when the stallion began calling out. He wasn't looking at us, so we knew we weren't the cause. We rode east as swiftly as we could and saw your battle, though I was as yet unaware who you all were. Though I know it now. For some of you I know well, some of you only by sight, and one of you not at all." Cynedyr bowed specifically to Rhiannon, his brows raised, his eyes alight with curiosity and something else.

At his regard Rhiannon's green eyes sparkled and she smiled at him. But before she could answer Gwydion stepped between them, his silver eyes snapping with imperfectly repressed irritation. "This is Rhiannon ur Hefeydd, whom I believe you know by reputation. The others I am certain you already know." In a milder tone he went on. "And we are grateful indeed for your help today. For I do not think that any of us would still be alive had you not come when you did."

Cynedyr bowed, obviously awed by Gwydion. "I am grateful in my turn for the chance to be of service to the Dreamer of Kymru."

"I would question, now, the prisoner your men hold."

"Of course." At Cynedyr's gesture two of his men brought the prisoner before Gwydion. Cynedyr's men held the man's arms in an unmoving grip and forced the prisoner to kneel before the Dreamer.

"Who are you?" Gwydion asked, his silver eyes glittering.

"I will not tell you, Dreamer, so there is no use in asking," the man said, his dark eyes hard and unyielding.

"What were your orders?"

"Ah, that I will tell you, for my master said I might. Our

orders were to kill Trystan ap Naf as soon as he crossed into Rheged."

"Why?" Trystan asked sharply.

"That I do not know. I know of you and personally bear you no ill will. I and my men did only what we must do."

"Who is your master?" Gwydion asked.

"That is my business, not yours," the man said proudly.

"You are wrong," Gwydion said quietly, his tone deadly. "It is my business. And I will know that answer. Be assured of that."

The man smiled and seemed to bite the inside of his lip. At that tiny movement Gwydion leapt forward, forcing the man's mouth open. But he was too late, for the mint scent of pennyroyal wafted from between his lips.

"Rhiannon!" Gwydion snapped.

But Rhiannon was already running to her horse and rooting through her saddlebags. She ran back, a small vial in her hand.

"Tip his head back," she ordered and she poured the contents of the vial down the man's throat. Gwydion closed the man's mouth, pinching his nostrils to make him swallow. After a moment, he did, and Gwydion released his hold. But the sickly smile on the prisoner's face told them their efforts were in vain.

"Sage," the man said softly, "was the right remedy. But there is not enough of it to counteract what I have taken. I am done for, as I mean to be."

"But why?" Amatheon said, taking the dying man's hands in his. "Why?"

The man's face broke out in a sweat. He arched his back in agony as the first convulsion took him. "I owed a debt," he gasped. "And did what I must do to repay it."

"Owed a debt to whom?" Gwydion demanded.

"That I will not tell you, Dreamer," he rasped. "That is for you to discover. If you can." At that he cried out, straining against the hands that held him. He bit his lips so hard that they bled, and blood flowed down his chin. His dark eyes stared at the sky above and tears glittered on his lashes. "Forgive," he whispered as the last convulsion took him. "Forgive."

Then he was dead, his eyes opened but unseeing, his last breath leaving his body with a sigh.

"Who would do this to him?" Rhiannon asked, her voice shaky. "Who would have such power over him?"

"I do not know," Gwydion said thoughtfully, speaking in a low voice so that the men of Cynedyr's warband could not hear. "Whoever it was they knew that Trystan was the next one to walk the past. If he was killed, our quest would be over."

"Who would know that?" Amatheon asked.

"Someone who was watching us," Gwydion said.

"Someone who profits by the continued absence of a High King," Rhiannon put in. "For without the sword a High King cannot come into his powers."

"Who might that be?" Achren wondered. "Who would not wish a High King to return?"

"Someone with things to hide," Gwydion said grimly. "Someone with plans that would benefit them, and not Kymru. Long ago the Protectors themselves came to me in a dream. And they warned me to be on watch for traitors among us. This is proof that they were right."

Gwydion turned back to Cynedyr, who stood with his men, patiently waiting for the low-voiced conference to be over. "You must not think us churlish, Cynedyr," Gwydion said politely. "We do not wish to offend."

"You do not offend," Cynedyr said swiftly. "The business of the Dreamer is not to be questioned."

Gwydion smiled with satisfaction until he saw that Rhiannon was rolling her eyes.

"Dreamer," Cynedyr went on, "I believe it would be best if me and my men stayed with you on this journey you are on, to guard you, though I do not pretend to understand what this is all about."

Gwydion suddenly noticed that Cynedyr's gaze was fixed on Rhiannon. Trystan, though he would have preferred Cynedyr's company, smiled to himself. He was in no doubt as to how Gwydion would react now.

"I thank you for your generous offer," Gwydion said evenly. "But we must refuse. For our purpose must be kept secret if we can make it so."

"I understand," Cynedyr said, clearly disappointed, but just as clearly not taking offense. "What, then, can we do for you all?"

"Will you and your men take on the task of disposing of these bodies?" Gwydion asked.

"We will, Dreamer," Cynedyr replied solemnly.

"Speak of what happened here today to no one," Gwydion warned. "I wish, for your sake, that you could tell the tale, for you saved our lives and we are more grateful than we can say. But it cannot be, for now."

"I do not need to puff myself up by boasting of my adventures. As a matter of fact, there are a number of things that my own father still does not know." Cynedyr grinned. "One more won't hurt him.

THAT NIGHT TRYSTAN volunteered to stand watch. To his

441

surprise, the others did not quarrel. Perhaps they understood his need to think of what had happened today and what would happen tomorrow.

They camped on the plain in the shelter of a ring of oak trees. Gwydion lit the fire using his gift of Fire-Weaving. Whenever they camped out Gwydion did so, calling the Druid's Fire in elaborate ways, forming fiery rose blossoms and swords, glowing horses and trees, anything that came to mind. They had all come to the point where they looked forward to Gwydion's nightly shows. All but Rhiannon. For she usually scanned Gwydion's face at those times thoughtfully, as though seeking to confirm something she had guessed long ago. But what that thing might be, Trystan did not know. He did not think the others knew either—even Cai who was so good at reading the truth behind men's eyes.

They had eaten a simple meal and had sat around the campfire for a while, speaking in desultory tones. At one point Amatheon and Angharad had risen and gone for a walk. They all pretended to believe as they had since Ymris, that a walk was all those two had in mind. It was true that they all seemed to have difficulty keeping a straight face at those times, but they did their best.

"Don't stray too far," Gwydion warned. "I have been Wind-Riding for the past hour or so and have seen no one. Nevertheless, be wary."

"Could I perhaps persuade you not to Ride in our direction?" Angharad asked with a grin as she took Amatheon's hand.

"But of course, Angharad," Gwydion said airily. "Your wish is my command."

The two had returned some hours ago and one by one Trystan's companions had fallen asleep in blankets before the fire.

Overhead the waning moon continued to rise in the night sky. Stars glittered coldly and thickly across the heavens. Trystan walked the perimeter of the camp, taking care to keep the campfire in his peripheral vision, but not to look directly at it, for it would ruin his night vision if he stared at the flames for long.

Movement near the campfire halted him and he crouched down, his hand on his knife. But it was only Gwydion sitting up. The Dreamer freed himself from his bedroll and sat looking into the fire. Trystan wondered if Gwydion had dreamt something and, if so, what it might be. A flicker of movement and Rhiannon, too, sat up.

"Did you dream?" Rhiannon asked, softly so as not to wake the others.

Gwydion nodded. "It is of no matter. An old dream. One I have had many times before."

"But one that still has the power to hurt you."

"Hurt me?"

"I can see it in your eyes," she said quietly. "Tell me."

For a moment Gwydion hesitated. Then, to Trystan's surprise, he answered her. "I am at Cadair Idris. It is night and the three High Kings come from their graves to stand before the Doors. They each draw a ghost of Caladfwlch from their scabbards and lay them on the ground. Arderydd, the High Eagle comes and tries to take them." Gwydion halted.

"And then?" Rhiannon prompted.

"And then the shadows of the plain rise. They moan and twist together. They cry out, threatening the eagle. I leap in front of the shadows, to try to protect the eagle. And then . . ." Again, Gwydion fell silent.

"And then?" Rhiannon pressed.

"And then the shadow reaches for me. It reaches into my chest and tears my heart. It is so cold. The pain is like nothing I have ever known. It is a pain that makes me wish for death to stop it."

"I am sorry," she said, gently laying her hand on his arm.

"Don't be," he replied harshly, as though already regretting the moment of intimacy. "I neither need nor want your pity."

"Don't start," she warned him.

"Of course pity is what you do best, isn't it?" Gwydion went on implacably. "Or is that running away?"

It seemed to Trystan that the slap she gave him would have wakened the dead but the others never moved from their sleep. Gwydion grabbed Rhiannon by her shoulders so hard that his fingers sank into the flesh of her arms. He opened his mouth to say something, but no words came out. He looked down at her and she looked up at him. For a moment neither one of them moved. Trystan saw Gwydion bend his head toward her. But he halted before even beginning the kiss he had in mind. He drew back, his face suddenly stern and unyielding. Rhiannon pulled away from him and he let her go. She turned away, going back to her blankets, turning her back to him.

So it was only Trystan that saw Gwydion did not take his eyes from her until morning.

Suldydd, Tywyllu Wythnos—late morning
AS THEY JOURNEYED west for the next few hours they saw the shores of the River Rhymney in the distance. Trees clustered the banks, their leaves of gold and flame blazing in the early afternoon sun.

Millponds branched off from the river and mills dotted

the banks, for Rheged was a land of golden grain, and the mill wheels turned constantly to grind the grain to flour. Occasionally they saw a cluster of houses near the river and crossed near field after field of rich grain. A number of the people they saw in the distance were winnowing grain. Using large baskets they threw handfuls of wheat into the air to separate the kernels from the chaff, the kernels, being heavier, fell back to the bottom of the baskets, the chaff floating to the top.

They saw a woman and her young children picking rushes by the shore for use in making candlewicks, for beeswax candles were another staple product of Rheged. Beehives dotted the plain, rising from the grasses like golden towers, bees buzzing gently in the cooling breeze.

Trystan spotted the tall, slender marker that stood in splendid isolation in the middle of the plain. The dark stone stood silently. The sides of the tower were carved with whorls and circles, while tiny figures did their deadly dance of battle in between. Yellow corydalis twined around the base of the obelisk, seeking, perhaps, to brighten the midnight stone.

They drew near to the marker and silently dismounted, coming to cluster at the stone's slender base.

"Tell us," Cai said, not taking his eyes from the stone. "Tell us exactly how it happened."

"Cadwallon and Caradoc were the twin sons of Rhys, the first King of Rheged," Gwydion began. "Their mother was Ellylw, the daughter of Govannon, the first Archdruid of Kymru. The twins had been very close as young boys. If one began a sentence, the other one had finished it. They were inseparable and their love for each other was pure and strong. Cadwallon, the elder by only a few moments, was destined to be King of Rheged, yet any jealousy the two boys were capable of remained dormant. Until the day that they met Eilonwy, the daughter of Gwydd, the second Dreamer."

The wind blew mournfully past the stone and the sun overhead seemed to draw back, paling slightly, taking some warmth from the golden afternoon.

"For they both loved her passionately the moment they saw her. And she returned the love of Cadwallon, but not that of Caradoc. Caradoc was devastated when Eilonwy agreed to become Cadwallon's wife. He convinced himself that the only reason she had done so was because Cadwallon would be King. If not for that Eilonwy would have loved him, Caradoc, and they would have been happy forever. So thinking he began to brood. He left Llwynarth for he was not willing to see his brother and his new bride so happy. He lived alone in a manor some leagues away from the city, and did not come often to see the couple. But then he took thought and realized that there was a way he could be King, in spite of his brother. So he rode to Ederynion and presented himself to the Rulers of that country, and caught the eye of Gwenis, their daughter and heir. He charmed her, he wooed her, and he won her. But he was not in love with her, although Gwenis understood this to her sorrow far too late.

"As the years went by the two brothers had children. Cadwallon and Eilonwy had two little girls, while Caradoc and Gwenis had two little boys. Eventually Rhys of Rheged died, and Cadwallon took his place as King. His mother, Ellylw withdrew from Rheged in sorrow, and went to live with her brother who was now Kymru's Archdruid in Caer Duir. Seven years later the King of Ederynion died, and Gwenis became Queen, so Caradoc was at last King.

"And still it was not enough. He had his wife's love, but

did not want it. He had sons, but did not care for them. He had the rule of a country, and it did not bring him joy. He began to try to persuade Gwenis to let him lead a force into Rheged. He pressed her, saying that he was truly the elder but the malice of his mother's serving woman had prevented it, for she had switched the two babies at birth, declaring Cadwallon the elder, though this was not so. And Gwenis, although she did not believe him, pretended that she did, for she still hoped to win his regard. Against her better judgment she gave him what he wanted, and called the muster, charging her husband to lead them into Rheged and take back what was rightfully his."

"I am surprised High King Macsen didn't do something then," Achren said. "He was Gwenis's brother and surely he knew what was happening."

"He did know," Amatheon put in.

"And he did indeed do something," Rhiannon said. "He—"

"Do you two mind?" Gwydion interrupted acidly. "Every time I try to tell a story of the Battles of Betrayal, you two jump in."

"I told you," Amatheon said earnestly, "we had a teacher that was very taken with the Battles. She would drone on about them all the time."

"Until we could drone on just as well as she," Rhiannon said. "But of course you want to be the center of attention, Gwydion. I must have forgotten that, though how I could do that is puzzling. Forgive me, and do go on." Rhiannon's tone was just as acidic as Gwydion's, clearly showing she had not at all forgotten about Gwydion's behavior last night.

Gwydion shot Rhiannon a hard look but did not chose to answer her. Instead, he continued with the story. "Caradoc took his army across the border into Rheged and they were met right here by Cadwallon and his army. The two lined up against each other a half league apart here on this plain. Caradoc had his Captain ride forward, declaring that his cause was just, declaring him to be the elder, declaring him to be the true King of Rheged. Cadwallon's answer was to throw back his head and laugh in contempt at this claim. Enraged, Caradoc gave the order to fight.

"The two armies began to gallop toward each other, weapons drawn, fierce battle cries on their lips. They engaged with a fierce clatter. Men and women began to fight and began to die. Suddenly, a wall of flame leapt up from the ground itself. Druid's Fire burned bright blue and orange and the heat seared the warriors, causing them to halt and retreat as quickly as they could. The wall of fire lowered, but still burned. From the west hundreds of black-cowled Druids poured onto the plain. They were led by two shrouded figures. One remained at the head of the Druids that now clustered on the side of the battlefield. The other marched forward to stand between the two armies as the flames sank and died to embers. The figure pulled back its hood, and the twins gasped. For it was Ellylw, their mother, and her face was stern and implacable. The figure that led the Druids also pulled back his hood and they saw it was their uncle, Sandde, the Archdruid.

"Ellylw walked forward in the sudden silence, stepping over dead warriors until she stood before Caradoc. He remained on his horse looking down at his mother who stood at his stirrup. 'My son,' she said softly, 'what do you do here?' And Caradoc tried to tell her that he was truly King of Rheged, but he faltered before her clear gaze; she who knew best of all that his story was a lie. She spoke gently to him as he fell

silent, of his days as a boy at his brother's side. She spoke of
the love they once had for each other, of the love she knew
still lived, though quenched and silent, as the Druid's Fire now
was, but ready to spring up again, as the Fire still was. Caradoc listened to her, his face bitter at first. But as she spoke,
reminding him of times past, his face changed. Tears gathered
in his eyes and began to spill down his white, drawn face. At
last he dismounted from his horse. He discarded his helmet,
his sword, his spear and his shield. He took the dagger from
his boot and plunged it into the ground. He took his mother in
his arms and gently kissed her forehead. Then he walked forward, unarmed, defenseless, skirting the dead and the dying,
walking toward his brother's army.

"And Cadwallon, seeing his brother coming, leapt from
his horse, instantly discarding his own weapons. Crying out
his brother's name he swiftly crossed the plain and the two
eagerly threw themselves into each other's arms, laughing and
crying at once. Caradoc begged his brother's pardon, offering himself up as prisoner to be killed or whatever Cadwallon
willed. But Cadwallon refused, saying that the best place for
his brother was back in Ederynion with the wife and children
who loved him so. And Caradoc agreed that this was where
he belonged, consenting to return home and saying that now
he would truly love the family that loved him. He needn't look
any further for his happiness. Their mother joined them there
and embraced them both, and the tears of all three mingled
on their faces. Caradoc, true to his word, returned home, his
heart released at last from its frost."

"And whose idea was the monument?" Angharad asked.

"Macsen's," Amatheon replied before Gwydion could
answer. "For with Macsen's power as High King the Druids

raised this stone from the bowels of the Earth that very day. And carved it, too, with the power of their minds amplified through Macsen."

"Who was, no doubt, holding the sword we seek at the time," Achren mused.

Gwydion nodded. "Yes, for all High Kings must do that for their powers to succeed."

"Then let us do what we must to find this sword, then," Trystan said. "For my turn has come and I am ready to take it."

Rhiannon, Gwydion, and Amatheon knelt and joined hands as they did so. Then Achren, Cai, and Angharad clustered around them, laying their hands on their shoulders, leaving space for Trystan to come forward.

Trystan took a deep breath. Cai and Angharad gazed back at him with sympathy, for they knew the feeling he would soon experience. Achren waited patiently, knowing her turn would soon come. Trystan walked forward, and placed his hands on the shoulders of the three Y Dawnus.

And the darkness swallowed him whole.

HE SAW TWO armies spilling across the plain, one from the north, the other from the south. Hundreds of warriors with their antlered helmets galloped to form two lines that stretched across the plain. Their hair was braided and bound for battle. The tunic and breeches of those from the south were red and white, while the clothing of those from the north was sea green and white. The warriors in red wore the badge of the rearing stallion, while those in green wore the badge of the white swan. Each man and woman, no matter which side they were on carried bows with quivers of arrows slung over their shoulders, as well as short spears, small shields, and swords.

Men and women seemed to be taunting each other, shouting the kind of cries that were preludes to battle. But Trystan could not hear them, for everything was silent. The silence in his ears seemed to press against him, thundering in his head.

Overhead the sky was clear, the bright blue unmarred by even the smallest cloud. The sun beat down almost mercilessly over the plain, as though Mabon, King of the Sun and Lord of Fire was himself displeased. As well he might have been for he was the god most revered in Rheged and that land had been invaded with no cause.

At last the warriors were ready and they faced each other, their weapons gripped firmly, their horses rock-steady as they waited for the signal. A man rode to the front of the line of the northern warriors. On his head he wore a helmet fashioned of silver in the shape of a swan with outstretched wings. The swan's eyes were two emeralds that seemed to glitter viciously under the golden sun and the entire helmet was studded with luminous pearls.

A second man rode to the front of the southern line. He wore a helmet of bright gold covered with gleaming opals and fashioned like the head of a fierce stallion. The stallion's eyes were fiery opals that flashed fire at the swan.

A herald rode forward from the northern line and spoke some words Trystan could not hear. The man in the golden helmet laughed, throwing his head back to the sky. The man in the pearl-encrusted helmet stood in his stirrups and shouted something. Then both lines were on the move, leaping forward to shed each other's blood. They engaged fiercely, and the blood began to flow, soaking into the once pristine ground.

Then a bright blue and orange line of fire sprung up from the very bowels of the Earth and the two armies halted, confused and frightened. Horses bolted and men could not control them. Brown robed Druids poured onto the plain, pooling like a shadow on the edge of the battle. One robed figure detached itself from its fellows and made its way to the center of the line of fire. Then the figure threw back its hood.

Her hair was rich gold, streaked with veins of bright silver and tumbling down her slender shoulders. Her eyes were like the blue of cornflowers but the expression in them was anything but flower-like. This woman was intensely determined. She would not be stopped, would not be turned aside. The warriors would bend to her will, and that was the end of the matter.

She walked forward toward the northern line and the man in the pearl helmet sat stiffly on his horse and watched her come. The two spoke for a long while and then the man leapt from his horse, tears streaming down his face, into the woman's arms. He threw down his weapons and walked forward, past the woman, across the plain, heading straight for the golden-helmed man.

When the man with the helmet of gold saw the first man coming, he instantly leapt from his mount, also divesting himself of his weapons. The two men met in the center and threw their arms about each other. They wept, their tears mingling together. The woman walked forward and joined them and they swept her into their embrace.

The woman said something to the two men and motioned them back from the spot they were standing. She signaled again, to the shadowy pool of brown-robed Druids. For a moment no one moved. Then Trystan felt a shaking beneath his feet. Men, women, and horses were tumbled about as the shivering plain struggled to give birth.

A crack appeared just at the spot where the two men had stood only a moment before. It yawned wider still, and from the depths of the Earth a huge, black stone rose, breaking through the Earth's crust, reaching for the sky. When it was as tall was three men, the stone halted and the Earth stilled.

At another gesture from the Druids the stone seemed to shape itself under the hammer of an unseen hand. Tiny whorls and circle appeared, covering the monument. Small figures of warriors sprang into being, brandishing their weapons up and down the side of the stone. Then the stone shimmered and solidified, the final surface glittering like dark glass. As one the warriors turned west, for they knew that this was Macsen's work, their High King and they bowed in reverence.

Then the scene shifted. The warriors, horses, and Druids were gone. A lone rider crossed the plain. His long auburn hair was bound at the nape of his neck with an opal clasp. Around his neck he wore an ornate torque of opal and gold. He came to a halt at the base of the stone and dismounted, looking long at it, unmoving.

At last his shoulders heaved with a sigh, and he turned to his horse, reaching into his saddlebags. He drew out something wrapped in a dark cloth and held it gently in one hand. With the other he gestured and a tiny fissure appeared in the base of the stone itself. He deftly slipped the slender bundle into the stone. He stepped back and, at his gesture, the stone neatly knit together again.

He turned away from the obelisk and remounted his horse. He sat his horse for a moment then looked over at the place to the side where Trystan stood. The man looked at him for what seemed like a very long time with his silvery, sad eyes. Then the man smiled. And the plain faded away.

WHEN TRYSTAN OPENED his eyes he was laying on the ground. Amatheon supported his head and shoulders while Rhiannon held a cup to his lips. He drank greedily, knowing that the contents would help prevent his head from splitting in two. Eventually.

He sat fully up, still cradling the wooden cup in his hands, his head bent. At last he looked up carefully at the others who clustered around them.

"Where?" Gwydion asked.

"In the base of the stone itself," Trystan rasped.

"And Bran?"

"Smiled at me. He did not weep this time. But his eyes were sad."

"He missed Lleu," Gwydion said softly.

"And always would."

Gwydion rose and went over to the base of the stone. "Show me exactly where."

Trystan supported by Amatheon and Cai rose and went to stand next to Gwydion. "There," he pointed, his voice still shaking and his knees weak from his enforced Walk between the Worlds.

Gwydion bent down, gently placing his hand on the place where Trystan had indicated. A gap appeared in the stone and Gwydion reached in and pulled out something that glittered in the sunlight.

It was in the shape of an arc, as the other two pieces were. It was made of gold and the curved border was rimmed with sapphires. At the top of one straight side 'eye of' was written in tiny emeralds. The pointed portion, like the others, shone with pearls outlined with tiny rubies. As with the others, a poem was incised in its golden surface. Gwydion read it aloud:

> *The sun rises when the morning comes,*
> *The mist rises from the meadows,*
> *The dew rises from the clover,*
> *But, oh, when will my heart arise?*

"Poor Bran," Rhiannon said quietly. "Poor man."

Gwydion did not answer, only went to his saddlebags and pulled out the other two pieces. He placed the three pieces together, with the piece from Gwynedd on the upper left, the piece from Rheged on the upper right, and the piece from Ederynion on the lower right. The three pieces were clearly forming three-quarters of a circle. The center of the upper portion now read: "Seek the eye of." But just what the object that the pearl and rubies at the center was forming, they could not be sure.

"One piece left," Trystan murmured.

"Mine to find," Achren said. "At Galor Penduran."

"The battle where Llyr our first Dreamer lost his life, where his wife, Penduran grieved," Amatheon said. "I do not envy you the sight of that, Achren. Not at all."

SOME LEAGUES TO the southeast a horse galloped across a plain in Ystlwyft. He ran freely, the wind rushing through his mane, the sun shining above, and the field glistening at his hooves.

Then, all at once, his heart gave a mighty leap and he came to a dead stop, his head cocked. For he had heard a call, a call he did not understand, but could not ignore.

It was time. It was time to go northwest, to journey to the special place.

He did not hesitate, for that was not in his nature. He

reared high; reaching for the sky, neighing fiercely then leapt forward, the leagues between him and his goal melting away as he ran.

Chapter Twenty

Llyn Mwyngil,
Gwytheryn and
Galor Penduran,
Kingdom of
Prydyn, Kymru
Collen Mis, 494

Gwaithdydd, Cynyddu Wythnos—late morning

Eight days later they neared Llyn Mwyngil, the huge lake that lay southwest of Cadair Idris. It had been on the shores of this lake, Achren recalled, that Bran had found the dying High King, Lleu Silver-Hand; had, perhaps, spoken to Lleu in those last moments. If so, history had not recorded what had been said, for which Achren was profoundly grateful—it was only right that some things remained private.

The lake before them glistened beneath the cold sun, the waters shimmering like a handful of azure sapphires. Off the far northern shore of the lake a large island rested. The isle was covered thickly with apple trees as far as could be seen. The time for the apple harvest had come and gone, and there were no apples left on the trees or on the ground, though no man had taken the fruit. Only the animals ate the apples there—the Kymri left Afalon strictly alone, for it was said to be a holy place. It was the chosen place of Annwyn, Lord of Chaos and his mate Aertan, Weaver of Fate, and no man or woman willingly encountered those two. Only the High Kings visited that isle, and even they had done so only at great need.

Behind them, to the east from where they had come, the long, now yellowing grasses of the plain were stirring beneath the hand of a chill wind. The sky overhead was a clear, crisp blue. It was so clear that Achren could still see the peak of Cadair Idris far to the northeast, and the topaz glow of Coed Llachar, the forest that abutted the deserted hall of the High Kings. The mountain had remained in sight as they had ridden across Gwytheryn over the past days, although it was many leagues away and they had not attempted to approach it. No one had even hinted that they wanted a closer look, for there was something about the cold, shuttered mountain that touched the heart, bringing a shroud of sorrow and loss to subdue the spirit. And that was something no one was eager to sample more closely without cause.

Within just a few days, Achren knew, they would cross out of Gwytheryn and into Prydyn, reaching the fringes of Coed Aderyn where the battlefield of Galor Penduran lay. And there she would likely see things that she had no wish to see. For that battle was surely the most heartbreaking of all the Battles of Betrayal. She was not looking forward to doing what she must do. But she would do it, for she had never turned away from her sworn duty.

And this was indeed a sworn duty, for her King had given his word that Achren would do whatever the Dreamer required of her. She had Rhoram's honor to uphold—a cause dear to her.

Life had been much better ever since the Dreamer had visited Arberth. It had been Gwydion's presence, his questions about Rhiannon, which had forced Rhoram to confront the truth of what he had become. It was that which had given Achren the impetus to shake Rhoram from his grief, to mock him back into life. Since that moment the Rhoram she had known years ago had returned.

He laughed again. He was enjoying life again with the old zeal—pursuing women, wine, and song without the underlying sadness he once had. And for that alone Achren was grateful to the Dreamer. For she had sorely missed the old Rhoram and was happy to have him back, once more interested in the world around him.

She knew he would wish to hear of everything—every word, every gesture, every expression—that her companions gave on this journey and so she had stored it all to tell him. When she returned they would spend many evenings drinking fine wine in the Great Hall and talking about this journey and other things until dawn surprised them.

At least, Achren thought, as she glanced ahead at her companions, the journey was now almost blessedly quiet, since Gwydion and Rhiannon were, once again, barely speaking to each other.

The silence had the merit of making it easier to concentrate. And quiet was necessary, for the land dipped without warning in this part of Gwytheryn. Achren was keenly aware that such terrain made them highly susceptible to ambush. The long grasses could easily conceal any number of warriors, and it was difficult to see what was beyond the next rise. Since Duir Dan they had all ridden warily, their weapons close at hand, their eyes sharp, their bearing alert. They were a formidable group, for four of them were the finest warriors in all of Kymru. The remaining three were exceptional in another

459

way, for they were all adept at Wind-Riding; they now scouted ahead and behind, able to send their awareness many leagues away to scour the countryside for signs of trouble.

The sound of singing drifted toward them from somewhere up ahead. Gwydion called a halt, his hand lifted. "Amatheon?" he called.

Amatheon, who had been responsible for scouting ahead to the west, blinked, pulling his awareness back from the Wind-Ride. "Yes?"

"Who is that ahead? Why didn't you warn us?" Gwydion asked sharply.

"It's just a farmer and his family," Amatheon said with a careless shrug.

"Doing what?"

"Plowing."

The singing continued, a cheerful song, sung without instruments in a rich and powerful voice.

"Is it a caller?" Cai asked.

"Indeed," Amatheon answered. "Singing the oxen along."

"I didn't think anyone lived around here," Angharad said.

"Very few people do," Gwydion said absently as he urged his horse forward to crest the rise ahead of them. "Most think the place haunted, since the death of Lleu so close by."

"And so it is," Amatheon said with a shiver. "Can't you feel it?"

"What have we to fear from Lleu?" Trystan asked softly. "For does he not know our errand?"

They crested the hill and saw a field stretched out before them. Half of the field was plowed, the newly turned earth glistening in dark russet furrows. Two huge oxen pulled a plow guided by a middle-aged man with dark hair. The plow's leather harness was strapped around his strong shoulders and his step was light as he guided the blade of the plow into the earth.

The caller, the man who sang ahead of the oxen, beckoning the animals forward, was an older man with long, silver hair. He had a smile in his voice as he sang in a rich, pure tone.

Saplings of the green-topped birch,
Which will draw me from the fetters
Repeat not they secret to a youth.

Saplings of the oak in the grove,
Which will draw me from my chains,
Repeat not thy secret to a maiden.

Saplings of the leafy elm,
Which will draw me from my prison,
Repeat not thy secret to a babbler.

The Wild Hunt with their horns are heard,
Full of lightning is the air,
Briefly it is said; true are the trees, false is man.

"Bran's song," Gwydion murmured, his face suddenly pale.

"It is a common song," Rhiannon said sharply. "Many sing it."

A young boy came bounding across the field, a jug in his hand. He drew up next to the two men and they halted. The dark-haired man smiled and took the jug from the boy, ruffling the boy's hair as he did so. He then handed the jug back to the boy who scurried over to the silver-haired man. The old man took the jug and drank. As he did so he clearly saw Achren and her companions at the crest of the rise. The man smiled as Gwydion rode forward down slight hill, coming to a halt at the edge of the field, the rest of them following.

"You sing a song of Bran," Gwydion said softly to the old man.

"I do," the silver-haired man said, his blue eyes alight with something Achren could not immediately name. His voice was rich and smooth with a hint of hidden power. "And you are well met, Dreamer."

"You know me," said Gwydion flatly.

"And all your companions," the dark-haired man said. "Amatheon ap Awst and Rhiannon ur Hefeydd. The great captains of Kymru—Cai ap Cynyr and Angharad ur Ednyved; Trystan ap Naf and Achren ur Canhustyr. You are all well met indeed."

The silver-haired man smiled, even as Gwydion stiffened and Achren and the other captains laid their hands on their swords. "I am Rhufon ap Casnar," he went on. "This is my son, Tybion, and my grandson Lucan."

Tybion inclined his head while Lucan bowed awkwardly, his sandy hair getting into his wide, bright, blue eyes.

"And we have been expecting you, Dreamer," Rhufon went on. "For we are of the Cenedl of Caine. The descendants of Illtydd, the last Steward of Cadair Idris."

"Illtydd was killed when Gorwys took Cadair Idris," Gwydion said flatly.

"But his son Samson was not," Tybion replied, his eyes glittering blue as sapphire.

"Bran himself gave us this land," Rhufon said, gesturing to the field and several like it that stretched out from the shores of Llyn Mwyngil. "When he had overcome Gorwys and shut up the mountain, he took Samson here. Bran charged him with continuing in his sworn task, as the heir of the House of Caine, to serve the High Kings of Kymru. And Samson wept, for the High King was dead, and he could not serve as he was born to do. But Bran said that was not so. That even in the absence of a High King the Stewards of Cadair Idris could serve.

"And we do. Every year we sow our crops. Every year we harvest them. Every year we grind wheat to flour. We cure pork and beef. We pluck apples and plums and other fruit. We brew ale and cider. And we take it all to Cadair Idris, against the day when the High King returns."

"When we bring the new food, we take away that which we have brought before," Tybion said softly. "All is always ready there, for when the High King returns."

"And just how," Gwydion said, astonishment written on his face, "do you enter the mountain? For no one can enter there, not unless the Doors open for them. Which they will not do without the Four Treasures."

"You are right," Tybion said. "For the Doors do not open for us."

"Then how do you enter?" Gwydion pressed.

"Ah," Rhufon said, his eyes alight, "now that would be telling."

Gwydion stiffened. The morning itself seemed to fall silent as the Dreamer and the Steward confronted each other. The birds had ceased to sing and even the oxen were stilled, frozen into place. Gwydion's silvery eyes bored into Rhufon's sapphire ones. But after a moment Gwydion relaxed. Achren did not know what he had seen in Rhufon's wise, azure eyes;

but whatever it was, it was enough.

"That would, indeed, be telling," Gwydion said softly. "And that, for one of the House of Caine, would be a tragedy."

"The Stewards of Cadair Idris are loyal to the High Kings of Kymru," Rhufon said quietly. "And to none other."

"So they are," Gwydion replied the hint of a smile in his voice.

"We know what you seek," Tybion said.

"Do you?" Gwydion said evenly.

"When you find Caladfwlch," Rhufon said, "you must bring it to us."

"Must I?"

"We will see to it that it is placed where it belongs."

"And that is?"

"In the golden fountain that lies in the center of Brenin Llys, the throne room in Cadair Idris. There it will stay, awaiting the touch of the High King," Rhufon said serenely.

"So it will," Gwydion said. "It will indeed."

Addiendydd, Cynyddu Wythnos—noon
THREE DAYS LATER they arrived at the battlefield of Galor Penduran. The confrontation had taken place on the fringes of Coed Aderyn, near the border of Gwytheryn and Prydyn. Coed Aderyn, Forest of the Birds, was aptly named, for birds speckled the trees, singing in their clear, sweet voices. Wrens and sparrows, thrushes and bluebirds sported through the flame-colored leaves, calling to each other.

"They seem to be restless," Trystan said, gesturing to the birds.

"They are welcoming Rhiannon back," Gwydion replied. "For Coed Aderyn was her home."

"Is my home," Rhiannon said sharply.

"Yes," Gwydion said blandly. "Is your home."

Achren shook her head, for these two never missed an opportunity to needle each other and she was not in the mood to put up with it. Truth to tell, she was nervous and she didn't like feeling that way, for she had little experience with such an emotion. "Not now, for the Shining Ones sake," she snapped. She had expected them to take issue with her but they did not. Perhaps they clearly understood and therefore declined to argue.

Trystan dismounted and went to her horse, offering his hand to help her dismount. Though she did not need the help she did not chose to disdain it, for it was kindly meant.

She stood still for a moment and briefly closed her eyes, gathering her strength. Then she walked forward and stood at the foot of the barrow that rested at the edge of the forest. Tall grasses fringed the ring of dark stones. Tiny rose-purple flowers of fireweed grew erect through gaps in the stones, like drops of blood. A yew tree, the tree of mourning, was planted at the head of the grave. Its needles were scattered in layers across the rocks as though the tree itself had wept for many years.

"So, this is Pryderi's grave," Achren said quietly.

"You have never seen it?" Cai asked softly.

Achren shook her head. "In Prydyn we do not speak often of Pryderi, our first King. His betrayal of the High King, his own father, is too shameful to be spoken of. We do not lightly invoke his memory."

"Yet Penduran herself, she who was most injured by Pryderi's actions, forgave him," Amatheon pointed out. "For it was she that insisted this barrow be raised. Pryderi was a traitor and the law said he must be left where he fell. But she said no."

"Penduran did indeed suffer greatly when Pryderi killed her husband," Rhiannon agreed softly. "Many years after Llyr died she wrote:

Tell me, men of learning, what is Longing made from?
What cloth is put on it, that it does not wear out with use?
Gold wears out, silver wears out, every garment wears out—
Yet Longing does not wear out.
Great Longing, cruel Longing is breaking my heart every day;
When I sleep most sound at night Longing comes and wakes me.
Longing, Longing, back, back! Do not weigh on me so heavily;
Move over a little to the bedside and let me sleep a while.

"She did love him so," Amatheon agreed. "And missed him sorely."

"And he loved her," Gwydion proffered softly. "For he was the Dreamer and he knew he would die at that battle, but did not tell her so."

"Do all Dreamer's know the time of their death?" Angharad asked.

"It is not given to all to see. Some do," Gwydion replied.

"Do you?" Rhiannon asked.

"No," Gwydion said. "At least, not yet. Were you hoping to hear differently?"

"No," Rhiannon said, flinching at the question. "I was not."

Obviously startled by her reaction, Gwydion began to step forward, perhaps to comfort her, perhaps to apologize. But whatever he had meant to do, he thought better of it, and subsided.

As he often did, Amatheon stepped into the breach that Gwydion and Rhiannon's enmity had created. "Llyr composed a poem about that, as I recall."

"I know that one," Cai said unexpectedly. "He wrote:

I'm helpless now,
And if they call me home
I cannot answer;
For the black, cold, bare, dank earth
Covers my face.

"He left that at Caer Dathyl and she found it after she returned alone," Cai went on. "She stayed in Caer Dathyl only long enough to bury him, I believe. She gave the governance of the Dewin over to her daughter, for she would be Ardewin no more."

"And then she went to Arberth, to rule for her grandson, Pwyll, Pryderi's son, until he came of age," Rhiannon submitted.

"And then she returned to Caer Dathyl, and died there," Amatheon finished. "Twenty eight years after Llyr's death." He put his arm around Angharad's waist, holding her to his side as he gazed down at the barrow. "A long time indeed to live without your love." Angharad smiled sadly and briefly laid her fiery head on Amatheon's shoulder.

"Tell us of the battle," Trystan said to Gwydion.

Gwydion, whose head had been bowed in thought since Rhiannon's last comment, straightened up and began to speak. "At that time the Great Ones of High King Idris were these: Llyr the First Dreamer and his wife, Penduran, the First Ardewin; their son, Llywarch, the Second Master Bard; and Govannon, the First Archdruid. Govannon, who was a very clever geneticist, had determined what proper matings were necessary in order to produce the next generation of Rulers and Y Dawnus. Therefore Annon, the daughter of Llyr and

Penduran, was sent to Arberth, to mate with King Pryderi. She did so and the couple produced a son, Pwyll. Annon left Arberth soon thereafter, returning to Caer Dathyl.

"But Pryderi was enraged that she had gone from him. For he had fallen in love with her. He rode to Caer Dathyl and begged and pleaded with Annon to return to him. But she refused him, as kindly and gently as she could. But she would not be swayed, for her heart belonged to Trinio, the son of Math, and they were soon to be married. At Llyr's insistence Pryderi finally left Caer Dathyl, but not before promising that he would get Annon back, one way or another.

"Pryderi went to his father, High King Idris, and poured out his heart. He begged his father to order Annon back to him, but Idris refused. Pryderi left Cadair Idris in a rage. His mother, High Queen Elen, journeyed to Arberth a few weeks later, hoping to help her son come to terms with what must be. But Pryderi was adamant. Annon would be returned to him or he would march on Caer Dathyl and take her by force. Sorrowfully, Elen returned to Cadair Idris, unable to sway her son from his destructive course.

"Pryderi attempted to find support among his brothers and his sister, the other Rulers of Kymru. But they, too, refused to further his aims. Then Pryderi sent for his uncle, Connan, Idris's younger brother. Now Connan had been jealous of Idris for many years, and he coveted his sister-through-marriage for himself. It was an easy matter for Pryderi to convince Connan that the High Kingship should be his. How Pryderi stomached Connan's plans for High Queen Elen was something no one ever knew.

"Even then it might have stopped there, but for Gilfaethwy. Gilfaethwy, Penduran's younger brother, had been in hiding for many years, ever since he had raped Goewin, High Queen Elen's sister. Gilfaethwy, ripe for anything that would turn the tables on Llyr and Idris, convinced the men to seriously challenge Idris's rule.

"And this they did. Pryderi, Connan, and Gilfaethwy marched on Cadair Idris, though Pryderi hid his true purpose, saying only that he was coming to his father for aid, and ensuring that Connan and Gilfaethwy were well concealed. He surprised his parents at Cadair Idris and even succeeded in driving them from the mountain for a short time."

"Which was long enough," Amatheon interrupted, "for Connan to attempt what he should never have attempted."

"True enough," Gwydion said. "For Connan, egged on by Pryderi and Gilfaethwy, gathered the Four Treasures and attempted to take his brother's place as High King, confident that he could pass the Tynged Mwyr, that test from which a man either emerges High King or dead. But Connan was wrong, for he did not pass the test. As he stood on the stone, the cauldron at his feet, the sword in the stone, the spear in his hands, he burst into flame, the energy in these implements turning him to ashes where he stood.

"But Pryderi would not give up, although his uncle was dead. He left Cadair Idris, sure that he was not safe in that fortress, knowing that his father knew of other ways in and out of the mountain. He marched west toward Prydyn; his plan to reach Caer Dathyl abandoned, for he knew he was not strong enough to take Annon by force. Yet he was too proud to surrender.

"Idris and his army caught up with Pryderi the next day. Idris had brought with him a formidable host, for his other children—the Queen of Gwynedd, and the Kings of Ederynion

469

and Rheged were at his side with their levies. Also with Idris were his Great Ones—Llyr and Penduran, Llywarch and Govannon, and a host of Y Dawnus. Idris was High King, and he had complete control over the Y Dawnus, able to use their combined gifts to his advantage.

"Before the battle began, High Queen Elen rode forth from her husband's army and pleaded with Pryderi to abandon his schemes. Pryderi heard her out until the end then smiled, almost sadly. 'Mam,' he said, 'are you sorry, then, that you ever gave birth to me?' 'Never,' she cried.' 'You should be,' he said gently. 'For if I can, I will kill you all.'

"Pryderi rose in the saddle, and threw his spear at his mother. But Idris was faster. He called on the power of the Druids and Shape-Moved the spear, causing it to miss Elen and fly high into the air. He then called on the Druids again and the spear burst into flame, the ashes harmlessly floating back to Earth.

" 'Father!' Pryderi called. 'If you wish to stop me, you must kill me!' With that Pryderi and his men leapt forward crying their fierce war cries. The battle began and it was ferocious, brutal. Men died by the score so fiercely did the men of Prydyn fight that superior enemy. Idris fought with Caladfwlch in his hands, cutting his way through the press toward his son. Llyr the Dreamer was by his friend's side, ensuring that Idris came through unharmed to confront Pryderi. The men who battled around them slowed and then halted as they stepped back to watch the confrontation between father and son, for they knew that this would decide the battle.

"Pryderi swiped viciously at his father with his sword, and drew blood from his father's side. But the wound did not stop Idris. Tears streamed down his drawn face as he lifted his sword to smite his son. But Llyr, wishing to spare his friend, leapt forward and furiously planted his dagger into Pryderi's heart. Fast as lightning, Pryderi dropped his sword and plucked the dagger from his chest. He lunged forward and plunged the dagger into Llyr's breast. The two men fell, clutching each other, their blood mingling together as they died.

"Penduran cried out and ran through the now still battle-field until she reached her husband's body. She lifted him up from the blood-soaked ground, cradling his head against her breast. Her tears flowed down her face and onto Llyr's. He tried to smile up at her, but he did not have the strength. Instead he whispered something to her, something that no one else could hear. Whatever it was, it seemed to comfort her, for she tried to smile back at him, so that, as the light fled from his eyes, her smiling face was the last thing he saw."

Rhiannon was openly weeping now. Trystan and Cai had bowed their heads, touched by this tale of grief. Angharad and Amatheon stood entwined, comforting each other with their nearness.

Only Gwydion did not seem to be having trouble, for his voice was firm and even. Achren glanced over at him and saw that she was wrong. For she saw the anguish, the echo of old grief in his silvery eyes even though it could not be heard in his voice.

She was the only one who seemed unmoved, for she stood dry-eyed. And that was not the case at all. The story always had the power to move her, but never to tears. Rather anger at the waste of it all. And shame for the first King of Prydyn.

"The battle was over," Gwydion continued softly. "The men of Prydyn threw down their weapons. Idris ordered that they be given quarter, for he had managed to stay on his feet, despite his wound. He ruled Kymru for only one year after that, and then died."

"From the physical wound or the wound to his heart?" Amatheon wondered.

"Both, I believe," Gwydion said gently. "Gilfaethwy, Penduran's brother, was captured a few days later, for he had run from the battlefield. He was brought to Cadair Idris, where Gwydd, Llyr's son, and the new Dreamer performed the rite that infused Gilfaethwy's spirit into the Doors of Cadair Idris. Though his body was dead his spirit was denied the chance to rest in the Land of Summer until his place would be taken by another traitor."

"I often think that is the most horrible punishment imaginable," Trystan murmured.

"So did Goewin, the woman Gilfaethwy had raped. It was she who thought of it," Gwydion said. "After the battle they burned the dead in pyre's. And, as we have said, Penduran insisted that Pryderi be properly buried. But she did not bury Llyr here. She took his body with her back to Caer Dathyl and buried him in Aelwyd Cerdinen, the burial mounds she raised for him in the center of the fortress. All Dreamers have been buried there since.

"They named this place Galor Penduran, Penduran's Sorrow," Gwydion finished, gesturing to the battlefield. "It is said that, in the night, just before dawning, if one listens closely, one can hear the sound of Penduran weeping still over Llyr's dead body."

"Do you believe that?" Rhiannon asked, her voice shaking.

He looked over at her for a long time before answering. "No," he said gently. "For Penduran and Llyr are surely joyous together in Gwlad Yr Haf, and she weeps no more."

Rhiannon dashed the tears from her face and tried to smile. "Perhaps you are right," she said.

"A first," Gwydion teased, much to Achren's surprise.

"So it is," Rhiannon agreed with a wider smile this time. "Don't get used to it."

"I won't," he promised.

"It's time," Achren said restlessly. "I am ready."

"Then let us begin," Gwydion said, holding his hands out to Rhiannon and Amatheon. The three Y Dawnus joined hands and the four captains took their places around them. Cai, Angharad, and Trystan, their eyes clear with understanding, waited for Achren to join them.

Achren stepped forward determined not to wait any longer. She would see what she would see. She would taste whatever grief and sorrow waited in the past and return to the light of day, bringing the knowledge they needed with her.

She was ready. So when the darkness took her the moment she laid her hands on the others, she was not surprised at its swiftness. Only at its ferociousness, as she plunged through time and out the other side.

THE PINPRICK OF light grew larger as it moved swiftly toward her through the tunnel of night. The light burst upon her, and she threw up her hands to shield her eyes. The brightness faded somewhat until she could focus her eyes on what was before her.

The meadow, still bright and fresh glowed strangely in the uncertain light from above, for a storm was brewing. Violet clouds piled overhead, and lightning laced the sky.

Men and women, their spears in their hands, their swords belted at their sides, arrayed in black and green, mounted their horses. They were a pitiful few compared to the host that faced them. Yet Achren felt a dim pride in them, she who had always been ashamed. For they faced the clearly superior foe and did not run.

The army they faced was indeed formidable. Warriors in the gold and silver of the High King, in the red and white of Rheged, the brown and blue of Gwynedd, the sea green and white of Ederynion, also sat rock-steady on their mounts, their weapons ready.

A pool of brown-robed Druids stood off to one side of the battlefield, joined by blue-clad Bards and Dewin in robes of sea green.

A man stepped out in front of the large host. His hair was dark and his gray eyes glowed in the lowering afternoon light. Around his neck he wore a massive torque set with a huge emerald, a pearl, a sapphire and an opal. In the center of the torque was a figure eight, the symbol for infinity, studded with dark onyx. His face was stern, although Achren could see grief in his silvery eyes.

The man's four Great Ones stepped out from the army to stand behind him. Achren saw a man in red and black with a torque of fiery opals at his throat and a cloak of raven feather clasped around his shoulders. He held the hand of a woman in sea green and silver with a cloak of white swan feather, a torque of pearls glowing around her proud neck. Next came a young man wearing a torque of glowing sapphires and blue and white robes beneath a cloak of songbird feather. Lastly came an older man in robes of forest green and brown, a heavy cloak of bull's hide and a torque of emeralds clasped around his powerful neck.

Then a woman made her way through the army, riding

a pure white mare. The woman wore tunic and trousers of silver and gold. She wore no ornaments and no cloak. Her rich, auburn hair, lightly touched with frost, was loose and flowing down her slender shoulders. Her eyes were fixed on the figure of a young man who stood to the forefront of the opposing army. She looked neither to the right nor to the left as she rode past the others. The dark-haired man with the silvery eyes reached out his hand to her as she rode by, but she did not halt and he let her go, slowly lowering his hand.

She rode across the meadow toward the army that stood there with the trees at their backs. The young man detached himself from the army and rode out to meet her. He wore tunic and trousers of black and green. The cuffs of his black leather boots were studded with emeralds. On his head he wore a war helm fashioned like the head of a wolf with emerald eyes, and a torque of emeralds hung around his neck. They faced each other in the center of the field. Although they spoke Achren could not hear them, for the entire vision was unaccompanied by sound.

Suddenly, swift as thought, the man drew back his spear and threw it at the woman. Although she could not hear, Achren saw the dark-haired man cry out. He lifted his hand and the spear shot up into the sky. He gestured again and the spear burst into flames. The woman turned her horse and rejoined the army. Tears rained down her drawn face and she halted before the dark-haired man. She reached out her hand and lightly touched his cheek. He took her hand and pressed a kiss on her palm. Then he released her and turned back toward the field.

He pulled his sword from the belt at his side and raised it high. At that moment lightning flashed and crawled over the blade. The hilt was fashioned like that of an eagle with outstretched wings. The eagle's eyes were bloodstone and its wings were studded with onyx. Precious jewels of emerald, pearl, sapphire, and opal covered the remainder of the hilt. The dark-haired man cried out what must have been the call to battle, for he ran forward and the rest of his host followed.

The two armies met in the center of the field with a clash that Achren could not hear but could feel, so powerful was it. The battle was fierce and brutal and blood immediately began to soak into the blameless ground. The dark-haired man, with the man in black and opals at his side, cut his way through the melee, making for the man with the wolf's helmet.

At last the two men met and as they did so the battle halted around them. The man with the wolf's helmet raised his sword and swiped viciously at the dark-haired older man. Blood spouted from the man's side and the younger man smiled, although the smile was tinged with latent grief, like a film of spiderwebs over fresh leaves. But the wounded man was strong and he raised his eagle's sword to strike. But before he could do so, the man in black and opals leapt forward and plunged a dagger into the younger man's heart. The man in the wolf's helmet threw back his head in pain. He whipped the dagger from his heart and plunged it into the breast of the man in black. The two men went down, even as the dark-haired man dropped his sword and reached out to cradle them both.

The woman in the swan feather cloak came running heedlessly through the litter of dead bodies that lay across the meadow. She sank down and took the man in black and opals into her arms. The dying man tried to smile, and spoke something, the woman bending low over him to hear his last message. She smiled down at him then and the smile remained fixed on her face until the light fled from the man's eyes.

She looked over then, at the man in the wolf's helmet. He was still alive and, as their eyes met, tears began to stream down his face. The woman reached out and gently laid her hand on the young man's cheek. The lines of rage faded beneath her palm and his face smoothed out as his eyes closed in death.

The woman rose and faced the dark-haired man who clutched his wounded side. He lifted his head and cried out soundlessly to the storm above. And the rains came down, as though trying to wash away the blood, the grief, and the horror of that day.

The scene faded and another took its place. Bonfires were lit to consume the dead, piled together in the center of the field. A cluster of people gathered around a barrow freshly dug on the fringes of the forest. The woman with the pearl torque stood at the foot of the grave, flanked by the dark-haired man and the woman in silver and gold. The three stood silently, beyond tears. At last the woman with the pearl torque loosened herself from her companions and turned to go. She mounted the box of a rough wagon. In the wagon was a body, shrouded in black cloth. The woman lifted her hand to the couple that stood at the foot of the grave, then turned away even as they returned her gesture of farewell.

Then the scene shifted again. The fires were long gone and the scarred ground was once again clean. The grass was long and green around the silent grave and tiny blossoms of fireweed glowed under the fresh, blue sky. A man wearing a robe of black and red rode alone across the meadow. Around his neck he wore a massive torque of opals and gold. His long auburn hair was tied back and fastened at the nape of his neck with a golden clasp.

He halted his horse next the grave and sat there for a few moments, looking down at it. At last he dismounted. He took something from his saddlebag. She could not see what it was, for it was wrapped in dark cloth. He went to the head of the grave, kneeling down at the base of the silent yew tree. He stretched out his hand and the earth opened up just enough to allow him to deposit his bundle. Then he rose and gestured again and the earth covered the item, rippling and flowing over it as though the hole had never been.

He stood for a moment, looking down at the grave. Then he raised his head and appeared to look right at her. His silvery eyes, so like Gwydion's, were filled with tears. His mouth was twisted, etched with the echoes of grief still lingering over the grave. His eyes held hers and she saw beyond the grief to the wisdom that was there. And when she did, he smiled. Then the darkness spiraled down.

WHEN SHE CAME to Cai was supporting her head while Rhiannon held a cup to her lips. "Drink," Rhiannon commanded while Angharad mopped Achren's face with a square of linen.

Obediently, Achren drank. "Why are you doing that?" Achren asked Angharad in surprise. "I don't have a fever."

"You were crying."

"I was?"

"Yes, Achren, you were," Gwydion said quietly. "Was he?"

"Yes," Achren answered. "He stood by the grave and wept. And then he looked at me. And I saw what was behind the tears."

"What?" Gwydion said, his tone eager. "What was it?"

"Wisdom."

"For which grief is the price," Cai said quietly.

"Is it worth it, then?" Trystan asked. "Sometimes I wonder."

"Sometimes we all wonder," Cai replied.

"Where is it?" Gwydion asked, abruptly.

"At the base of the yew tree," Achren answered wearily.

Gwydion rose and went to the tree, kneeling down at its base. With a gesture the ground split neatly. Gold winked at them, and Gwydion reached down and pulled the last piece of the puzzle from the earth.

Like all the others it was in the shape of an arc, what they now knew to be the final quarter of a circle. The golden, arched border was covered with sapphires. On the lower portion of the arc were the letters "Nants" filled in with emeralds. The pointed portion was covered with pearls, outlined on one side with rubies.

Rhiannon, looking over Gwydion's shoulder, read the poem aloud:

Into his grave he is gone,
No more talk about him;
Earth's crop,
Which generation by generation
Slips away into oblivion.

"Poor Bran," Trystan said.

"But strong," Achren put in. "So very, very strong."

The other captains nodded, for they, too, had seen Bran, and had sensed in him the same trait that Achren had detected—an implacable will, potent enough to lure them into the past.

"Put it with the others, Gwydion," Rhiannon said. "And then let us see what we have eyes to see."

Amatheon pulled the three other pieces from the saddle-bags and brought them to his brother. Gwydion held all four pieces in his hands, pressed tightly together. He bowed his head and closed his eyes. For a moment the gold seemed to shimmer in his hands. The broken lines melded together, once again forming a single piece.

Gwydion held out the now whole circle for them to see. At the top were the words "seek the eye of," with "Nantsovelta" written at the bottom. The pearls and rubies at the bottom of each pointed piece now clearly formed an apple, split in half. At the center of the apple was a pentagram outlined in onyx and filled with fiery opal.

"Afalon," Gwydion breathed.

"Apple-Lane," Amatheon agreed. "Of course."

"The eye of Nantsovelta," Rhiannon put in, "means a well. Nantsovelta, the Goddess of the Waters. Eyes are metaphors for wells."

"A well at Afalon," Amatheon said, wonderingly. "What better place to hide the sword than on the isle where no one ever goes? Do you all realize what tomorrow is?"

"Calan Gaef," Cai said. "The winter festival. The festival of the dead."

"The festival of Annwyn and Aertan," Trystan said.

"Lord of Chaos and the Weaver of Fate," Angharad put in.

"The god and goddess to whom it is said the High Kings owe their allegiance," Gwydion said.

"And Afalon is their island," Amatheon said gleefully. "It all fits. We've done it!"

THE WOLF SPRINTED through the woods of Coed Aderyn, hunting for his dinner. He moved swiftly and silently through the trees, like a silent shadow after his prey. The scent was strong and he followed it, sure-footed and graceful.

The rabbit bounded from cover up ahead and the wolf leapt. But the call took it by surprise and he twisted in mid-air at the strength of it.

He landed on all fours, crouched, his head cocked, his green eyes wide, his dinner forgotten. For it was time. Time to go northeast, to the place whence the call came, to the place he had been born to go.

He howled once, his head thrown back and lifted to the lowering sky. Then he turned away from his prey and loped off through the woods.

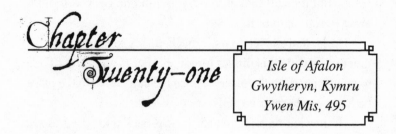
Addiendydd, Cynyddu Wythnos—noon

"Not so fast," Gwydion said at Amatheon's statement of victory. "The well itself has yet to be found."

"And the Guardians subdued, whoever they are," Rhiannon reminded them.

"That is the task of the captains of Kymru," Achren said proudly. "In this, as in all else, we will not fail."

"None of us will!" Amatheon declared, his eyes shining.

Gwydion's face became suddenly stern. "Us?" he inquired, his brow raised.

Amatheon's bright smile faded. "Gwydion—"

"You are not going with us to Afalon," Gwydion said firmly.

"You can't do this!" Amatheon cried.

"Can't I? Did you not promise me that you would leave us at my command?"

"Yes, but—"

"I command it. You will not come with us to Afalon."

"But you need me there! The verse says:

482

The trees covered the beloved dead,
And transformed the Y Dawnus,
From their faded state,
Until the two were one,
In strength and purpose,
And raised up that which they had sought.

"Only two of us are needed to raise the sword from that well," Gwydion pointed out. "Rhiannon and I can do it without your help."

"Gwydion," Amatheon said, his face pale. "You can't mean to send me away."

"You promised," Gwydion said implacably.

Amatheon's bright blue eyes pleaded with Gwydion, to change his mind, to not do this thing, to forget the last stanza of the song that spoke of death.

But this Gwydion would not, could not do.

Amatheon turned and mounted his horse. Angharad, her face pale, went to him, reaching up her hand to gently touch his face. He bent down and kissed her, long and slow. At last he released her. "When you are done send for me at Hetwin Silver-Brow's court. I will come to Dinmael as soon as may be."

"I will," Angharad said softly. "Safe journey to you."

"Rhiannon," Amatheon said, "take care of my pig-headed brother. He needs looking after." Before she could reply he turned to Gwydion. "Good-bye, brother."

"Good-bye," Gwydion replied his face still stern.

Amatheon turned his horse and rode east. Gwydion never took his eyes from his brother until the Earth's curve took him out of sight. His face never changed as he watched Amatheon go.

It was his eyes that betrayed him.

Calan Gaef—early afternoon

TYBION WAITED PATIENTLY on the shore of Llyn Mwyngil. He knew the Dreamer and his companions would arrive any moment now. He knew that the instant they would have realized Afalon was their final destination they would have ridden hard, stopping only when too dark to continue. They would have risen at first light this morning, which would put them here at any moment.

He was right, for he saw them crest the rise on the horizon. There were only six of them now, for Gwydion had already sent his younger brother away, as Tybion had known would happen.

Tybion dismounted from his horse and walked to the boat moored at the edge of the lake. He loosened the rope that bound it to the shore. This was not the first time this morning that he had done this, of course. Earlier today he had rowed a passenger across the lake and to the shore of Afalon. He hadn't wanted to, but he had been given no choice. For what would be, would be, as his father was fond of saying, and it was not Tybion's place to affect events.

Still, he wished he could have prevented the passenger from going to the isle. And he wished he could warn the Dreamer.

But he could not. So when they reached him he silently handed the rope to Gwydion. Gwydion did not even bother to ask him how he had known to be there, how he had known to have a boat ready and waiting.

Without a word Tybion mounted his horse and left the Dreamer and his companions at the water's edge.

For what would be, would be.

484

THE BOAT TOUCHED the coast of Afalon with a gentle bump. Cai and Trystan jumped from the boat and easily hauled it up onto the shore. Gwydion gestured for Rhiannon, Achren, and Angharad to exit the craft first.

He rose and set his feet on the shore of Afalon. That was when he knew, beyond all doubt, that this was the place. Power seemed to emanate from the very soil. He could feel it throbbing beneath the soles of his feet. Even the others seemed to feel it. Rhiannon was somewhat pale and the hands of his other companions hovered near their weapons.

Although his brother had left them only yesterday, Gwydion already missed Amatheon more than he had thought possible. He missed Amatheon's cheerfulness, his bright eyes, his ready smile, and his laugh. Sometimes Gwydion thought that Amatheon had been given all those things that life had denied Gwydion—love, laughter, companionship. And even as he thought this he realized that life had not denied him those things—rather Gwydion had denied himself.

But what was done was done, and it was far too late to change. In any case, now was not the time to be thinking of those things. Although he had—ever since that night that Rhiannon and he had spoken together by the dying campfire. For that night Gwydion had almost forgotten his duty to Kymru. He had almost forgotten his obligation to find the sword, to keep Arthur safe against the day that he would be High King. He had almost forgotten all of it in Rhiannon's emerald eyes. But he had stopped himself before it was too late, for to give into the lure of a woman was to abandon duty. His mother had taught him that.

"Are you sure we can do it?" Rhiannon asked sharply.

"What?" Gwydion said, for he had not heard the first part of Rhiannon's question.

"I said, are you sure that without Amatheon we can still do what we are supposed to do?"

"We must," Gwydion said simply.

"And where is the eye of Nantsovelta?" Cai asked, gesturing to the thick grove of apple trees that covered the island. Wind played through the trees, and the rustling of leaves made it seem as though the trees were whispering, gleefully holding a secret in their depths.

Gwydion looked at Rhiannon, for he had an idea that she would be the one who would lead them to it. For Rhiannon was Dewin, and Nantsovelta was the goddess they most revered. "Rhiannon?" he asked.

"Yes," she replied. "It pulls at me. As I think you knew it would."

"Then lead on," he said. "And we will follow."

She led them, without hesitation, through the trees. Overhead the sky was gray and overcast. The wind was cold and tugged at their cloaks, moaning in their ears. The apple trees grew thickly and the underbrush was dense. Although Gwydion was sure there were a number of animals on this island they neither saw nor heard them as they made their way forward.

As they walked, Gwydion called to mind every word of the Battle of the Trees.

On winter's first day
Shall the trees
Face the Guardians.

On winter's first day

486

Shall the trees
Do battle.

The alder tree, loyal and patient,
Formed the van.
The aspen-wood, quickly moving,
Was valiant against the enemy.
The hawthorn, with pain at its hand,
Fought on the flanks.
Hazel-tree did not go aside a foot
It would fight with the center.

And when it was over
The trees covered the beloved dead,
And transformed the Y Dawnus,
From their faded state,
Until the two were one,
In strength and purpose,
And raised up that which they had sought.

On winter's first day,
The one who is loved shall die.
And tears will overwhelm
The lonely heart.

Today was Calan Gaef, the first day of winter, and the first day of the New Year. In other parts of Kymru right now people were beginning to gather for the festival that would honor Annwyn, Lord of Chaos and his mate Aertan, the Weaver. These two ruled Gwlad Yr Haf, the Land of Summer, the place where the dead went to await rebirth. The festival celebrated the time of year when Annwyn and Aertan walked the Summer Land, touching those chosen to return to Earth with a branch of yew wood. Tonight the Kymri would gather and call out the names of the beloved dead, in hopes that the two Shining Ones would choose those spirits to return.

According to the song, the Captains would face the Guardians. And they would do battle. In that battle someone who was loved would die. Now that Amatheon was gone, Gwydion faced that prospect with a less mournful heart. He would not wish death on any of his companions; but clearly, one of them would die today. Gwydion might be the one to take the journey to the Summer Land. He hoped not, for if he did he would feel his duty undone. But if it must be, it would be. As long as Amatheon was safe, that was all that mattered.

At last they reached a small clearing in what seemed to be the center of the island and they halted, looking around them. In the center of the clearing, was a pool of dark water. It was impossible to see what it held in its depths, or exactly how deep it was, for the weak light from the gray sky did not illuminate the well. Gwydion took a step forward and immediately halted as a hawk flew into the clearing with a fierce cry and came to rest between the well and Gwydion. Then a huge swan swooped down from above and joined the hawk. Next a golden horse entered the clearing and reared up, neighing aggressively. Last, a black wolf stepped from the trees, snarling.

"These, then are the Guardians. And the Captains are to fight them?" Rhiannon asked in a low tone as Gwydion slowly backed away from the well.

"The song says we will do battle today," Achren replied. "But I have no stomach for one against these."

"I do not think we are to fight them," Cai said quietly.

"The song says—"

"That we will do battle today. But not, I think, with them."

Cai stepped forward, warily eyeing the hawk. The bird spread his wings and hissed at Cai's approach. Cai slowly divested himself of his weapons, all the while never taking his eyes from the hawk. He pulled his sword from his scabbard and laid it on the ground. He gently set down his spear and shield. He pulled two daggers from his boots and laid them down also. Defenseless, he faced the fierce bird.

"Hawk of Gwynedd," Cai said softly, "you know me. I am Cai ap Cynyr, Captain of Gwynedd. Uthyr ap Rathtyen var Awst is my lord and my master. In the name of Uthyr Pen-Hebog, he who is the Head of the Hawk, I command you to step aside."

For a moment there was silence. Then the bird spread his wings and cried out. He launched himself into the air and came to rest in the branch of a tree.

After discarding his weapons Trystan stepped forward and addressed the golden horse. "Horse of Rheged, I am Trystan ap Naf, the Captain of Rheged. In the name of Urien ap Ethyllt var Gwaeddan, the PenMarch, the Head of the Horse, I command that you step aside."

The horse bent his proud head and moved back away from the well.

Then Angharad came forward, also laying her weapons on the ground at her feet. "Swan of Ederynion, you know me. I am Angharad ur Ednyved. My lady is Olwen ur Custennin var Elwen, she who is the PenAlarch, the Head of the Swan. In her name I command you to step aside."

The swan hissed, snaking its graceful neck toward Angharad. Then it, too, backed away from the well.

Achren, her spear and her daggers on the ground, addressed the wolf. "Wolf of Prydyn, I am Achren ur Canhustyr, Captain of Prydyn. My master is Rhoram ap Rhydderch var Eurneid. He is the PenBlaid, the Head of the Wolf, and in his name I command you to step aside."

The wolf growled, then slowly backed away from the dark water.

Gwydion and Rhiannon started forward toward the well.

HE WAS WATCHING through the bushes, careful not to betray his presence. He saw the Captains call off the animals that guarded the well, one by one. He saw Gwydion and Rhiannon step forward, for they knew, now, that the water held that which they sought. He wondered, as he had often done during the last months, just what battle would transpire today. And who would die.

The buzz of the arrow was the only warning he had. He knew in that split second where the arrow was headed. And he knew he could not let it reach its destination. So he leapt up and stepped in the arrow's path.

And that was when he felt the burning pain in his gut. He looked down to discover that the arrow was protruding from his side, to discover that blood spurted from his wound and splashed the leaves.

To realize, indeed, just who was going to die that day.

THE FOUR ANIMALS—the hawk, the swan, the horse and the wolf—suddenly tensed and cried out. The hawk screamed, the swan hissed, the horse whinnied, and the wolf howled. Gwydion and Rhiannon halted, sure that the animals were ready to attack.

And they did. They leapt into the forest. Gwydion and

490

the others could just make them out through the trees as they closed in on a man who held a bow in his hands. The man tried to run, but the horse cut off his retreat. He turned to run the other direction, but the wolf was waiting for him. He turned again, and the hawk and the swan fell on him from above. The bird's cries mingled with the man's screams. The horse reared up and lashed out with his hooves, breaking the man's bones. Then the wolf leapt forward, snarling, tearing the man's throat out.

Suddenly the clearing erupted as men poured from the shelter of the dense undergrowth, launching themselves at Gwydion and Rhiannon.

As one the four Captains, the best warriors in all of Kymru, leapt for their weapons. Cai rolled and grabbed his daggers. As he rose he stabbed the first assailant in the gut with his left hand and slashed the throat of another with his right.

Angharad darted for her sword, grasped the hilt and swung it up in one, fluid motion. The blade caught one man in the stomach and he fell. She continued to turn, kicking out behind her with her right foot, catching another man in the jaw. As he flew back she reached forward with her blade and buried it in his guts.

Trystan leapt toward his weapons and grasped his spear. Rolling to the left he brought the point up and impaled an attacker. He raised his foot and pushed the dead man off the spear shaft to the ground. He whipped around and plunged the spear into another man's back. The man arched in agony then swiftly died as Trystan yanked the spear out.

Achren, too, had leapt for her weapons but she found her way blocked. She lashed out with both feet, diving into the man who stood in her way. The air rushed out of the man's lungs as he went down. Still rolling Achren grasped a rock and brought it against the side of the man's head as he began to rise. His head cracked open and he collapsed. She grabbed a dagger from the dead man's belt and turned, slashing up, burying it in the stomach of the next assailant.

Eight men were down in a matter of moments, and the last two were still running toward Gwydion and Rhiannon. The two Y Dawnus stood their ground, each taking a dagger from their boots.

But suddenly the two men halted, frozen in their tracks. The first man had Achren's dagger and Trystan's spear through his back. And the second man had Cai's dagger and Angharad's sword in his guts. They both fell, dead.

For a moment the clearing was silent as they started at the bodies of the ten dead men who littered the once peaceful glade.

That was when Gwydion heard a sound, a faint call, a cry of agony. For many years—indeed, until he died—he would hear that cry echo in his soul. For he knew that voice as he knew the beat of his own heart.

The bushes rustled and a figure staggered out into the clearing. He lifted his arms toward Gwydion, pain in every line of his bloodied, suffering body.

"Brother," he rasped as Gwydion rushed forward and caught him, gently lowering him to the ground.

"Amatheon," Gwydion gasped.

Rhiannon put her hands to the wound and closed her eyes. Gwydion watched her face hopefully as she concentrated. But she opened her eyes from the Life-Reading and shook her head. The damage the arrow had done to Amatheon was too great to turn death aside.

"I came back," Amatheon whispered. "I didn't want to be left out."

Gwydion tried to speak but could not.

"I heard the arrow. I knew it was for you. I had to stop it."

"Oh, Amatheon," Gwydion rasped. "Oh, my brother."

"I am glad you weren't hurt," Amatheon said. "But I am sorry to leave you. And to leave Angharad." He looked up and caught sight of her flame-colored hair. She sank to the ground, taking his hand in hers.

"*Cariad*," Amatheon whispered.

"Beloved," Angharad replied softly. "Farewell." Tears steamed down Angharad's face, but her green eyes were steady as she gazed down at Amatheon.

Amatheon's bright blue eyes, now growing dim, fastened on Rhiannon. "Take care of my brother," he gasped. "Take care of him."

"I—" Rhiannon began, but Amatheon did not wait for her answer. He turned back to Gwydion. "Good-bye, brother."

"Good-bye," Gwydion replied steadily. His eyes were dry, for this was a disaster beyond simple tears. This was a blow too strong for the conventional signs of grief.

He watched as Amatheon's blue eyes dimmed, as his spirit fled his body and began the journey to the Summer Land. He watched as his brother left him irrevocably alone. He watched as a piece of his heart withered and died.

Now he knew why the shadows in his dreams always tore out his heart.

Now he knew, because now it was happening in the waking world.

His nightmare had come true.

CAI, TRYSTAN, AND Achren came forward to join Angharad beside Amatheon's dead body. Gently Achren pulled Rhiannon to her feet, while Cai and Trystan helped Gwydion to stand.

Angharad leaned forward and gently kissed Amatheon's cold forehead, smoothing back his dark hair. Achren reached out and gently closed Amatheon's eyes. Without speaking, the four positioned themselves around Amatheon's body. Achren and Angharad took his arms while Cai and Trystan grabbed his legs. They lifted him gently and carried him to the well and laid him down beside the dark water.

Angharad went to her pack and pulled out a square of white linen. She returned and knelt again by Amatheon's body. She gently laid the cloth over Amatheon's now lifeless, cold face.

Then the four of them rose and recited the death song of the Kymri:

In Gwlad Yr Haf, the Land of Summer
Still they live, still they live.
They shall not be killed, they shall not be wounded.
No fire, no sun, no moon shall burn them.
No lake, no water, nor sea shall drown them.
They live in peace and laugh and sing.
The dead are gone, yet still they live.

They stood silently for a time after the song was done, each in their grief, although no one's—even Angharad's—was as profound as Gwydion's. Yet still he could not weep. He thought it would be long and long before he did. He thought that his heart would remain cold and dead forever. There were still those that he loved who still lived. There was Uthyr, his half brother. There was Cariadas, his daughter. There was Myrrdin, his uncle. Only those three still had the power to touch him. Only those three, and nobody else now that Amatheon was gone.

Suddenly it seemed to him as if his father was dying again. The pain was back that he had felt on that awful day that he had discovered his father's body, when he knew that one who loved him was gone, forever beyond his reach. But then he had had Amatheon to help him bear it. And now Amatheon was gone.

It was enough that there were three others whose loss could hurt him so. There would never be more.

Never.

"GWYDION."

He would not answer. If he didn't they would leave him alone. That was all he wanted now, was to be left alone.

"Gwydion."

The voice—insistent, implacable—would not leave him be.

"Gwydion."

"What?" he answered at last, only to stop the sound of his name on her lips.

"The sword," Rhiannon went on. "Remember the sword."

"What of it?" he asked dully.

"We must find it."

"We?"

"The verse, Gwydion. Remember the verse:
Until the two were one
In strength and purpose,
And raised up that which they had sought."

"The Shining Ones will wait a long time until we are one," he muttered.

"Gwydion—"

"No," he said harshly. "Leave me be. Haven't you done enough?"

Rhiannon drew back from him, shocked. "What have I done?"

"You let him come!" Gwydion shouted. "Back at Caer Dathyl, you told him he could come!"

"I didn't kill him!" she cried. "You did! You sent him away! If he hadn't been forced to sneak back, if he hadn't been hiding, he might still be alive!"

"You killed him!" he screamed back at her. "You killed him!"

"Gwydion," Cai said stepping in front of Rhiannon. "Stop. Stop this now."

Gwydion turned away but Trystan was there. "Gwydion," Trystan said quietly. "It wasn't her fault."

Again, he turned away, only to face Achren. "She didn't kill him."

Again, he turned, and Angharad was there. "And neither did you."

He halted, staring at her, unable to speak.

Angharad's face was drawn and her mouth set with grief, the tracks of tears on her cheeks. But her green eyes were steady as she looked at him. "He was killed by the person who has tried to stop us all along from retrieving the sword."

"Will you let that person win?" Cai asked.

"Will you let the sword remain hidden?" Achren asked.

"Will you fail?" Trystan asked softly.

The silence in the glade was complete as Gwydion stood there, surrounded by his companions. The four Guardians were gone, and it seemed to Gwydion that the five men and women that stood here in this clearing with him were the only living things left in Kymru.

He did not count himself, for much of him had died today.

Duty was all he had left, really. The Shining Ones had given him the duty to find the sword. He would finish what the gods had started. He would finish it. Because duty was all he had, all he had ever had.

Wordlessly he made his way to stand before the well. The dark water was still and silent. He turned his head to look back at Rhiannon. At first she did not move. Her emerald eyes were filled with grief at Amatheon's death, with rage at Gwydion's accusation, with the fear that there was truth to it.

"Rhiannon," Cai said gently when she did not move to stand before the well. "He needs you."

"He needs no one," she said bitterly.

"He does, although he does not know it," Achren said softly.

"I do not care," Rhiannon said between gritted teeth.

"Think of it not as Gwydion's need, then," Trystan said. "Think of it as Kymru's need. The sword, Rhiannon. We must have the sword."

"Do not let Amatheon die for nothing," Angharad said with a catch to her voice. "Do not let it be meaningless."

All the while Gwydion held her with his eyes and did not let her look away. At Angharad's words she flinched. At last she stepped forward and came to stand beside him. They both knelt down by the still water. He reached out and took her hands in his.

HE SAW A figure step into the clearing. The man had long, auburn hair that hung lankly around his shoulders. He wore an ornate torque of gold and opals around his neck. He was dressed in worn, dusty, black riding leathers. An old blood-stain covered the breast of the tunic, as though someone had lain his head on the man's chest to die. He carried a sword sheathed in a scabbard decorated with runes of gold and silver. The hilt of the sword was fashioned like an eagle with out-stretched wings. The eagle had eyes of bloodstone and wings studded with onyx. Light flashed off the emeralds, pearls, sapphires, and opals that were scattered across the hilt.

The man came to stand on the other side of the well, and stood looking down into the water for some time, his head bowed, his face hidden. At last the man released the sword. It plunged cleanly into the water with a bell-like sound that rang through the clearing.

Then the man lifted his head and looked straight at Gwydion and Rhiannon. Tears spilled down Bran's drawn, set, grimy face. He gazed at them both then lifted his hand to them—in salute, in farewell, in the knowledge that they shared calamitous grief.

Then he was gone.

GWYDION WRENCHED HIS hands from Rhiannon's. "It's here," he said. "I can raise it."

"You need my help," she said.

"I don't," he snapped. "The sword is at the bottom of this well. The only thing needed to get it to come up is a Shape-Mover. Which you are not."

"And you are," said Rhiannon in a monotone. "Nonethe-less, you will need my help. The poem says—"

"I am done with that," Gwydion said harshly. "I am done with it all. I will bring this sword back to Kymru. I will complete my duty. Alone."

He turned back to the well and put forth his hands. He felt the sword beneath the water, slowly rising. But then it seemed to slip from his mind-hold, sinking back. He shook his head impatiently. He had lost his concentration, something that he hadn't done in many years. Again he put forth his hand and called the sword to him. Again he could sense that it began to rise. Then again, he felt it slip away from him.

And then he knew. There did not seem to be any end to the cruelty of the Shining Ones. He turned to Rhiannon and opened his mouth to ask—or, perhaps, to beg.

But she had unsolicited mercy for both of them, and came to stand beside him before he even spoke. Her face was hard and angry, and she did not talk. But she took his hands in hers and gave him what she had.

And it was enough.

The sword rose from the well, whole and shining, as water streamed from the scabbard like a flow of bright diamonds.

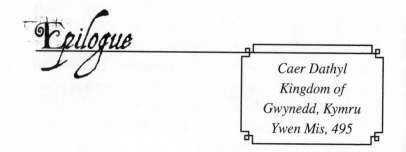

Addiendydd, Lleihau—early afternoon

N ow," Gwydion said, his hands on the cold stone.

Uthyr, his palms also on the rock, his fingers grasping the edges of the stone slab pulled along with Gwydion. The stone door opened with a grinding moan.

Uthyr and Gwydion stepped back from the now open door of Aelwyd Cerdinen, the tombs of the Dreamers at Caer Dathyl. At that moment a cold wind swooped from the sky, emitting a low moan of its own. The flame-colored rowan trees in the sacred grove of Nemed Cerdinen shivered in the breeze.

Taran of the Winds had come to say farewell.

UTHYR HAD ARRIVED at Caer Dathyl only that morning, and had greeted his brother with a bear hug that would have made Gwydion weep if he had yet been able to. Yet the sight of his remaining brother comforted him somewhat.

He and Uthyr had gone up to the Dreamer's Tower so that

Uthyr could pay his respects to Amatheon. When Gwydion had returned to Caer Dathyl two days ago he had Amatheon's body laid on the pallet in Ystafell Yr Arymes, the Chamber of Prophecy. He had wanted his brother to rest there for a while, beneath the glass roof in the room where Gwydion's dream's had begun. It had seemed fitting, somehow.

Uthyr and Gwydion had sat with the body for a few hours. Gwydion had told Uthyr the whole story of what had happened.

"And after I raised the sword from the well—" said Gwydion.

"After you and Rhiannon had raised the sword from the well," Uthyr corrected.

Gwydion ignored Uthyr's comment and went on. "I took it to Rhufon the Steward, as he had asked me. Now the sword lies in the golden fountain in the empty throne room at Cadair Idris."

"Waiting for the touch of my son's hand," Uthyr said quietly.

"Waiting for that," Gwydion agreed.

"And the others? Did they go with you to see Rhufon?"

"No," Gwydion replied. "We rowed back across the lake to the eastern shore. I told the Captains that they could return to their masters. I told them that they could tell the story to them, but to no one else."

"When I got your message Cai had not yet returned. I left Tegeingl as soon as Susanna gave me the news."

Gwydion did not answer, merely looking down at Amatheon's shrouded form.

"What about Rhiannon?" Uthyr pressed.

"What about her?" Gwydion asked absently.

"What did you say to her?"

"Nothing," Gwydion said in surprise. "Why, what should

I have said?"

"How about thank you?" Uthyr answered. "Or, perhaps, I'm sorry?"

"Sorry?"

"For what you said to her. For accusing her of killing Amatheon."

"It is best that Rhiannon and I not be on speaking terms, brother," Gwydion said before he had really thought it through.

"Because?"

Gwydion fell silent, unwilling to explain. But Uthyr, who knew him so well, did not need an explanation to understand.

"I see," Uthyr said softly.

DINASWYN'S FORMAL ROBES of black and red whipped and tossed in the fierce wind. Her long silvery hair streamed out behind her. Her silver eyes were undimmed by tears, her face frozen in a smooth mask, even as she knelt down beside the shrouded body that awaited internment.

Deep inside herself, Gwydion knew, Dinaswyn was mourning, weeping bitter tears in the stone fortress of her heart, where no one could see. He knew this, for did he not do the same? Had she not been his teacher in all things, even in this?

Not for him the tears that streamed down Uthyr's drawn face as they lifted Amatheon's body. He envied Uthyr's ability to grieve. He would have liked to do the same, but it seemed he could not. He had not shed one tear since Amatheon's death almost two weeks ago.

He wondered now if he ever would. He wondered now if he ever could.

Carefully cradling Amatheon's body the three of them

entered the tomb. Both Dinaswyn and Gwydion evoked Druid's Fire at the same time, and flames danced in the air, illuminating the darkened chamber.

Ivory bones glimmered as the light danced over the niches carved into the stone walls. The bones of all the Dreamers of Kymru decorated the walls, each lying within their proper niche. If he went far enough back through the stone chamber, Gwydion knew, he would come to the bones of Llyr himself. And those of Penduran. For although Penduran had not been a Dreamer she had chosen to lay next to Llyr in death.

Gwydion resolutely did not look at the niche that contained his father's bones. That was another body who had been buried here that was not a Dreamer. But Gwydion had insisted, all those years ago, that Awst be buried here in Aelwyd Cerdinen. He had also insisted that his mother's body be laid to rest elsewhere. He would not under any circumstances permit his father to lie next to his murderer.

Gwydion, Uthyr, and Dinaswyn gently laid Amatheon's body on the empty niche just beneath Awst's bones. Gwydion noticed that as they did so Dinaswyn's eyes refused to even flicker to Awst's final resting-place. That meant something, he knew, but he was too tired, too uncaring to pursue it.

They stepped back, not taking their gaze from the shrouded form.

"He gave his life for that sword," Dinaswyn said, an underlying bitterness to her tone.

"He gave his life for me," Gwydion said, his voice steady.

"He loved you," Uthyr said with a voice full of tears. "He loved all of us."

"If I knew exactly who was behind his death I would swear vengeance on him," Dinaswyn said fiercely. "He would owe a galanas so high that the Shining Ones themselves could not pay it."

"The Shining Ones do not care about a little thing like justice," Gwydion said bitterly. "They do not care about us at all."

"Brother," Uthyr said quietly, putting his hand on Gwydion's shoulder.

Gwydion subsided, but in his cold heart a rage was growing.

"I loved him, too, Gwydion," Uthyr went on.

At first Gwydion did not answer. But he knew that his brother deserved a response and so he spoke, not bothering to choose his words. "When we were children, it was just Amatheon and I. Our mother did not care for us, she only noticed us when she wanted to use us to punish our father. Awst rarely saw us, for he let our mother drive him away time and time again.

"Amatheon was the only thing that kept me from loneliness. He was the only warmth in my life, the only love, the only laughter, the only cheerfulness in my existence."

Gwydion fell silent for a moment, and then forced himself to speak to Uthyr beyond the grief lodged in his throat. "You had a mother and a father that loved you. Amatheon and I only had each other. And now he is gone."

"I know, Gwydion," Uthyr said softly. "I know."

"And now you and Cariadas and Myrrdin are all I have left."

"And Dinaswyn," Uthyr pointed out with a nod to Gwydion's aunt.

"But Dinaswyn and I, we come from the same cold place, and so cannot warm and comfort each other. We are the same, she and I."

Dinaswyn's mask did not even slip as Gwydion spoke. Gwydion knew it would not, for he knew his aunt well. He even loved her, if truth were told. But it was also true they were too alike to be of any aid to each other. And Dinaswyn knew that too well to dispute it.

"So now all I have left is my duty as the Dreamer. That is the only solid rock left for me on which to stand. Do not tell me, brother, that it is not enough. I know it is not. But it is all I have."

"Gwydion—" Uthyr began.

"All that I have. All that I am likely to ever have."

The three of them stood there silently; gazing down at Amatheon's still shrouded form.

"Sing his song," Gwydion said quietly. "Sing my last gift to him."

Dinaswyn began to sing in a minor key:

He was a vessel of silver filled with pleasing wine.
He was a sweet branch with its blossom.
He was a vessel of pure glass filled with honey.

Uthyr's rich baritone echoed in the stone chamber as he sang next:

He was a precious stone with its goodness and beauty.
He was a brilliant sun round with summer.
He was a racehorse over a smooth plain.

Lastly Gwydion sang:

He was white-bronze, he was gold.
He was all that was good and strong.
He was my brother, Amatheon.

When they were done Gwydion gestured for the other two to leave. He stood looking down at Amatheon for a moment. He reached out his hand and laid it gently upon the side of Amatheon's still face beneath the linen shroud.

"Farewell, best of my heart," Gwydion whispered. "Farewell."

Gwydion turned and stepped out of the tomb. At his gesture, the stone door closed, shutting with a finality that would echo in his lonely heart for years to come.

Glossary

Addiendydd: sixth day of the week

aderyn: birds

aethnen: aspen tree; sacred to Ederynion

alarch: swan; the symbol of the royal house of Ederynion

alban: light; any one of the four solar festivals

Alban Awyr: festival honoring Taran; Spring Equinox

Alban Haf: festival honoring Modron; Summer Solstice

Alban Nerth: festival honoring Agrona and Camulos; Autumnal Equinox

Alban Nos: festival honoring Sirona and Grannos; the Winter Solstice

ap: son of

ar: high

Archdruid: leader of the Druids, must be a descendent of Llyr

Arderydd: high eagle; symbol of the High Kings

Ardewin: leader of the Dewin, must be a descendent of Llyr

arymes: prophecy

Awenyddion: dreamer (see Dreamer)

awyr: air

bach: boy

Bard: a telepath; they are musicians, poets, and arbiters of the law in matters of inheritance, marriage, and divorce; Bards can Far-Sense and Wind-Speak; they revere the god Taran, King of the Winds

bedwen: birch tree; sacred to the Bards

Bedwen Mis: birch month; roughly corresponds to March

blaid: wolf; the symbol of the royal house of Prydyn

bran: raven; the symbol of the Dreamers

Brenin: high or noble one; the High King; acts as an amplifier for the Y Dawnus

buarth: circle

cad: battle

cadair: chair (of state)

caer: fortress

calan: first day; any one of the four fire festivals

Calan Gaef: festival honoring Annwyn and Aertan

Calan Llachar: festival honoring Cerridwen and Cerrunnos

Calan Morynion: festival honoring Nantsovelta

Calan Olau: festival honoring Mabon

cantref: a large division of land for administrative purposes; two to three commotes make up a cantref; a cantref is ruled by a Lord or Lady

canu: song

cariad: beloved

celynnen: holly

Celynnen Mis: holly month; roughly corresponds to late May/ early June

cenedl: clan

cerdinen: rowan tree; sacred to the Dreamers

Cerdinen Mis: rowan month; roughly corresponds to July

cleddyf: sword

collen: hazel tree; sacred to Prydyn

Collen Mis: hazel month; roughly corresponds to October

commote: a small division of land for administrative purposes; two or three commotes make up a cantref; a commote is ruled by a Gwarda

coed: forest, wood

Cynyddu: increase; the time when the moon is waxing

Da: father

dan: fire

derwen: oak tree; sacred to the Druids

Derwen Mis: oak month; roughly corresponds to December

Dewin: a clairvoyant; they are physicians; they can Life-Read and Wind-Ride; they revere the goddess Nantsovelta, Lady of the Moon

Disglair: bright; the time when the moon is full

draig: dragon; the symbol of the Dewin

draenenwen: hawthorn tree; sacred to Rheged

Draenenwen Mis: hawthorn month; roughly corresponds to

late June/early July

Dreamer: a descendent of Llyr who has precognitive abilities; the Dreamer can Dream-Speak and Time-Walk; the Dreamer also has the other three gifts—telepathy, clairvoyance, and psychokinesis; there is only one Dreamer in a generation; they revere the god Mabon, King of Fire

Dream-Speaking: precognitive dreams; one of the Dreamer's gifts

Druid: a psychokinetic; they are astronomers, scientists, and lead all festivals; they can Shape-Move, Fire-Weave, and, in partnership with the High King, Storm-Bring; they revere the goddess Modron, the Great Mother of All

drwys: doors

dwfr: water

dwyvach-breichled: goddess-bracelet; bracelet made of oak used by Druids

eiddew: ivy

Eiddew Mis: ivy month; roughly corresponds to April

enaid-dal: soul-catcher; lead collars that prevent Y Dawnus from using their gifts

eos: nightingale; the symbol of the Bards

erias: fire

erydd: eagle

Far-Sensing: the telepathic ability to communicate with animals

ffynidwydden: fir tree; sacred to the High Kings

Fire-Weaving: the psychokinetic ability to light fires

gaef: winter

galanas: blood price

galor: mourning, sorrow

goddeau: trees

gorsedd: a gathering (of Bards)

greu: blood

Gwaithdydd: third day of the week

gwarchan: incantation

Gwarda: ruler of a commote

gwernan: alder tree; sacred to Gwynedd

Gwernan Mis: alder month; roughly corresponds to late April/ early May

gwinydden: vine

Gwinydden: vine month; roughly corresponds to August

Gwlad Yr Haf: the Land of Summer; the Otherworld

gwydd: knowledge

gwyn: white

gwynt: wind

Gwyntdydd: fifth day of the week

gwyr: seeker

haf: summer

hebog: hawk; the symbol of the royal house of Gwynedd

helygen: willow

Helygen Mis: willow month; roughly corresponds to January

honneit: spear

Life-Reading: the clairvoyant ability to lay hands on a patient and determine the nature of their ailment

llachar: bright

llech: stone

Lleihau: to diminish; the time when the moon is waning

lleu: lion

Llundydd: second day of the week

llyfr: book

llyn: lake

llys: court

Lord/Lady: ruler of a cantref

Mam: mother

march: horse; the symbol of the royal house of Rheged

Master Bard: leader of the Bards, must be a descendent of Llyr

Meirgdydd: fourth day of the week

meirig: guardian

Meriwydd: seventh day of the week

mis: month

morynion: maiden

mwg-breudduyd: smoke-dream; a method Dreamers can use to induce dreams

mynydd: mountain

mynyddoedd: mountains

naid: leap

nemed: shrine, a sacred grove

nerth: strength

neuadd: hall

niam-lann: a jeweled metallic headpiece, worn by ladies of rank

nos: night

ogaf: cave

olau: fair

onnen: ash tree; sacred to the Dewin

Onnen Mis: ash month; roughly corresponds to February

pair: cauldron

pen: head of

Plentyn Prawf: child test; the testing of children, performed by the Bards, to determine if they are Y Dawnus

rhyfelwr: warrior

sarn: road

Shape-Moving: the psychokinetic ability to move objects

Storm-Bringing: the psychokinetic ability to control certain weather conditions; only effective in partnership with the High King

Suldydd: first day of the week

tarbell: a board game, similar to chess

tarw: bull; the symbol of the Druids

tarw-casgliad: the ceremony where Druids invite a dream from Modron

telyn: harp

teulu: warband

Time-Walking: the ability to see events in the past; one of the Dreamer's gifts

tir: earth

triskele: the crystal medallion used by Dewin

ty: house

tynge tynghed: the swearing of a destiny

Tynged Mawr: great fate; the test to determine a High King

Tywyllu: dark; the time when the moon is new

ur: daughter of

var: out of

Wind-Riding: the clairvoyant ability of astral projection

Wind-Speaking: the telepathic ability to communicate with other humans

wythnos: week

yned: justice

Y Dawnus: the gifted; a Druid, Bard, Dewin, or Dreamer

ysgawen: elder

Ysgawen Mis: elder month; roughly corresponds to September

ystafell: the Ruler's chambers

ywen: yew

Ywen Mis: yew month; roughly corresponds to November

A Special Preview of *Memories of Empire*
by Django Wexler

chapter 1

> "The fundamental flaw in their culture is a certain
> stubbornness, a continued resistance to the world as
> it is. The clearest example is their religion, worship-
> ping ghosts six thousand years dead, but this trait
> runs throughout their entire culture. It makes them
> fearsome in times of strength but pathetic in times of
> weakness, and it leaves them unable or unwilling to
> adapt to changing conditions . . ."
>
> —Kabiru Shun, *The Fall of the Sixth Dynasty*

THERE'S ALWAYS ONE perfect moment, when the mind has just
awoken and consciousness has yet to fully engage—still
half-wrapped in dream, eyes open but uncomprehending, until
the weight of the world crashes down with all its harsh reality.
That moment, Veil had decided, was something to be savored.
It slipped away all too quickly. The very act of thinking about it
kicked her mind into action, and what had been mere patterns
of light and shadow resolved into familiar objects. She managed
one clean breath, held it for one perfect moment.

Then memory returned, and Veil settled in for a nice long
scream.

ONE MAN. IT didn't seem possible.

The scream was very uncharacteristic of Veil. She was not,

1

as a rule, a person who screamed or cried or threw tantrums. Growing up in Kalil's massive household had taught her a number of important lessons about life, and not the least of these was that screaming and crying rarely accomplished anything.

But, in this case, she felt she deserved a good scream. It helped to burn off tension, that was the main thing, And, once she was done, she was able to look at the situation with a great deal more equanimity. Under other circumstances she might have been worried about her reputation, but since there wasn't another human being for at least fifty miles in any direction that was also not a concern.

The sun was up, having just cleared the eastern horizon, and was beginning to make itself felt. The day promised to be a scorcher—the sky was blue from edge to edge, not even a wisp of cloud to blunt the heat. Veil could feel the sand, gritty and cold against her back, but already starting to drink in the sun's rays. In a few hours it would be too hot to touch.

Mahmata lay on top of her, and blood from the wound in the fat woman's belly had crusted over Veil's legs. Once she was done screaming, Veil set about freeing herself. This took some time, since Mahmata was quite fat and Veil might have described herself, charitably, as 'wiry.' Eventually, though, she managed to wriggle out from underneath the corpse and survey what was left of the camp.

Most of Bali's men were sprawled on a blood-soaked stretch of sand halfway to the bluff. Low as it was, it was the only decent shade for miles; it was no surprise they'd run into someone. That was where they'd confronted the stranger, and it didn't look like any of them had gotten more than two steps. Veil wandered over to inspect them, in a stunned state of idle curiosity. Dead bodies didn't bother her—the spirits were gone, after all, settling into the Aether or snapped up as food for something bigger and meaner.

So what was left to be afraid of? They were all dead—seven men. Vosh, who'd boasted so around the campfire, hadn't even gotten his sword out of its scabbard. Vosh had voted to pass Veil around at night, as a kind of bonus for the guards. Thankfully Bali had overruled him—apparently her virginity was worth more than a sellsword could offer—but Veil gave Vosh's corpse a kick anyway and felt a little better.

The other slaves had died, too, tied together and unable to even run. Veil hadn't known the pair of dark-skinned aborigines very well, since they spoke no Imperial and only a few broken words of Khaev, but fair-haired Silel had come from a clan to the west of Kalil's. Veil had gotten to know her in a month of traveling—a pretty, empty-headed thing. It was no wonder her father had gotten rid of her; still, she hadn't deserved to be slashed open like a Mourning fowl, spilling purple and black on the sands. Veil looked at her a moment, and shook her head. In clan lands the corpse would already be covered with flies, or torn apart by coyotes, but nothing lived in the high desert. Not even insects.

Bali, himself, had gotten the farthest. She assumed he'd started to run as soon as his sellswords started falling like trees in a sandstorm, but he'd made the mistake of stopping at his pack to dig out his purses. She found him there, slumped over his gold, run through from behind. Blood had coated the open purse and dulled the gleam of the coins.

She thought about kicking Bali, too, but he was so pathetic in death that adding further insult to his corpse seemed pointless. Instead she bent down to look in the purse. It was filled to bursting, a not-inconsiderable load for a grown man and a hopeless encumbrance for a girl of fifteen. She reached in, delicately, and extracted two fat golden eyes. That had been the slave-price Bali paid her father; more than the usual one-six he paid for children, she remembered, because there was a shortage of virgin girls in Corsa and the brothels were paying double.

Veil tucked the coins into the pocket of her ragged shorts and sat down heavily on the already-warming sands, trying to decide whether or not she wanted to die.

Even that was a bit egotistical, she had to admit.

It's not as though I have much of a choice. A hundred miles from home, in the middle of the trackless high desert, with no food and no water other than what she might salvage from the wreckage of the camp. The right thing to do, the logical thing, would be to lie down in the sun, enjoy the warmth, and slowly wither to a mummified corpse. Either that or, if she was feeling brave, borrow a dagger from one of the guards and end it herself. *That would be the logical choice. No food, no water, no help, no chance.*

On the other hand, why not? Veil's life had ended two months ago, when Kalil lost a war against Siorn and came up short on the reparations. *And yet, I'm still here. Might as well make the most of it. What's the worst that happens:, I die in the desert?*

She permitted herself a tight, sarcastic grin and went about stripping the bodies. She acquired a white cloth robe, suitable for desert wear, from Mahmata; it was a bit used and had a bloody hole through the middle, but Veil felt she wasn't in a position to pick and choose. From Silel, after a brief internal struggle, she took shoes —real bound-leather shoes, better by far for loose sand than the sandals Veil was wearing. The two biggest water skins - which Bali had been carrying - she hoisted over one shoulder. The little canteens that everyone had carried she drained, drinking until she squelched at the edges. There was no food—presumably the stranger had taken it. Veil shrugged. *If I live long enough that food becomes an issue, I'll have gotten farther than I expected.*

She hesitated over the last item. It seemed pointless, really—there wasn't a human for miles and miles , except for maybe the stranger, and there were no animals in the high desert. Nevertheless, she finally unstrapped Vosh's short sword and slung it awkwardly over her other shoulder. It was only a piece of pointed steel, but it made her feel better.

That left one last choice to make. *Which direction to go?*

Two options presented themselves. She could backtrack, heading west toward the Red Hills and home. That did not sound promising—the hills themselves were rife with bandits and rebels, and soldiers hunting both. Not to mention it was at least two weeks' walk through the high desert that way. *And if I turned up again at Kalil's door, what would he do? Probably chastise me for being disobedient and sell me to the next caravan that passed by, counting himself lucky to get paid twice for the same girl.* Veil's memories of her father were understandably colored by recent events, but, even in the past, Kalil had not been the kindliest of men. Not that he'd been particularly cruel, either—he didn't have time, with seven wives and uncounted children to manage, and there had been nannies and tutors to dispense the punishments. But she remembered him as distant, and cold.

Still, she hesitated. There was someone at home who would welcome her. *Kyre.* He was her truebrother, sharing both a father and a mother, born almost two years to the day before her. He'd cried, a little, when Kalil announced that she was to be sold. Afterwards, as she'd sat on her bunk in stunned silence, he'd kissed her lightly on the cheek and told her not to worry. *Kyre would be happy to see me.*

The other choice was south. The trail was clear enough, for the moment, a line of footprints running straight as an arrow across the sand. The first wind would obliterate them, but the baking air had barely stirred. The stranger had gone that way.

Bali had been heading vaguely south, she knew. There were oases, and little towns where you could buy water. She'd searched his body for a map, but either the slaver had navigated by memory or the stranger had taken it; probably the former, since Bali was—had been—only barely literate. Go south far enough, and the desert ran out. The city of Corsa was out there, somewhere. Every vile, nasty story Veil had ever heard had been set in Corsa; apparently the place was populated entirely by slavers and pirates, and operated beyond the reach of Khaev law.

It was ultimately curiosity that helped her to make up her mind. *One man against seven.* Her memories of the fight were confused, a blur of blood and flashing steel, but she remembered the stranger. All in black, and he'd moved like a phantom. *He won't last, in the heat. He'll have to rest. I can catch up with him, and he has the food.* He'd killed everyone, even the women and slaves. *He didn't kill me.* In all likelihood, he hadn't even noticed her—Mahmata had fallen on top of her, and Veil had fainted. *But, still . . .*

The sun had climbed higher, and the sand was getting hot. Veil struggled to her feet, water skins clonking heavily against her breast, and started south. *One step at a time, one foot after the other.*

JUST AFTER MIDDAY, when the sun was at its hottest, she finally caught sight of him.

The air felt like it had been cooked, so dry she could feel her skin cracking every time she moved. It was like the inside of the bakery, back home, when she was standing next to the oven and feeling the waves of heat it threw off; except here the oven was the whole world, and she couldn't duck outside the hut for a quick break. Everything Veil wore—her new boots, her flimsy shirt—was soaked in sweat.

Her burden felt heavy, so heavy. Taking the sword had been a mistake. Just carrying the water was hard enough; the sword flapped against her back at every step, as though chastising her for her errors. She couldn't summon the energy to reach back and get rid of the damn thing, either. It would have meant putting everything down to rearrange the straps, and if she stopped walking, Veil was certain she wouldn't start again.

The dunes went on forever. At the crest of each one, she felt as though she could see to the end of the world—the desert receded eternally to the blue-hazed horizon. Only on her right, in the east, was anything else visible: the dim shapes of the Cloudripper range rode like ghosts on the edge of vision.

By chance, she crested a dune at the same moment he did. A tiny black ant, ten or twenty dunes ahead, crawling across the boiling sands. Veil stopped and shouted herself hoarse, trying to get his attention, but if the ant shifted in its progress she couldn't see it. She spent the next hour damning him in every way she could think of, coming up with creative torments the spirits of the Aether could subject his soul to before devouring it utterly. She saw him again a couple of hours later, a bit closer than she remembered—this time, when she shouted, the distant speck definitely paused for a moment to look back at her. Then he continued on his way, unconcerned. Veil rasped her tongue over cracked lips, took a swallow of precious water, and started down the dune.

ISBN#1932815147
Silver
Price $14.99
Fantasy
September 2005
www.bloodgod.com

For more information

about other great titles from

Medallion Press, visit

www.medallionpress.com